THE cold between

THE cold between

ELIZABETH BONESTEEL

HARPER Voyager
An Imprint of HarperCollins *Publishers*

HarperCollins books may be purchased for educational, business, or sales promotional use. For information please e-mail the Special Markets Department at SPsales@harpercollins.com.

FIRST EDITION

Harper Voyager and design is a trademark of HarperCollins Publishers L.L.C.

Designed by Paula Russell Szafranski

Library of Congress Cataloging-in-Publication Data has been applied for.

ISBN 978-0-06-241365-9

16 17 18 19 20   OV/RRD   10 9 8 7 6 5 4 3 2 1

For Debbie

THE cold between

PROLOGUE

*S*ixty seconds to detonation. Please evacuate the area."

Kate ran toward the *Phoenix*'s infirmary, grumbling with frustration. When she'd told Captain Kelso they could evacuate quickly she had expected more than five minutes' notice, and now there was no way they'd transfer everything in time. They had moved their patients and started shifting the most essential drugs, but she had fewer than half her everyday remedies, and almost no tools at all. At this rate, she would be practicing frontier medicine on the nine-week trip back to Earth. If anyone had a heart attack or a compound fracture in that time, Andy Kelso was going to be dealing with some injuries of his own.

She passed one of her clinicians running in the other direction, his arms full of vacuum-sealed pouches. "Last of the antigen packs," he told her.

"I'll get the scope," she called over her shoulder. "Stay in the res wing."

"Aye aye, Chief!" She heard his pace pick up.

"Fifty seconds to detonation. Please evacuate the area."

She turned and entered the infirmary, frowning at the number of people still rummaging through the shelves. "Didn't I tell you people to get the hell out of here?"

Amy was shoveling topical healers into a bag. "Big bang," she said tersely. "People will be bleeding."

"Not if it goes as planned," Kate reminded her, opening a cabinet and pulling out a portable medical scanner. Her scalpel kit followed, and she took a moment to strap it around her arm.

"What part of this mission has gone as planned?"

Kate was not the only one who laughed at that. Tension release, she knew; they'd all be less manic once this was over, and they had the long ride home to reflect. She would have time to digest what had happened, and figure out how to tell Tom the story without scaring the hell out of him. She didn't want to end up using all her precious shore leave dealing with his feelings of protectiveness, but she supposed it served her right for marrying a man who hated the Corps.

"Forty seconds to detonation. Please evacuate the area."

"Okay, that's it," she declared, clapping her hands. "Everybody out. Now. That's an order. Move your ass or I write you up."

The others tightened their arms around their loads of supplies, and turned to leave. Amy glanced back at Kate. "You coming?"

"You think I'm planning on dying here while you assholes run off?"

Amy waited while Kate grabbed the microscope. The two women ran up the hallway together, heading for the bulkhead separating the residential wing from the ship's main engine room and weapons locker.

"Thirty seconds to detonation. Please—"

"'—evacuate the area,'" Kate and Amy finished simultaneously. They exchanged a smile and passed through the open bulkhead, following the long hallway through the residential area and into the main cafeteria. There they found the medical staff seated around one long table, strapped into the sturdy chairs. Raban, Kate's head nurse, had saved her a seat.

She would tell Greg all of it, Kate decided, no matter what she censored for Tom. Her son loved all of this just as she did, danger be damned, and he pestered her for every detail whenever she was home. She had felt from the day he was born that the Corps was his destiny, but now—twelve years later, watching him tread the line between stringy little boy and thoughtful young man—she *knew* she was right, in ways she had never imagined. He would be part of all this soon, and he would be the one bringing home fantastic stories for her.

She stowed her rescued equipment under the table and sat next to Raban, flashing him a grateful smile. He often reminded her of her son, although he was twice the boy's age: effortlessly handsome, with dark, thick hair and serious gray eyes. When Greg had been a baby his eyes had been blue, but time had drained them of color, and left behind a stormy shade streaked through with black. Exotic eyes. Tom's eyes. Greg had her fine features—and her mercurial temper—but he had his father's eyes.

"You okay?" Raban asked.

He was perceptive like Greg, too. She gave him a tight smile. "I feel like I've just abandoned my childhood home."

"You could have said no," he reminded her. "It had to be unanimous, remember?"

"It's worth it," she said. He kept looking at her, and she made herself smile more easily. "Besides, it never hurts having a man like Andy Kelso owe you a favor, does it?"

"He already owes you," Raban pointed out, but he smiled back, letting her off the hook.

"Twenty seconds to detonation. Please evacuate the area."

Raban clutched the edge of the table, frowning as he looked around the room at people spinning in their chairs, running around and changing places in the last seconds available. "We work with idiots, did you know that?"

Kate watched the people she served with, the people who knew her better than her own family. "We work with people who know when to have fun," she corrected. On impulse, she put her hand over his, and gripped it hard.

"Ten seconds to detonation."

In the distance, she heard the heavy bulkhead creaking as it lurched closed. She wondered if it would hold; as far as she knew they had never used it before.

"Nine."

There was a comforting *thunk* as the bulkhead locked into place, and she took a breath.

"Eight."

She realized, belatedly, that along with her infirmary, the gymnasium was on the wrong side of the bulkhead as well. It was going to be a *very* long trip back.

"Seven."

So many missions she had been part of, in her years with the Corps. So many causes, so many battles.

"Six."

So many missed opportunities. So many mistakes.

"*Five.*"

But not this time. This time . . . they had been soon enough.

"*Four.*"

This time, they were right.

"*Three.*"

She thought of Meg, her daughter, her beautiful young woman, and what she looked like with the sun silvering her wild, dark curls. She thought of Greg, still mostly a boy, and the twinkle in his eyes when he was trying not to laugh.

"*Two.*"

She thought of Tom, her husband, her soul mate, who watched her leave time after time and still waited for her, patient and constant and full of love. Sometimes she missed him more than life.

This time, when she got home, maybe she'd stay a little longer.

One.

PART I

CHAPTER 1

Volhynia

"Another round, please," Elena said to the bartender.

The man's expression did not change, but she thought he looked at her a moment longer than necessary. She resisted the urge to roll her eyes at him. She knew what he was thinking; she was thinking it herself: *They've had too much to drink already.*

Her eyes caught a familiar face in the mirror behind the bar, and she turned, singling out Jessica. Her friend was in her element: surrounded by rowdy, cheerful strangers, red curls bouncing as she laughed and joked with the crowd. Jess thrived as the center of attention. Elena wished she had more of Jess's confidence, wondering again why she had agreed to spend her meager shore leave in a crowded place where her dearest wish was to be ignored.

Because it was better than staying home.

She had to admit that Jessica had done her research. Volhynia's capital city of Novanadyr was crowded with tourist traps, but Byko's, despite the crowd and the noise level, had an air of sophistication. The bar served not just the flavored beers so often favored by tourists, but also a wide variety of subtler brews the colony did not export. Indeed, there were a number of local patrons, and even one man in a PSI uniform, drinking quietly at a corner of the bar, as serene as if he were the only customer in the place.

There were plenty in the crowd who were loud and stupid at this hour, but the atmosphere seemed upbeat, the music was bluesy and seductive, and the smell of fresh hops filled the air. Elena had spent interminable evenings in environments far less inviting, but the environment hadn't put the knots in her neck. No, it was not the fault of the bar that her nerves were so frayed.

Sitting here, amid the amiable chaos, she found herself wondering for a fleeting moment if she shouldn't have taken Danny up on his invitation to spend the evening with him instead. He had broached the subject just that morning, approaching her nervously after breakfast, palpably relieved when she had agreed to listen.

"There's this scientists' bar," he told her. "Eggheads and weak drinks. Quiet, they say, although they'll rip you off like everywhere else in the Fifth Sector." She had laughed at that, and almost said yes. But she did turn him down, albeit gently and with some regret. Now she thought he would at least have been someone she knew.

The locals, of course, had come out in force when *Galileo* had taken up orbit. Jessica hadn't warned her, but Elena realized she had been foolish not to figure out for herself what would happen. Volhynia was a well-populated colony world— there were nearly four thousand in Novanadyr alone—but there was nothing like new blood.

They knew we'd be here, Elena thought irritably. *And they're hunting us like wildebeest.*

Not that it didn't go both ways. Most Corps starships had downtime every twenty days, sometimes more often, but *Galileo*'s crew had been six weeks without formal shore leave. Ordinarily they encountered something to shake up their fine-tuned routine—diplomatic crisis, terraformer malfunction, crop failure—but the Fifth Sector was largely prosperous and free of conflict. Six weeks of peace, it turned out, was mind-numbingly dull. Elena could not blame her crewmates for seeking out something—anything—that was new. Had she been a different sort of person she might have enjoyed this place with her friends, instead of wishing herself away from them, wandering her starship's wide, empty halls.

She slipped a finger behind her ear to query her comm for the time: 2350. Too early and too late. At midnight the city's power grid would be shut down for almost a full hour as the nearby neutron star swept the planet with an electromagnetic pulse. She would never make it to the spaceport in time, and she doubted the dispatcher would take kindly to her loitering until the lights came back on. Her eyes swept the crowd again, and she wondered if the dispatcher was open to bribes.

She had almost resolved to head for the spaceport and plead her case when she heard a step behind her. She closed her eyes, mustered a polite smile, and turned.

He was taller than she was, with straw-yellow hair and an indisputably nice smile, and he bore a heart-wrenching resemblance to Danny. Damn Jessica—what had she been thinking, sending this one over? She wasn't usually so oblivious.

"Can I help you with the drinks?" the man asked.

He had a nice voice, a little dark and grainy, with that broad accent they spoke with here. He was handsome, friendly, not entirely pie-eyed—and he left her cold. As she looked at him, thinking of what to say, she realized she was done pretending to have fun.

The regret in the smile she gave him was genuine. "You're very kind," she said, willing all the flip sarcasm out of her voice. "Actually, you can take them back to the table for me. I'm afraid I'm not staying."

This news took a moment to penetrate. "You sure?" he said, still genial, still easygoing. "Your friend, there, she seems to think you could use some fun and games. Doesn't have to, you know, *be* anything."

He was nice, this one. Under different circumstances, with more time . . . *he would still look like Danny.* "My friend," she told him, "has a good heart and a deaf ear. If you think of it, please tell her to enjoy herself without being concerned for me."

He flashed her that smile again. "If you change your mind . . ." he offered, then moved away, and she turned back to the bar to settle the tab. She was struggling to remember how much one was supposed to tip in Novanadyr when a voice came from the corner of the bar.

"You were very kind to him," said the man in the PSI uniform.

He had not moved since they had arrived, seated comfortably on his own, nursing something served in a small, smoke-colored glass. He was dressed in black from head to toe, clothes fitted and well-worn, black hair pulled back from his face into a tight, short braid—the uniform worn by PSI in all six sectors. An anomaly in the crowd of tourists and natives.

"He was polite," she replied. "There was no reason not to be."

She wondered, as she had when she had first spotted him, if he was an impostor. Real PSI soldiers were rarely seen on colonies, living primarily in nomadic tribes, many of them spending their entire lives—birth to death—on massive generation ships that isolated themselves from Central Gov. Central maintained authority over colony worlds, supporting local government while regulating interstellar trade and rule of law, but PSI as a people kept mostly to themselves, appearing only to deliver supplies to colonies in need . . . or, as was rumored, at least, to steal necessities from a passing freighter.

On a wealthy colony like Volhynia, PSI would be seen as anachronistic, even threatening; a PSI soldier at a local bar would be an attraction. Or, more likely, a wasp to be provoked. But if he was an impostor, she would have expected him to be making the most of it: courting attention, and drinking a good deal more than what the bartender had poured into that tiny glass.

She waited, wondering if he would say something else, then finished paying for the drinks. When he spoke again, she almost jumped.

"May I offer you some advice?" he asked.

His pronunciation was clipped and exotic, his speech mannered and slightly slow, as if he was translating in his head before he spoke. Most PSI were reputed to be multilingual, and some joined as children, or even young adults. She would have no way of guessing on which colony this one may have started his life.

"All right," she said.

"You should not keep company with children."

He was staring straight ahead, not looking at her. He had an angular profile punctuated by a substantial, aquiline nose and a neatly trimmed mustache. A masculine face, and yet his lips were full, almost feminine. His eyes were wide and deep set, and in the dim light of the bar looked jet-black; but they caught light from all around, giving him an expression of intelligence and good humor. She could not, if asked, have honestly called him handsome; but there was something in his bearing, something immediate and physical that she suspected made people watch him even when he did not move.

"Are you offering me an alternative?"

At that he smiled, although he still did not look at her. "I take my own advice."

The amusement in his eyes was not cruel, but she still found herself annoyed. "Do I seem so young, then?" she asked him.

"My dear lady, you *are* young."

He had a nice voice, almost impossibly deep, with a hint of music. She wondered if he sang. "I'm not *that* young."

He took pity on her at that, and turned to meet her eyes. His direct gaze was sharper, and she realized that whatever he was drinking had not intoxicated him at all. "What age are you?" he asked her curiously.

"Thirty-two."

He gave a brief, dismissive snort. "When you were born," he said, "I was well into my twenties, and I had seen more horrors than you will all of your life." He turned away again.

By her estimation, she had seen enough horror for anyone, but he would have no way of knowing. "So if I am so young," she deduced, "then surely I'm in the right crowd. Me and all these boys."

"Possibly," he allowed. "But these boys can do nothing for you."

"That's not what *they* think."

He scoffed again, still good-humored. "These boys believe that because they know the mechanics, they know how to make love to a woman. They are wrong."

She thought for a moment, an old memory surfacing. "My cousin Peter used to say something about young men," she remembered. "'Too busy loving themselves to effectively fuck anybody else.'"

At that he put down his glass and let out a loud bark of laughter. She could not help but smile herself. "He tends to be crass," she said, half-apologetic.

"Observant, though," he said, favoring her with a genuine smile. She saw him focus, as if he had not really looked at her before. "Tell me, dear lady," he asked her, curious. "Why are you here?"

Those dark eyes of his, in addition to sharpness, held a genuine warmth that pleased her more than she would have expected. "I thought we'd established that," she tried, but he shook his head.

"You told that boy you were planning to leave," he reminded her. "I believe you meant it."

This time she was the one who looked away. "I came here because I promised Jessica," she confessed, waving toward her friend. "She says I've been irritable lately. She's a big believer in sex to treat . . . everything. Irritability, exhaustion, insomnia, the common cold. She doesn't understand that it doesn't work for everybody."

"So you came here to placate her."

"I figured I'd stay for a while, then creep out to a hotel somewhere and let her yell at me in the morning when she's too hungover to put much energy behind it."

"So if you are not interested in drunken children in spaceport bars," he asked, "what do you do? Surely there are people on your ship."

That was not a short-answer question, and it was a far more personal subject than she should have been comfortable discussing with someone she had just met. "Shipboard . . . can get messy. There's only two hundred and twenty-six of us, and it gets very insular. You either have to be serious, or casual like Jess."

"And can you not find true love on board your ship?"

How easily he leapt from sex to love. Strange, how familiar he felt to her. "Sometimes." She thought of Danny, of his crooked smile as he tried to charm her that morning. It would have been easier than she wanted to admit to say yes to him, to have met him tonight, to have fallen right back into everything that had gone wrong. "But reality tends to strangle it."

She caught sympathy in his eyes, and braced herself, but he was perceptive enough to let it go. *Definitely not a boy.*

"So on your ship you must choose from casual lovers or untenable affairs," he said. "I can see why you were persuaded to come down here."

"It did make some sense at the time," she told him, relieved to have the subject return to the present. "In practice, though—my God, is there anything less alluring than a pack of strangers so drunk they won't remember their own names, not to mention yours? How do people *do* this?"

"There are alternatives to drunken fools, you know."

"You already said you weren't interested."

"Ah, yes," he said, lifting his drink. "I'd forgotten." But he couldn't suppress the half smile on his lips.

She began to understand what they were doing. "Story of my life," she said lightly. "The only men worth talking to aren't interested."

And at that they were looking at each other, and something inside of her turned. And she understood, in that moment, what came so effortlessly to Jessica in places like this.

She dropped her eyes, and saw him set down his small glass, looking back into the mirror behind the bar. "How much time off do they give you?" he asked her.

"Twelve hours, by the clock," she told him. "I have to report back by oh-nine hundred hours tomorrow." She took a breath; nerves had come upon her.

"That is not a lot of time," he remarked, and she wasn't sure whether to attribute his tone to disappointment or disapproval.

"It's enough for some," she said. "Usually it's enough for me."

He looked over at her again, and she felt her face grow hot before she looked up to meet his eyes. His gaze, no less intense, had become serious, and she thought perhaps he was finding her unexpected as well. He shifted a little, turning toward her.

Without warning the lights went off, and a rowdy cheer rose from the crowd. Elena blinked, disoriented; the dark, while diluted by the bioluminescent sidewalks outside the bar's windows, was more absolute than anything she ever experienced back home, where the ship's operational lights were everywhere. She had forgotten to watch the time, and now they had hit the Dead Hour. Everything but emergency systems would be off-line for nearly an hour.

After a few seconds the bar's interior was lit with a bank of portable lamps mounted high on the walls; the room was nearly as bright as before, but the light was cooler, and everything was faded to monochrome. Her companion was painted with light and shadow, lending drama to the strong angles of his face. He looked pale in the blue-white glow, and strangely unreal; she found she wanted to reach out just to see if he was really there.

And then she was startled by a man lurching between the two of them, his hands slapping into the bar as he kept himself from stumbling to the ground. He had bright blue eyes and hair as jet-black as her companion's, but his eyes were rheumy and unfocused, and he wore a deep scowl. She did not recognize him—he was not part of the entourage that had coalesced around Jessica—but he must have been in the pub for a long time. He was very, very drunk.

He straightened himself up against the edge of the bar, and turned to look at her. "You do realize what you're talking to," he slurred, his voice overloud.

This one she was less inclined to be nice to. Beyond his attitude, his timing was abysmal. "You do realize *who* I'm talking to is none of your business," she snapped.

It was a tone that had effectively driven away many men over the years. This one was too drunk to listen. "You *military* types," he spat bitterly. "You come here and you flood our city and you talk to us because we're *quaint*. I'll bet you think pirates are *quaint*. But he's nothing but a thief and a murderer."

Her companion cleared his throat. "I believe what she means is that this conversation does not concern you." His words were polite, but there was ice in his tone. "Perhaps you'd like to return to your table."

"Fuck off," the man shot over his shoulder; and then he took a step closer to Elena, millimeters from touching her. "You like bad boys, little girl? I can be as bad as you want."

And at that, her temper flared. "What I like," she said deliberately, holding her ground, "are people with the brains to *get lost* when they're not wanted."

At her words his face grew ugly, his brows drawing together, his lips pressing into a thin line. "If you think I'm going to let you walk out of here with this"—he spat out a word in the local dialect that she didn't understand—"you must be a bigger whore than he is."

None of which made any sense, she realized, but then he clamped a hand over her arm, and she got a sense of his strength, even inebriated. He moved toward her, and she felt the heat of his body and smelled the liquor on his breath, and she had just enough time to think *Oh, hell, I'm going to have to hit him,* before she caught a movement out of the corner of her eye and his hand was wrenched off of her, and then he was on the floor.

Her companion stood over him, arms and legs relaxed, his hands tightened into fists. "This woman," he said clearly, as the drunk stared up at him, "has made her wishes very clear." His eyes, so light and amused when talking with her, were full of a dangerous calm. "If you ignore them again, I swear to you, you will not see the sun rise."

She took in the two men, saw the drunk shift against the wood floor, and then drop his eyes. He rolled, with more dignity than she would have thought possible, and climbed to his feet; then he brushed past, not looking at either of them, heading toward the exit with some haste. Her companion's eyes followed him, deadly and dangerous, until he had disappeared.

The room, which had gone quiet when the drunk had fallen, began to buzz with conversation again, the confrontation already old news. Elena felt heat rising to her face. *Holy shit.*

The man watched the door for a moment. "You are unhurt?" he asked.

She made a small affirmative sound, and he turned, meeting her eyes. The danger in his expression had been replaced by ordinary annoyance—and a shadow of regret. "You believe I have overstepped."

He was standing closer to her than he had been. He smelled of spices—cardamom, she thought, and maybe rosemary—and something sweet she could not identify. "Um," she managed, then took a breath. "No, actually. I would have had to break his arm. Your way, at least he goes home in one piece."

"Hm." He turned back to the door, still frowning. "Now you are making me wish I had let you deal with him."

Minutes ago she would have laughed at this, and resumed their light flirting. Now she could do nothing but stare at him, distracted by the way he shifted as he stood, by wondering what his hair felt like or whether he needed to shave. After a moment he looked back at her, his expression still dark. It should have made her shrink away, but she found she could no longer move.

He seemed to realize then how he looked, because he shook himself, and the last of the irritation fell away. He studied her face, absorbed. "But there is still something wrong," he observed, and she nodded.

"It's just—" This was all so odd, and yet it felt so familiar, as if she had been here before, would be here again. "I came here," she explained, "thinking I knew what I wanted. I'm not sure I know anymore."

He kept studying her, and she felt herself blush more deeply; but she wanted to look back at him, wanted him to see what she was thinking. Something flickered momentarily over his face, fierce and hungry, and it was all she could do not to reach out to him, to fall toward him, just to see what he would do.

"Perhaps we should discuss it somewhere else," he suggested.

She could have left then. She could have told him, honestly, that she was not brave enough. That was true, for a part of her. But that part of her was being shouted down, and she did not want to listen to it anymore.

She nodded.

He turned to the bartender and paid his tab, efficiently but not hurriedly. Then he met her eyes again and waited.

Elena pushed away from the bar and headed for the door. The man in black followed her out.

Chapter 2

I t was foolishness, of course. Trey was clear on that. Even as he followed her out of the bar, distracted by the easy sway of her hips, he knew he should walk her back to the spaceport and send her home.

He also knew he wouldn't.

He had watched her since she arrived at the pub, trailing behind her boisterous friend like a silent and elegant shadow, uncomfortable and out of place and simply breathtakingly lovely. It was her beauty he had dwelled on, at first: her tall, slim figure, elegant and regal in her telltale gray and black uniform; the curve of her jaw; the dark hair tumbling in curls into her wide, expressive brown eyes. It took him longer to recognize the depth of her discomfort, and longer still to detect the intensity of her desire to escape. She was laughing and joking with the others, but she was not drinking liquor, and he realized she was deflecting more than making conversation. When she had come up to the bar he had admired her walk, but he had noticed how careful she was not to touch anyone as she worked her way through the crowd.

He had not planned on talking to her—during his years with PSI he had learned not to socialize with Central Corps soldiers—but watching her, he had become curious. Listening to her gentle dismissal of the flirtatious young man, intrigued. And upon speaking to her . . . She was so refreshingly direct, and, much to his astonishment, *interested*. He tended to dismiss romantic attention as a by-product of his past, but she had said nothing of his former profession, and had not even reacted when that jackass Luvidovich had brought it up.

Damn the man. Trey would have to kill him someday, he was certain. He could not bring himself to view that eventuality with much regret.

The evening was cool, and felt cooler lit only by the faint glow of the bricks edging the sidewalk. "Are you cold?" he asked, looking down at her. In the dim light she looked exotic and alien, a strange creature from another world.

She shook her head and smiled, glancing at him with that odd mix of shyness and desire he had noticed in the pub. "I grew up outside of Juneau," she explained. He must have looked confused, because she laughed. "It's in Alaska. On Earth. Very far north. This would be a warm summer night."

"I have never been to Earth," he told her. "Is it all so cold?"

"No. In fact, most of it isn't. A lot of it's hot, even uninhabitable. But I lived in a nice place."

"Do you miss it?"

"Never."

He stopped, and turned to her, and watched the wind tug at her hair. "May I kiss you?" he asked.

Even in the dark he could see her blushing, the color warming her cheeks and her jaw and her throat, and he wondered how much of her that blush was covering. Her eyes were still shy, but she nodded anyway.

He took a step toward her. A lock of hair blew across her cheek; before she could brush it aside he caught it, rubbing the silky curl between his fingers, then tucking it carefully behind her ear. He looked into her eyes, letting his fingers trail across her jaw. Her skin was cool and smooth, and he traced the line of her cheekbone, then reached up to smooth her hair from her forehead. She moved toward him, first a small step, then leaning into his touch, almost imperceptibly. Her lips parted slightly, and he heard her breath quicken.

He lifted his other hand, placing his palms on either side of her face, tangling his fingers in her soft, dark hair. Her eyes drifted closed, and he studied her long lashes, shadowing her moonlit skin. He took a breath, inhaling the scent of her: clean, feminine skin, something floral in her hair. His own eyes closed as he brushed her lips with his own.

Her mouth was warm and soft, and she made a small sound, kissing him back. Their exploration was gentle at first; but when she pulled his lower lip between her own, tasting him with a feather-light touch, the electricity within him flared bright and sharp. His hands tightened in her hair and he kissed her harder, parting her lips with his, tangling his tongue with hers. She leaned into him, pulling his tongue deeper into her mouth, passionate and hungry. He felt her hands running over his shoulders, felt her palms on the nape of his neck, running up over his hair, pulling his head closer. Unable to resist any longer, he reached around her waist and pulled her against him, and he felt the warmth of her all along his body. She pressed herself closer, wrapping her arms around his neck, and he knew she could feel how much he wanted her.

What seemed remarkable was how much she wanted him in return.

It was so easy, kissing her here on the street, with the moonlight and the luminous sidewalk and the cool breeze, lost in the heat of her. It would be easy, as well, to pull her into the shadows, to shove their clothes aside and take her, fast and hard, in the alley just meters away. As she kissed him and touched him and pulled at him, he even thought she would be willing.

But he knew it would not be enough.

He pulled away from her, keeping his arms around her, and they swayed together, disoriented. He opened his eyes to look at her, and found all of the shyness gone.

"My flat is a block away," he told her, surprised at the unsteadiness of his voice. "Will you come home with me?"

"Yes," she said, breathless, and she let her fingers wander over his eyebrows and across his temples. He closed his eyes, savoring her touch, and after a moment he reached up to take her hands in his.

"If you do not stop that," he told her, smiling, "we will not make it that far."

She laughed, delighted. She was so open, and so lovely, and he wanted his hands on her more than he had wanted anything in a long time. He kept her right hand in his left and turned, and they walked down the sidewalk together. They did not speak again, but somehow he felt lighter and more comfortable than he had with anyone in the six months since he had returned to Volhynia.

When they reached his building he led her up the front stairs. She looked around, curious, eyes darting from the steps to the window to the fingerprint lock on the door.

"Old technology," he said, following her eyes.

"Still harder to hack than a voice lock," she remarked, "and a lot cheaper."

She was right, but it was not a fact he would have expected her to have at her fingertips. He realized, then, that he did not know what she did on this ship of hers.

He did not even know her name.

He opened the door, finding the entryway lit by the moon shining through the skylight. The stairs did not bother her at all; she was not even winded when they reached the top. Instead she was looking up through the window in the ceiling. The moon lit her face in the dark, and she smiled. "It's so beautiful," she said softly. "I never miss the sun. But moonlight . . ."

"This does not surprise me," he said to her. "It suits you, the moonlight."

He stood aside for her and she moved into the flat, leaning against the wall by the alcove. The light of the moon turned the room blue-gray, casting cool shadows against the planes of her face. The door closed behind him and he stood opposite her, the kitchen at his back. He felt strangely formal, like he was missing part of a ritual. Like it would have been so much easier if they had stayed outside.

"Can I offer you something to drink?" he asked.

She shook her head. "No," she said, and it crossed his mind that now she, having made up her mind, was more at ease than he was. "But you could come here. If you like."

She held out her hands, and he took them. "What is that scent in your hair?" he asked, longing to bury his hands in it again.

"Lilac," she told him. She let his hands go and laid her fingers at his waist, and he felt suddenly how thin his shirt was, how much he wanted to feel her fingers against his skin. "It's Jessica's," she admitted, and looked briefly embarrassed.

"It is lovely," he told her. He pressed his lips to her forehead, then nuzzled her hair, inhaling the scent. "But what you are doing to me has nothing to do with flowers." He moved his lips down her cheek, along her jaw, to the pulse on her neck. He heard her inhale sharply, and her head fell back, baring her throat to him. He kissed her smooth skin, then nipped at her; she moaned, just a little, at the touch of his teeth, and that was enough.

He moved to kiss her lips, but this time there was no preamble of gentleness, no feeling each other out. The kiss was fierce, devouring, and he leaned against her, pushing her hard against the wall. Her arms reached around him, and her hands went to his head; she pulled the leather tie from his braid and let his heavy hair fall around her fingers. One of her hands trailed down, and he felt her pulling the tail of his shirt from his trousers. When her fingers touched the skin of his back, all reason disappeared. He unzipped her shirt, and she managed to let go of him long enough to shrug it off and toss it to the ground; he dispensed quickly with her undershirt, and then he had her breasts in his hands, and he kissed her over and over, pressing his hips against her, so hard his clothes were hopelessly uncomfortable.

She moaned as he touched her, his thumbs brushing over her stiff nipples as she arched against him. On impulse he released her mouth long enough to drop his head and pull one nipple between his lips, tugging on it with his teeth. She held on to his head and pressed her breast to his mouth, and whispered *harder,* and he sucked as hard as he dared, biting down enough he would have thought it was painful. But she did not object. She said *God, yes* and *please* and *anything you want* and he could not wait any longer.

Somehow they rid themselves of the rest of their clothes, and he took a breath, feeling the heat of her skin against his, painfully aware of his raging erection brushing against the cleft in her skin. She was wet and slick, and, he noticed, just the right height.

"Here?" he asked her, and she beamed at him, a gorgeous, bright-eyed smile.

"Oh, yes," she said.

He slid one hand over her ass and down one toned thigh, and pulled her knee up alongside his hip. She wrapped her leg around him, pulling him closer; and with little maneuvering, he pushed himself inside of her.

She cried out, an unmistakable sound of pleasure, and he felt her muscles tighten around him. He found himself groaning as well. She was tight and warm and so lovely, so soft, and he drove into her again and again, grateful for the wall holding her up, riding the wave of pleasure higher and higher, and every moment he thought it was going to break, she pulled him in deeper, devoured his mouth, ran her hands over his back, into his hair . . . *Good God, I would drown in her if I could,* and that was his last coherent thought. When she finally gasped and called out, over and over, her body convulsing, clutching at him, inside and out, surrendered completely to pleasure, he went over the edge with her, pounding again and again, oblivious to everything else, letting the waves wash over him as she moved with him, hanging on for dear life, until all was spent into stillness.

They stood, unmoving, wrapped around each other, for several minutes. Trey was not entirely sure he could do anything else. As he came back to himself he found her stroking his hair and nuzzling the inside of his neck. He glanced down at her and she smiled, her eyes light and contented.

"I may fall down," she confessed.

He laughed. "Let us see what we can do about that." He pushed away from her a little, testing his legs; they seemed to be willing, for the moment, to hold him up. He reached for her again, and she put her arms around his neck. He wrapped his arms around her waist and lifted her; she wrapped her legs around him, linking her ankles behind his knees. It seemed as practical a way as any to travel.

He carried her past the bathroom door into the bedroom, enjoying the weight of her in his arms, her limbs so unselfconsciously embracing him. Gently he deposited her on the blanket-covered bed, and managed to lie down next to her without letting her go.

He closed his eyes, pleasure still warming his blood. It was not as if his recent life had been without women, he reflected. It had just been so long since he had been with one who had given herself over so completely. Since Valeria, perhaps. More than a year.

He had no inclination to linger on the past.

He pulled her closer, and she draped a long leg over him, tucking her head under his chin. "If I had known you were coming," he told her, one hand skimming her waist to come to rest on her hip, "I would have ordered a skylight in here as well."

She laughed, and he felt the vibration of it against his chest. "You should have one anyway," she said. "It's easier to sleep if you can see the stars."

"I will tell you," he admitted, wondering at his newfound gregariousness, "I have never had trouble sleeping. Out there, I was well-known for it. I could sleep on my feet if there was a need. But I did know a few, like you, who needed windows."

She shifted against him, and he was surprised to feel a twinge of desire returning. "I used to fall asleep in the engine room," she told him. "There's this catwalk there, with these big floor-to-ceiling windows. They take them out for maintenance some-times, when she's docked, but the rest of the time, it's the best view on the ship. A few months in, the captain heard about me sleeping there, and he found this little unused storeroom with one windowed wall and had it converted for my quarters."

"He is thoughtful, then? Your captain."

She was quiet a moment. "In some ways," she said. He was not surprised she found it a complicated question. Command required separation, and often callousness, and even those who understood were not always comfortable with being on the receiving end. "Mostly . . . he is observant, and he is good at knowing what keeps us efficient." She looked up at him. "I used to think, sometimes . . . There are these moments, in life, when you just stop and realize that everything is just as it should be. Everything. I had that, a little. For a while. But even now—I try to remember that life doesn't have to be perfect to be valuable."

He brought his hand to her face again, brushing his knuckles against her cheekbone. "Are you always so kind?" he asked her.

"Only to people I'm in bed with."

Her hand was resting on his rib cage, and he felt the heat of her fingertips and wanted to pull her on top of him. Somehow this woman was turning him back into a teenager. "It seems to me," he observed, lacing his fingers in hers, "that you are not the sort of woman who should be finding herself in bed alone."

"Now you sound like Jessica," she said.

"She is right on the cure," he told her, "but not the problem. You are a beautiful woman. Regardless of your ship's short-sighted population, you should be worshipped, not sent out to try your luck at a spaceport bar."

"My luck worked out well this time," she pointed out.

"I am serious." Actually, he was outraged, but that seemed presumptuous. "This fool, that you were in love with. What happened?"

A shadow crossed her face. He had seen it before, in the bar, when she had dismissed the possibility of true love surviving on a starship; but either he had missed the depth of her pain, or he simply read her better now. "The usual," she said, and he thought her lightness was feigned. "He lied, and I found out. I tried to forgive him. I failed."

"How long ago was this?"

"Two and a half months."

He winced. "Damn. I am sorry, my dear. I did not mean to remind you of fresh grief. Especially here."

She shook her head. "But it doesn't hurt to remember it here."

"I am your first lover since then."

"Yes." She smiled, and some of the wickedness was back. "You do not remind me of him at all. And that is a compliment."

Just then he heard a sound, and realized it was her stomach rumbling. "Good Lord, is that you? Are you hungry?"

"Starved, actually," she admitted, looking embarrassed. "I was too nervous earlier to eat much supper."

"*This,*" he declared, "I can fix." He sat up, and her hand slid over his arm to rest on his back. "On your feet, woman," he commanded. "I must give you fuel. I have every intention of your needing it."

She followed him out to the kitchen. He leaned down to retrieve his clothes, pulling on his shorts and handing her his shirt. She shrugged it on, not bothering to button it, and he took a moment to take her in. He was never going to be able to look at that shirt the same way again.

Shaking himself, he turned and opened the refrigerator, a cool draft escaping into the darkened room. "You have a sweet tooth," he assumed.

"God, yes," she said, moving in behind him to look over his shoulder. "What do you have?"

He retrieved his latest experiment from the top shelf. He was only on the second stage—he was still deciding whether to wrap it in pastry, or to thicken it and coat it in some expensive, off-world chocolate—but he thought, so far, that it was rather wonderful on its own. He pulled open a drawer to retrieve a spoon, and scooped a little out of the bowl.

"Here," he said, holding the spoon out to her. "Tell me what you think."

She took it, glancing at him, then gamely took a taste. In an instant her expression changed to something not unlike what he had seen a few minutes ago by the alcove.

"Oh my *God,*" she breathed. "What is that? Cream, and lemon, and . . . hazelnut?"

"You have a discerning palate," he told her, pleased. "I've

also added a splash of rum, just to deepen the fruit flavor. I was worried it was a bit too much."

She shook her head. "No, it's perfect. Lovely. Is there more?"

So he handed her the bowl, and they wandered into the living room, and he sat next to her on the couch while she consumed his experiment. "You made this," she said, as she ate it all, bite by bite.

He nodded. "It is my profession. I am a dessert chef."

"My goodness, yes you are," she said. She scraped the bottom of the bowl and looked into it sadly. "I suppose that was all," she sighed, and he laughed.

"There are a few others at earlier stages," he told her. "Incomplete. I experiment, a bit, on my own."

"Have you done this long?"

"Off and on, for about thirty years," he told her.

"Was that your profession with PSI? Did you cook for them?"

He shook his head. "I was an officer," he told her, deciding not to elaborate. "But Fyodor—he was our captain, and for most of my life there my mentor—loved to make desserts, and on the longer journeys he would always try something he had never made before. He would have me help him. After he retired, I kept on doing it." It had been a comfort, one thing he had been able to keep constant after everything around him had changed.

"Is that why you came here?" she asked. "To be a chef?"

He paused. "In a way," he told her at last. "I was born here. My sister has never left. Her husband died last year, and she asked me to come back and help her run her business. She has a café, so cooking for her made sense." He felt a strange sense of relief, and of exposure; he had not spoken of Katya to anyone since he had come back.

He waited for her to ask why he had left, why he had stayed away for so long; but it was Katya that had caught her imagination. "Are you close to her?" she asked, with something like wistfulness.

He shook his head. "She was very young when I left. I wrote to her . . . but I was a stranger. Now she asks that I tell no one how we are related." It was not the whole truth, but it was enough.

"Why?"

He raised his eyebrows at her. "We are not always thought of with charity," he told her, although he was certain she knew it. "Katya believes PSI is full of evil, selfish thieves, running from their responsibilities." He regarded her, suddenly curious. "I'm rather surprised you do not." He had always assumed Central Corps collaborated with PSI only grudgingly, when left with no other options. It had not occurred to him that Central, mistrust notwithstanding, might recognize the value in an alternate approach.

The woman's eyes narrowed a little as she considered her next words. "I know what people say," she admitted. "But I know what they say of us as well. There is truth and lie in all of it. I may be loyal to Central, but I know enough to understand why some would want nothing to do with them. And given my own choices, people choosing to live their lives and raise their families on a starship instead of a dusty bit of rock makes a lot of sense to me. Out here . . . you may think I'm naive, but I have seen things. I have seen people starving. I've seen the remains of colonies that turned to civil war when they ran out of food. And I have seen people who have survived this fate, or dodged it entirely, only because PSI intervened when we couldn't. You are called thieves, and perhaps strictly speaking that is sometimes true," she concluded. "But I don't believe thievery is always wrong."

It surprised him, her vision of his family, and he felt vaguely ashamed of his own assumptions. "I would not have expected a Central soldier to have such a subtle perception of reality," he admitted. "I would not think you were allowed."

She grinned, and her eyes danced. "We are not *all* bored idiots with guns," she told him. "The truth is, out here we see everything. And on a ship as small as ours . . . we must all agree, at least on some level, about right and wrong, no matter what the regulations say. The captain follows the rules when he can, but he's also pragmatic. If it saves lives, he orders us to do the sorts of things PSI does every day, damn Central Gov, and he doesn't lose a moment's sleep over it."

"I think I like this captain of yours."

"You might, but for one thing: he has no sweet tooth."

"I am outraged," Trey declared. "Or perhaps I should feel sympathy."

"I think it's wonderful," she told him. "When they ship us chocolate, he lets us have his share."

He laughed. "I must admit, you soldiers appear to be less different from us than I have thought."

"Because of chocolate?"

"Because the pleasures of being human," he said, "seem to appeal to us all."

She drew up her legs and knelt on the sofa, moving closer to him. "When you said, earlier, that I would need the fuel," she asked, "what exactly did you mean?"

He took the bowl from her hand and leaned forward to place it on the table. "I should have thought that was obvious."

"Tell me anyway," she whispered.

He leaned back on the couch and reached his arm around her waist. Wearing his shirt, one oversized sleeve slipping off her shoulder, her breasts peeking out from behind the buttons, she looked somehow more enticing than she had completely nude. "I should like to make love to you," he told her, drawing her closer, his free hand finding her breast and hefting it gently. "Here, on the sofa. Or the floor, if you prefer, although my preference would be first one, and then the other." She had crawled into his lap, and he kissed her once, gently, tasting cream and hazelnut on her lips. "I would like to continue this until the sun rises and the day reclaims us both." He moved to kiss her neck, nuzzling the hairline behind her ear. "Do you find this suggestion agreeable?"

She responded by moving closer until they were hip to hip, and she kissed him, deep and long and satisfied, and he thought the pleasures of being human would be a fine way to pass the night.

CHAPTER 3

Galileo

*W*hat is the half-life of the radiation produced by the destruction of a hybrid nuclear starlight engine?

Captain Greg Foster read the message again, then turned away to look out his office window. The planet of Volhynia filled the viewport, green plains and azure seas dotted with swirls of clouds, the stars shifting behind it as *Galileo* paralleled its orbit. All planets looked beautiful from up here, he reflected, no matter what lurked beneath the atmosphere. One of the loveliest planets he had ever seen was Liriel, an emerald jewel in a stable, six-planet star system. But Central's fleet had struggled to evacuate the fifteen thousand colonists before the failure of their terraforming equipment had surrendered the surface to sulfur and methane. They had lost civilians. Few, in context, but Greg knew every name. He had been decorated for his work on Liriel, but he still counted it a personal failure.

The most important lessons, his mother had taught him, *are the ones that go wrong.* At least whatever was wrong with Volhynia was not in its atmosphere.

He turned back and reread the question. Mathematically it was a simple problem, one every Central Corps officer was expected to be able to solve without the aid of a computer. Depending on the size of the engine, radiation from the explosion would drop to tolerable levels anywhere from three to seven years later. That was a big reason nobody ran hybrid engines anymore; beyond the efficiency gains that had been made in pure starlight tech, the risks of failure were too high. Nobody wanted to block a travel corridor for such a long period of time, never mind irradiate a habitable planet. The hybrid design was inherently unstable, and nobody had been sorry to see it abandoned.

Curious, though, that only one Central starship had ever lost a hybrid engine. Curious that twenty-five years later, the site of the *Phoenix*'s destruction was still too hot for travel.

Conspiracy theories abounded. Everybody seemed to think Greg ought to care, that he ought to seek absolute proof of what had happened to his mother's starship. When he was young, he had been caught up in unproven government conspiracies and rumors of alien invasion. He had almost let it destroy his life. Now he had been part of Central Corps for fifteen years, nine as captain of his own ship, and he had learned that the simplest answer was almost always the truth. Central did not have the resources for an expansive cover-up, even if it would have provided some benefit—and there was no discernible benefit to the loss of 456 trained soldiers.

What is the half-life of the radiation produced by the destruction of a hybrid nuclear starlight engine?

He swept his hand through the message, and it disappeared. "*Galileo*," he asked, "what's the current radiation level at the site of the *Phoenix* disaster?"

There was an almost imperceptible pause as his ship queried

the larger net. "Current radiation levels at location 345.89.225," *Galileo* told him in her warm androgynous voice, "are ambient 13, critical 22.2."

Meaning you'd melt before you got anywhere near it. Greg put his thumbs over his eyes. "A nuclear starlight explosion nets what, sixteen, eighteen?"

"Nuclear starlight explosion yields are dependent on size, configuration, attendant materials, fuel levels, ionic—"

"Okay, okay," Greg said, and the ship fell silent. Officially the *Phoenix* had not been carrying cargo. *Deep space exploration* had been her charter: the elusive search for alien life, which no one anymore thought would be successful. Boring stuff. Even the wormhole at the center of the *Phoenix*'s patrol territory was uninteresting, the meager secrets of its unapproachable entrance having long since been exhausted. His mother, before she left, had seemed unenthusiastic, despite her love of space travel.

There was no data on the *Phoenix*'s fuel levels, or anything else. Despite twenty-five years of long-range scans, the unique audio signature of the ship's flight recorder—which might have provided them with everything from engine status to last-minute comms—had never been detected, despite the extensive debris. The recorder should have had sufficient shielding to survive the hybrid blast. Yet another anomaly that had never been explained.

"Assume one-half fuel level on a sixteen-ton D-10 config. What yield does that give you?"

His ship answered promptly. "Sixteen point one seven, repeating."

Greg did some quick math. Assuming the maximum seven-year half-life, the *Phoenix*'s residual radiation should have hit ambient eight less than twelve years ago, ambient four six years after that. "So here's a question," he said. "What type of cargo might spike the previous explosion to produce radiation of fifty-six?"

"Armed hybrid torpedoes," *Galileo* returned promptly. "Ellis Systems terraforming modules 16 and 45. Twelve kilos of dellinium ionic solids. Seventy tons of—"

"Stop." The dellinium rumor was old, based on readings right after the explosion that had been corrupted by the nearby pulsar. Once the initial shock wave had passed, they found no evidence of dellinium at all, much less twelve kilos of the stuff. The *Phoenix* had carried no terraformers, and even if she had, Ellis had been a tiny research company at the time, not yet building heavy equipment. Weapons seemed the most likely conclusion . . . but then he was back to conspiracy theories. If the *Phoenix* had been hauling weapons, surely something, somewhere, would have come out about it; an exploratory mission never carried that much firepower.

There were no answers. There would never be answers. He should have learned to live with it by now. He *had* learned to live with it, even in the face of messages sent to him, year after year, by lonely and desperate people convinced the Corps knew more of the accident than they were telling. It had been years— decades—since he had given those theories any credence. And yet . . . there was something different about this message, sent anonymously, and the two that had arrived before it, spread over less than two weeks. He could not believe that it was coincidence that they had diverted to Volhynia, so close to the site of the disaster, at the same time as the messages started to arrive.

Someone knew something—was trying to tell him something—and he could not work out what it was.

It unnerved him to realize how easy it would be for him to fall into that abyss all over again.

After his mother died, he worked toward joining the Corps because it was what she had wished for him. He had been in the field nearly two years, barely a lieutenant, before he had accepted she had been right: he belonged here. He had saved lives. He had ended wars and transported engineers to repair failing terraformers and weather converters. He had made food and medicine drops, carted researchers and humanitarian workers to worlds where people were struggling to make the unlivable into a home. He had made a difference, just as his mother had always told him he would. Despite that, though, all he ever saw at night—as he lay awake awaiting whatever meager portion of sleep would be granted to him—was her name among the dead.

The low chime of his office comm shook him out of his glum thoughts. A message ident flashed before his eyes: *Adm. Josiah Herrod, Central Admiralty, Earth.* Greg frowned. A real-time call from the Admiralty, and vid at that: they wouldn't have allocated the bandwidth unless something was up. Out of habit he straightened, and felt a moment's relief that he had been avoiding alcohol for the last two weeks. Off-duty or not, he didn't want to talk to Herrod while he was drunk.

"Connect," he told *Galileo.*

A moment later the admiral's face appeared before him. He was seated at a desk similar to Greg's, but instead of stars, the window behind him revealed a span of green grass and the wall of a blue-gray brick building. The light was dim, and Greg was not sure if it was early morning where Herrod was, or evening. "Admiral Herrod, sir," he said formally, and saluted.

"At ease," Herrod said automatically. Herrod was roughly twice Greg's age, although his gray hair still retained much of its original dark brown. He had a broad face, a broad nose, and a perpetual frown, and Greg had the impression the man did not like him much. For Greg's part he found Herrod too often stiff and uncompromising. Of course, this was not an unusual affliction for Corps brass who had been long out of the field, and it had been more than thirty years since Herrod had been off-planet. Still, he tolerated Greg's idiosyncrasies, albeit with less grace than some of his peers; and if he sometimes lacked subtlety in his decision-making, he had been known, when presented with evidence, to change his mind. He was not the most nagging of Greg's superior officers, and he had never been prone to vid comms across five sectors for no reason.

"What can I do for you, sir?" he asked.

Herrod's hands were folded on the desk before him, and Greg saw his fingers clench. "What you can do for me, Captain," Herrod said, "is explain to me what you're doing loitering over Volhynia."

Greg frowned again. Herrod would know; their presence here was official. "We took on *Demeter*'s cargo on Aleph Nine, sir," he explained. "Volhynia was the last drop."

"I'm aware of the cargo transfer," Herrod snapped, and Greg thought perhaps this was not some kind of test after all. "What I want to know is why you're still there."

At that Greg became annoyed. It was easy for a man stationed on Earth to ask such a thing; he had no real idea of what life was like for a starship crew. But Herrod had spent time among the stars, albeit decades ago, and Greg was frustrated by how much the admiral seemed to have forgotten. "My people have been out for nearly half a year, Admiral, and they haven't had a break since Aleph. You want to explain to me why you're using a live vid signal to complain about my crew taking shore leave?"

"You want to explain to me why your crew is taking shore leave when we're in the middle of a diplomatic incident?"

All of Greg's irritation vanished. "I'm unaware of what you're talking about, sir."

"Your ship was briefed on approach, Captain Foster," Herrod said severely. "If you've been ignoring Central's reports—"

"No, sir," Greg said. His gut felt cold and hard; he knew what had happened. He should have dealt with Will months ago. "There have been some . . . internal communication issues lately. If you could brief me directly, sir, that would probably be most efficient."

Herrod looked away, and Greg could see him weighing whether or not he ought to waste time taking Greg to task. In the end he stuck with the problem at hand. "We're on alert in the Fifth Sector," he told Greg, "from Volhynia around the pulsar through the hot zone. The public story is that *Demeter* went in for repairs at Aleph because they were attacked by Syndicate raiders. In truth they were hit by PSI."

Hit by PSI. Greg could not let that go unchallenged. "That can't be right, sir. Someone miscommunicated something, or Captain MacBride is playing a joke that got out of hand. PSI's not going to hit one of our ships. Above and beyond the fact that they're on our side, we outgun them, sir, and not by a little bit. It'd be suicide for them to engage one of ours." A cold fear struck him. "Are they claiming casualties, sir?"

"They're not claiming anything," Herrod told him. "They're not talking to us."

So it wasn't a joke. *Christ.* Relations with PSI had always been light on dialogue, but it had been more than eighty years since any kind of live fire had occurred between Central and the nomadic group. Central maintained bureaucratic structures to facilitate aid and distribution to the colonies spread sparsely throughout the galaxy's six mapped sectors; PSI preferred a more ad hoc style of providing assistance. Despite the humanitarian goals PSI shared with Central, their solutions were too different to facilitate camaraderie, but most Corps soldiers would never think of seeing a PSI ship as a threat. Something had set them off, and Herrod didn't seem to know what it was. "What is Captain MacBride claiming?" Greg asked.

"MacBride *reports* that the PSI ship *Penumbra* approached them adjacent to the hot zone, and fired on them unprovoked."

"For what? Their cargo?" If Central thought PSI had been after *Demeter*'s cargo, they would have made sure Greg was properly warned instead of simply loaning him twenty-five members of *Demeter*'s crew to handle the shipment.

Herrod was shaking his head. "MacBride said they took their shot and then retreated. No demands for cargo, no comms at all."

"But that doesn't make any sense."

"No," Herrod agreed, "it doesn't. Which brings me back to my original issue. We need you to be scouting for PSI activity in the area."

Greg was already querying *Galileo*'s sensors. "We're showing all four PSI ships outside of this vicinity," he said. "Closest is *Castelanna,* but even she's six hours out, and she's not moving. They're all stationary. *Galileo,* what's the local time?"

"Local time is Dead Hour plus thirty-eight," the ship said smoothly.

"What the hell's Dead Hour?" Herrod asked irritably.

"Artificial power outage," Greg explained. "The colony's power grid isn't reinforced to withstand the EMP from the pulsar, so they take the waypoints down for about an hour every night while they get hit. It doesn't always save their equipment, but it keeps the pulse from traveling along their connections."

Herrod shook his head. "They've got more money there than half the First Sector," he grumbled. "Why the hell don't they update their grid?"

"Tourism," Greg replied, although he shared with Herrod an impatience at the planet's odd decision. "When we come out of the pulse, sir, I'll get my people on recon." He hesitated. "You want me to pull them home, sir?"

Six months away from the First Sector, away from most of their families. Six weeks since they had had any time that was their own. They had barely nine hours before they were due back. He could recall them, and they would come, and they would do their best for him; but they had so little left. Most of them didn't even really understand how close to the edge they were running.

Herrod appeared to be weighing the option. "Your discretion, Captain," he said at last. "As long as PSI's ships aren't moving, we'll stay off high alert. But I want you away from there in the morning, do you hear me? Find out what PSI is doing in the sector. Get them to talk to you if you can—but put it together. I want to know why they fired on *Demeter,* and I want to know if they're going to do it again. Understood?"

"Yes, sir."

"I want a report in twelve hours. Directly to me, Captain."

"Yes, sir."

"And fix your communication problem," Herrod finished. "I don't want to hear again how a starship captain isn't getting his orders."

Damn, damn, damn. "Yes, sir," he said. "It won't happen again, sir."

"You're damn right it won't. Herrod out."

The vid vanished. "*Galileo*, let me know when Novanadyr comes out of the Dead Hour. And get me Commander Valentis."

Galileo usually acknowledged his orders, but this time the ship simply opened the connection to Will Valentis without saying anything. He thought perhaps it knew he was angry.

Will could have taken the entire night for shore leave, but he had returned early. Greg had wondered about that. Six months ago he might have asked, might have encouraged his first officer to take more time to relax. Now he was just glad the man was back on board . . . and within reach, in case Greg found he had to strangle him. When the connection completed, Greg did not wait for Will to speak. "My office," he said. "Now." And he cut the line.

Will reported promptly. Will always reported promptly. Seven years they had served together, and Greg could not think of a single time his second-in-command had been late. He could not think of a time that Will had neglected to pass on relevant information, either, but he knew why it had happened now.

And he was entirely out of patience.

Will stood at attention, and Greg let him stand, stiff and rigid and staring straight ahead. "I just got off the line with

Admiral Herrod," he told Will. "You have something you need to tell me?"

"No, sir."

Not an oversight, then. "The admiral seems to think I was supposed to know about a general alert in this sector," he said, "because *Demeter* was hit by PSI. You know anything about that, Commander?"

Will blinked, and his eyes shifted briefly. "Sir, I—" He stopped and regrouped. "I'm sorry, Captain. I should have briefed you."

Which was a reminder that it was Will who had been briefed on the situation, and not Greg. Will was enjoying his temporary power trip far too much. Greg let lie, for the moment, the fact that such vital information had not come directly to him. "You want to tell me why you didn't?"

Will hesitated again. "Sir, you know there are things I can't explain."

And that was the crux of it. Six months earlier, when they had been on Earth, Will—perennially ambitious and stagnating as Greg's first officer—had been tapped by Shadow Ops for a secret investigation. Greg had been notified of the fact of Will's assignment to Central's intelligence branch, but not the details. As a result, he had been required to give Will extensive leeway on comms and internal reporting, and in return Will provided him with a heavily redacted copy of his monthly report to S-O.

Greg had not been gracious about this. He should have been happy for his old friend, a man who had never been destined for command. In fact, intelligence seemed better suited to his talents, and might actually provide him with his long-sought avenue for advancement. But the secrecy had bothered Greg, despite having no concrete reason to mistrust Shadow Ops. Perhaps worse, Will enjoyed far too much leaving him out of the loop.

It was Bob Hastings, the ship's senior medical officer and Greg's oldest friend, who had made Greg stop and think. "He's seven years older than you, Greg, and he's spent all this time in your shadow," Bob had pointed out. "Let him be good at this. Let him have something that isn't a subset of you for once."

So when they had arrived at Aleph Nine alongside the damaged *Demeter* and Will had asked him to have *Galileo* fulfill *Demeter*'s cargo obligations, he had agreed, despite the fact that it was prolonging their mission another three weeks. MacBride was providing twenty-five members of his crew to do the actual work of delivery, and it would take *Galileo* to a planet well-known for its recreational value.

The decision had made sense at the time. Now he wondered what had really been behind Will's request.

"How about you redact what you need to redact," he told Will, "and explain to me how you thought the sector being on alert was an important point to conceal."

Will shifted uncomfortably. "The alert was relevant to *Demeter*, sir. You put me in charge of that mission."

"I made you supervisor of her crew while they were on board." Greg had no doubt the man understood the distinction. "Regardless, the alert is relevant to all ships in this sector. This is the safety of my crew we are talking about, and you chose to say nothing to me."

"Sir, if I can explain—"

"No, Commander, you cannot." He rounded his desk and stood before Will. Will was one of the only people on board as tall as Greg himself, but he kept his eyes on the opposite wall as Greg glared at him. "Out here, on my ship, I am the law. Not Shadow Ops. Not the Admiralty. Not you, Commander Valentis. This omission of yours, whatever excuse you concocted in your head, is feeling awfully close to mutiny for my taste. You think I'm going to be putting up with mutiny, Commander?"

Will swallowed. "Sir, I have no intention of being mutinous."

"That's encouraging to hear," he said. "But your intentions are irrelevant. If I find out you've concealed anything else from me that affects the safety of this ship and this crew, I will write you up, regardless of any orders you feel you might have from S-O. Is that clear, Commander?"

Will reddened, a sure sign he was angry, but all he said was "Yes, sir."

"You have anything else you need to be telling me, Commander Valentis?"

"No, sir. Nothing else."

"Then you're dismissed."

Will snapped up straight and saluted, then turned and stalked out of the room. Not once had he met Greg's eyes.

Only when Will was gone did Greg allow himself to react to what Admiral Herrod had told him. War with PSI. Son of a bitch. As long as he had been alive PSI had been a source of help and intelligence. Their people did not mingle with Central's— they dealt more with colony governments and freighter captains than they did with Central Gov—but they had helped with everything from evacs to firefights, always on the side of Central and the colonies. The only groups they were actively hostile toward were the Syndicate tribes, and since the Syndicates often attacked PSI ships directly for their cargo, Greg could hardly blame them. PSI brought food to the starving, and equipment to planets losing their terraformers; they served as a refuge for homeless children, and often for adults who felt they had nowhere else to go.

But Central knew almost nothing of them. They had pieced together enough intelligence to make a guess at some of their patterns and rituals, but little more. For their part, PSI seemed singularly disinterested in engaging with Central. Why would they fire on *Demeter*? Had MacBride done something stupid?

Or was PSI changing their tactics?

His eyes returned to the window. *Galileo* flew between the pulsar and the planet, her shielding protecting her from the EMP. Her shuttles would be similarly protected, had they been allowed to take off during the blackout. Central should have insisted Volhynia upgrade their system years ago, but the government wasn't inclined to push the colony to do anything. Central needed the bulk of the human population—most still living on Earth, or on the densely populated First Sector colonies—to believe prosperous worlds like Volhynia were the rule rather than the exception, and with widespread starvation in the Third Sector, they didn't need Volhynia publicizing how little Central had to do with their success. Greg had spoken to the officials on the surface to arrange the cargo drop-off; they were smug bastards, and it had taken most of his energy to be polite to them. They seemed to think the dumb luck of their ancestors, who had managed to find a planet that was natively adapted to human life, somehow implied merit. Greg had little patience with such arrogance.

His father had always seen it differently. "A man who has never lost can't understand what it is like to be without," he said. Greg found that a weak excuse. He had always had food and clothing, diversions and transportation, friends and opportunities. He had led a charmed life. He still did. And every day, every time he inhaled, loss clawed at his throat and threatened to suffocate him. Nothing that Volhynia had was certain. Life could drop out from under you with no warning at all. Those officials were fools to believe they would never need Central's goodwill.

With a silent apology to his people, Greg signaled the recall of the infantry down on the surface. He could not solve the *Phoenix* disaster—not now, maybe not ever—but he could find out what was going on with PSI. And maybe, if he could do it quickly enough, they could avert a war.

CHAPTER 4

Volhynia

Elena walked along Novanadyr's wide streets, the bright morning light casting long shadows. She could not remember the last time she had stayed up all night for anything beyond her job. Back when she was in college, she thought. Before she enlisted. Back when it was easy to ignore her worries and be carefree, at least for a few hours.

The night would catch up with her, she knew. In this moment, however, she could not remember ever feeling so delightfully wide-awake.

Traffic picked up as she neared the spaceport. A few quiet solar mass-transit trams slid past along the center of the street, and she caught sight of some private shuttles speeding politely over the low rooftops. She realized, as numerous pedestrians smiled at her and wished her good morning, that she was wearing a wide grin. Well, so be it: for once she could be part of the crowd who had enjoyed shore leave.

They had made love as the sun rose, and then he had washed her hair, and found her an elastic she could use to tie it back. She caught him watching as she looped her hair into an efficient knot at the nape of her neck, and when she asked he had smiled.

"I had never realized," he told her, "how lovely a woman could be in a soldier's uniform."

It was hyperbole, she knew; he had grown up around women in uniform, and she was certain many of them were far more beautiful than she was. But somehow, in the moment, she believed him.

Despite the early hour the spaceport floor was crowded, numerous visiting shuttles lined up against the walls. *Exodus One* rested undisturbed where Elena had left her the night before. She began her preflight check, and caught herself humming; dancing was impractical when she was leaning down to look at the undercarriage, but every part of her felt full of music.

"Why are you so goddamned cheerful?" a voice growled behind her.

She turned and grinned at Ted. "Good morning, Lieutenant," she greeted him. "How does the day find you?"

Ted Shimada was, at most times, a good-looking man, lean-muscled and hearty, but this morning he looked haggard. "There's a remote possibility I had too much to drink last night." She laughed aloud, and he winced. "Fuck, Lanie. Seriously." He squinted at her. "You *are* cheerful, aren't you? Who'd you spend the night under?"

"Some guy I met in a bar."

"You? Picked up some spaceport cruiser? I don't believe it."

"He wasn't a cruiser," she told him. "He was PSI."

That shocked most of the hangover right out of him. "Seriously? You picked up a *pirate*?"

"Well," she said, a little alarmed at his response, "sort of. He's retired."

Ted's expression froze, and his eyes took on a cunning look. "You picked up an *old* pirate."

"Old my ass," she declared, turning back to her task. "I didn't sleep."

"Yeah? How long?"

"Six hours, give or take."

He shook his head in wonder. "Jessica is going to tell everyone on board, and the comms guys are going to stare at you like cats in heat for a *month*."

She stopped and turned back to him. "Actually," she said hesitantly, "I was thinking of telling Jess I hid in some dive hotel alone all night."

"You think you can sell that?"

"Can't I?"

"Let's see." He considered her. "Stop smiling so much."

She drew her lips together and tried to look serious.

"Stand up straighter. Be military."

She stood at attention.

"Now stop humming."

She had not realized she was still doing it. Swallowing a grin, she complied.

He shrugged. "That's not bad. Of course," he added, as she went back to the preflight, "that big-ass hickey on your neck pretty much gives the game away."

Elena put a hand to her throat. Sure enough, there was a tender spot under her left ear. She glared at Ted, who put up his hands in self-defense.

"Don't yell at *me*," he objected. "*I* didn't bite you."

The others trickled in as she worked, ticking their names off at the wall terminal. Fifteen minutes from departure she had twenty-one; not a bad showing from a roster of thirty. Most of the stragglers were from the *Demeter* crew; the few who had already arrived waited outside the shuttle for their friends, talking to each other in low voices and falling silent every time a *Galileo* soldier walked by. Elena did not understand them. Enthusiastic friendship was hardly required, but *Demeter*'s borrowed soldiers seemed intent on open hostility between the two crews. She should have asked the bay officer to assign them a dedicated shuttle, but she supposed that made her no better than they were.

Belatedly it occurred to her that Danny might be on this shuttle as well, and would hear how she had spent her evening. Well, she had made it clear to him when she turned down his invitation the day before that he had no claim on her any longer. He had thrown that away all on his own.

She had finished her check of the ship's air seals and was turning to look for the dispatcher when she came face-to-face with Jessica, who had crept up silently behind her. Despite the fact that Jessica was likely just as hungover as Ted, she looked perfect: coppery hair tamed away from her face, expression bright-eyed and alert, the picture of a disciplined officer. Except that she was staring at the bruise on Elena's neck, her expression cheerfully curious.

"So," she asked, "did you find someone else?"

Elena shook her head, and saw her friend's eyes widen slowly. "*Seriously?*" she said, nearly shrieking. "You fucked a *pirate*? Those guys are *dangerous*." Jessica was looking at her friend with naked admiration. "You are out of your mind. So how was he?"

Elena thought of all the ways she could answer that. She thought of the night behind her, of how he had touched her, of how he had spoken to her. She searched until she found the right word.

"Thorough," she said.

Jessica stomped with impatience. "Elena Marie Shaw, after all the years we've known each other, all you're going to give me is 'thorough'?"

Elena considered. "Extremely thorough," she amended.

Departure time neared and they were still down four. It was Jessica who cleared up the discrepancy for her. "Someone said Foster pulled the infantry guys back early," she said. "Didn't say why."

Elena frowned. Jessica seemed unconcerned, but Elena didn't think Greg would have pulled any of them back early without a solid reason. If it had been an incipient emergency, he would have told all the senior officers, but she could not shake her unease. He would be awake when they got home; no matter how acidic he insisted on being, she would have to ask him.

Greg never took shore leave—captain's privilege, he always said. Six months ago she would have cheerfully stayed home with him, enjoying his quiet company. As things stood, though, it had been easy for her to decide to leave. Their friendship had been strained for half a year, and the public argument they'd had two weeks ago had undone the last of her equanimity. If she had stayed behind, she would have run into him, and he would have goaded her into shouting at him again. Losing Danny should have hurt more than losing Greg, but she had so few true friends in her life. Lovers were easy; she felt she had left Danny behind already.

Greg was not so easily replaced.

She climbed onto the shuttle and settled into the pilot's seat to steer them out of the main hangar. The morning sun blazed through the front window, and in deference to Ted's quiet groan she engaged the polarizer. She angled them upward, keeping the incline gentle as they transitioned from the planet's gravity to the ship's artificial field. The sky darkened quickly as they rose through the clouds, and then the stars came out. She brought them around to the planet's night side, and there, sleek and streamlined, graceful as a swan with wings outstretched, drifted the CCSS *Galileo*. Her ship. Her home.

Galileo had been state-of-the-art once, seven years ago, when she had first been christened. Even now, with all of the larger, faster ships that had been deployed since, the little craft was a gem, although Elena acknowledged she might not be entirely objective. Certainly the ship's hull bore some battle scars, the sleek metallic surface discolored and battered here and there; but she could still outfight a vessel twice her size, and even with a slower top speed, she was faster off the mark than any ship that had been built since.

Demeter was both newer and larger, outfitted with cutting-edge tech out of Ellis Systems' research branch, and Elena overheard her crew make disparaging comments about *Galileo* from time to time. She let it go, aware of where her own loyalties would lie if their positions were reversed. They were lucky they didn't have to deal with Commander Jacobs, her old boss, who would have slapped them down publicly and succinctly, and with more than a few insults. Jake had always been impolitic and passionate, and in the year since his death she found she missed that part of him the most.

Only a year ago. Just a year. A year ago Jake, not Elena, had been chief of engineering, and she had been content working for him. A year ago she had had Danny to keep her warm, and Greg to keep her sane. Now she had none of them, all lost, one way or another. In recent months she had considered transferring off of *Galileo*, leaving behind all of the pain and alienation and starting over on another ship. But on this morning, flying home with a night's worth of warm memories, that choice seemed ridiculous. How would her life look different if she went somewhere else? Leaving was an overreaction. It was giving up, and she had never been one to quit.

She hailed her ship. "*Galileo,* this is *Exodus One* requesting hangar access."

"*Exodus One, Galileo.* Shuttle hangar seven. Welcome back, Lanie. You missing anybody?"

"Nobody but the infantry."

"Well, you're ten minutes late. Hurry up before you all miss breakfast."

Elena glanced around the cabin. "I don't think you're going to have a lot of takers on the food."

The comms officer cackled, and beside her, Ted groaned again. "Would you people *please* stop laughing?" he said plaintively.

Elena resisted the urge to pat him on the head, then transferred the shuttle's control to *Galileo* and let the autopilot bring them home.

Trey took his time walking to work. It was nearly 6:30, and he was already an hour late. Katya would be irritable; but then, Katya was always irritable with him. It bothered her that his former profession was an asset to her restaurant. She still insisted he stay in the kitchen, invisible to the diners; but word had spread that Katya Gregorovich had a pirate for a chef, and curiosity had brought customers in droves. He liked to think they kept returning because of his cooking, but realistically he knew that most of them were just hoping to catch a glimpse of him. It gave him an odd sort of satisfaction, knowing that strangers thought better of him than his own blood.

He walked along the sidewalk past the restaurant window, and caught the shadow of someone moving inside. Katya would not open for another half hour, but she would have been there since 5:30, preparing. Trey thought back: at 5:30 he would have been washing the woman's long, dark hair.

Since his return to Volhynia, he had been approached by men and women alike, attracted by strange misconceptions of the life he had led. This woman had not spoken to him as a PSI soldier; she had spoken as an equal, as a friend. As someone interested in him, and not the uniform he used to wear. He had actually felt glad, for the first time in months—perhaps years—to be what he was.

He began to hum again.

He stepped into the alley behind the restaurant. The kitchen was in the basement, and the separate entrance helped Katya preserve the illusion that he was some paid stranger, and not her family. He had always excused her treatment of him, even felt deserving of it. Today, though, he found himself tired of penance. Perhaps it was time he stopped apologizing for his choices. Perhaps it was past time to face the world as it was, the good with the bad.

The wind shifted, and he froze, still thirty meters from the entrance.

Not here. Not my home . . . When he was fifteen years old, *Castelanna* had been hit by a Syndicate raider. Trey, who had not yet seen battle, had run haphazardly into the middle of the fighting. By the time he arrived there was only one raider left alive, and before he had a chance to do anything Fyodor had used a pulse rifle to blast off the man's shoulder. The invader had dropped, dead before he hit the floor. Trey had been hit with a spray of human blood and flesh, and it was days before he stopped smelling death.

Forty-two years later, he smelled it on the wind.

He crossed to the opposite side of the alley, his back against the wall. He could see, just beyond the basement entrance, a heap that might have been a man, and a dark shadow on the pavement that had nothing to do with the morning light. He inched closer, alert for movement. Nothing. The odor told him that whatever had happened had been over for hours.

When he got close enough to get a good look, he began cursing and did not stop. The man was young: thirty, perhaps thirty-five. In life he had been handsome, slender and fit, his yellow hair striking against his olive-gold skin. Now all trace of animation was gone. He stared straight up with pale brown eyes that were already sinking back into his head, long-congealed trickles of blood tracing from the slash across his throat onto the cement beneath him. His torso and abdomen were a mass of haphazard cuts and slashes—much of him was now indistinguishable from any other piece of meat—but even underneath the blood Trey recognized the same black and gray uniform he had sent the woman away in that morning.

The dead man was one of hers. And Trey, the outsider, was going to have to deal with it.

CHAPTER 5

Galileo

Greg watched the shuttle pull in, easing to the floor of the hangar without a bump. The autopilot, he supposed; even Elena, as obsessive as she was about flying, allowed *Galileo* to handle the artificial gravity transfer. Still, it was a testament to her flying skills that he could not tell by sight. He had watched her fly through atmospheric turbulence and antiaircraft fire, her hands steady and true, her mind always on the task before her, no matter what waited on the other side.

He was dreading the task before him, but at least it was action. *Galileo* had been fortunate enough to suffer few losses through the years, but in the Corps death was an inevitability. To Greg, losing one of his own crew always felt like a missed opportunity, some horrible mistake he had no way of correcting, and the futility of it enraged him. All he could do now was break the news to her compassionately, give her as soft a landing as he could. What waited for him on the other side was the search for answers, and the vain attempt to convince himself that justice would mean anything at all. Justice, he had found, was a flimsy illusion used to stave off anger, and anger always won in the end.

He kept his eyes on the ship as the hangar was sealed from space and oxygenated, and as the massive outer bulkhead closed. The shuttle settled to the floor and powered down, and the side door opened, disgorging a mix of his crew and *Demeter*'s, all lumbering with a lack of sleep. He saw Jessica Lockwood, as crisp and composed as she had been the night before, and Ted Shimada, looking slightly green. Elena came out last, her eyes scanning the shuttle's hull, reflexively checking for damage.

Wherever she had been, she had changed her hair; it was knotted at her neck, more loosely than usual. When she left the night before it had been down, and she had fussed with it, self-conscious about the change. Now she seemed relaxed, almost liquid, as if movement were effortless; she shot a smile at the ground crew sergeant that nearly shattered Greg's calculated detachment. She was not, he knew, a great beauty by any objective measure, but he was years past any kind of objectivity about her. He wished he could stop the universe and keep her frozen in this moment before he had to break her heart.

He wondered if it would have been easier or harder six months ago, before he had needed to retreat from her. She might have already been home on *Galileo* when he received the news, sitting with him in the cafeteria over an early breakfast. He would have had time to take care of her before he had to focus on anyone else; he could have held on to her for a while, steadied her until she could stand on her own. She would not have been isolated from him, unable to take comfort, unable to hear anything in his words but the failure that had let a man die.

Harder. Definitely harder.

"You could say hello, you know."

He looked down at Lieutenant Lockwood. Unlike Elena, Jessica was a classic beauty, wide-eyed and round-faced, and she used it like a cudgel when she needed to; but what he always noticed first about her were her shrewd green eyes. He suspected few people bothered to lie to her. He could not start now.

She had seen it in his face already, and her expression sobered. "Is this about the recall, sir?"

Anger flared, and alongside it guilt. He should have recalled everyone, not just the infantry. He should have immediately pursued any officer who did not respond. He should have thrown Will Valentis in the brig for insubordination. It all would have been too late anyway. "No, Lieutenant," he told her, keeping his voice neutral. She would hear the whole truth soon enough. "But if you could start gathering people in the pub, I'm going to have to make an announcement."

She went white under her freckles, but he saw her straighten. "Yes, sir," she said. She hesitated for a moment. "Do you need me to stay?"

She had followed his eyes and was watching Elena as she ran her hands along the shuttle's exterior. "That's all right, Jess," he replied, more gently. "Just get the others together."

She gave him a salute and disappeared out into the hallway. He closed his eyes for a moment, wishing for the last six months of his life back, then entered the hangar.

Elena looked up at his step, and she stiffened, all that liquid grace gone, waiting for him to reach her. He caught sight, as he drew closer, of a bruise on her neck—no, he realized, momentarily disconcerted, not a bruise. She had found company. It surprised him—it was unlike her to move on so quickly from a broken love affair. He wondered who it was; he had not noticed her showing an interest in anyone since her breakup with Danny Lancaster. Then again, he had always done his best not to look.

He stopped in front of her, and unlike Will Valentis she held his gaze, her dark eyes steady. She had never shown him any deference, even years ago when she was just another ensign under his command. And just like she had every time he spoke to her, in every conversation they had had for seven years, she saw it in his face before he made a sound. Her eyes widened with dread.

"Who is it?"

Of course she would know what had happened. There was a particular flavor to it, the death of one of their own. "I'm sorry, Elena," he said. "It's Danny. He's been killed."

He watched her face change, stage by stage: astonishment, doubt, denial, anger. Her eyes flashed, sharp and flinty. "Are you sure?"

"They have his ident. I'll send Doctor Hastings down to verify, but there's really no question."

Her fingers convulsed against the ship. She turned away and then froze, as if she was trapped in a small space. "What happened? He drinks too much, all the time, was that it? Did he—"

Damn all colonies straight to hell. "He was murdered, Elena. I'm sorry."

For a moment she did not react at all, and he thought he would have to repeat it. But then she said, "*What?*"

He looked away, reflexively running a hand over his short-cropped hair. "He was knifed. His comm was taken. For what it's worth they've arrested a suspect—someone they've been watching for a while." He left it at that; she did not need to know the rest. The rest he would take up with Will after the news of Lancaster was public and he did not have to rein in his emotions anymore.

"So you're telling me he was mugged. That Danny was killed over *money*." She pushed herself away from the shuttle, turning her back to him, her arms wrapped around herself. Her spine was stiff, but he could see how fast she was breathing. Rage and grief; he had been through it with her before, when Jake had been killed. When they had still been friends. "How long will they let us stay?" she asked, her voice low.

They meant Central. Elena knew the rules. "I haven't spoken with them yet." Mindful of Herrod's order to depart that morning, he was waiting for more intel from the Novanadyr police department before he informed the admiral of his intent to remain. He thought he knew how Herrod would respond, but despite his hard line with Will, he was not beyond a little insubordination himself. They could do their part monitoring for PSI movement while they were in orbit, and if Herrod didn't like it, he could haul his aging ass off of Earth and relieve Greg in person.

She shook her head. "We've already been out six months. What's a few more days?"

He did not answer. She knew as well as he did what long tours did to soldiers, how events like one little night of shore leave became the difference between efficiency and anarchy. Greg believed he had the best crew in the fleet, but he knew a few more days might break them. A few more days might break her, too.

"Why did we come here, Greg?" she asked, in that same quiet voice.

It had been weeks, he realized with some surprise, since she had used his first name. Since their argument. "You know why," he answered, confused. "*Demeter* needed repairs, and we took on her delivery. We—"

"I know *what* we did, Greg. I want to know *why.*" She turned to face him, and her rage hit him like a slap. "What was so critical about their cargo? Their timeline? Some two-bit *trawler* hauling for some overfed liquor merchants adds *three weeks* to our schedule, and you don't even blink?"

"Elena—"

"No, let me guess," she snapped. "You can't tell me. Some *need-to-know* bullshit. Well Danny is dead, Greg, because of your *need-to-know* bullshit. Over *money,* for God's sake, that paltry ten thousand that was all he ever managed to save, no matter how many times he won at cards, no matter how much—"

She stopped, and he saw the reality of it begin to sink in, and he wanted to throw away his rank and his detachment and his pointless self-involvement and put his arms around her, pooling her grief with his own. He had long since abdicated any right to offer her comfort, and for a moment his composure threatened to disintegrate in the face of a wave of self-loathing. Dammit, he should have had someone else tell her. He had forgotten, after all these months of avoiding her, how easily she could dismantle him.

He watched her expression close, her breathing steady, her posture straighten. Little by little she hid herself from him again, tucking away all her rage and bitterness.

"Thank you for telling me, Captain," she said calmly.

This was worse, he thought: this deliberate separation, this rejection of anything he might offer her. "Elena, if you need anything—"

"*Don't.*" The word was a choked whisper.

He nodded. "I'll be informing the rest of the crew in a few minutes. Just so you know."

She looked away from him, and he turned back to the door, grasping at the shards of his anger. He needed it back. His rage helped him to forget how entirely pointless his presence was, how useless he was to her, to his crew, to the dead man.

There would be justice, and it would make no difference.

He shook off self-pity and left the hangar to tell his crew their comrade was dead.

He spoke to them in the only area large enough to hold the entire crew: the massive VIP conference room, years ago repurposed as the ship's pub. He kept it brief and factual, talking about justice and love and losing one of their own, and he saw in some faces, at least, that it helped. They believed in him, and they believed he would find justice for Danny. After all, he was the man who made things happen, who circumvented regs and logic and the goddamned laws of physics when it suited him. His reputation, as exaggerated as it was, worked in his favor. When he finished they were shocked and grieved, but reassured that he would get to the bottom of it all.

When Greg turned to Will at the close of his speech, his first officer looked pallid and shaken, unable to hide his shock. Will had played some poker with Danny—Danny excelled at losing money, and was popular at the gambling table—but Greg had not thought they were so close.

It was a rare crack in Will's armor, and Greg thought he could use it.

"With me," he said stiffly, and walked out, trusting Will would follow him. There were too many people still milling about to risk having this discussion in public.

Will trailed into Greg's office after him and sat in his usual chair without asking. Greg leaned against the edge of the desk, arms crossed. Will met Greg's eyes, already defensive.

"I hate coincidence, Will," Greg told him.

"I don't know what you mean."

"I'll spell it out, then," he said, still calm. "One of my men gets killed in the middle of a cargo mission *you requested,* right around the time I get my ass handed to me because *you decide* Shadow Ops has somehow given you the authority to keep me out of the loop on a general alert. Which coincidentally involves some *fairy story* MacBride is telling about being attacked by PSI. And here's the most interesting thing about that. Do you know who Novanadyr is holding for Lancaster's murder? Some PSI expat who just settled there. Who somehow manages to kill a trained fighter with an old-fashioned, low-tech blade." Greg leaned forward, looming over Will's chair. "Lancaster was nearly decapitated, did you know that? I didn't tell the crew, but I've got that picture in my head. A thirty-five-year-old man, with a sister and four nieces, bleeding out in seven seconds on an alien planet."

He had not raised his voice, but Will had flinched. "So let me reiterate, Commander Valentis: I hate coincidence. Explain to me why I shouldn't shut down your investigation *right now* and tear up the concrete on that rock down there until I find out what happened."

"You don't have the authority," Will said, his voice dry.

So much for sympathy. "We are ten days away from the closest Central hub, Commander," he returned. "Five months away from Earth, if we take a straight shot. I can do whatever the fuck I want out here, and every soldier on this ship will back me up." He leaned back. "Try again."

Will swallowed, and looked away. "I don't believe Lancaster's death is related to my work, sir," he said.

Greg stood up and circled behind his desk, parsing that. "Why not?"

"Sir, I—dammit, Captain, I'm under orders here. From people who outrank you." He sounded desperate. "I can't just give you this investigation. It'd be my career."

"It always comes back to your career, doesn't it, Will? It's never about the crew, or even the mission. It's always what's in it for you."

Will had reddened. "That's not fair, Captain. What I'm doing for S-O is important."

"Yes," Greg said icily. "I'm sure it is. So important you can't tell a living soul, so now we've got a dead one."

"You're not putting Lancaster's death on me."

"Then tell me who to put it on, Will."

Will exploded. "I've told you! I—" He looked away, then got to his feet, agitated, running his fingers through his short black hair. He was graying here and there; Greg had not noticed before. "Lancaster spoke a lot with the *Demeter* crew, yes." He began to pace. "You know what he was like; he wanted everyone to get along, and most of our crew hasn't exactly welcomed them with open arms."

Greg thought that went both ways, but he let it pass. "Would they have discussed anything proprietary with him?"

Will had stopped at Greg's window and was looking down at the planet. "They shouldn't know anything proprietary," he said at last.

That had cost him, and Greg tried to remind himself to appreciate that. "But if they did," he pressed, "would they have told Lancaster?"

"I won't speculate." Will's expression had closed, and Greg thought that small admission was the only thing he was going to get.

Greg allowed himself to rub his eyes; there was no point in posturing anymore. Will had told him all he needed to know about how deeply *Demeter* was involved in all of this. Any further investigation was going to have to be his own. The problem was how to ensure he could investigate unencumbered. He did not want to make an enemy out of Will, not in the middle of a crisis. It had crossed his mind, however, that they might be beyond that point.

"Here's what's going to happen, Commander." He spoke calmly, wanting Will to understand that his decision was not made in a temper. "We're going to stay here as long as it takes to get Lancaster's death resolved. That means more than just Novanadyr charging his killer; it means we find out *why* he did it."

"Central won't allow that."

"You let me worry about Central." There were delaying tactics he could use, everything from semantic arguments to outright lies. If he achieved his ends, he thought the Admiralty would forgive him, or at least not come down on him too hard. "But in the meantime . . . I'm shutting you down, Commander. Your investigation stops right now. S-O gets nothing until we find out what happened to Lancaster."

"You can't do that, Captain!" Will turned on Greg, shouting into his face. "They are not just my superior officers. They are yours as well, and this will *not* be tolerated!"

Greg held on to his temper. "Maybe not," he said evenly, "but that's on me, Will. I'm revoking your external comm privileges, effective immediately."

And to his astonishment, Will laughed. "They'll bust you for this," he said, with certainty.

"Maybe." Greg wondered exactly who Will's allies were. "But if they do, it'll be after we get answers for Danny Lancaster."

Chapter 6

Jessica sat before a cup of bitter coffee, surrounded by her silent and somber friends. After the captain's speech, about half of them had stayed in the pub: more than a hundred people, including the *Demeter* crew members. They might be self-satisfied jackasses, but their distress seemed genuine. Danny had spent a lot of time talking to them, even Lieutenant Commander Limonov, widely known to be half-mad. Danny had listened to the man's ravings, all his tin-foil-hat theories of aliens and government conspiracies, with what had always seemed to be genuine interest. Now Limonov sat with his crewmates, scowling miserably into a clear glass of dark liquid, and Jessica reflected that everyone needed someone to listen once in a while.

"Excuse me."

Along with the rest of the table, Jessica looked up. Captain Foster stood over them, his demeanor grave and military, unrecognizable from the hollow-eyed, resigned man she had left in the hangar.

Damn, he's a good actor.

"I'm sorry to interrupt," he said, "but I need to borrow Lieutenant Lockwood for a moment."

The others murmured excuses and one by one removed themselves from the table. Jessica wondered at that; surely she and the captain should have been the ones to leave. But it was deference to him, she realized: no matter how big a jerk he was to Elena, no matter what sorts of rumors persisted in the hallways, Captain Foster's crew adored him. She adored him a little herself, which irritated her sometimes; she did not like to think she was subject to military psychology. But she had to admit, no matter how well she got to know him, no matter what stupid mistakes she saw him make, she would always be willing to walk into death for him.

He waited for the others to leave, then dropped into a chair next to her. He was a good-looking fellow, her captain. A bit on the thin side, sure; but he had a handsome, chiseled face just this side of perfection, well-muscled arms, and lovely, long-fingered hands that gestured gracefully when he was speaking. And his eyes, of course. Those eyes, light gray and black, strange zebra-stripe eyes, laser-bright against his dark skin. She had thought, when she met him, that they were a cosmetic affectation. It had not taken her long before she realized affectations were alien to him. He dealt purely in somber reality, although she caught flashes, sometimes, of lightheartedness. As she looked at him now, he seemed weary and defeated, and she wondered how much was Danny, and how much was Elena.

Jessica did not understand it at all. For months Elena had seemed to recognize, on some level, that Foster needed to keep away from her, and had tried to give him space; and then everything had blown up a few weeks ago in the pub. Jessica did not believe he had really meant the things he had said, but she knew how Elena held a grudge. He was going to be a long time rebuilding that bridge, if he could do it at all, and she did not think having to break the news of Danny's death had eased any tension.

"Did Commander Valentis say anything useful?" she asked him.

She had seen the look on his face when he had left with Valentis. Five months ago Foster had handed her the first of Commander Valentis's reports to Shadow Ops, with a carefully worded request for her to see what she could make of the parts that had been redacted. Without explicit authorization to decrypt, she had simply documented the algorithms, and how long it might take a competent hacker to break them.

When he had shown up with the next report, she had asked why he was confiding in her, and not Commander Broadmoor, his security head. "Because you're more loyal to me than to the rules," he had told her.

She had never been sure what to make of that, but she couldn't disagree.

He unfolded his long legs under the table and crossed them at the ankles. "Not so you'd notice," he replied. "Double-talk about Lancaster and the *Demeter* crew, and how it's all just a coincidence it happened on this cargo drop."

"You believe him?"

To her surprise, he paused. "I don't know," he said at last.

On top of everything else, she found herself hit with a wave of unease. "You think his story is credible."

"I think," Foster said slowly, "that 'credible' and 'true' are not the same thing." He looked over at her, and she saw a familiar sharpness in his eyes. "How comfortable would you be digging into the life of a dead man?"

The breach of privacy should have horrified her, but it was action, and it might actually prove useful. "Parameters, sir?" she asked.

"No parameters, Lieutenant. I want everything."

"What if I run into something locked?"

"We'll clear it after the fact."

She held his gaze for a moment. "Locked" could mean tagged as private, or it could mean classified and sealed under threat of court-martial. She wondered briefly if her captain was testing her. Greg Foster got creative with regulations sometimes—she had heard him interpret orders with impressive semantic gymnastics—but there were lines he just didn't cross. It occurred to her to ask him if he understood what he was suggesting. She had learned over the years, though, that he missed almost nothing. He knew exactly what he was asking her to do, and how good she would have to be to do it.

This was more than circumventing regulations. This was working around the Admiralty, around Shadow Ops, around Central Gov itself. Regardless of her intentions, she could be charged with treason. There was something bigger happening, something he had not told her yet—and he didn't trust his own command chain to handle it. That he trusted her was both flattering and daunting, and she had no intention of letting him down.

"She spent the night with someone, didn't she?"

It took her a moment to recognize the change of subject, and she grew immediately wary. Like every practical, pragmatic man, he had a blind spot, and his had been the same as long as she had known him. "Why do you ask?"

She knew he had heard her bristle. He always heard it when she bristled. "This guy—do you think they're at a point where she'd lean on him? No matter what she thinks she needs, at some point being alone is not going to work."

Oh, hell, he thought it was someone on board. "It wasn't one of ours, sir," she told him. "He was a stranger. Some guy she met at the bar."

"That doesn't sound like her."

"You think I'm making it up?"

"Of course not. I just—you know her as well as I do. You're telling me you're not surprised?"

She thought back. She had been pleasantly tipsy when Elena had left the group, but she remembered the pirate, how he had leaned toward her friend and smiled, how Elena had laughed, her whole body relaxing for the first time all night. "Not with this guy," she told him. "He was tall, dark, and handsome, and looked like he'd had his nose broken a half-dozen times and didn't care about getting it fixed. He even wore the uniform, which seemed a little weird at a local pub, but it looked good on him."

"Uniform? You said he wasn't one of ours."

Oops. "No, sir. He was PSI."

Foster became utterly still, and for one disconcerting moment she could not read his expression at all. "Are you certain of that, Lieutenant?"

All of her alarm bells were going off. "Certain? No. He was wearing all black, and he had his hair pulled back in a braid, like they do. Of course, he was friendly, at least with her, so maybe he was just playing the part." Jessica thought of her friend—tall, dark, and lovely—and did not wonder that anyone, even a PSI soldier, would warm to her. "What is it about PSI, sir?"

"We don't know anything about them," he tried. "We don't know why this man was there. None of our intelligence suggests they do shore leave like we do. What could he want on Volhynia, then?"

She took in the anxiety on his face. She was beginning to think this wasn't about jealousy after all. "Don't bullshit me, sir. I know you. You don't get paranoid about PSI. Hell, you're not shy about working with them when we need them."

"That's in the Fourth Sector. I don't know them here."

"But they're on our side, sir. Aren't they?"

He was silent for a long time, and her spine began to tingle again. PSI was an acronym pulled from a dead language, which roughly translated meant *freedom, truth, intellect.* In her experience, they lived up to the sentiment. Like many people who had grown up on a world with limited resources, she viewed PSI as a positive force, sometimes heroic. PSI supply drops had kept her warm and properly fed as a child. It had never occurred to her before that she knew nothing of them at all.

"It's more than just Danny," she said quietly, "isn't it?"

"Yes."

"And you can't tell me."

"No."

She took a moment to silently curse rank and regulations, then nodded. "I'll get on Danny's records, sir," she said formally. There was little she could do for Danny, but she could do this.

"Thank you, Lieutenant. And as soon as I can—" He was interrupted by a chime from his comm. "Yes?"

Jessica heard nothing; he had it set to private audio, the patch behind his ear flashing dimly as he listened, but by his lack of response she knew the message was not from a person, but from *Galileo* herself. She saw the color drain from his face, and his eyes grew hard and determined. Before he was finished listening, he was on his feet. She stood as well, and wished she hadn't; the difference in their heights seemed less dramatic when she was sitting down. "Sir?" she asked.

"They've released the killer's name," he told her tersely. "I need to talk to the chief."

Chapter 7

Elena sat on the floor between her bed and the window, staring out at the stars. She could so easily imagine being out there in the icy darkness, weightless, airless, soundless. Sometimes as she watched she held her breath; but she could still hear her heartbeat, and under that the soft, constant thrum of *Galileo*'s systems. The ship made a different sound when they were in the FTL field at speed, but even at rest it sang, gentle as a lullaby. That song always made Elena think of Jake, and for a long time it had left her sad; but in recent months, despite her battles with Greg, it had made her feel strong, and less alone. Even after she broke up with Danny. Especially after.

She tried to feel grief, but all of her rage, all of the intensity that should have been about Danny was focused on Greg. Why had he brought them here? He hated tourist planets. She had wondered about his mother, about being close to the wormhole and the site of the *Phoenix* accident; but the man she knew wouldn't have kept tired troops out another three solid weeks just to get three billion kilometers away from where a starship had been blown to pieces twenty-five years ago. There was something else happening; she had seen it in him. Only there was no way for her to ask him, this man who had become a stranger to her, what was really going on.

The anger was childish and pointless. She was stupid. And more than anything, she wished for the Greg she had known six months ago, who would have sat here, as he had after Jake died, asking nothing of her, just staring with her out at the stars.

She climbed to her feet, turning her back to the window. "*Galileo,* have you got a Novanadyr news feed?"

"Twelve feeds are available, six on the stream."

That surprised her; stream feeds usually meant tabloid journalism, and Volhynia didn't seem like the kind of place that would encourage such a thing. "Find me one with a decent news reputation."

"Standard or local dialect?"

The local language, like Standard and most of those spoken in the Fourth and Fifth Sectors, was a derivative of ancient Russian. Elena knew enough to get by, but she did not want to risk losing the subtleties. "Standard," she said.

The vid flared to life in the air half a meter before her eyes. She saw a low building made of yellow sanded brick lit by the planet's unfamiliar, anemic sunshine, an overlay identifying it as the police station. For a moment she thought the picture was static, but occasionally the small shrubs planted by the foundation stirred in the wind, and eventually a bland, accentless voice-over explained that they were waiting for a promised update from Yigor Stoya, the chief of police.

"Is this all they're showing?" she asked, after several minutes without change.

"A summary of earlier updates to this story is available," *Galileo* told her.

Elena dropped into one of the chairs that sat at her little table by the door. "Let's have that, then."

A selection of news clips began playing: the initial report of the murder, identifying him only as a tourist; some reaction shots from a selection of local merchants; a brief statement from a sturdy, barrel-chested man in his early forties identified as Chief Stoya. He had iron-gray hair over weary eyes set in pale skin, and she was almost certain he was an off-worlder. There was something in how he moved that set him apart from the natives she had seen, something familiar that she could not place. The set of his mouth gave him a look of ruthlessness, and she wondered if that ruthlessness applied to his pursuit of justice.

She opted to watch the full vid of the arrest of the suspect. Oddly, he had been at the station at the time, reporting finding the body. *What a strange way of trying to divert suspicion,* she thought; and then she watched as the police hustled the man, in old-fashioned handcuffs, through the low yellow building's open front entrance.

And her blood went cold.

His hair was loose, hanging over his face; but she could see one bruised, half-shut eye, and his lip was split in several places. Blood had dripped onto his clothes: white and pristine that morning, she remembered. His knuckles were clean; he had not fought back. She supposed, knowing something of the local laws, that would have been close to suicide. He glowered at the cameras, his dark eyes irate, but she caught a resignation in them as well. A man like him, PSI for most of his life, would not be surprised to find himself railroaded by colony law.

He was marched forward far enough for the news crews to get a good look at him, and then he was bundled around to the back of the building and out of sight. The shot switched, this time to a different police officer, identified as Lieutenant Commander Janek Luvidovich, investigator in charge. He spoke with intelligence and deliberation, diverting the press with articulate non-answers . . . and had it not been for the edges of a hangover tugging at the corners of his eyes, she might not have recognized him as the incoherent man who had grabbed her arm the night before.

She swore, leaping to her feet. "*Galileo,* how old is that clip?"

"Two hours sixteen minutes."

Two hours. *God.* They would have been beating him again, almost certainly. They would want a confession, and he had nothing to confess. "Is there an ident on the suspect?"

Galileo flashed a name, and she froze. "Truly?" she said faintly.

"Suspect has confirmed to police."

She swept her hand through the video and hurried out of her room, heading back in the direction of the pub. "Where's the captain?"

"Captain Foster is in the atrium."

She emerged from the narrow corridor that housed her quarters into the bright, wide atrium area, the center of the ship. Six levels high and fifty meters wide, the space was lit with full-spectrum mid-morning light, making the day on Volhynia look like a winter afternoon. With its gardens full of vegetable plants and fruit orchards, the atrium had always provided her with enough of a sense of open space to keep her happy; in the center of it, she could deceive herself that it was a park on a colony somewhere, and not the central hub of a starship.

Elena scanned the paths before her, oblivious to the beauty she passed. She did not have to search long. He was walking toward her, his stride businesslike, and she had the impression that he had been coming to find her.

"Captain," she said as they approached each other, "I need to talk to you."

"I need to talk to you, too, Chief."

He stopped, glaring at her, and she felt a flash of exasperation. So much for their recent argument diffusing his pent-up anger. He was annoyed with her again, for God only knew what, and she did not have time to tiptoe around his temper. "Captain, I've got to go back down."

"The hell you do." She could not tell if he was more incredulous or annoyed.

Why does he never just listen? Ignoring his outburst, she said, "I need a shuttle, and I need to get down there right now, because they've been beating him up already, sir, and it's only going to get worse."

"You are not going *anywhere* until you tell me about this PSI officer you spent the night with!"

There were not a lot of people in the atrium: half a dozen that she could see, huddled in groups, hanging on to each other as they processed the shock of Danny's death. Greg's outburst had secured the attention of all of them.

She didn't care. "I'm *trying* to tell you, sir. They've got the wrong man, and that investigator isn't going to let him go, and I have to get down there and untangle it or they're not going to do a goddamned thing to find Danny's killer."

"They've got his killer. And I want you to tell me what the hell PSI is doing dropping people on Volhynia."

She replayed that in her head, and could not make it comprehensible. "What are you talking about?"

"That man you were with last night? I want to know who he was, and what he was doing there, and how in the hell Treiko Tsvetomir Zajec ended up on Volhynia *murdering* my crewman."

"That's what I'm trying to tell you!" She wanted to shake him. "He didn't, Greg. He couldn't have. He was with me when Danny died, and for hours afterward. What the *hell* are you talking about?"

Slowly his eyes widened, some of his anger and frustration dissipating. "You're telling me the suspect—Captain Zajec—*that's* the PSI officer you spent the night with?"

"What did you think?" she asked irritably. "That there were hordes of them down there, and one of them diverted me while the others hunted down Danny?"

He was staring at her, but she knew the look. That was exactly what he had been thinking. "Come sit down," he said at last, and took a step toward a bench next to the herb garden.

Now *you want to keep this private?* "We do not have time." But she followed him, and she saw the others turn away, losing interest in the argument.

When she sat, he turned toward her. "Tell me."

"That man they've arrested. Treiko Zajec. He's the man I was with last night. And unless they completely bollixed up the time of death, he could not have murdered Danny."

"You're sure of this."

"Yes."

"He didn't step out, comm someone else? What about while you were sleeping?"

"We didn't sleep." He looked away, and she felt like shaking him again. "Greg, the ident. Are we really sure it's him?"

"He's the right age," he said, "and he's apparently known to the local PD." He rubbed his eyes, and for a moment she glimpsed his extreme fatigue. She wondered if he had commed Danny's sister yet. "Elena, what the hell is a PSI captain doing in a place like Novanadyr?"

The Fifth Sector was not their usual patrol. *Galileo* took the Fourth Sector, and was familiar with the PSI ships that shared their territory. Greg had met all of the officers, had even befriended a few of them; Elena knew most of their names. But even outside of the Fifth Sector, everyone in the Corps knew the names of its PSI captains: Piotr Adnovski, Valeria Solomonoff, Aleksandra Venkaya, and Treiko Zajec.

The dark-eyed chef. Her lover.

"He's retired," she told Greg. "He said about six months."

"Why Volhynia?"

"He was born there."

"Why'd he leave?"

She thought of the sister who did not want to acknowledge him. "He didn't say. Greg, why does it matter?" She shifted, wanting to run to the hangar and get moving. "He didn't kill Danny, and I need to make a statement, or they'll hang it around his neck."

"I've talked to the cops," he said. "Stoya, and that kid they've got in charge of it. They're not stupid. You really think they're just going to hang it on an innocent man?"

"That kid they've got in charge of it is part of the problem," she said.

His face grew wary. "Why?"

She told him.

"Oh, that's fucking *marvelous*," he snapped. "The chief fucking investigator, knocked on his ass by the most notorious pirate in the sector, over *you*."

"So you see why I need to make a statement."

He shook his head. "Elena, you can't go back there. What do you think they're going to say when they find out you and Danny were lovers? You really think that's going to help the guy?"

"What are they going to do, call me a liar? With Central backing me up?" He just looked at her, and after a moment her stomach dropped. "Oh," she said.

"You go down there, you're just going to make it worse."

"You're telling me Central doesn't care who killed Danny?"

"It's not about that."

His expression had closed again, and she clenched her teeth. *God, this secrecy is bullshit.* "Greg," she asked him, "what's going on?"

"You know the political situation with Volhynia."

Everyone knew the political situation here. Volhynia: the planet that didn't require terraformers, had a healthy, growing population, was a tourist center, and a scientific hub. Central needed people to believe that Volhynia was not the exception: that humanity was able to thrive out here, that they weren't fighting a losing battle against score after score of hostile environments.

But she could not believe Central would let the murder of one of their own go unpunished. "I don't believe it," she said flatly. "It's something else, Greg, something that you're trying not to tell me." *I'm going back with or without your permission,* she told him silently, *so give me something to work with here.*

He was staring at her intently, eyes serious, evaluating her. He frightened some people when he was like this, but she knew better. He was trying to understand, trying to read her mind, trying to figure out how much he really needed to say. Before, he would not have hesitated; he would have known he could trust her. In all fairness, before, she would have trusted his advice without needing to know why he gave it, too.

Now, she needed to know. After a moment he looked away. "This is command-level intel, Elena," he said.

"Who the hell am I going to tell?"

He shot her a look. "MacBride is reporting that *Demeter* was hit by PSI."

She thought for a moment he was joking. "Bullshit," she said.

"He is reporting," he told her, "that they approached the PSI ship *Penumbra* outside the *Phoenix* hot zone, and when they asked what the ship was doing there, they were fired upon."

"*Penumbra*." She had a vague memory of having heard the name. "That wasn't Captain Zajec's ship."

Greg shook his head. "Solomonoff's."

"She doesn't have the reputation for being crazy."

"None of them do."

"But Central is still letting MacBride file this work of fiction."

His lips tightened. "He's an experienced Corps captain, Elena, and a die-hard patriot. And why in the hell would Niall MacBride make up a story that makes him sound like a coward?"

True enough . . . MacBride was all ego and bravado, but he did his job, and he did not have a reputation for running away. "So Central thinks something is up with PSI."

"Central is watching very carefully right now."

"So carefully they will let Volhynia convict a man for murder who had *nothing to do with it*."

His face took on a careful expression. "Kind of a coincidence," he said, "that of all the people in that bar, Zajec talked to you."

Bastard, she thought, but something had occurred to her. "Listen—I'll allow for the possibility that it wasn't my wit and charm that made him take me home." She hated saying it. She certainly did not believe it—not after last night. "But think about this: let's suppose, for a moment, that PSI has some secret scheme that involves making MacBride look chickenshit, and picking off our mid-level infantry grunts one at a time. Does Central really want Captain Zajec in the hands of the authorities on Volhynia? Where by the end of the day they'll have him locked up in some room so far belowground he'll never see sunlight again? It makes no sense, does it?"

Please, she thought at Greg. *Please understand what I'm saying.*

He was staring away from her, his eyes aimed at the herb garden, seeing nothing. "Why do I feel like you'd say anything to get me to agree to this?"

"Because I'm right," she told him, "and you know it."

He closed his eyes for a moment. "Central won't want him locked up on Volhynia," he said, "but they're not going to want him running around free, either."

That was an angle she had not thought of. "But—"

"You can't have it both ways, Elena. You tell me he's useful? I agree. That means we use him."

"He's *retired,* for God's sake," she snapped. "He doesn't know what happened to *Demeter.*"

"And you know this how?" He opened his eyes and stared at her, his gaze hard. "This isn't some guy you picked up at a school dance. This is a PSI captain who runs into you while we are on alert. Central isn't going to buy 'he's retired.'"

"And you don't, either, do you?" She felt anger taking over again. "It's so easy for you to believe that he could have fooled me, that I could have turned a blind eye to some fucking *conspiracy*."

"And it's so easy for you to dismiss the possibility because the guy's got some personal charm." Before she could object, he added, "Will you fucking *think* for a second? You want to believe this guy? Fine. But think about how it looks from the outside, to people who've never met him. We need to talk to him, Elena. This isn't about tact or diplomacy, this is about people *shooting at each other*."

"So you want me to arrest him."

"I want you to do what you have to do to get him up here," he told her. "Appeal to his better nature. I'm sure he doesn't want war any more than we do."

And yet we're the ones talking about taking prisoners. She shook her head. "I'll get him released, Greg. But if you want him up here, either he comes willingly or you send someone else down to grab him. I won't do it."

She saw his jaw set and his fists clench, and she wondered if he would risk giving her a direct order.

She wondered what she would say to him if he did.

At last he nodded, and she felt a flood of relief. "You go down there," he told her, "you give your statement, you get him out. And you do your damnedest to convince him *Galileo* is the safest place he could be right now. Whether he says yes or no . . .

you don't piss around down there, Chief. You deal with the immediate situation, and you haul ass back here. Clear?"

"Clear, sir."

"And I'm sending Bob down with you."

The relief vanished. "Doctor Hastings? Why?"

"I want him to validate their postmortem results," he told her. "And it's a plausible excuse to have someone down there keeping an eye on you. You stay with him, you understand? Have him treat Zajec's injuries, if it makes you feel better, but do not go anywhere without him."

"Fine," she agreed. "But he's got five minutes to make it to the hangar, or I leave without him." She turned and started to walk away.

"Elena."

She stopped.

"This isn't going to change what happened."

Nothing would change what happened. Danny was dead, and that was reality, and when all of this was untangled she would have to sit down and have a good hard look at that fact. When Jake had died she had spent days cleaning up the engine room, clearing burnt debris left over from the blast, repairing what she could and writing up invoices for the parts that needed replacing. It had not brought Jake back, but it had needed doing, and when his loss finally hit her she had been able to surrender to grief without having to worry about duty.

She would do her duty for Danny as well, and see his killer come to justice.

"Five minutes," she repeated, and headed for the hangar.

CHAPTER 8

Volhynia

forget," Doctor Hastings said as they glided back down toward the planet, "do you deal with this sort of thing head-on, or are you the type to swallow your feelings?"

"You know exactly what type I am," she told him. Bob, as it happened, was one of the few people who would know for certain.

"You've been swallowing a lot lately."

Not now, she thought, shoving a bubble of grief back down her throat. "Maybe I wouldn't have to if my friends weren't being such assholes."

"Did it ever occur to you that he's even worse at dealing with loss than you are?"

"Did it ever occur to you that that's no excuse for his behavior?"

"Didn't say it was an excuse." Bob always spoke mildly, as if nothing he ever said was of any import. "I'm just suggesting that when someone who copes poorly makes the mistake of getting intoxicated in public, he's not going to handle it well."

Annoyance began to blunt grief, and she clung to the topic.

"He's a grown man," she said. "He has a tantrum, and I'm supposed to shrug it off and forgive him?"

"It's really that bad between you?"

"You were there," she reminded him. "What do you think?"

Everyone had been there. Bob had been at the bar right next to her, talking with Emily Broadmoor until Greg's yelling drew their attention. She had retorted, for all the good it did—there was no real comeback to what he had said. His outburst had crossed a line she had thought long crossed. He had hurt her, when she had thought there was no more room for hurt in her life. At least she wasn't spending any more time trying to figure out how to forgive him.

Bob had known Greg for years; knew his father, his sister, his wife; had known his mother before she died. Duty notwithstanding, Elena knew where his loyalties lay.

"If I asked you, as a personal favor, not to close the door on him," Bob asked, "would you do it?"

For a moment she thought quite seriously of screaming at him. Instead she bit her tongue, and took a mental step back. Underneath her irritation, her guilt, her grief, there was bone-deep exhaustion. She had not slept, she had not eaten, she had too much left to do, and none of that was the fault of the physician. "I didn't close anything," she said, with more civility than she felt. "But he sure as hell did."

Novanadyr's traffic control guided them through the atmosphere and onto the spaceport's tarmac, keeping them hovering until they were waved into the hangar. The deck coordinator assigned them a spot right by the back door. She appreciated the placement—she always preferred to be close to the exit, even on a developed colony—but she suspected they were simply hoping that Central wouldn't leave their representatives on the surface for long.

They took one of the public trams to the police station. Elena was aware of stares. She kept her face expressionless and her eyes forward; both of her hands gripped the railing, but she was conscious of her handgun at her hip. Next to her Bob leaned into the wind, a half smile on his face. At one point he turned to a woman standing behind them and said hello. The woman looked startled and moved away; Bob gave a low chuckle.

"We need to be efficient," she told Bob as the tram slowed in front of the station. "Once we walk in there, the press will descend like vultures." She hopped off, Bob at her heels.

"A proper postmortem is going to take me at least an hour," he warned her.

"You do what you need," she said. "If we get separated, you can go ahead and take the shuttle back up."

"He'll skin me alive if I do that, Chief."

"He'll skin me alive, too. But I'm not sticking around here if it means dealing with stringers." If she had to choose between Greg's anger and the full force of the press corps, she would face her captain's rage.

His lips thinned, and he shook his head. "Stubborn," he murmured, and she knew she'd won this one.

As they were walking up to the station's entrance, a wide gap open to the building's lobby, she caught sight of a man halfway up the block, slouching against the wall, eyes looking ahead at nothing, as if he were listening to a comm. He was absurdly thin, absurdly tall, and absurdly handsome.

She cursed.

"Bloody Ancher," she said to Bob's look. Ancher was a stringer: a professional journalist who had covered the Corps for years. He was tenacious, good-natured, and entirely without ethics. "Someone's leaked that the dead man is a soldier."

"Then we'd better get it done," Bob said wearily, and opened the door.

The desk officer, a young man with disapproving eyes, checked her weapon and directed them upstairs to the main office, a wide, airy room spanning the width of the building. Behind the reception desk stood a young woman, pale and petite, like Jessica; but her hair was dark, her skin was free of freckles, and she lacked Jess's palpable exuberance. She watched them patiently, and Elena stood back, allowing Bob to handle the social aspects. "Good afternoon," he said to the officer. "We're here to see Chief Stoya."

He flashed her a smile that Elena had long ago noted many women—even as young as this one—found charming. Elena saw the pale cheeks color a little, and her dark eyes warmed. "Of course," she replied easily, giving Elena a perfunctory glance. "I'll let him know you're here." She walked off toward the private offices that lined the room's interior walls.

One of the office doors opened, and the weary-eyed Chief Stoya emerged. In person he seemed smaller, although he was easily Elena's height. She thought the illusion came from the way he moved, compact and efficient, threading himself between the desks with ease. He scanned the room with wary intelligence, and despite his cold expression she wondered if he would prove more flexible than she had assumed.

She did not have to wonder long. He shot her a look of open dislike, then let his gaze settle on Bob. "You are Doctor Hastings," he said. His rigid mouth thinned. "Doctor Velikovsky is waiting for you downstairs in the morgue," he said. "Officer Keller will escort you."

That accent again, different from that of the locals she had heard in the city, and still vaguely familiar. He sounded like some of the traders she knew, and she wondered if he had spent time in the Fourth Sector. Cygnus, maybe, or Osaka Prime. Someplace with money.

Bob favored Keller, the young woman at the desk, with a pleased smile. "That's very kind of you, Chief," he said, and Elena thought his warmth was sincere.

As Keller made her way around the desk, Stoya locked his eyes on Elena. They were cold, those weary eyes; ice-blue and clear, but barren of any emotion at all.

"Captain Foster says you are a material witness," he said. "You will make a statement, on the record?"

She nodded, and caught a flicker of emotion in his face, too quick to identify.

"Very well. Luvidovich!" he shouted.

Another office door opened, and Luvidovich emerged. She saw him hesitate, his confident expression wavering, and then his face darkened as he realized she was about to ruin his day. She had wondered if he would remember her.

It was still not payback enough.

He kept his eyes on her as he approached. "Yes, sir," he said to Stoya when he was close enough.

"This woman," Stoya said, "claims she can provide Zajec with an alibi. Set up the polygraph and take her statement."

Luvidovich flushed, and she saw his teeth clench. "That is not possible."

Stoya gave an impatient sigh. "If it is not possible, she will fail the polygraph. And then, if you wish, you may charge her with obstruction of justice. But until that happens, do as you are told." He added a phrase in the local dialect; Elena, despite her passing familiarity with the language, missed it entirely.

Luvidovich, however, did not miss it at all. He colored more deeply, but straightened up, composing himself. He glanced back at Elena, then looked away as quickly as he could. "Follow me," he told her.

Elena turned and met Bob's eyes; he nodded at her, and she followed Luvidovich out of the room.

Luvidovich took her statement in a small, dank, and poorly lit basement room, with the help of an ancient polygraph. At times he seemed to believe he was interrogating her, challenging the sequence of events and accusing her of saying things she had not said; but after a quarter of an hour it struck her that however hostile his delivery, Luvidovich was doing his job, and fairly well. She thought she might have misjudged him, at least a little. No professional police officer would release a suspect lightly.

But it was not until they had left the polygraph behind and were heading up the stairs to the lobby that he asked her anything about Danny himself.

"Did you know the dead man well?"

She could not see his face, but his tone was overcasual, and she tensed. "There are just over two hundred and fifty people on board right now," she told him. "We all know each other well." It was only a slight exaggeration.

"Did you speak to him about Volhynia before you came?"

The question threw her, and she felt a glimmer of relief; she had been expecting something more personal. "He was talking to people about the planet's history—its stability, agriculture, how the population dealt with the pulsar. Not much else, though." He had sounded like a tourist the first time away from home; they had all teased him. Something rolled over in her stomach, and she bit her tongue to quiet it.

"It was the pulsar that interested him?" Luvidovich's tone had sharpened.

"He mentioned it," she repeated. "But he spoke of a lot of things." *He has found something.* Despite his earlier hostility, she could not keep from pressing him. "What is it?"

He was silent as he climbed the last few steps, and when he turned as the door opened, she thought he was going to answer her. But she became abruptly aware of the audience that stood beyond the doorway: a dozen members of the press, gathered in a polite crowd in the station's foyer. Before them, his hands behind his back like a field admiral, stood Chief Stoya. Luvidovich's expression went flat.

"I must ask you to wait, Commander Shaw." The police chief's voice was even as he stepped forward to face her down. Elena watched him warily; next to her, Luvidovich did not move. Stoya had not acknowledged his subordinate at all. "Are you aware of our laws governing obstruction of justice? I should like to know why Central is choosing to champion a known criminal."

He had listened in as she made her statement, of course—she had expected nothing less—but his response to it was puzzling. Hadn't she just advanced his case by eliminating a suspect? Why would he try to discredit her? Especially in front of the press?

Beside her Luvidovich shifted, his eyes quickly scanning the reporters before resting unhappily on the open entryway beyond. She did not really expect him to challenge his superior in public, but he seemed reluctant to engage Stoya at all. She was missing something.

Whatever Stoya's reasoning, if he thought the presence of reporters would make her back off and leave, he was going to be disappointed. "It has nothing to do with championing anyone," she said. "We wish the criminal to be brought to justice, and Captain Zajec is not responsible for this murder. You're not going to find the one who killed my crewmate by pursuing some personal vendetta against one of your own."

That caught Luvidovich's attention. He turned on her, face reddening, his stiff discomfort erupting suddenly into rage. "He is *not* one of our own!" That same quick temper from the night before; she wondered if his problem was with Captain Zajec, or if he disliked all foreigners. She found her curiosity becoming an annoyance; when had this stopped being about Danny?

Deliberately, she took a step toward Luvidovich. "And what is your standard for that? Because he grew up somewhere else? So did your own police chief, and that doesn't seem to bother you at all."

Out of the corner of her eye, she saw Stoya's face flicker with surprise, and she felt a moment's satisfaction. He had not expected her to know.

"You make me wonder if this is typical on Volhynia," Elena continued. The anger that had been building since she had learned of Danny's death began to rise in the back of her throat. Luvidovich knew something, dammit, and she couldn't understand why he was stonewalling her. "That you would fabricate evidence against someone simply because you dislike him, and then try to discredit someone who points out your error. Perhaps your department hasn't the skills to do the job properly. Is that the problem? Or is it just that the case has been botched by your off-worlder police chief?"

She knew she was deliberately provoking Luvidovich, but she was utterly unprepared for his response to the remark. His face went purple, and his hands were shaking, but he was not looking at her anymore. He was staring over her shoulder at Stoya, and she thought what she saw in his eyes was desperation.

For the first time that day, since Greg had told her of Danny's death, everything came abruptly into focus. She thought of Zajec's bloodied face, of the look of resignation in his eyes, of Luvidovich mentioning Danny only where Stoya would not overhear. Something hot and sharp began to grow in her stomach. "You're not going to investigate this at all, are you?"

Luvidovich turned to her and opened his mouth to retort, but she shook her head. "No, that's why you didn't ask me about Danny in the interrogation. None of this is about him at all. This is about *someone you don't like*." She turned to Stoya; his stony expression had not changed. A wave of revulsion overcame her, and suddenly she didn't care that the press was there, that the whole conversation would get back to Greg, who would almost certainly yell at her again. "What kind of people are you?"

"Let me assure you, Commander Shaw," Stoya said with infuriating calm, "we have no intention of abandoning our investigation."

"You are a *liar*, Stoya." Behind her she heard the reporters murmuring, but she was done with tact. "You've got an off-worlder corpse and an off-worlder suspect, and the only reason anyone is focusing on your manufactured case instead of an incompetent off-worlder police chief is that PSI makes an easy target. What in the hell is wrong with this place?"

Stoya stood back, his expression stoic, but Luvidovich was furious. "Chief Stoya has done more for Volhynia than you and your useless soldiers have done in five hundred years!" he shouted. "Who do you think you are, coming to our world and accusing an honest man?"

"You started it," she snapped.

At that Luvidovich lunged, but before he could reach her, Stoya held out an arm, and the younger officer stumbled against it. She had not even had time to flinch. "It is Stoya who has been fighting for this city, for this world," Luvidovich continued, fists still clenched. "*You* are the one who is letting a murderer go free!"

"Perhaps we should all calm down," Stoya said. He fixed his cold gaze on Elena, still holding off Luvidovich. "As far as our case against Captain Zajec is concerned, there is still the possibility of conspiracy—"

"Oh, bullshit," she said. "If you had anything on him, you wouldn't have cared what I had to say. He's innocent, and you know it, and all of those people"—she gestured toward the reporters—"know it, too. While you're idly persecuting an innocent man, there's a *killer* wandering around. Is that your way of 'fighting for this city'? Do you really think Central Corps is going to sit on their hands while you waste time fucking this up?"

It was a baseless threat, and she suspected Stoya knew it. At the same time . . . whatever her arguments with Greg, however angry he would be with her for losing her temper, she could not believe he would sit by and watch the police do nothing. Greg had been Danny's captain. In the end, Danny had belonged to Greg more than he had to her.

Stoya raised his eyebrows at her mention of Central. "The citizens here *chose* me," he said. "They have not chosen Central. What kind of goodwill do you suppose you would gain by trying to take over?"

Goodwill. She almost laughed. "I rather imagine the Corps will take *justice* over *goodwill,* especially when it comes to the death of one of their own. Are you going to release Captain Zajec, or not?"

He stared at her a moment without moving: one last gesture of control. But in the end he shrugged, and nodded. "There is no need for a Central invasion, Commander Shaw," he said. "We will release Captain Zajec. Our investigation will continue."

She didn't believe him. Danny meant nothing to him. The murderer meant nothing to him. She didn't know why, but Stoya was hell-bent on pinning the crime on Zajec. And Luvidovich, for all his doubts, couldn't get far enough past his own biases to listen to his instincts. If she were not angry enough to choke the pair of them, she might have felt sorry for the young man.

Stoya, on the other hand, could go straight to hell.

With some effort, she controlled her temper. That she no longer believed that Zajec's innocence would make a difference to the police did not change the fact that she needed to get him out of prison. As far as justice for Danny was concerned . . . it seemed possible, she had to admit, that Stoya's insistence on framing the PSI captain was not coincidence. Greg was wrong about what Captain Zajec had wanted from her, but she was beginning to share his fear that PSI was a piece of this somehow.

"Excellent," was all she said aloud. "I look forward to the successful resolution of this case." Her eyes flicked dismissively to Luvidovich, still vibrating with anger; despite herself, she could not resist a parting shot. "But you may want to call off your dog before somebody puts him down."

She turned away from the two men, ignoring the silent stares of the press and the open-mouthed gape of the desk officer. Her comm chimed insistently as she headed up the stairs.

She did not answer it.

Chapter 9

I t was only when he began to see lights before his eyes that
Trey realized there was something unusual going on.

In the six months since he had returned to Volhynia he had
been arrested a handful of times, albeit on charges far less serious than suspicion of murder. Each time the interrogations
had been carefully restrained, designed more to intimidate and
demoralize than cause injury. Luvidovich, who could not have
known Trey's experiences as a child, seemed to believe Trey
ought to be learning a lesson, and Trey was always surprised
at how quickly his stoicism crawled under the officer's skin. It
was petty, but he took a grim pleasure in that small, useless act
of defiance.

This interrogation was different, though, and Trey began to
wonder if his innocence mattered at all.

Trey had been escorted to one of the dark basement interview rooms and shoved into a hard chair. Luvidovich had spent
the first hour of the interrogation doing nothing but hitting
Trey, who knew enough of Volhynia's authoritarian rules to
refrain from hitting back, even when his vision tunneled and
he began to feel nauseated. The questions, when they finally

arrived, included predefined answers, and Trey realized Luvidovich was dictating his confession. After attempting to assert the truth—no, he did not know the victim; yes, he had been home all night—he had stopped answering and started to listen. His head was alarmingly foggy, but even so he could see how thin the story was: Luvidovich was suggesting that he had, for unknown reasons, followed the soldier into the alley behind his own workplace and killed him for an unknown sum of money that had not been found.

"Do you know," Trey said at last, unable to restrain himself, "that is a remarkably foolish story. If you have the need to frame me, you had best come up with something more substantive. Not even the courts in Novanadyr would believe this nonsense."

That had earned him a further beating, but he had minded less.

When Luvidovich finally left, Trey seriously considered putting his head down on the table and surrendering to unconsciousness. He tried and failed to remember anything about Volhynian criminal law. He might be entitled to a lawyer, and a trial, but he was not sure. Certainly the court of public opinion would not be on his side. Most of them believed he was an off-worlder, and after forty-four years, he was in all meaningful ways. They would desperately want to believe that this had nothing to do with their friends and neighbors. He would likely be railroaded, with or without a trial, and no one would ever find out what had really happened to that poor boy.

The thought of what Katya might believe nearly drove him to despair.

The lock turned, and he tensed, lifting his head; but it was not Luvidovich who came through the door, it was Chief Stoya.

Trey sat back, knowing better than to be relieved. Stoya was more observant than Luvidovich, and far more ruthless. He understood people where Luvidovich did not, and never had to resort to physical abuse. Even Trey was careful of him.

Stoya stood before the open door, frowning at Trey, his gaze thoughtful. "A woman has come here," he said, "who claims you have not committed this crime."

There was no way, he realized, that Stoya could miss his surprise. She should have trusted him to look after himself, should have left Volhynia to its own business. He thought of that dead boy in the alley, thought of her passion, her empathy: *I know what people say. There is truth and lie in all of it.*

Of course she had come back.

Deliberately, he straightened his shoulders, shifting in his chair as if he were stiff from sitting still instead of having been beaten. "Excellent," he said. "When can I go?"

Stoya's jaw twitched—a rare betrayal of emotion. "Luvidovich has taken her statement. We will be releasing you. For now."

Luvidovich. *Good God.* Had it only been the night before that he had reminded himself he would kill Luvidovich one day? "There was no need for Luvidovich to speak to her, Stoya. She is a soldier. She knows how to make a report."

"And now you are worried for her. This is curious, given that she says you did not meet until last night."

Damn. He must have been more exhausted than he thought. He dropped all pretense. "Luvidovich is a thug," he said seriously, "and she came here only to help. You know I am innocent of this."

Stoya was younger than Trey by fifteen years, but even so Trey was taken aback by the man's quickness. He was abruptly in front of the table, leaning toward Trey, his face so close Trey could see the shadow of stubble on his chin. "I know you are a killer, *Captain Zajec*," he hissed. "That woman may absolve you this time, but she does not know what you are. She does not even know your real name, the name you gave up when you fled this place. You cannot become something else so easily. You may not have committed *this* crime, but we will have you. Whether it is today or tomorrow makes no difference to me."

Trey kept his expression mild, and when he moved he was slow and careful. He pushed his chair back from the table and stood, the ache of his legs keeping him focused. Standing, he was taller than Stoya, and he allowed himself to lean forward, just a little, to look steadily into the police chief's eyes. "But you do not have me today, Stoya." He straightened, then walked around the table, avoiding Stoya's eyes, and headed through the cell's open door.

She was still beautiful, Trey thought, tall and elegant and patrician, waiting for him by the main office door. But if the night before she had seemed self-conscious, here she stood with an unconcerned composure that suggested she had no expectation of being thwarted. A performance, almost certainly, but an effective one; he supposed it was an indispensable skill for a soldier. When he caught her eyes he saw her blush faintly, and he remembered standing with her in the moonlight and thought perhaps he had not been beaten so badly after all.

He stepped up to the desk, where Reya Keller had his paperwork ready. "Just here," she told him, gesturing at the thumbprint square. When he moved to approve it, she spoke more quietly. "There are reporters outside," she whispered. "A lot of them."

He looked at her. Reya was a girl of about twenty, and considered a good police officer, if inexperienced. Unlike many of the others, though, she treated him with respect every time Luvidovich dragged him in. Once she had slipped him a small bottle of analgesic on his way out; he had plenty of the stuff back in his flat, but the gesture had touched him.

"Thank you," he said, and she nodded, a smile flickering across her face before she backed away.

Trey turned, and took a step toward the woman. She looked guarded, and a little hesitant; he supposed he looked the same. He wanted to tell her he was pleased to see her again. He wanted to tell her to go home. Instead he said, "You did not have to wait for me."

She looked away, and he wished he had been more welcoming. "I did, actually," she told him. "It seems your police department has no intention of investigating properly."

He was surprised Stoya had tipped his hand in front of her. "You believe you can make up for their deficit?"

"That's my intent, yes. Does this place have a back door?"

"You wish to avoid the press."

Her face warmed again. "I already have their attention. I'd just as soon avoid entertaining them again."

He had missed more, it seemed, than just her arrival. "There is a rear exit," he told her. "But we will need someone to let us out."

In the end it was Reya who helped them, escorting them down a poorly lit back stairway. He fell into step next to the woman—the soldier, he realized. She moved differently here, confident and unhesitating. She was a good deal more forbidding than she had been the night before, and he wondered once again exactly who she was on her starship. At thirty-two, she was young for command, but she carried herself as someone accustomed to being obeyed.

Valeria's voice echoed in his head. *It is not women you like; it is power.* He had laughed at her and told her it was powerful women. That exchange had been decades ago. It seemed his tastes had not changed.

Reya left them briefly at the back of the building to retrieve the woman's weapon from the desk sergeant. She released the door's voice lock, and Trey stepped through into an alley. He began walking toward the street, the woman next to him, the afternoon sunlight a balm against his face.

They had taken no more than two steps on the main sidewalk before he heard footsteps running behind them. "Hey, Chief!" a man's voice called. Not all of the press had missed their surreptitious exit, apparently. Trey glanced at the woman; she neither slowed nor reacted, and he followed suit.

After a moment the man caught up, falling into step next to Trey. Tall, slim, with vid-ready good looks, he wore a perpetual manic grin that was almost absurd enough to distract from the shrewd gleam in his eyes. He held his hand out to Trey.

"You're Treiko Zajec," the man said. "Cholan Ancher, Corps press corps." He laughed at his own joke.

Trey considered, then took the offered hand. "How do you do, Mr. Ancher?"

Ancher's grin widened. "Better now. You're a legend, you know. It'll be something, telling people you shook my hand."

"What do you want, Ancher?" the woman finally said.

Trey looked at her again. Her demeanor had not changed, but he thought he detected a hint of annoyance in her voice.

"You're always so suspicious," Ancher said cheerfully.

"That's because I know you."

"Are you *still* holding a grudge?" She said nothing, and this time the reporter didn't laugh. "I was doing my job, Chief."

"So was I."

And damned if Ancher didn't look uncomfortable.

"Well, maybe I can make it up to you," he told her.

"How would you do that?"

"I have an ID on your dead man."

And that stopped her. Trey watched her look over to the reporter, and wondered if she had the authority to back up the murder in her eyes.

But Ancher did not back off, or stand down. Instead, his face softened into something almost human. "I know who he was, Chief," he repeated. "And I know who he was to you."

Trey saw her turn ashen, then go red; she looked away for a moment. When she turned back she met Trey's eyes, and she was the woman he had known the night before: vulnerable and transparent. The sadness he saw in her told him all of it. *That boy,* he thought, remembering what he had found just a few hours before. Alive, he would have been tall, young, handsome.

The boy she had loved.

"My dear lady," he said gently, "I am so sorry."

Her eyes brightened for a moment, and then she shook her head. "He was not mine," she told him. "Not anymore. He's not for me to grieve. But if it gets out . . ."

" . . . the alibi you have given me will look quite different."

"Wait," Ancher said. "She's your alibi?"

PSI did not have journalists who followed them, like Central did, but Trey recognized the tone of a reporter who had landed on a story. How to best handle the situation depended on the reporter, and he did not know this one. This woman—Chief, Ancher had called her—seemed to have some sway over him, though. Trey opted to give the man a chance.

"If you would give us a moment, Mr. Ancher," he said.

The reporter looked suspicious, but when Trey stepped aside, the woman following him, Ancher let them be.

"What will your crew say when the police talk to them?" he asked her.

She grasped her elbows. "Depends on who they talk to. The *Galileo* crew won't be inclined to share, but we have some loaners on board that we borrowed to deliver cargo. Danny . . . he was tight with them, and they don't like me much."

"So it will come out." When she nodded, he said, "Would your friend Mr. Ancher spin the story for you?"

"Would it matter if he did?"

"No," he admitted. "They will use it as an excuse to detain me again, and possibly you as well."

"That excuse or another, they'll find a reason." Her eyebrows drew together. "We've got to find out what happened before they come after you again."

"My dear, I think we had best rid ourselves of your reporter before we discuss this more deeply."

"Don't worry about it," Ancher called over. "My ears aren't that good."

She gave Ancher a look, then turned toward him, pulling him into their conversation. "Why haven't you gone public with this?"

"I told you," he said. "I figure maybe I owe you one. But I can't sit on it forever, Chief. Someone else will find out, and they'll broadcast."

"How much time can you get me?"

"Five hours, maybe six." He began to sound like a reporter again. "What do I get for it?"

"What do you want?"

"An interview." His gaze took in Trey. "With both of you. *And* Captain Foster."

"No deal. Leak it, and I'll take my chances." She turned and began to walk away, and Trey moved to follow her.

"Wait, wait!" Ancher scurried to catch up. "Just you, Chief. But an exclusive. Nothing for those streamer scavengers, okay? Not a word."

Her reply was just as prompt. "Done," she said. "But if I hear so much as a rumor anywhere on comms in the next six hours, Ancher, you are shut out for good. Not just on this, but on everything. You understand?"

That, Trey knew, was a serious threat for a reporter, and she delivered it sincerely. But Ancher just gave her that cocky smile again. "Loud and clear, Chief." He winked at Trey. "You kids have a nice day." He turned, and walked off the way he had come.

They both watched him until he was well out of earshot, and then Trey turned to her. He could see the shadows under her eyes, and her expression held a hint of desperation. Closer to the edge than she was letting on. "What of Central?" he asked. "Will they get involved?"

She paused before answering, and he wondered if that was good or bad. "Not in a way that will help," she said at last.

"Central's rigid when it comes to troops on Volhynia, and I didn't do myself any favors by losing my temper in front of the press. There's a good chance they'll demand I leave, which means we need to—"

Her comm chimed, and she muted it, but almost immediately the tone was repeated. This time she frowned, resigned. "I apologize," she said to him.

"For what?"

"For this," she replied, and completed the connection.

"You have fifteen seconds," a man's voice said, low and menacing, "to explain why you cut me off. *Twice*."

Her response was terse. "I was busy."

There was a pause before the man replied. "You were *busy*?" His incredulity was palpable. "Was this five seconds ago, or while you were *having a tantrum* in front of the fucking chief of police, not to mention every goddamned streamer in this sector? You realize your entire chain of command is watching that right now?"

She swore, looking chagrined.

"Yeah, *now* you're thinking about it, after it's out on the public fucking stream! Now how about you answer the question, Chief, before I bust you back to ensign for insubordination?"

This, Trey realized, had to be her captain, and he was using a tone Trey, who'd had to use it on occasion, recognized very well. What was curious was her complete lack of deference. "How about this?" she snapped in return. "How about I knew all you were going to do was *shriek* at me, and I had better things to do than listen?"

"You—are you forgetting my direct order? The one where you give that pirate his alibi, and get your ass back to the ship? The one that *did not* include threatening the local cops with authority *you don't have* before you snuck out the back door?"

Trey's stomach turned. She did not know the people she was dealing with. "What did you say to the police?"

She looked away. "I told them Central would take over the investigation if they didn't do it properly."

"Who are you talking to?"

"Captain Zajec, sir."

Another pause on the line. "Captain," the man said formally, as if he had not been threatening his officer a moment before, "we haven't been introduced. I'm Captain Greg Foster, CCSS *Galileo*."

Trey knew his name, of course, and a little of his reputation, but he did not think the circumstances were shedding the best light on the man. "A pleasure, Captain," Trey told him, "but I do not use my title any longer. May I express my condolences on the loss of your officer."

This time Trey heard him sigh. "Thank you, Mr. Zajec," Foster said, and he sounded old and tired. "And may I say, I am sorry you've become tangled in all of this. Our only goal is to see the killer brought to justice."

Glib and practiced, Trey thought, but not necessarily insincere. "Thank you, Captain. Although I do not think our police are yet convinced they should look elsewhere."

"Why did they suspect you to begin with?" Foster asked.

Trey closed his eyes and ran a hand over his face; he did not want to have this conversation now, but he could not see Foster allowing him to put it off. "A number of reasons, actually," he told the captain, feeling the woman's eyes on him. "One is because I was PSI, and Volhynia has an uneasy relationship with us. Stoya was appointed, in part, due to the tension between PSI and some of the local Syndicates who are moving to become legitimate traders. Another is simply because I am a stranger, and this is a small colony." He took a breath. "Mostly, though, it is because I committed a crime here when I was a child, and they cannot prosecute me for it."

"What did you do?"

Ah, well. It's not like I'm ashamed of it. "I killed a man," he said.

Trey felt rather than saw her grow still.

"If they know it, why can't they arrest you?" Foster asked him.

They could, of course. They could arrest him, and he could confess, and even on Volhynia—even in Novanadyr, where he had so few friends—no jury would convict him. "They cannot make a case," he said simply.

"So instead, you're just the guy they arrest whenever they need a warm body?"

Trey risked a glance at the woman; her eyes had gone wary, and he was surprised how much that stung. "In this case they were not without reason. I found your officer outside the kitchen of the restaurant where I work. And yes, Captain, it would be a remarkable coincidence, except that the body was moved there." He had wanted to tell her earlier, when Ancher was still there, but something had told him this was as important a detail to keep secret as her relationship to the dead man.

"How do you know?"

Trey chose as few words as he could. "There was not enough blood."

"How can you be sure?"

"I know death." And he thought, captain to captain, that he would not have to say anything more.

"I think Luvidovich knows it as well," the woman said. "Stoya is keeping him from investigating properly. I don't know why, but Luvidovich isn't happy about it."

"I doubt that matters," Foster said. "After your impromptu press conference, they're going to start asking about you as well as Danny, and they're going to spin it as a very neat setup. I can protect the chief, Mr. Zajec, but I have no influence over the treatment of Volhynian citizens. If you'd consent to visit *Galileo,* we could offer you protection."

Her expression had changed, grown wary again. This time, however, Trey did not think she was being wary of him. There was more to this conversation than he was seeing. "Thank you, Captain," he said formally, "but I prefer to take my chances. My family is here."

"We could protect them, too, if it comes down to it. This whole thing should be cleared up in a few days, and it'd be one less thing for us all to worry about."

Odd, Trey thought. *First an offer of help, then manipulation.* The woman was looking away, squinting into the afternoon sun, her lips thin. "I will consider your offer," he said at last. It was the truth, at least. "But for now, I would like to remain home."

"The offer stands if you change your mind. Chief, I'll expect you back here in—"

"I'm staying, Greg." She said it quietly, and with complete conviction.

There was a long pause. Based on Foster's behavior so far, Trey would have expected the captain to start shouting again. Instead, when he spoke, his voice was immeasurably more gentle, and Trey began to wonder at the relationship between the captain and his subordinate. "We've discussed this already, Chief."

"We haven't," she told him. Her voice was tight, as if she had swallowed something thick. "I owe him."

"You don't owe him *anything*."

"*We* owe him," she said, her voice growing stronger. "The police aren't going to do a damn thing, and I'm not going to leave this alone while a murderer goes free."

"That's not your call, Elena. It's not mine, either."

"If it was me who'd been found dead," she asked bluntly, "what would you do?"

Foster was silent.

"I want to find out where he was last night, what he was doing there, and what he was into that made someone want to kill him."

"You know it may have just been a robbery." Foster was considerably more subdued.

"With the police covering something up?" Her tone had softened; this, it seemed, was detente. "Please, Greg. Just a little more time."

The pause was longer, and Trey took the time to study her. With Ancher she had been practiced, composed, unconcerned with his reaction. Here she stood, tense, her face bleak, desperation in her eyes. Heart on her sleeve. It mattered to her, what her captain was going to say, and Trey thought it went far beyond whether or not she received permission.

"His financials show he was at that bar he'd been talking about," Foster said at last. "Gregorian's. His last charge was fifteen minutes before he was killed. That's where you want to start. I'll give you six hours. You dig up what you can in that time, and then you come home. And if the cops twig your connection with Danny, you come up sooner, understood?"

She closed her eyes. "Understood, Captain."

"I want a report in three hours, Chief. No excuses. You cut me off again, it better be life or death, or I'm writing you up, and I'm not kidding. We clear?"

"Yes, sir," she said, composed. "We're clear."

The captain signed off. When she looked up, she did it slowly, and the eyes that met his were guarded. "Who did you kill?" she asked him.

All the questions he had for her, all the things he needed to understand about the conversation he had just heard. Well, if he was to ask her to trust, perhaps he would have to trust first. "My stepfather," he told her.

"Why?"

"He was beating my sister," he said. "He had beaten me for years, but I suppose he was getting bored. One night he turned on her, and I stopped him. As it turned out, I stopped him forever."

He looked away. It was an old story to him now, and it was difficult for him to feel anything around it but sadness.

He could feel her looking at him, and out of the corner of his eye he saw her arm move—toward him, not away. He looked up, and found the guarded look had shifted.

"That is not a crime, you know," she said. "That is self-defense."

"He was not hitting hard enough to kill," he told her. "He never hit terribly hard. Most of the time I was not even badly hurt. When I hit him back—I had never done that before."

He remembered how it felt, heaving the little portable heating unit that had been the first thing his hand had found, hearing the unmistakable sound of a skull being crushed, seeing the man drop, eyes open, switched off like a light. "I cannot say I did not mean to kill him. I can say I am not sorry I did." He searched her face. "What kind of man does that make me, do you think?"

Her arm dropped back to her side, but she took a step toward him. "I think you must have been a brave child." He saw sadness in her eyes—and something he recognized as admiration. Something small and bright flared inside of him, and he straightened.

"I did not feel brave," he confessed. "But over the years, I have come to believe I was strong." With some effort, he shook off the past. "Elena. Is that what you prefer to be called? Or is it Chief? Chief of what?"

She accepted the diversion. "I am Commander Elena Marie Shaw, chief of engineering," she said formally. "Elena, if you like, or Lanie. What do you prefer? No title, I understand."

"My friends call me Trey," he said. On impulse, he held out his hand. "How do you do, Elena?"

She laughed a little, and took his hand in hers. Her fingers were warm, and he felt a ripple of electricity; he should have asked her name the night before. And yet, it had been rather delightful *not* knowing. "It is a pleasure to meet you, Trey," she said, and his name sounded warm on her lips.

He dropped her hand, somewhat reluctantly, and said, "I know Gregorian's. It is not far, and there is a place on the way we can find something to eat, if you are hungry." He did not imagine she had had much time for food.

"Food is your answer to everything, then," she said.

Not everything, he thought, but now, perhaps, was not the time to remember the night before. "We will both be the better for it, I think. Elena." He turned her name over in his head. "That is a Volhynian name, you know." He began walking, and she fell into step beside him.

"There are more Russians in Alaska than in Novanadyr," she said.

"So you must have known a great many Treikos."

She looked over at him, and he had a brief memory of the night before, the wind tugging at her hair. "Actually," she remarked, sounding shy, "you are the first."

He could not imagine why that would please him, but it did.

CHAPTER 10

Galileo

"Coffee, Lieutenant? Something stronger?"

Jessica Lockwood, perched on the edge of the chair across from his desk, gave him a look. "Hell no, sir. I just came from the pub, and I've watched enough people getting drunk for one day. Including Commander Valentis." She watched as he stood and poured himself a cup of coffee. "He's in kind of a complaining mood. A loud one. Do you like pissing him off? Because one of these days he's going to take a swing at you, and it'll be your own damn fault."

Greg would have bet most of the money he had saved over the years that Will would never do something so wildly against the rules. "He used to have more of a sense of humor. Do you remember?"

"You're romanticizing him in your memory, sir. He's always been a stiff. The difference is he used to laugh at your jokes, and he doesn't anymore." She glared at him. "There's a lot of that going around."

Greg had learned, in recent months, when and why Jessica would start snapping at him. She was as dispassionate as any field-seasoned admiral, and she only lashed out when she was particularly tired or upset. This time, he guessed a little of both. "How are you doing with all of this?" he asked.

Her lips tightened, and for an instant he caught real grief in her bright green eyes. "I don't like death, and I don't like unknowns," she replied. "So naturally, I'm hugely fucking pissed off, and not fit company for anyone. Yourself, sir?"

Greg had just finished talking to Danny Lancaster's sister. He suspected his current state of mind was written deeply into his face at the moment, but the last thing he wanted to do was discuss it. "I managed to get Admiral Herrod to let us stay," he told her instead.

"No shit. I didn't think he had a heart."

"It's not heart, it's regulations." *Which is,* Greg thought, *a little unfair to the admiral.* Herrod had responded with no sarcasm at all when Greg had told him he wanted to keep *Galileo* where she was until the crime was solved. He had, however, quoted Greg the exact line from Central's treaty with Volhynia that outlined Central's authority to do exactly nothing to interfere. Herrod had used the word *nothing* a number of times.

"I also talked to the chief."

Jessica crossed her arms. "Did you tell her yet that she's not getting any help?"

"You know we won't leave her on her own."

"Which is a sideways way of saying Central is happy to drop her in the soup, because Volhynia is some kind of untouchable public relations gem that makes everybody forget how many colonies need our help, which is somehow a good thing." She frowned, and he waited her out; he was familiar with her political views—he even shared them, despite his obligation to be officially neutral. Eventually she said, "What's he doing there, sir?"

That was not the question he had expected. "You mean Captain Zajec?"

She uncrossed her arms and waved her hands at him. "*Yes, sir,* I mean Captain Treiko fucking Zajec, who has kicked more Syndicate tribes in the teeth than all the Fourth Sector PSI ships together. What the hell is he doing on Volhynia, planet of the wastrels?"

"That's a little harsh, don't you think?" She glared again, and he relented. "He was born there. And he doesn't use his title anymore."

"You talked to him?"

"Briefly." Greg thought back to the conversation. Zajec had come across as pragmatic and sincere, and Greg could understand why Elena doubted his involvement. Zajec's reputed shrewdness had been apparent as well, as Greg was fairly certain the man knew exactly why he had been offered asylum.

"When is she coming back?"

"A few hours yet," he told her. "She's working with him."

"You gave her permission to stay." It wasn't a question.

"I did."

Jessica held very still for a moment. "Have you *ever* said no to that woman, sir? She's not an investigator. She's not even infantry."

"She's a certified combat pilot," he reminded her.

"She is a *mechanic,* sir, and no matter how well she flies in a war zone, this is not something she can cope with on her own."

"She's not on her own."

"Screw Valentis, sir, *I* am going to hit you." Her arms folded again. "Were you not explaining to me a few hours ago how we couldn't trust PSI? And now you've left her down there, without Central backup, with nobody to lean on but a PSI officer, never mind that he's retired? You explain yourself, sir, or I'm going down after her myself."

He briefly considered pulling rank and shutting her down. He was not in the habit of explaining orders. But right now . . . right now he needed someone who would ask the right questions, without being afraid of how he would respond. *That used to be Elena,* he thought ruefully; but Elena was not the only good officer he had. "The conversation we are about to have never happened, Lieutenant. Understood?"

"Yes, sir." She did not even blink.

He told her first about *Demeter,* and waited until she had stopped swearing. "Between you and me, Lieutenant," he said, "I agree with you." He tried and failed to remember if he had told Elena the same thing. *Probably not,* he realized. "MacBride's story is bullshit, but I'm less worried about his lousy lie than I am about who he is protecting. There are too many coincidences to let it go."

She shook her head. "You want coincidence? Ask me what I've found out about Danny."

He leaned back and folded his arms. "You telling me he was investigating *Demeter,* too?"

"No, sir. He was investigating the *Phoenix.*"

For a moment he rolled her words over in his mind, trying and failing to make them fit into what he knew of the world. "Explain," he said at last.

She leaned forward, elbows on his desk. "I can't, sir," she said. "But it started a couple of days after we left Aleph Nine with the

Demeter crew and cargo. He hauled up all the public records: official reports, crew manifests and schematics, old news stories, retrospectives—even whacked-out conspiracy theories."

More than most people would have bothered with, Greg realized, although less than he himself had seen. "Did he have an angle?"

"That's harder to say, sir," she hedged, some of her enthusiasm ebbing. "He wasn't much of a diarist. He was doing some scientific research as well, but that may have been unrelated."

"What kind of scientific research?"

"Electromagnetism. Pulsars. Specifically, Volhynia's pulsar. He seemed particularly interested in the research that was done at the observatory down on the planet."

Novanadyr Observatory, Greg recalled, had been the first station to report readings from the *Phoenix* explosion. "That may not be as unrelated as you think." She raised an eyebrow at that, but he wanted the rest of her report first. "What else?"

"Well, he had an appointment set for today, sir. With Commander Valentis. At fifteen hundred hours."

The anger that lit his gut was becoming familiar. More secrets. "Had Commander Valentis acknowledged the meeting?"

"Acknowledged and accepted, sir. He didn't tell you, did he?"

"He's not required to tell me." She knew that, of course, but he was reminding himself as well. Lancaster might have asked Will to keep the meeting to himself. Which would explain why Greg had not known of it when Lancaster was alive, but offered Will no excuses at all now that the man was dead.

What the hell had Lancaster found?

"I need you to find out who he's been talking to," he told her. "Everything. I want to know who he had breakfast with, who he played cards with, all of it. I want to know why he was hanging out with the *Demeter* crew."

She shifted in her chair. "They don't like me, sir."

"Surely you can charm your way past that."

"I don't like them, either. And I'm not very good at faking it."

He had not thought of that. He found it oddly pleasing to think that if she ever decided she disliked him, he wouldn't have to guess. "All right, then, get Ted Shimada to help you." Shimada was easygoing and facile, and a good friend of Elena's on top of it. Greg found his unrelenting good cheer irritating, but he could not deny that the man could get along with almost anyone. "But there's another piece to this, and I don't want him in on it."

"If you tell me there's something worse than an escalating conflict with PSI, I may throw things."

He paused, trying to figure out where to start. "I don't know if it's worse, Lieutenant," he said seriously. "But it's another thing that's too much of a coincidence to be ignored. Just before we put in at Aleph Nine, I received an anonymous message. The first of three. About the *Phoenix*."

She frowned. "Did you trace it?"

"They've been coming in on the Admiralty channel with an ident that's garbage. I can't even trace them back to their closest routing point." He paused. "Anonymous messages aren't new. They come in every year around this time. But I've never had one I couldn't trace before."

He thought she would ask what the bogus ident told him, or what the messages said. Instead she asked, "You get these messages *every year*?"

She stared at him, and he tried to keep his expression neutral. He was acutely aware that everyone on the ship knew his history, and that every year around the anniversary of his mother's death, they gave him a wide berth so he could brood in peace. In the midst of this mess, it all seemed like foolishness. "Some years more than others," he told her.

"What's in them?" she asked.

"Questions. Innuendo. Conspiracy theories. Nothing definitive."

"But these—the bogus Admiralty messages—they're different."

He looked away from her. He had spent years following madness, had nearly lost his life to it. He could not say for certain he was not falling back into the abyss. "The ideas they're floating don't seem completely insane." *Except that they almost certainly are.*

"Ideas about what? It was engine failure."

She would have been less than ten years old, he realized, and not affected directly. She had not even been on Earth. "There was a lot the public was never told," he said, and left it at that. "But me getting these messages now, in this sector, so close to the site of the accident—" It sounded thin when he said it out loud.

"You said they started before Aleph. How long before?"

Thank God, she was thinking. "Twelve hours before we arrived."

"But after we were diverted." He nodded, and she sat forward. "Someone knew we'd end up here, didn't they?"

"Which suggests the bogus Admiralty code is hiding a genuine Admiralty code. Think you can break it, Lieutenant?"

"Of course I can." He saw it in her eyes, the challenge, the thrill of the hunt. "It's all connected, sir, isn't it? The messages, the *Demeter* bullshit, poor Danny—it's not a coincidence, is it?"

"It could be, of course," he allowed. "Except for two things. One, this planet that we've never been to before—that little pulsar that so unspectacularly EMPs it every night? That was the navigational signpost used by the *Phoenix* when they went off to investigate the wormhole."

"And the other?"

"What was *Demeter* doing by the hot zone, Lieutenant?" He watched her expression changing as she began piecing it all together. "That wouldn't be a bad place for you to start."

"And I'm going to find this out by charming the *Demeter* crew."

He knew what she was asking. "This conversation isn't happening, remember? Which means any methods you might need to utilize to find out what you need to find out aren't happening, either."

She beamed at that, as if he had just released her from prison. "I will tell you nothing, sir," she promised.

"Don't tell me if you install a back door, either." If he were trying to dig into Admiralty data, the first thing he would do would be to open a proprietary port into the ship's comms core, just in case his ordinary routes were locked out. It occurred to him, after he said it, that she might have something set up already.

He stood, and she stood with him, turning to the door, eager to start her work. They all needed a mission, he realized, especially now. He wished he liked his better. "Lieutenant," he asked, before she could leave the room, "do you know why they broke up?"

She was still for a moment before she turned around, and he could tell by the expression on her face that she didn't want to tell him. "Respectfully, sir," she said cautiously, "this isn't relevant to the investigation, is it?"

"You *do* know."

"She's my best friend, sir."

"She's mine, too."

At that, Jessica's temper flared. "Not lately she's not, sir, and it's your own damn fault. Why should I tell her secrets?"

He couldn't argue with her. "It matters, Jess," he said quietly. "He hurt her, and I don't know why, and it matters."

"Well, you hurt her worse." He gave her a look, but she didn't back off. "It's true, and you know it. Why should I give you something else you can use against her?" She had raised her voice, and he couldn't remember ever seeing her so angry. "What does it matter why she finally cut him loose? You tell me why you've been a flat-out dickheaded bullying asshole to her for the last six months, and then maybe, *maybe* I'll trust that you don't want to hurt her again."

He didn't want to talk about it. He didn't want to think about it. He had not intended to hurt her, but she knew him too well. All he had wanted was for her to give him room, but somehow he had let it go further than that. He was only beginning to understand the extent of the damage he had done.

He shrugged, and made his way back around his desk. "Found out last time we were on Earth that my wife was cheating on me."

In retrospect, he had to admit it shouldn't have caught him off guard; he was lucky if he made it home six times a year, and then only for a few days. But if Jessica thought he was an idiot, she hid it well. "I'm sorry, sir," she said, her expression all sympathy. "What did you do?"

Turned tail and ran, he thought. "Not much. She said . . . she thought it was understood, with me being away so much. She didn't seem to think it was a big deal. I suppose you're on her side on that one."

"Don't be an ass. Drifting through—what is it, eleven, twelve years of marriage?—and then saying 'Oh, honey, didn't I tell you?' That's a big fat lie, not an open relationship."

"Yeah, well, that's what she wants," he said.

"And you don't."

It was nothing like that simple. "Did you know, Lieutenant," he said, "that there are women on my ship?"

"It hasn't escaped my notice, sir."

"An awful lot of them are good-looking. Well, all of them, really. Not knocking the rest of the crew, you understand, but these last six months . . . I'm finding it hard to miss how good-looking the women are."

"But it's not you," she said gently, "is it, sir?"

He felt a flicker of annoyance that she would know that about him. "I don't want to cheat on my wife. No matter what she thinks she promised, I *know* what I promised. The fact of that promise hasn't changed."

"And Elena gets too close," she said, and he thought she knew what he was keeping to himself. She shook her head. "Respectfully, sir, you're handling this end of it the wrong way."

He had no doubt of that. Two weeks before, he had handled it as badly as he had handled anything before in his life. He remembered Elena walking into the pub, remembered wanting, as he did every time he saw her, to tell her everything, as futile as it was. He remembered needing to strike at her, to get her away from him. He remembered drinking; he did not remember stopping. Well, he'd already exposed himself as hopelessly naive and a moralistic idiot; he was unlikely to make himself look worse. "What did I say to her, Lieutenant?"

Jessica's eyebrows shot up. "You really don't remember."

He recalled Elena's reaction, the flash of hurt in her eyes before it disappeared behind that icy, splintered rage that had not left her since. "No."

She told him.

He swore, and put his elbows on the desk, running his hands over his head. "On the record, Lieutenant, I am never drinking again."

"That's nice, sir, but how are you going to fix it?"

"Hand it over to Bob, probably, and tell him not to—"

"How are you going to fix it with *Elena*?" she clarified patiently.

Ah, right. That, of course, was more problematic. *I have no idea.* "How the hell do I fix something like this?"

"I'm partial to sincere apologies myself," she said. "In Lanie's case . . . you could try telling her the truth."

"How would that help?" he snapped, before remembering he hadn't told Jessica what the truth was. Well, she wouldn't be the first person in his life who had figured it out . . .

"Might not," she agreed. "But you broke it, sir, into little tiny pieces. It's not going back the way it was. You tell the truth, at least you guys are starting level. And it might give her some perspective on what you said." Her expression softened, and he realized she must have seen something in his face. "She doesn't hate you, you know. If she hated you, she wouldn't be so angry with you."

They startled him, those brief words of kindness. "I'll fix it when this is done," he promised. And he would, he was certain of it. She had forgiven him so much over the years; she would forgive him this. "You know there's a rumor floating around that she was in on Danny's murder," he said.

"Floating around the *Demeter* crew, you mean."

"Yes."

"See, the one *I* hear from them," she told him, "is that maybe *you* killed him."

Anyone could have done it, Bob had said. No particular strength required—just the ability to get close enough to Lancaster without triggering the man's fight reflex. Someone he knew. Someone he trusted.

That was a long damn list.

Jessica was watching him, her expression far too astute. "Is this your life all the time, sir?" she asked. "Responsible for everything, and suspicious of everyone?"

"Pretty much."

She shook her head. "Rank is looking less attractive, sir."

"You don't know the half of it, Lieutenant."

She gave him a look he was beginning to recognize as sympathy. "I'll let you know what I've got when I've got it, sir," she told him, and saluted before she left the room.

CHAPTER 11

Volhynia

Mmay I ask you a personal question?"

They had caught a tram in front of a bakery where he had procured sandwiches, and were seated together in a corner of the small car. He had told her they had enough time to eat—nearly fifteen minutes, he said, to travel to the edge of the city. Despite her hunger she found it difficult, but she had caught him watching her out of the corner of his eye as he ate his own food. She had consumed the sandwich methodically, like medicine, and was surprised to find it cleared her head.

It was on the tip of her tongue to tell him that after last night, he should feel free to ask her whatever he liked; but she did not know what he was thinking about that. They had not thought to see each other again; they had not even exchanged names. And she had returned to let him know that the dead man was her ex-lover—she was lucky he was speaking to her at all. "Of course," she replied.

"What is your agenda here, Elena?"

She thought of Greg's plan to use Trey for intelligence on PSI. Trey was right to mistrust her. He might be retired, but he had not survived twenty-six years as captain of a Fifth Sector generation ship by being a fool.

And she had survived eight years in the Corps following orders, the last seven trusting Greg with her life. She gave Trey as much of the truth as she could.

"I'm not sure I know," she said. "It's useless, really. He's gone. Forever. I can't fix that. I can't go back." Oh, all the things she would change if she could go back. "But I can find out what happened. It's nothing—it's meaningless—but it's all I can do, and I have to do *something*."

"You may fail," he said, but his voice was kind. "You may never know."

"I need to try."

"You may find out something you do not like."

"The truth is always better than the unknown."

At that he smiled at her. "I do forget how young you are."

"I've led a sheltered life."

"Have you really?"

His voice was low and quiet, and she became aware suddenly of how close he was sitting, how broad his shoulders were; his arm brushed against hers, just a little, every time someone stepped on or off the tram. She was aware of stress and exhaustion, and she knew she was running on little more than adrenaline, sandwich notwithstanding. She closed her eyes and tried to focus, but instead her mind filled with memories: his hands on her, his skin against hers, his hair as she tangled her fingers in it . . .

When her comm chimed, she felt a surge of relief. "It's Bob," she told Trey. "Doctor Hastings." She completed the connection, leaving it loud enough to be audible to them both.

"You've done a fine job pissing off the old man," Bob said irritably. "And now I have to fly myself home? You know I hate flying."

She had no intention of engaging in an argument with him. "You've finished the postmortem," she said. "What did you find out?"

There was a pause, and she remembered that he had just spent an hour with a dead man. "Their report was accurate, although we got a little more precise on the times. He died of sudden, catastrophic blood loss, via a severed artery in the neck. It would have been very quick, Elena," he added gently. "Close to painless."

She wondered how that made it better. "What about the other wounds?"

"Postmortem, all of them, by more than half an hour."

"Made by the same person?"

He hedged. "Same weapon, certainly. And the cuts didn't take any more strength than the killing stroke. But either way, Chief, none of them would have required unusual power."

"You're saying he knew his killer. Or was caught by surprise."

"I don't draw conclusions."

But she could not think of any other way a trained infantry soldier could have had his throat cut by an ordinary person. "Did you find anything to suggest that he was moved after he died?"

"Lividity is uneven enough to support that, sure," he said. "Why?"

She glanced at Trey. His eyes were on the floor as he concentrated on Bob's words. "Mr. Zajec found the body," she said, "and he seems to think so."

"He say what gave him that idea?"

Trey met her eyes, and for an instant she saw his age, and the weight of everything he had seen in his life. He looked at her steadily as he spoke. "There was not enough blood," he said. "And what was there was in the wrong place. It was pooled beneath his torso, not below the killing stroke. And it—" He stopped, and looked away from her. "An arterial cut would have sprayed," he said roughly. "There was no spatter, no spread at all."

Her mind produced a vivid image: Danny standing, talking to someone, turning his back, relaxed, trusting . . . and then one cut, and brief surprise, and the end. She swallowed the ball of rage flaring in her stomach. *Later,* she told herself, harshly. "Does that fit with what you found, Bob?"

She thought her voice had been steady, but Trey was looking at her again, face full of concern. She sat up straighter; it would not do to have him worrying about her. She needed his mind on Danny.

"It does," Bob said, unaware of their silent exchange.

"I thought you didn't draw conclusions." This was from Trey.

"Generally I don't," Bob admitted. "But those postmortem cuts—they bother me. They've got all the hallmarks of rage—apparently random locations, obliteration of identifying marks, unnecessary violence. But they're all the same depth, within a few millimeters. And the entry points are smooth, not torn as they would be with a violent strike. As if someone chose each location carefully. This was made to look like a crime of passion, but I don't think it was. I think someone staged this with great deliberation." He paused. "Where did you find him, Mr. Zajec?"

"At the kitchen entrance of my workplace," Trey told him.

"Somebody doesn't like you," Bob remarked dryly.

Trey made a sound that was almost a laugh. "A great many people do not like me," he said.

"We're going to talk to the people Danny was with last night," Elena added, trying to sound confident. "With luck that'll clear up some of the ambiguities."

"You're not a detective, dear. You're a mechanic."

"It's debugging, Bob, like I do every day. Start with what's wrong, and go backward until you find the cause."

"You're not infantry, either."

Being infantry hadn't helped Danny. "If I were infantry, Volhynia would have thrown me off-planet by now."

She heard him sigh, but he let it go. "When are you supposed to check in?"

She checked the time. "Two and a half hours, roughly. If you could fill the captain in on the crime scene—"

"You can't keep avoiding him, Chief."

"Yes I can." With the two of them ganging up on her, there was no way she was talking to Greg any earlier than she had to. "I will check in with him at the appointed time, and not before. Have a safe flight home." She disconnected the comm.

Trey was studying her curiously. "You did not tell him about the reporter."

"I don't want that getting back to the captain."

"Hm." The sound was speculative, but he did not press the point. "Can you tell me, Elena, what the police will hear about you and Danny?"

"That depends on who they talk to," she replied. "Someone will tell them how hard it had been for Danny lately, or how everyone had been trying to cheer him up."

"It was you, then, who called it off."

"Yes."

"Why?"

She opened her mouth to tell him. She had told no one. Even Bob Hastings, who thought he knew, did not know all of it. She told herself Danny was dead now; surely telling couldn't matter. But when she spoke, she told him not why she had ended it, but why she should have. "He wanted to retire," she told him. "He wanted a house on some colony. Marriage. Children."

"And you did not."

She shook her head, swallowing the knot in her throat. She could not bring herself to tell him more. "We were bad for each other, Trey. Maybe not at first, but very much so by the end. If I'd confronted him sooner, maybe—"

"Maybe what?" he interrupted. "Maybe he would not have come down on shore leave? Or spent so much money, or wandered off on his own? Even if you believe such things, Elena, you must remember: Danny's death is not your responsibility. His death is on the conscience of the one who killed him, and no one else."

"Now who is being naive?" But she said it gently; he was trying to make her feel better. She turned to look at him. His face held frank concern, and something else, something watchful in his eyes that she did not know him well enough to interpret. She looked away, letting her eyes stray through the window, and was relieved when she felt his gaze drop. Kindness was more than she could take.

Trey was not sure Elena was lying, but he was quite certain she was leaving things out. There had been a precipitating event that had caused her to leave the dead man, but she was still protecting him. She thought it did not matter, but so often it was the small, personal details of a life that led to murder. She could not know. He would leave her that secret for as long as he could.

The offer of protection was another matter. He remembered the look on her face, the careful neutrality that suggested to him Foster's offer was not a surprise to her. He would need to figure out what exactly it was Central thought he knew.

What was more immediately curious was the dynamic with her captain. There was more there than simple antipathy. He thought of the conversation he had overheard, and how skillfully they had struck at each other. What had she said? *If it was me who'd been found dead, what would you do?* That one had hit its target, and gained her exactly what she wanted. The casual cruelty of it had shocked him. She had not seemed cruel. Direct, perhaps, but not cruel.

I know so little of this woman. He wondered if she had been cruel to Danny Lancaster. He wondered how the dead man had felt about Captain Foster.

"How much did Danny spend at Gregorian's?" he asked.

"Thirty-three thousand," she said. "More than usual. He'd been winning more at cards lately; everyone was talking about it, but I didn't realize it was this much."

"Even at Gregorian's he could not have spent all of that money alone."

"He had a tendency to buy for the house," she said.

"They have regulars there," he told her. "If he was spreading his money around, there will be those who remember him."

The tram reached the outskirts of the city, and there were fewer and fewer people with them on it. Those who remained sat far away from them, and it occurred to Trey that they might be reacting to her uniform. Given the city's dislike of off-world authority, it made him wonder if anyone at the bar would talk to her at all.

Not that he would fare any better. He had patronized Gregorian's twice, despite preferring whiskey to beer, both times in the company of his friend Ilya Putin, who sometimes consulted at the observatory. The staff had treated him with the same friendly courtesy they treated the rest of their customers, but cheerfully taking his money was not the same thing as sharing secrets. "We would be better off if we brought an astronomer," he mused aloud.

She glanced over at him. "I hadn't thought about that," she admitted. "They won't want to talk to me, will they?"

"Perhaps not," he said, "but that is not what I meant. The bar is popular with the astronomers and cartographers at the observatory. Most of the regulars study the pulsar. If we had an astronomer, we could at least engage them in conversation."

She was frowning. "Is it mostly the scientists? Do they really drink enough to keep the place in business?"

"It does better than you would think, given how far away from the center it is. The local citizens like it in part because it is usually missed by tourists. There are exceptions, of course," he told her. "Some weeks ago there was another of your ships in orbit, and they apparently caused a fair amount of chaos. It seems they were not shy about spending their money, but they were less sanguine about leaving when asked."

He had meant to reassure her, but her eyes had gone sharp. "The ship," she asked him. "Do you remember which one it was?"

He did remember. Trey had never dealt directly with Captain MacBride—he had been part of Valeria's watch, and Trey had happily left her to deal with the man—but he had followed the ship's movements for a decade. "It was *Demeter*," he told her. "She usually prefers Shenzhu, or at least used to, so I was a little surprised when she took shore leave here. Elena, what is it?"

All of the color had drained from her face, but when she spoke, her voice was strong. "*Demeter* was here? How long ago?"

He thought back; he had been with his niece when he heard the news, a few days before she was due to start school. "About four weeks."

She was staring at him, her eyes searching his face, desperate for something, he could not know what. "I asked you before," she said to him, "if you trusted me. You said you had no choice."

"Elena—"

"Can I trust you?"

He looked down at her, into her dark eyes—so determined, so intelligent, *so lovely*. He should have said no, told her that her doctor was right, that she needed to go back to her ship and let her angry captain exercise diplomacy. She should leave him here, where he would not look at her and remember how it had felt to kiss her. Where he would not find himself trusting her when everything he had ever learned about the universe outside of PSI was telling him he should not.

"Yes," he said. "You can trust me."

She looked away, brushing a wisp of hair off her forehead. "*Galileo* wasn't meant to come here," she told him. "Volhynia is far beyond our territory."

He knew this. *Galileo* was a Fourth Sector patrol ship, and was well thought of. He might even have heard people speak of Elena, although he could not remember.

"We were in at Aleph Nine about a week and a half ago. Provisioning and repairs. We were supposed to go to Shenzhu, give people some time off; we'd been out more than five months already, and tempers were getting short. Greg was barking at everybody, trying to get us out of there as quickly as possible. And then *Demeter* came in, limping. She'd been hit, on her way to Volhynia to drop cargo. They'd fought off their attackers, but they were going to be two weeks in port. Captain MacBride asked Greg if we'd take the delivery. As anxious as he had been to leave, I was surprised when he said yes. We took on twenty-five of their crew to help with the extra work, and a whole hangar bay full of food and materials cargo. We diverted three weeks out of our way for this drop."

"I see the coincidence," he said. "And I can understand wondering why they would need to deliver cargo if they had just been here. But surely there is nothing unusual in the attack itself. The Syndicates strike ships all the time—even here, although it is true they are rarely bold enough to hit a Central warship."

"But that's the thing, Trey," she told him. "The Syndicates didn't hit them. They are claiming they were hit by PSI."

He opened his mouth to challenge her, but something in her face made him stop. Suddenly the idea of being deliberately framed for murder seemed a small and insignificant thing. "You believe this," he said.

"I think Captain MacBride is an arrogant asshole who would happily lie if he thought it would save face. But that's the problem. This isn't in the public incident report. It's part of his classified write-up. I'm not even supposed to know."

"And yet you do." There was something seriously wrong with Central's chain of command rules. "How do you know this?"

Her eyes shifted away, and he knew before she said it. "Greg told me, before I came down."

"To convince you to bring me back to your ship." When she nodded, he swore. "So I am to be Central's prisoner instead of Stoya's."

"*No.*" She looked miserable. "I wouldn't do it. I wouldn't have done it. He didn't give me a direct order, Trey. And even if he had, even if you'd wanted to come, I'd have told you all of this. I wouldn't have taken you back."

He knew he was glaring. "You would use me against my own people, imprison me over some skirmish of which I know nothing." He shook his head. "You should have stayed away from here."

"I came back here to get you out of jail."

"You came back here because you believed I was involved with the assault on *Demeter.*"

He saw her jaw set; he had made her angry. "You say you trust me, and now I'm a liar?"

He was aware of being unfair, of feeling unmoored, as if the world had dropped from beneath his feet. "You make this accusation about my people—my *family,* Elena, as much as *Galileo* is yours—and I am to put my fate in your hands?"

"What do you want me to say?"

"I want you to explain yourself!" he shouted. The other passengers glanced worriedly in his direction; he did not care. "I want to understand how you can face Luvidovich one moment in defense of the truth, and then turn and lie so easily. I want to know how you can speak with such casual disrespect to your commanding officer, and then tell me that you trust him. I want you to explain how you could so easily feign concern when you are no better than the local police. And before you answer that," he added when she opened her mouth, "remember this: I was an officer for *thirty years*. I have seen every kind of officer there is, including insubordinate mechanics, and I know a lie when I hear one." He hoped that last declaration was true.

To her credit she did not look away. Her eyes were still angry, but when she spoke her voice was steady. "I have not lied to you," she said. "I never thought you were involved. But I *was* the one who suggested to Greg that Central might not want you incommunicado in police custody. That was the only way I could think to get him to let me come back. If you had taken him up on the offer, I would have told you all of this while we were still here. All I wanted was to get you out, and get the police back on track. I didn't know they had no plans to find Danny's killer, and I sure as hell didn't know how *Demeter* played into all of it. As for Greg—" She took a breath. "Yes, I have been disrespectful, and no, there is no excuse that would withstand official scrutiny. I will only say that I trust that he would not have told me what he told me unless he believed it."

And that, he realized, was what was angering him: not her inconsistencies, not his uncertainty about her motives, but the very real possibility that the story was true. All of his outrage deserted him, leaving behind gut-level dread. *Dear God.* "It would be an exceptionally foolish thing for us to have done," he said. He wondered if MacBride had fired back, if he would have heard if anyone had died. "For this to be true—such an act would threaten all of us. We are aware that Central has more firepower than we have, should we ever end up on opposite sides. I cannot imagine what might provoke such an act." He felt abruptly old and exhausted. "I should not have shouted at you."

"Of course you should have." She reached out, and her fingers brushed his arm—a small gesture, of forgiveness or atonement he was not sure. "For what it's worth, when he told me my first response was that it's bullshit."

"Which is part of why you think it may be true."

She acceded the point with a nod. "I can't think of a good reason why MacBride would make this up. Scurrying away after getting shot at by PSI hardly fits the heroic image he likes to cultivate."

"So you think this incident may explain why someone placed that poor boy on my doorstep." He shook his head. "I do not like being convenient." In particular, he did not like being convenient to Central. Stoya had position and power, but he was only one man. *Speaking of men in power* . . . "Why are you angry with your captain, Elena? It is not only because of me."

For a moment he thought she was not going to answer. "He was probably the best friend I had," she said at last. "And six months ago, he stopped being my friend at all. I don't know why. It's a loss, Trey, and I can tell myself that it's his fault, that he changed, that I don't deserve any of it, but the truth is I miss him."

"So you hit him however you can."

"It's not like it hurts him."

"Do you really believe that?"

" . . . I don't know." She sounded as tired as he felt. "I hit him because I can't stop hurting, and then I end up feeling small and cruel, which is worse. And then he does something else, and I want to hit him again. It never ends." Her next words were quiet. "I would not have let them take you prisoner, Trey."

He turned to find her looking at him, and he flashed back to walking next to her in the cool evening, before he kissed her, wondering at this beautiful woman by his side. He wanted to take her hand in his, but he was already aware of how little objectivity he had left.

He looked away. "It is in the next block," he told her, and focused on their approaching exit.

Gregorian's was on the outskirts of the city, a short walk from the squat, institutional observatory buildings. It was high enough on the hill that even inland it benefited from some of the sea-mist fragrance that pervaded the city, and offered a panorama of the skyline that attracted guests staying at the fancier hotels. Wealthy tourists notwithstanding, though, the observatory staff gave the place almost more business than it could handle. Ilya had told him he dropped by once or twice a month, but talking with a server the last time he was there led Trey to believe most of the regulars were there nightly. They served consistently fine liquor and good food, and if Trey had been more comfortable spending his money on ephemera, he might have joined Ilya more often.

Through the bar's wide front window they could see the staff preparing to open: someone setting up chairs and tables, someone behind the bar arranging bottles with long-practiced efficiency. A woman looked up from the front desk and met Trey's eyes through the window; she raised her eyebrows in question, and when Trey nodded at her she left her post to open the front door.

"Can I help you?" she said to them.

He remembered her: the bar's floor manager, a young woman, although likely not as young as her pale hair and waifish figure made her look. She had treated him just like any other guest, a trait he had learned to value highly since he had returned.

Elena replied to her. "I hope so," she said, more subdued than she had been, and he recognized the effort to downplay her uniform. "I am trying to trace one of my colleagues—he came in here last night. I am wondering if I could speak to anyone who might have been working while he was here."

Watching the young woman's face, Trey saw the exact moment she put Elena's uniform together with the day's news. Her blue eyes grew huge, and the practiced calm on her face dissolved. "Oh, my God," she said, her voice wavering. "It was him, wasn't it? The dead man. It was Danny."

CHAPTER 12

Galileo

Ensign Enkhtuyaa seemed like a nice enough kid, Jessica had to admit. She was the least standoffish of the *Demeter* bunch, and when Jessica had found her in the pub, she had been moving from table to table, grieving and commiserating with crew from both ships. Now she was sitting next to Ted Shimada, weeping openly. Jessica sat across from the pair, making sympathetic noises.

Jessica thought the girl was more angry than sad, and for that she could not find fault. One of their own had been killed, almost certainly by a civilian. It was intolerable. Joining the Corps meant fighting for something larger than yourself, being willing to sacrifice. An ordinary killer was an insult to all of them.

"I hope they find the bastard and fry him in the street," the girl fumed through her tears. Jessica silently handed her a tissue, and Enkha blew her nose. "I'm sorry about the crying. I always cry when I'm pissed off. Not that I'm not sad, because dammit, he was a good guy. I mean a *good guy,* you know? Nice. Honest. Cheerful. But people die on this job. If I sobbed over all of them I'd never do anything else with my day. If he'd been killed in action, I'd get stinking drunk and toast him all night. But this? Murder. Fucking *murder.* On some planet where they charge three hundred for a fucking beer." She dissolved again, and Jessica handed her another tissue, meeting Ted's eyes over the girl's head.

"The captain'll get the killer," Ted said reassuringly.

Enkha just glared at him. "Oh, really? That's not what they're saying. They're saying he's wasting time digging up dirt on that pirate that his woman was fucking."

So much for camaraderie. Even the least standoffish of these *Demeter* soldiers, Jessica reflected, was still an invader in her home. "Who told you the captain was digging up dirt?"

Enkha had unusually large eyes, and they lent her an air of innocence Jessica had always thought was feigned. "Commander Valentis said so."

Jessica had not realized Valentis's complaints in the pub had escalated to undermining Foster's credibility. The shift made her uneasy. She knew the captain was not inclined to think of Valentis as an enemy, but this kind of talk was creeping uncomfortably close to insubordination, and it wasn't going to do anything to quell the rumors that Foster had been jealous of Danny. "The captain is just being thorough," she said, trying to sound practical. "That pirate couldn't have been killing Danny while he was with the chief."

"Unless they were in it together."

One rumor or the other, she thought, exasperated. "I don't think she was *that* mad at Danny."

Enkha gave an indignant snort. "He was sure mad at her, though. Said she was all business, all the time, like he hadn't handed her his heart every day for two years."

That sort of poetry didn't sound at all like Danny. "When did he talk about her?"

"Over cards, mostly," Enkha said. "He'd drink too much and get maudlin. It wasn't good for him to be alone when he was like that."

"Is that why you guys let him win all the time?" Jessica asked her.

Enkha looked surprised, and Jessica downgraded her estimate of the girl's intelligence. "We didn't let him win," she tried, but she must have seen something on Jessica's face because she looked away. "Well, maybe now and again somebody threw a hand. We wanted to help."

Jessica had been wondering about that. Danny had been winning more lately—everyone had remarked on it. But he had been playing more conservatively as well, and Jessica had just thought Danny was a better card player than he had let on. *Maybe a combination of both.* "Was it just the chief he talked about?"

Enkha shrugged. "Kind of, yeah. When he talked at all. Mostly he'd prompt people, let them tell stories. He was really nice about that," she said, and teared up again. "He let me go on and on about my mom, and he listened to all of us about the attack. He even listened to Limonov." She laughed a little. "Even *we* don't listen to Limonov. Danny was a good guy. *We* appreciated him."

Jessica remembered Limonov from that morning, sitting at a table with his comrades, next to them, but separate. None of the others had been speaking to him. She wondered what he had been talking about with Danny.

Before she had a chance to ask, Ted spoke up. "You guys

have been running this sector for a while. Do you know Captain Zajec?"

If Jessica was any judge, Enkha was none too pleased to be pulled off the subject of Danny. "Not personally," she said. "I expect Captain MacBride met him once or twice, but that would've been before I joined."

"What's his reputation?"

She shrugged. "Aren't they all the same? Violent, standoffish, disinterested in anything we have to say."

That didn't fit Jessica's impression of PSI at all, but she was aware some crews held a more traditional view. "Violent how?"

"They run down Syndicate raiders," Enkha said. "Little ships, two- or three-person crews. They blow them out of the sky."

"Aren't the raiders usually trying to board them?" Jessica didn't have to fake the puzzlement in her voice.

"Half of what PSI hauls is already stolen," the girl insisted. "The Syndicates are just trying to get it back. Sell it properly, introduce it into the economy. They're not monsters, and they're not stealing anything."

Well, *that* was a warped perspective if Jessica had ever heard one. Not that she hadn't run across it before; there were even folks on *Galileo* who were happy to see the Syndicate tribes pushing out of black and gray markets and into the legitimate shipping channels. Jessica, who had spent the first fifteen years of her life on a small, constantly hungry colony, was less impressed by this belated attempt at lawfulness. By her estimation, once a pack of thieving bastards, always a pack of thieving bastards.

But that perspective wasn't going to get Enkhtuyaa to talk. "So he hit raiders," she said, and tried to mold her face into some kind of outrage. "What else?"

"Well." Enkhtuyaa's outrage deflated a little. "Pretty much that. Sometimes . . . some of the PSI ships would sometimes help us," she admitted. "When we were moving large shipments, or the couple of times we needed to shift some of the big Ellis terraformers. We didn't have a lot of emergency missions out here, which is why I don't understand why—" She broke off, and she reddened.

"Did something happen?" Jessica prompted.

Enkha looked at Jessica, then over at Ted. Her face took on a conspiratorial look. "Can I trust you guys?"

Oh, you poor kid, Jessica thought. *The Corps is going to eat you alive.* "Of course you can," she said.

"That hit we took, that sent us to Aleph Nine? That got us stuck on your ship, with all our cargo?" She glanced around, checking to see if they were being overheard. "It was a PSI ship that hit us."

"No fucking way." This came out of Ted's mouth before he could stop it, but by the time Enkha had turned to look at him, he made it look like outrage instead of disbelief.

Jessica resisted the urge to kick Ted under the table, and hoped he'd have the sense to shut up. If this little girl was telling them here in the pub, Jessica realized, the whole story was going to be out before the end of the shift. "What happened out there?" she asked.

"All I know," Enkhtuyaa said, "is that Captain MacBride put us on alert, and the next thing I know the artificial gravity is fluctuating and I'm trying to keep our cargo from falling over."

"Where were you?" Ted asked.

"Out by B1829," the girl said. "You know. That wormhole in the radiation zone."

Well, hell. If Enkhtuyaa knew, they had all known. Ted, of course, was still behind. "I thought you guys were at Shenzhu," he said.

"That was the plan," Enkhtuyaa said. "At least as far as they told me. I'm just a cargo jockey, after all. But we were all pissed off, because usually we take liberty on Shenzhu, and instead we end up on Volhynia. Do you know what they charge for wine down there?"

The conversation ran off the rails at that point, as Ted expended some energy trying to figure out why Enkhtuyaa would bother to order wine on a planet known for beer. By the time the ensign finally left them to head to the next table—giving Ted a quick kiss on the cheek for comfort—Jessica knew what she had to do next.

"You need to introduce me to Limonov," she told Ted.

He looked tired, she realized, and only some of that was holding up his end of their interview with Enkhtuyaa. He and Lanie went back a long way, and it occurred to her that he might be worried. "That could be a problem," he told her, sitting back and sipping what she was almost sure was water. "Limonov doesn't like me."

"Apparently he doesn't like anybody," Jessica observed. "But he liked Danny. Can't we use that as an in?"

"It won't work." At her look, he threw up his hands. "It won't, Jess. I tried, believe me. I poured on the charm from Day One with that crowd, and he was the only holdout. He's kind of . . . strange. Off-putting strange. They think so, too. They don't even know why MacBride sent him on this mission, especially as the senior officer."

"What, no theories?"

He shrugged. "Limonov's a good mechanic, I guess," he said. "And they tell me he and MacBride seemed friendlier after they took damage."

"So, what—shared trauma?"

"Sounds thin, doesn't it?"

She stood. "Which is why I have to meet him." He may have been disliked by his crewmates, but both Danny and MacBride had apparently taken pity on the man. He was smelling a lot like a clue.

They tracked Limonov down in engineering, where Lieutenant Dogara, the shift supervisor, had assigned him to test the calibration of *Galileo*'s long-distance sensors. "It was the only way I could keep him out of the way," Dogara told them, after Ted protested. "I'll double-check his work. But if I hadn't put him over there, he'd have done nothing but loom over people with that black look on his face, talking about curses."

"Curses?"

Dogara gave Jessica a look. "You haven't been exposed to this guy for the last two weeks," he told her. "Everything is cursed. The sensors are cursed, the engines are cursed. My grandmother is cursed, apparently. Also some types of sandwiches." He shook his head. "I don't know what you want to ask him, but nothing he says is going to make any sense."

Limonov almost certainly heard them approaching, but he did not look up from his work, meticulously matching the light metering on the sensor display with a set of equations displayed next to his head. Up close, Jessica could see that a lot of his dour expression was etched into the shape of his face: he had narrow, deep-set, paunchy eyes, and a sharp jaw that tugged down the corners of his mouth. He looked up as they came closer, and she thought she saw a flicker of irritation pass over his austere features. He paused the meter easily enough, though, and turned to face them.

Ted cleared his throat. "Commander Limonov, sir. I don't think you've met Lieutenant Lockwood."

"I have not." His voice was rough, as if he had had some throat damage earlier in his life. He nodded at her affably enough. "Pleasure, Lieutenant. I'm sorry about your man. He was a solid fellow."

That, Jessica thought, was possibly the most respectful epitaph she had heard about Danny all day. "Thank you, sir," she said, then wondered how to begin. She had no angle at all, beyond the truth, so she began with that. "I know the two of you spent some time together, and I'm wondering if you could tell me what you were talking about."

"Why?" Neither his tone nor his expression had changed.

She cleared her throat. "Well, sir, I'm trying to find out what he was doing before he was killed. What might have happened to him."

Limonov turned back to his work, firing up the meter again. "You don't want to know."

She felt Ted giving her a don't-say-I-didn't-warn-you look. She ignored him, stepping forward. "I do, sir. It matters to me, what happened to Danny."

"You were not his friend." Still even, still casual.

"No," she admitted, "I wasn't. I didn't know him well, and I didn't try to get to know him well. But he was one of us, sir. You know what that's like, don't you?"

He was staring at the light meter, but she did not think he was really seeing it. "This is not a good business, you know," he said. "The Corps. There are so many omens . . . and nobody sees them."

It was strange, Jessica thought. Somehow she had expected raving. He sounded quite normal—if a bit inclined to bounce off-topic. "What sort of omens?"

He shook his head. "That wormhole," he said. "There's something wrong with it. It took the *Phoenix,* and when we were there, it nearly took us."

"I thought it was that PSI ship that clobbered you," she said.

He did not seem surprised that she knew. "It tried to take the PSI ship, too. It will take all of us, eventually. The *Phoenix* was only the first. Captain MacBride—he knew before we went there. For years he was blind, but something opened his eyes. Danny knew. Danny was never blind. You want to know what we were talking about? He was listening. He was understanding. He was seeing the patterns, asking the right questions . . . and now he is gone. You think that is coincidence, Lieutenant Lockwood?"

"No," she told him. That was the truth.

He nodded, approving. "It is that thing, that wormhole. It is dangerous, and we need to stay away from it. It will lure us to it, and one by one, it will destroy us all."

"And how will it do that?"

Limonov glanced briefly at Ted, then back at her. Slowly he leaned down until his face was close to hers, until he could speak to her without Ted overhearing. His huge, deep-set eyes were intense, beseeching—what he was about to tell her was important.

"*It sings*," he said.

Ted cleared his throat and put a hand on Jessica's arm. "Thank you, Commander. I'm sure you're busy. We're sorry we bothered you." He pulled on her, and she took a step back.

Limonov straightened, his face returning to its sad mask, and turned back to his work. Jessica pulled her arm free, trying to think of something to say. She thought at any moment she would start shivering. "Thank you, Commander Limonov," she said. "I appreciate your candor." But he did not turn around, and after a moment she turned and followed Ted out of engineering.

"I told you," Ted said, as the door closed behind them. "He's nuts. Not useful. Who are we talking to next?"

Jessica's mind was reeling. None of it made sense, and yet somehow it did. Danny had seen something in the man's ravings. Certainly not a warning, but something he had taken for information. *It will take all of us.* How was that possible, when nobody could get close to it? But it all tied together, she realized. Solomonoff's PSI ship. *Demeter.* The *Phoenix.* Whether or not the wormhole was cursed, an awful lot of dramatic events seemed to happen in its vicinity.

Damn, she was beginning to think like a crazy conspiracy theorist.

"Anybody you can get," she told Ted. "Anybody who will talk to you. See if you can find out if they overheard anything between Limonov and Danny, maybe something more coherent than what he just said."

"You really think there's something there?"

"I don't know. Probably not." Her heart was racing, and the

tingle down her spine had not quit. "But Danny sure as hell did, and I'm betting whatever it was has something to do with what really happened to him. Find out, Ted."

"What are you going to do?"

"I'm going to report to the captain," she told him. *And maybe,* she thought, *get some useful information from him for once.*

CHAPTER 13

Volhynia

He came in a little before ten," the young woman said, her fingers wrapped around a mug of hot coffee. Despite the steam rising from the liquid, her fingernails were white, and Elena could see her hands trembling. The bartender had tipped some dark liquid into the cup along with the coffee. Elena hoped it was something potent.

Elena had let Trey deal with her. He had become instantly solicitous: helping her into a chair, calling to the bartender for assistance, intently focused on her well-being. A detached part of Elena found this impressive, because within seconds the young woman was clutching at his arm, leaning on him, hanging on as if he were the only solid thing left in her universe.

They would not need to worry about anyone here mistrusting PSI.

Trey had extracted her name—Ynes Bardzecki—and accepted her offer of coffee for them both before asking her his first gentle question. Elena sat back and let him lead. It was strange, hearing this tiny young woman talk about Danny as if she had known him. If Elena had come in with Danny, Ynes would never even have learned his name.

"He asked for a table by the window, but he didn't stay there," Ynes recalled. "He ordered one beer, and drank about half before he got up and started going from table to table, talking to people."

"That seems odd," Trey said.

Ynes nodded. "We're a social enough place, but it's almost always the research teams from the observatory, and they tend to stick to their own. I kept an eye on him in case he started bothering people, but everybody seemed pleased to talk to him. Everybody. It was weird; he'd introduce himself and sit down, and within about three minutes whoever he was sitting with was smiling and chatting as if they'd known him for years."

That sounded like the Danny Elena knew: the collector of stories. He had collected her stories, too. It had been lovely, at first, to have someone so interested. Only after Jake's death had she come to realize he did not always understand what the stories meant. "Do you know what sorts of things they talked about?" she asked.

"Mostly he was asking them about their research," she said. "I didn't understand a lot of it, but it was the same sort of thing they always talked about."

They must have been fascinating for some other reason, Elena thought. Danny had been able to muster an interest in most topics, but anything even remotely mathematical made his mind skitter off onto something else. "My dad was an accountant," he had told her, "so of course I have as little to do with numbers as I can." She felt briefly grateful that Danny's parents had not lived to see their oldest child lost.

"When did you begin speaking to him?" Trey asked.

"Just after the lights went out," she replied. "I watch people when the Dead Hour starts; it says a lot about them, how they react. He didn't even blink. Mostly he seemed surprised that everybody else went quiet."

"What did the two of you talk about?" Trey asked.

"We didn't talk about anything serious, not really. He asked me about my job, and what I liked about it. I asked about his, and he said he thought he was better at it in his head than in the real world. I liked that," she said quietly. "Who hasn't thought that about their job?"

Elena's heart twisted. Danny, the perpetual underachiever. It seemed that he had known it.

"He talked about this woman, too," Ynes added. "He said he'd asked her before to meet him here, but he was glad she turned him down this time."

Elena did not dare look at Trey.

"That must have been unwelcome," he said. "To have him bring up another woman." He shifted his hand on the table, just a little, and his fingers brushed Elena's wrist.

"It was me who brought it up," the hostess admitted. "There's a look they get, when they're not really free. Only he said he'd screwed it up. I thought that was nice, too, that he said that. Most guys? They want to complain about the ex, talk about how awful she was, all the ways I'm not like her. You know? But he said it was his own fault, and then he went back to asking about me."

He had liked this woman, Elena realized. She remembered how he could be, when he was trying; he had been the same with her, early on, when she was deciding whether to risk dating someone on board. He had asked her about herself, and he had listened. More than that, he had *remembered*. She looked at

Ynes, young and uncomplicated, and thought how much better suited she would have been to Danny.

"He even asked me about that ship from before," she said.

Coincidence again. Elena shook off self-pity. "You mean *Demeter*." When the woman nodded, she asked, "Did he ask anything specific?"

"It's funny," Ynes said, "because it's sort of what you're asking about him. He wondered why they had been here, in this bar, instead of the usual tourist haunts by the spaceport."

"Did you know? With them all being so drunk?"

The woman looked embarrassed; she seemed unused to criticizing her customers. "It wasn't all of them, not really," she said. "Just most of them, and that was the problem. By the time the police got here, Stanis wanted them all out. But there were two I can remember. One of them was . . . strange-looking. Like his face was falling in on itself."

Elena wondered if *Demeter* had anyone else who fit that description as well as Limonov.

"He spent most of his time in a corner, talking to one of the researchers. That old fellow." She looked at Trey. "The one you've come in with a couple of times. Ilya."

Elena knew Trey well enough to recognize surprise in his eyes, but all he did was smile at the hostess. "You have an excellent memory," he remarked, and Ynes blushed again.

"You're easy to remember," she told him. "And your friend—he doesn't come in often, but he's always nice. They aren't all, you know. The researchers. Some of them think I'm a dim-witted city girl, but he never talks down to me."

"Do you know what they discussed?" Elena asked, refocusing her.

Ynes shook her head. "I didn't listen in. I kept an eye on them, just in case, but they were fine. They'd left before the police showed up."

Elena filed that away to ask Trey about later. "Who else stayed sober?"

"One grim-looking older guy. I think he was the one in charge," she said, "but I don't know how that works, really. They seemed to pay some attention to him, but he didn't help when they started getting unruly. And he wasn't sober all night, either. He started drinking just before the Dead Hour. Right after he got a comm. He seemed . . . worried, after that. Like he stopped seeing what was going on around him."

"And he spoke to no one?" Trey asked her.

Another blush. Elena wanted to shake her. "He spoke to me, a bit," Ynes admitted. "I stayed behind the bar for most of the night, and he was sitting there, talking half to himself. I remember he asked me a lot about life here in Novanadyr. The culture, he said. He wanted to know about immigration."

Elena frowned. That made no sense. "What sort?"

"PSI, mostly," the hostess said. "He asked about the local Syndicates, too, but he didn't seem as interested in them. Mostly he wanted to know what kind of a relationship we had with PSI, whether we thought of them as allies. It's funny," she added. "When I asked him why he was curious, he said he'd always thought of them as allies, too. It . . . seemed to make him sad."

A well of dread was opening in Elena's stomach, along with something else she did not want to examine. "How long ago was this?" she asked. "Precisely. Can you remember?"

"Let me look it up." Ynes touched her comm and pulled up a calendar, scrolling backward. "A month," she said. "Three weeks and five days, actually. But what does this have to do with Danny?"

Elena shook her head, unable to speak, and looked at Trey. He was still watching Ynes, but he kept his fingers on her skin, and she had to resist the urge to grasp his hand. MacBride had been talking about PSI in a public bar less than twenty hours before they had been attacked by a PSI ship. She didn't like the man, but he was no fool. How classified could his orders have been? How classified could the result of his trip out to the wormhole really be? What had really happened out there?

And how much had Greg not told her?

"We are not at all sure which events are relevant," Trey was telling her smoothly. "But we must follow what trails we have. When did Danny leave?"

Ynes looked suddenly crushed, and sympathy almost pulled Elena out of her haze. "It was still the Dead Hour," she said, her voice quiet. "His comm went off."

"Do you know who he spoke to?"

"I don't know. He wasn't happy, though. Very cagey with whoever it was."

"No vid, then?"

"It's not widely used here, especially for local comms," Ynes told them.

It would only be local comms, Elena realized, that they could enable with the grid down—low-tech, short-range wireless. She blinked aside her numbness and tried to focus. "Can you tell me what you remember about the comm? Even if it seems meaningless to you?"

Ynes frowned, concentrating. "He was irritated when the signal came through, I remember that. Waited to answer it. He spoke politely, but he was . . . detached. I wondered for a minute if it was his girl tracking him down, but he seemed a little cool for that. Then I wondered if he'd had one of his friends call him, so he'd have an excuse to leave."

"He wasn't like that," Elena said reflexively. "He'd have left if he wanted to, and been honest about it."

And yet, she did not know if even that was true. Before everything had fallen apart between them, she would have stood up for his character to anyone, even Greg. Afterward, she had gone over every word he had ever said to her. She had not thought herself easy to deceive—and yet she had been. She had thought Danny's deception had been an act of desperation, and not who he was, not really. Just as she had tried to tell herself Greg's anger, his exclusion, was due to something unrelated, something that had nothing to do with her. That if there was something important going on, Greg would become himself again, would tell her what she needed to know.

She had been a damn fool.

"He said it'd be quick, that he'd be back before the hour was up," Ynes told her. "When he didn't come back—well, it happens. I'm usually careful, but it still happens sometimes. Even so—I cried," she said, embarrassed. "Not a lot. But I hid in the bathroom and let go for a few minutes. It had seemed different with him."

Elena's mind flashed a picture: Danny and Ynes, in one of the lovely row houses Volhynia built overlooking the sea, a herd of yellow-haired children running through the yard. He would have none of that now, with anyone. She looked away.

Trey asked Ynes if she could give him a list of everyone who was there the night before, and Elena thought his goal had been to get her to leave. Elena watched her cross the room, a good-hearted, obtuse young woman. She was caught between the desire to put her arms around her—reassuring her she could not have known, that she was not responsible for what happened—and shaking her until her teeth bounced right out of her head. Surely there was something she could have said: she could have warned Danny of the danger, seduced him to keep him in the bar . . . anything other than stand there like a scorned schoolgirl while he wandered off, unconcerned, to his death.

Her hands felt cold and she clasped them together, rubbing her fingers. No, Ynes could not have warned Danny. She could not have known anything. Elena, on the other hand . . . no, not even she could have saved him. Her pathological liar of a lover, who she always thought was too stupid to fool her. If she had met him here, it would have been her, and not sweet, innocent Ynes, who let him go off to meet a stranger.

Trey broke into her thoughts. "You said your ship came here in lieu of *Demeter*."

Twenty-five of them, Elena thought. *Twenty-five of those people on* my *ship.* "This trade drop was their scheduled mission. That earlier trip—that was something else."

He waited until she was looking at him to answer. "I believe," he said gently, "that there is a larger plan here than you have been told."

Well, at least he wasn't accusing her of trying to kidnap him anymore. "Greg would have told me."

"You are sure of this?"

Yes, she wanted to say. *Not just because he is a captain, and I am an officer, and he would not let me walk into this defenseless. Because I have known him more than seven years, and I matter to him, and he would have told me because he tells me these things.*

But she couldn't say that. Instead, she shook her head. "I'm not sure of anything," she told him. "But . . . the man she was talking about, the old man at the bar. That had to be Captain MacBride. I think—Trey, I think that comm MacBride took was about PSI."

She was saved from elaborating by Ynes, who returned to the table and opened a document before them. "There were sixty-two regulars I could remember," she told them. "I am pretty sure this is it, but I couldn't swear to it."

"Thank you," Elena said, but she was not sure she meant it. She did not want to talk to astrophysicists, did not want to rummage through other people's memories of Danny. She was no longer convinced what he had done with his evening had anything to do with what had happened. All of this was madness.

Trey, fortunately, had retained his manners. He stood, and held a hand out to the young woman. "Yes, thank you," he repeated. He sounded so sincere. "You have been a great help to us, Ynes."

"Will you find him?" Ynes asked, her huge eyes, wide and trusting, on Trey's face.

Elena opened her mouth to say they would try, but Trey spoke first. "Yes," he replied. He reached out and took the woman's hand between his own. "We will find him."

Chapter 14

Why did you say that to her?" Elena exploded, as they headed up the sidewalk. "You've no idea if we're going to catch anyone. If this is some big Central cover-up, we're not going to find anyone. These people are *professionals*. You can make all the promises you want, but it's not going to find us a killer."

Trey looked over at her. She was walking fast, oblivious to their direction, and she would not look at him. "I do not think there is any harm in offering her hope," he said. "What has made you angry, Elena? It is not what I said to Ynes."

"It is, though. Who are you to decide what she should and shouldn't know? She's young, but she's not a fool. Of course she should worry, and she knows it, and you're telling her what she knows is wrong."

"But that's not the only thing, is it?"

She shook her head. "It's just like with Greg. 'No, Elena, MacBride's totally on the level, this bullshit story he's telling is the *truth*, of *course*,' and the real problem is that I'm just not understanding the circumstances. 'Just be cautious, Chief, and I'll look into it.'" She spat the last sentence out. "He doesn't have to lie to me at all, does he? He just tells me half truths and pats me on the head like I'm a fucking *idiot,* and why wouldn't he think so, because I *am.*"

He put his hand on her arm, and she shrugged him off, stopping in the street to glare at him. "Danny was *stupid,* did you know that? I figured *stupid* meant *sweet,* that he'd never lie to me, that I was such a bloody marvelous judge of character he'd never be able to pull it off. But Greg is right, Trey. I *am* an idiot. I *don't* understand the circumstances. And Danny knew that, and he used it, and I should have known he would, I should have seen it—"

She buried her face in her hands and collapsed against the corner of the building. He moved closer to her, wanting to touch her again, uncertain of what she would do. He could hear her breathing through her hands. He did not think she was crying. He wondered if she had cried for Danny at all.

"I trusted him," she said, her voice muffled by her hands. "Even when he kept after me over and over about retiring, settling down, living on some bloody piece of rock—I *trusted him.*"

"Elena," Trey said softly. "*M'laya,* what happened to you? Tell me."

She lowered her hands and closed her eyes, dropping her head back against the wall. Her eyes were swollen; he thought perhaps she had been crying after all. But when she spoke, her voice was calmer. "About three months ago," she said, "I had a miscarriage."

At that Trey reached out and put his hand on her arm. "My dear," he said, "I am so sorry. Had you been trying for a long time?"

She did not answer at first. "I was sick for two days. I couldn't work. First time in my whole career. I told everyone I had the flu, and I hid in my room until it was over. It was entirely unexpected. I have never wanted children," she told him. "But to lose it . . . Doctor Hastings told me it was nothing I'd done or hadn't done, that sometimes it just happened like this, that if I wanted to I could—could still have a child. And I know it, in my head. But in my heart? It's like . . . it couldn't stand to be with me. That something about me made it leave." The tears spilled over, but she still did not sob.

"I take it Danny did not handle this well," he said, keeping his hand on her arm.

At that she laughed, and he could not remember when he had last heard a sound so bitter. "Oh, no, he was lovely," she told him. "Stayed with me, took care of me, held me while I cried, told me over and over it wasn't my fault. But he was never much good at sitting with difficult emotions, and after a few days he started trying to cheer me up. He kept saying we could try again."

Trey wondered at the mind-boggling stupidity of the boy. "His timing was unfortunate."

"He didn't understand," she said. "I wanted to explain that I hadn't changed my mind, that I still didn't want a baby, but it hurt so much and I feel—I felt so guilty, so I told him how mad the odds were, with both of us on the shot, and he said, 'Well, about that.'"

Trey swore under his breath and looked away from her. Not stupidity then; irredeemable selfishness.

"We'd been on Cygnus a month before, and he said he'd bought this drug. He said he'd been taking it daily and he hadn't had any side effects at all, and clearly since I got pregnant it had worked. He said even with my allergies it wouldn't hurt me, but we could talk to Doctor Hastings if I was worried. And he had no idea why I got so angry with him." She met Trey's eyes, and he almost shrank from the intensity of her rage. "He did that to me. *On purpose*. He made me pregnant, and when I lost it all he could think about was doing it to me *again,* making me go through all that loss *again,* and he thought I'd be glad because that explained everything, didn't it, him going off the shot, and wasn't I pleased it would be so *easy*?" He watched as the rage in her face dissolved into agony. "I trusted him with everything. I had no one else. Jake was gone, and Greg was horrible, and Jess was too busy doing her duty. He was all I had, and he tore it all away from me, all because he wanted to turn me into someone else." She finally began to sob.

Trey was done second-guessing himself. He reached out and put his arms around her, pulling her against him, one hand cradling the back of her head. After a moment she wilted, wrapping her arms around his back, and she buried her face in his shoulder and cried. He whispered to her, kissed her hair, and let her weep. The tears went on for a long time.

"Have you talked this through with anyone?" he asked her, when she began to quiet.

She shook her head. "Doctor Hastings is the only other person who knows, and he doesn't know all of it."

"Would you have told your captain, if you had still been friends?"

She gasped with laughter. "God, Greg would have put him out an airlock before I even finished the story."

Trey thought perhaps he might like Captain Foster after all. "You protected Danny," he observed.

She nodded against his shoulder. "Sort of. I didn't want people talking about me. I knew it was going to be bad enough, just breaking up with him. On a small ship, gossip is cheap entertainment. And I didn't think—" She swallowed. "I've always figured I was hard to fool, or that my friends were lousy liars. But they don't have to be, Trey. They don't have to lie at all. They tell me the truth—just never enough of it."

He kept his arms around her. "Your captain may not know the whole truth to tell you, Elena."

"If *I* can figure out MacBride was following some PSI-related order when he got hit, you can bet Greg knows all of it."

She spoke with absolute confidence, and he had no reason to disbelieve her. She knew Captain MacBride better than he did. But there was someone else who knew him as well, and it was past time he spoke to her. "There is more than one side to this story, *m'laya*," he said.

She pulled back, studying his face. She had heard something in his voice. "You don't have to," she told him.

He had not been in touch with any of his people in six months. When someone left PSI, contact generally decreased; but there were letters, and sometimes visits, like those of a child after leaving home. He would not have chosen to sever ties himself, and now it seemed he needed to reconnect them. Something stirred in his heart: despair, defeat, relief, he was not sure. On some level he had always known he would turn back to them. He belonged with them more than he ever had belonged in this place, despite how long he had dreamed of coming home. He was as alone as Elena was; it had just taken him more years to see it.

"We must comm from my flat. She will not be monitoring the main network." *And with the way things were between us when I left, I'm not sure she will answer even then.*

She shifted away from him, sliding one palm down his arm as she moved, and instinctively he caught her hand and laced her fingers in his. She looked briefly surprised, but he was almost certain she was pleased as well, and they turned together and headed back up the street.

They were back on the tram, still hand in hand, before she spoke. "That word you used back there," she said. "*M'laya.* I don't know that one. What does it mean?"

"Hm." He felt his face grow warm; she had caught him out. "It means darling, or sweetheart. One who matters. My niece, Sarah—my sister's daughter, who is twelve. She is also *m'laya.*" It mattered, somehow, that she understand the word did not connote a lover, necessarily, but there was no escaping that it implied a closeness he had no right to claim.

She smiled, and he thought she was blushing again. "It's a nice word," she said. "Warm. Is it gendered?"

He shook his head. "Like all good terms of endearment, it speaks to everyone."

"I'm sorry I shouted," she told him. "I'm not angry at you."

"I am thinking you should have shouted sooner," he said, and squeezed her hand. "You are carrying a lot of anger."

She sighed. "I suppose I am. I forget. Day to day, there's too much to do."

"And you have no one to talk to."

"Not really, no." She looked away. "It's not that I'm without friends. It's just most of them are used to me being competent. I tend to hide before I fall apart. After Jake . . . I fell apart around Greg, but that was all. Most of the crew cursed and got drunk for weeks. I just hid."

"Who was Jake?"

"Commander Jacobs. Chief of engineering before me. I knew him from way back, when I was working as a mechanic for my uncle. I came up under him." She moved closer to him. "We were trying to stop this skirmish. A couple of traders getting stupid enough to shoot at each other. One of them hit us. It was a one-in-a-million shot; it hit a heat vent, and shot straight into the machine room." She met his eyes. "It was strange. He was standing there, like he always did, and we were grumbling about having to mediate this stupid fight, and there was a sound, just this quiet noise in the wall, and then this blast of flame went right through him. My eyes went to the opposite wall, like he would have been thrown by the force of it . . . but he wasn't thrown. He was incinerated, right there, right in front of me, this man I had been talking to seconds before."

He wanted to put his arms around her again. "You were close to him."

She nodded. "I always thought of him as my father, really, although most of what we talked about was professional. He was always pushing me to learn more. He was never shy about telling me when I'd screwed up, either, so when he told me I'd done well, I knew he meant it." Her voice grew soft. "I was happy with him."

So she'd had a family, of sorts. A father who was proud of her, and a lover. One friend who understood, another who pushed her to try things she would otherwise not. She had lost so much so fast. He wanted to tell her that life would settle down, but he did not know that it was true. He had spent four decades seeking normalcy with PSI, then tried to find it by coming home. And yet, to this day, the closest he ever got was when he was trying to teach Sarah to cook.

"How long afterward did you argue with your captain?" he asked her.

She gave him a sad smile. "We never argued," she told him. "That was the thing. We went back to Earth a few months after Jake died, and when we left again, he was different. He completely shut me out."

"You do not know why?"

She shook her head. "I didn't think much about it at first," she said. "He's often moody when we come off Earth. It's not so uncommon, really; a lot of people are like that when they leave their families, and he doesn't get to see his wife more than five or six times a year as it is. But this time it lasted, and after a couple of weeks I came to realize it was just me, that with everyone else he was pretty much back to normal. But now—I wonder, Trey, about what else is going on here. If maybe that's part of what has been bothering him."

She was trying so hard to understand.

"Did you ask why he changed?"

"Oh, of course. But it just started getting worse and worse, to the point that people would leave the room if he and I were both in it. He was sarcastic and mean, and I hate that kind of thing. He knows I hate it." Trey could feel her tensing. "And why, if it was a professional problem, would it just be me? A few weeks ago I tried to have it out with him, but he shut me down. Told me we were never really friends, that he'd felt sorry for me all these years."

Her dark eyes looked sad and resigned. Whether or not this was a bigger loss than death, it certainly hurt her more than losing her lover. Trey released her hand to put his arm around her waist, pulling her closer. "I must believe," he said, "that whatever happened is nothing to do with you, my dear. For him to change so much—we all have our own demons. You simply ran afoul of his."

"Oh, I know," she said, and gave him an unconvincing smile. "But it's the same thing. I do not forgive him. The reasons don't matter anymore."

"You are a holder of grudges." *Just like Valeria*, he thought, but he was past the point where such observations surprised him.

"I take it you are not."

"If I were to say that," he told her, "I would not be entirely truthful. On the whole, I do not easily take offense, but there are things I have not forgiven, and probably never will."

"Like the police arresting you for everything."

"For that, I think perhaps I will hold a grudge," he said, smiling. "But I will fix the blame squarely on the shoulders of the chief investigator, and not the junior officers doing as they were told."

"As I am the holder of grudges," she told him, "I will blame them for you, if you don't mind."

"That seems an equitable division of labor," he agreed.

They fell silent again, and he kept his arm around her waist, acutely aware of his hip brushing hers at every shift of the tram, and he did not realize until later that any doubts he had had about her had vanished.

Chapter 15

The police had been thorough in searching Trey's flat. Everything he owned, everything that had been neatly shelved or stacked in drawers the night before had been pulled down and tossed to the floor without any pretense of organization. Clothes were strewn in a path from the entryway to the bathroom; in there, they had opened the walls around his water generator and left it in pieces. Elena went in to give it a quick once-over; she thought all the pieces were there, and that she could probably repair it without much effort.

Trey was clearly not thinking about repairs. He called from the living room, where he was clearing debris off of the coffee table. "In the bedroom," he said, "there is—there was a small figurine. Clear resin. It looks rather like a cat. I kept it on the windowsill. Can you see if you can find it?"

She left the bathroom and headed into the bedroom. The bedding had been tossed to the floor, and the wardrobe opened, all of his clothes and spare linens scattered in a heap. She began sorting items by type as she dug for the figurine.

She should not have felt so calm after her outburst. She hated losing control, and she had lost it completely, in front of a man she barely knew. But he had listened, and been kind, and had made no excuses for anyone, and somehow all of the festering anger and pain had thinned. She did not feel strong, precisely, but she felt quiet inside, waiting for whatever happened next, and she thought, if he kept holding her hand, she might get through it.

What is it, she wondered, *that makes him so much easier to trust than Greg?*

She lifted a pillow and tossed it onto the bed, and out of the pillowcase rolled a small figurine. Retrieving it, she held it up to the window. It was foggy white, and partly translucent, and although it did not resemble anything in the real world, she understood why he had described it as a cat. It had a sinuous grace, a plump inertia about it, that was distinctly feline. As a work of art, it was both crude and remarkable. She carried it back into the living room.

He had cleared the coffee table and most of the couch, and was sitting, studying the table's polished surface. He looked up at her. "Is it damaged?" he asked.

"I don't see any chips or cracks," she said, "but I also don't know what it looked like before." It would have been there, she realized, last night; she had not registered many details beyond him. "It's pretty. Where is it from?"

"Sarah made it for me at school, when I first returned." He held the cat up to the light, studying the base of it, then placed it in the center of the table. He studied it anxiously, unmoving, and she wondered what he was waiting for.

After a moment there was a blue flash in the corner of the table's surface, and then a pulse of violet light radiated out from the figurine. The polished tabletop became traced with faint blue instruments, crude touch interface controls, laid out with elegant efficiency. She drew in a breath; like all engineering students, she'd had to manufacture an off-grid system as part of the mechanical curriculum, but hers had been far less sophisticated. This one was a work of art, its interface clean and instantly comprehensible, containing exactly what it needed and no more. She watched him frown at it, and felt like she was seeing him for the first time: he had made this thing, this beautiful machine, and she'd had no idea it was there.

He glanced up, then looked surprised at her stare. She crossed her arms and frowned at him. "If I'd had any idea," she told him, "I'd have been a lot more careful with your coffee table last night."

His expression rippled, and she thought he was trying not to laugh. He had laughed the night before, when their utter failure to balance on the table had ended up with both of them on the floor in a graceless heap. "My dear," he said to her gravely, "this comm will be difficult enough without such marvelous memories in my mind."

She felt her face warm; she should not have said it. She made her way around the table and sat next to him, feeling his eyes on her face; she watched the interface, looking for the inputs. "How do you connect?" she asked him.

"It uses a combination biological and cryptographic code," he said. "I have a key that will encode the message so it can only be read by someone who has a corresponding key. If I want to target it specifically, I add the destination bio key to my own, and their signature is verified as well."

"How do you know the crypto keys?"

"They are taught to us," he told her. "They rotate fairly frequently, but you get used to remembering."

"Will the one you're using still be active?"

"No. But she will recognize it, and she will take the message anyway."

She looked over at him; he was still frowning. "Why will the comm be difficult?"

For a moment his face took on a puzzled look, as if he were translating in his head again. Then he said, "Valeria does not like me."

She wondered what he had left out of that statement.

It took well over a minute, but he saw a subtle violet pulse traverse the table, and then she heard a voice speak a single word she did not recognize. The voice was a woman's, calm and cool and uninviting.

Trey spoke, and she heard him say his name. When the woman replied, Elena started piecing the words together: it was another Russian derivative, and some of the articles were similar to the language Stoya and Luvidovich had spoken at the police station.

She was not going to pick up much in this conversation, though. They were bickering, and speaking quickly. Just when the woman's tone became most heated, Trey spoke in Standard: "And you know I would not have contacted you had there been another alternative."

The language switch, she suspected, would have clued the woman in to the fact that he was not alone. She caught his eyes, and he nodded at her. "Captain Solomonoff," she said formally, "I am Commander Elena Shaw of the CCSS *Galileo*." She was nothing but nerves; it had been easier talking to Trey in a crowded bar.

"What is it I can do for you, Commander Shaw?"

Valeria Solomonoff's Standard was unaccented, but the ice in her voice was unmistakable. Elena did not react to it. "One of my people was murdered last night here in Novanadyr," she said. "We have found some information that suggests what happened might be tangentially related to something that happened several weeks ago."

"And what is the reason you believe I may be interested in this?"

Elena had spoken to enough officers in her career to know when one did not want to talk to her. "The incident involved your ship."

Valeria was silent for a moment. "Why is it you believe I will discuss anything with you?"

"Because I am looking for the truth."

It was a weak argument, and Elena was not surprised that Valeria scoffed at it. She began arguing with Trey again, and Elena saw the ire rising in his eyes. Whatever reason Valeria had for disliking him, Elena suspected they knew each other very well.

"Wait, please," she interrupted. Trey stopped and looked at her, his expression apologetic. "I am doing this wrong," she said quietly.

He took her hand, and she tightened her fingers around his. "Be direct," he told her, and she looked into his steady dark eyes and started again.

"If you know my ship," she said, "you know we do not patrol the Fifth Sector. We are here delivering cargo for another ship that took some damage. The CCSS *Demeter*. Her captain claims you attacked them."

"If I had," Valeria replied, no longer trying to hide her hostility, "why do you suppose I would speak of it to you?"

"Valeria—" Trey was annoyed, but Elena squeezed his hand again.

"It's all right, Trey. Why would she trust me?" She was going to have to trust first. "Captain, I'm off the record here. I have heard so many stories at this point I don't know who I am supposed to believe. I have heard a story about PSI firing on *Demeter,* and I can't think of a single logical reason why that would happen. I'd be inclined to ignore the story entirely, except that I can't think of a reason Captain MacBride would lie, either. None of this may have anything to do with anything," she concluded, dispirited, "but it's the only lead I have, and I don't want this killer to escape. I know you don't know me, but I am asking you, Captain. Please help me."

The line was silent, and for a while Elena thought the woman would not answer her. When she did, her voice was entirely different: all antagonism was gone, and she sounded as exhausted as Elena felt.

"We did fire on *Demeter,*" she said. "But they fired on us first."

Elena closed her eyes. She had suspected it—it was the only way PSI's behavior made sense. "Did you take casualties?" She desperately wanted no more dead.

"Minor injuries only," Valeria said, and Elena thought she appreciated the question. "My field generator, on the other hand, is currently being held together by goodwill and hope."

Trey squeezed her hand again, and she held on tightly. "Do you know why they shot at you?"

Valeria sighed. "Perhaps you can tell me. It makes very little sense from our side. We were headed for Cygnus, and were recharging our batteries out by the wormhole, well outside the hot zone. *Demeter* appeared, and I did not think much of it. Certainly it seemed off of her usual path, but we like the spot because it is quiet, and I saw no strangeness in them choosing it for the same reason.

"But then Captain MacBride contacted us—on an open line, so all in the area would hear—and commanded us to remove ourselves from the proximity of the wormhole, or he would fire on us."

"You did not believe him."

"I do not have the luxury of disbelieving such a threat," Valeria said. "I have almost one thousand people on my ship. But I was puzzled. I have known Captain MacBride for many years, and this seemed uncharacteristic. If he had needed us to move for some operation he wanted to stage, he need only have asked. So I asked him what the issue was, and he replied by shooting. We defended ourselves."

Valeria had a point, Elena thought. If the only requirement had been for *Penumbra* to move, he could have accomplished that without any altercation at all. "Did he leave when you shot back?"

"He did not retreat. We did."

"Why?"

"His second message was not over the main comms channel," Valeria said. "It was tunneled directly to me. He said, 'Please, you have to go.' Do you know Captain MacBride, Commander Shaw?"

"Only by reputation."

"He is not a man who says 'please.' I took him at his word. He fired at us as our field was forming, which is why the generator is currently unreliable. I do find myself wondering if his bad aim was deliberate."

"Do you think he was coerced?"

"I do not know. I do not believe, based on his behavior, that he was being coerced directly. But I was given the distinct impression that he was not happy doing what he was doing."

Orders, then. It was the only answer. "I know it changes nothing, Captain, and I cannot speak for anyone but myself right now. But what was done to your ship—it is against every order I have ever been given, every oath I have taken, and everything I personally believe. It was an act of war, and no one I know would condone it."

Valeria changed languages again, and said something Elena thought might have been *That is a very practiced speech.*

Trey answered her in Standard. "She means it, Valeria."

There was silence on the line again, and Elena realized what Trey's change of language had done: he was telling Valeria that he trusted her, that Valeria could trust her, too. "Does this information help you with your murder?"

It didn't. It was baffling, random, tangential. And it was the only thing she had stumbled on that seemed large enough for someone to kill for. "It means," Elena replied, "that something is very wrong, and I don't know what it is yet."

"How was he killed, your man?"

"His throat was cut," Elena told her. "And then his body was dumped on Trey's doorstep."

"You have been implicated, Treiko?" Valeria sounded worried, and Elena thought her dislike could not run very deep.

"I have been framed," he corrected. "And although I can think of a great many reasons why I might have been a useful target, I cannot rule out the facts of my childhood as the cause."

"Which would mean the authorities are involved."

"I have dealt with the authorities before," he said dismissively. Elena suspected the woman knew him well enough to know it was bravado. He changed the subject. "Where was Rosaria, with *Castelanna*?"

"We left them at the pulsar," Valeria said. "We did not think we would need them. We could signal them easily enough from where we were settled. The EMP helps, sometimes; it can filter out some of the low-quality stream traffic, at least briefly."

Elena wondered how long Valeria had been with PSI. "Did you know the *Phoenix,* Captain Solomonoff?"

There was a pause. "That was a very long time ago, Commander Shaw. Why is it you ask?"

"Her chief medical officer," Elena told them, "was my captain's mother."

"My condolences to your captain," she said. "But is it relevant?"

"It is a coincidence," Elena said. "I don't like coincidences." Her head was spinning. "I appreciate your candor about *Demeter,* Captain."

"I wish you luck on your investigation," Valeria said. And then, after a pause: "Treiko."

"Yes?"

"Stay away from the authorities. Look after yourself." She added one more phrase after that, in her own language; Elena thought it was *Don't do anything foolish.* Elena saw a flicker of warmth in Trey's eyes. He said something in response, gentle and soft, and the table went black.

Elena squeezed her eyes shut, thinking. If MacBride had been under orders, why had he lied? Or perhaps he hadn't lied; perhaps he had told as much of the truth as he could. He had been under orders, after all. Perhaps Greg was under orders as well. There had been a time when he would have told her everything, regardless of restrictions; but now she had no such expectation.

"Six months ago," she said, opening her eyes, "I would have told you with absolute conviction that my captain did not know anything of this, that if he knew of any such orders being given he would have raised holy hell and done everything he could to stop it from happening. Now . . ." God, she was tired. "I don't know who has been telling me what anymore."

"You are exhausted," Trey said to her. "You need rest, *m'laya*. Just for a little while."

So did he, but she shook her head. "There's no time."

"You could return to your ship," he suggested.

She picked up her head and looked at him. "And leave you to be arrested?"

He shrugged. "I have been arrested many times," he reminded her. "I would survive it."

She was less sure of that. "No," she told him. "And not just because of you, Trey. Because it's more than Danny. Whatever this is, it's big, maybe as big as Central. I can't go back there and close my eyes and wish it away. I can't keep working for an organization that might have done something like this. And I won't let them sweep it into your lap, not if I can stop them."

He was studying her with that same intensity he'd had earlier, his eyes hard and hopeful all at once. "I could elude you," he told her. "We could go out onto the street, and I could leave you behind, and you would not be able to find me again."

"Is that something you'd do?"

Something desperate crept into his gaze, and she thought she could spend hours just staring into his eyes, reading his thoughts, falling into them. He lifted a hand and brushed her hair away from her face, tucking a stray lock behind her ear. He had done that the night before, she remembered, right before he kissed her, and she felt herself blushing again. "I should do it," he said softly. "I should tie you up and leave you here and call your people to pick you up and take you home."

"But you won't."

He sighed, and dropped his hand. "Ilya lives around the corner," he said. "I believe he is home. I do not wish to comm him in advance to check."

"I thought local comms weren't recorded."

"They are not, but that does not mean they cannot be traced while they are active, if one knows what one is looking for."

Reluctantly she stood, her eyes down on the dark tabletop. "I have this wish," she said, half to herself, "that your friend will tell us something that will make this all make sense. But I am afraid of it as well. Is that crazy?"

He reached out to her and slipped his hand into hers, and she held on to him, her only lifeline. "It is human, *m'laya*. And under the circumstances, perhaps the only logical response."

She looked over at him. "I am less naive now, I think," she said.

The ghost of a smile flickered over his lips. "I have concluded, my dear, that I am the one who was naive. So perhaps we have both learned something."

Hand in hand, they left his chaotic flat behind.

CHAPTER 16

Galileo

Greg had set the precedent early on in *Galileo*'s run that in the pub, rank was not acknowledged. Here the crew members were just people, no saluting, no rules of hierarchy. While he was never quite afforded the status of comrade, they had learned to relax around him, and behave with each other as if he were not there. Now, sitting in a dark corner with his hand curled around a glass, he was fairly confident he was seeing their genuine reactions to the day.

Despite the morning's hangovers, there had been drinking throughout the afternoon, all of it in Lancaster's honor. On the whole it had been an affectionate wake. People swapped stories both humorous and sentimental, and the general impression he got was that Lancaster would be deeply missed. It was impossible not to feel some guilt at the fact he had not liked the man; but in that respect, Danny Lancaster had been no different from any of the men Elena had become involved with over the years.

Professional grief was another thing entirely, and more than once he wished he was drinking scotch. This whole thing was wrong, and the closer he looked at it, the less sense it made.

Galileo's biography on Captain Treiko Zajec had failed to suggest in any way, shape, or form that the man might be involved in anything hostile. Zajec had been thirty when *Castelanna* had fallen under his command, and there were regular reports of both trade with corporate freighters and skirmishes with Syndicate tribes. His record with the Syndicates was brutally one-sided, and the tribes had filed hundreds of formal complaints with Central Gov, but Zajec had never been charged. Every time the Syndicates produced evidence, a freighter captain would claim to have witnessed the initial Syndicate hostility and insist that *Castelanna*'s retaliation was self-defense.

It might have been true, but corporate freighter crews were notoriously closemouthed and risk-averse. That they had spoken up suggested they had liked Zajec. They had trusted him. Greg had no great admiration for corporations, but freighter crews—who often ended up in war zones with no one to rely on but each other—had little use for politics. They would not have defended someone intent on one-sided hostilities.

Zajec had been viewed, throughout his career, as the de facto leader of the Fifth Sector PSI tribes. No leader who followed him would have risked the goodwill he had obtained from the freighter crews. Which implied that what had happened with *Demeter* was not one-sided, and Greg was not yet sure what to do about that.

The mystery of Zajec's childhood crime had bothered him until *Galileo* had traced Zajec's original name: Ivan Rostovich. He had been thirteen when his stepfather had died, and the police had flagged the boy as a missing person, but it was clear from Novanadyr's records that they believed he was guilty of murder. They also believed his stepfather had been beating the children, but Rostovich's mother had refused to let them speak to her eight-year-old daughter. Her statements suggested she was content to let her son take sole responsibility for the death. Zajec had sent his sister comms nearly every week for the forty-four years he had been away from Volhynia, but she had never answered.

It all added up to one thing: Elena had been right about Zajec. She had been right, and Greg should have trusted her. If he had listened, he might have considered a far more frank discussion with Zajec from the start, and he might have more to ask Admiral Herrod than *What the hell is really going on?*

Twenty minutes before her scheduled check-in. He suspected, if he tried to comm her early, that she would cut him off again. His thoughts were interrupted by Jessica, who dropped into a chair next to his without waiting for an invitation.

"May I?" she asked, gesturing at his glass. Silently he handed it to her, and she took a sip; after a moment she grimaced and handed it back to him. "You might have warned me, sir."

He had forgotten how much Jessica disliked tea. "What's got you needing a drink?" he asked.

"Well, sir. I just got finished talking to a crazy person, and I'm a little worried that he's not crazy at all."

She had to mean Limonov. He'd had a few complaints about the man, mostly from the younger crew members. "I wouldn't think you'd be bothered by superstition, Lieutenant."

"Begging your pardon, sir, but I don't think it's all superstition. The trouble is I can't decode it. And then it occurred to me that maybe you could."

He leaned forward. "What have you got?"

She closed her eyes for a moment. "Danny was digging around about pulsars, right? This specific pulsar. The one you called a signpost. And I thought it was Volhynia he cared about—how it was affected by the pulsar—but Enkha said he listened to Limonov, even though nobody else did. So I talked to Limonov, and he talked like that wormhole was alive. Said it had taken the *Phoenix*. Said MacBride knew."

"Knew what?"

"That's what's unclear, sir, although he implied Central was involved as well. But he said it would take all of us, and when I asked him how that would happen, he leaned over, so nobody else could hear him, not even Ted. And he said, 'It sings.'"

Everything inside of Greg went still. It wasn't possible, not after all this time. "Did he say what it sang, Lieutenant?"

She shook her head. "I got the hell out of there, sir. He seems almost normal when you first start talking to him. Hearing something like that—it makes it worse."

He wondered if Limonov could actually know, or if it was just the ranting of a madman. Greg had been told shortly after he was deployed, and he had only repeated the information once. His own father did not know. For Limonov to have sources seemed unlikely, since he wore his conspiracy theories on his sleeve, and nobody at Central was going to trust him with much. He was a talented mechanic, but his mental state had restricted his career.

Now Greg began to wonder if that was unjust.

"You know what it is," Jessica said, watching him closely, "don't you, sir?"

He didn't know. He couldn't know. It was insane. *And yet* . . . "I have a guess," he told her. He met her eyes, and he thought she might have guessed herself. "Have you ever noticed that everything they've told us about the *Phoenix* doesn't really come to anything?"

"I figured it was just the Corps being the Corps."

He nodded. "That, too. They didn't want anyone panicking, didn't want to lose funding or sponsorship, especially when they were in the middle of phasing out the old drives. Starlight was unproven. Blaming the explosion on the *Phoenix*'s engine was useful . . . but they don't know, Jess. Because they never found the flight recorder."

She would know what that meant, how blind Central would have been without the mission data stored on the flight recorder. She would realize that all of the Corps' public statements about the *Phoenix*, for the last twenty-five years, had been guesswork, misdirection, and flat-out lies. He saw her eyes widen. "You think that's what's singing?"

"Yes. No." Radio signals were not uncommon in space, but *singing* implied something melodic, like a flight recorder signature. "Why would Central hide it, if it was? But what the hell else could it be?" What if this was what Lancaster had found?

And, if so: Why would he be killed over a flight recorder?

"Sir, I—"

His comm chimed, and he was not sure if he was relieved or annoyed at the interruption. "Who is it?" he snapped at his ship, and *Galileo* obligingly projected the name in the air before them.

Lieutenant Commander Janek Luvidovich, Novanadyr PD.

He met Jessica's eyes; she looked as anxious as he felt. "What can I do for you, Mr. Luvidovich?"

The vid appeared before him, crisp and clear. Luvidovich was seated at a desk, his hands folded, unsmiling. Despite his professional demeanor, though, he couldn't hide the smug look on his face. Greg's veins turned to ice. "We have come across a piece of information," Luvidovich said, "that holds some interest for us."

Greg worked to keep his expression neutral. "And what would that be, Mr. Luvidovich?"

The man did finally smile, but there was a coldness in his eyes Greg suspected never left his expression. "It seems the alibi produced for our prime suspect is . . . in question."

"Why?"

Luvidovich's face turned ugly. "You had best stop assuming I am an idiot," he snapped. "You know precisely to what I am referring. Did you send that woman down here to make fools of us? We small, provincial colonists? Did you believe we would not find out?"

"And what is it you think you have found out?"

"That woman. Your engineer. She was involved with the dead man." He seemed annoyed Greg had made him spell it out.

"Maybe if you'd asked her some real questions instead of trying to frame someone you don't like," Greg said, his tone menacing, "you wouldn't have had to stumble on the information like a fucking *amateur*."

Luvidovich's lips tightened. "We know she is in Novanadyr. Where is she?"

"Why the hell should I tell you?"

"Because if you do not," Luvidovich said, leaning forward, "I will contact your Admiralty, and I will tell them you are obstructing our investigation into the death of one of your own men."

Shit.

But he wasn't going to let Luvidovich see his vulnerability. "I *am* the Admiralty out here, Mr. Luvidovich," Greg said coldly. "And before you threaten me again, I suggest you consider the fact that the weapons on this ship are precise enough that I could take you out right where you are without anybody around you seeing a damn thing." Luvidovich opened his mouth to retort, but Greg talked over him. "I will contact Commander Shaw, and let her know you'd like to speak to her. But if you start slacking off on this investigation again, I will be down there with infantry, and I will shut down your whole fucking city until you get me my killer. I don't want to hear from you again until you have more than bullshit speculation." He disconnected and stood, Jessica standing beside him.

"He's right, sir," she said. "The Admiralty isn't going to like this at all."

"Of course he's right." He headed for the door, Jessica at his side, and he noted that she had no trouble hustling to keep up with his longer stride. "But I'm done fucking around with this. Whatever fixation he's got with Zajec, it's not finding us Lancaster's killer." They moved into the hallway, and he turned to head for his office.

"What are you going to do?"

"I'm going to warn Elena," he said grimly. "I'm going to get her ass off of that planet. And then I'm going to find an excuse to blast that smug son of a bitch cop into fucking *dust*."

CHAPTER 17

Volhynia

The night air was cooler, and Elena shivered. Trey tugged her closer as they walked, and slipped an arm around her waist again; gratefully she reached around to share his warmth. It was courtesy, certainly, like his gentleness with her earlier; but she had no time for pride. She had come back to free him, and she would do it, and then she would shake his hand and say farewell to him.

But she did not know what she would have to go back to.

Her mind was spinning with possibilities and doubts, and she was not capable of sorting any of it out anymore. She found it easier to sit with the idea of Central lying to her, of her work all of these years having been a deception. Every time she thought of Greg, of her seven years of service with him—of her belief, even as their friendship dissolved, that he was a decent and noble man—her mind danced away, toward Danny, toward Trey, toward the evening stars.

You know nothing, she reminded herself. *One question at a time.*

Trey stopped at a busy street corner before an older building. Like his flat, it sported print locks and high windows; but the stairs were steeper, and the entryway was narrower. They climbed, and as they reached the top, he hit the door chime. "Ilya, it is me. I have brought someone to meet you."

After a moment the lock disengaged, and Trey pushed open the door.

The interior was done in old-fashioned blues and browns, but it was clean and well lit, and unlike Trey's building included an elevator at the back of the hallway. But it was the door of the first-floor flat that opened, revealing a small, slight man of indeterminate age. He had a full head of white hair, and a face so wrinkled it was difficult to read his expression; but his eyes were bright and clear, and he smiled when he saw them.

"This is not your usual time, Treiko Zajec," he said, but he was looking at Elena.

"I am sorry to bother you, my friend," Trey said. "I am wondering if you would have a few minutes to talk to us."

"Of course," he told them. "Come in." He stood aside.

The entire flat consisted of one room, with a door to a bathroom in one corner, but it was packed with furniture. A long sofa and an overstuffed chair stood against one wall, and the rest of the space, apart from the small kitchen, was covered in vintage floor lamps. The lampshades were in bright, varied colors; she did not think any two were designed to work together, but the overall effect was one of good cheer and artistry. He had artwork on the walls as well, in the same scattering of styles. She recognized one artist that Jessica collected.

"Elena," Trey said formally, "this is my friend Ilya Putin. Ilya, this is Commander Elena Shaw, of the Central starship *Galileo*."

"It is a pleasure to meet you," Elena said, and took his offered hand.

"And you, Commander." His smile widened. "May I offer you something? I have some wine, or some very nice bourbon."

Elena smiled back. "Thank you, no, not for me."

Trey cleared his throat. "I do not mean to be ungracious, but we may be against something of a deadline," Trey said. "Did you hear about the young man who was found dead this morning?"

The gleam vanished from Ilya's eye. "I have been watching the news. I am sorry, Commander Shaw, that you have lost a comrade. Such tragedies are senseless."

"The thing is," she said, "you may have spoken with him last night, before he was killed. Do you remember, at Gregorian's, talking with a soldier?"

Before she finished the question, his face lit with recognition, and then sadness. "That boy was the one who died?" He shook his head. "He seemed like such an innocent."

She turned the word over in her head. Despite Danny's lies, it was not entirely inaccurate.

"Do you remember what you discussed with him?" Trey asked.

Ilya looked mildly annoyed. "I am not so old, you know," he replied, and she caught herself smiling at Trey's chastened look. "You have time to sit down, at least."

They took the couch, and Trey reached out and took her hand in his without looking. "He seemed curious, mostly, about the surge," Ilya said.

"Surge?" Elena asked.

He raised his bushy eyebrows. "I suppose this would not have been news where you were at the time. Either of you," he added, nodding at Trey. "About six months ago, our pulsar had a surge. We were washed for three days straight. Eighty percent of the uncaged electricals in the city were damaged or destroyed. Riga was without power entirely. There were riots."

"That could not have been long before I returned," Trey said. "Why does no one speak of it?"

"You know the answer to that, Treiko Zajec. People have habits, and when they are able to indulge them, disruptions are forgotten. The researchers, though, are trying to see if they can predict when it might happen again. It may be a thousand years. It may never happen. But they are nervous. I find I think only that it is good no one died, and it might be time to update our grid, despite how pretty the wireless transfer stations look."

"Is that why Volhynia is powered this way?" she asked. "Artistry?"

"At the start it was necessity. They did not have enough hardware to cage all of their equipment, so they created the model we are still using today. It is kept, they say, because it brings tourists, but I think it is simply laziness and fear of change. They worry our cities will lose their charm if we do not expose ourselves to this natural phenomenon. Not to mention the expense. Ellis is the only big manufacturer, and the power equipment subsidizes their terraformer business. There is actually some public debate on the topic," he said, looking at Trey. "I am surprised you have heard nothing."

"I have heard some," Trey said. "Mostly Katya complaining about the changes she would have to make to the restaurant. Is this what you spoke to the boy about, Ilya?"

Ilya shook his head. "We did not get to local politics. He began by buying me a drink, and then asking me about my career. He spoke to all of us like that. Most felt he was just a gregarious tourist. But I thought . . ." He trailed off, glancing briefly at Elena. "He was . . . polished. He wanted something from me, and when he listened he seemed to see that as payment. As if I owed him a confidence, because he had shown me kindness. I apologize, Commander," he added, and his face reflected real regret. "I see these things in people. I am sometimes wrong."

She shook her head. "I think you put it very well," she told him. Surprisingly, all she felt was sadness. This stranger had seen in one night what she had not recognized in years.

"What did he ask you?" Trey prompted.

"General things at first," Ilya answered. "What pulsars do, the effects of electromagnetism. He asked a great deal about radiation, and electromagnetic waves. But when he asked me what sort of audio signals might be carried on such a wave, I knew what he was getting at. He was wondering about the Singing Star."

Elena's mind capitalized the words. "What is that?" she asked.

"There have been stories, now and again, over the years. Some people think it is a myth, or a result of staring into space for too long," he related, with some amusement. "But myths often have a grain of truth. I heard it myself, the first night of the pulsar surge," he confided. "Just for a moment. I wondered if I was imagining, if had stayed up too late, but my head was quite clear."

"Where is this Singing Star?" Trey asked him.

"From here, it is on the other side of the pulsar," Ilya told them.

And Elena knew before he said it. "The wormhole," she said. "You have heard music from the wormhole."

He nodded. "Your friend Danny said he had spoken to someone else who had heard it, although they were not on Volhynia. He seemed pleased that I confirmed their story. He thanked me, and he moved on, and shortly afterward he spent some time talking to that lovely young woman who seats people there."

Stars made sounds, she knew. Radiographers could play their waves, and computers could translate almost anything into audible tones. *Galileo* had her own music: the gentle pulse of the engine, irregular but repeating. Different for every ship, thanks to the grown crystals that were a unique part of each machine. Elena fell asleep to that pulse; the lack of it now was making her edgy.

But she did not think that was what Ilya meant.

"How did you hear it?" she asked him.

He understood her immediately, and the genial old man became a sharp-eyed scientist. "It was a comm-level audio wave," he told her. "It had a melody, and it was repeated."

"Man-made."

"Created, almost certainly," he agreed, "although it would not be unlike the human mind to hear a repeating set of notes and assign some kind of intelligent order to it."

"Can you remember it?"

"I can do better than that," he told her, a twinkle in his eye. "I can play it for you." He stood. "Come upstairs and I will show you."

Elena glanced at Trey. What she was thinking was madness. This was some bit of debris, some artifact catching an odd sort of energy and scattering sounds through space. It could not possibly be what she thought it was. After twenty-five years of nothing . . . it would be a remarkable coincidence.

Like everything else that had brought her here.

They stood, and followed Ilya out of the door.

Ilya ignored the elevator and headed for the stairs, climbing steadily. Elena revised her original impression: the slowness of old age was, at least partly, a front. Danny would have seen through it, she realized. He had always been good at reading people, and knowing how to approach them. It had worked with her. That Ilya had seen through Danny's self-serving charm said a lot about the old man's powers of observation. *And not much for mine,* she thought.

Greg had never liked Danny. He had never said anything to her, and, more than that, he had always treated Danny the same as he did the rest of the crew. But whenever Danny's name came up, Greg became guarded—just a little, nothing anyone else would have noticed—but enough to make her change the subject. She wondered, now, why that hadn't bothered her more at the time. She had told Trey she and Greg never spoke of personal things . . . and yet they had, especially before Jake was killed. He knew all about her family, and how often she felt guilty for not missing them, and she knew all about his mother, and the *Phoenix* accident, and the things they had only told the families, and no one else.

Like the fact that they had never found the ship's flight recorder. Like the specific melodic transmission, unique for each Corps starship, that would identify the recorder from the *Phoenix.* The recorder was engineered, upon activation, to emit nothing but that brief repeated radio signal, until a Corps ship with appropriate authorization came close enough. The recorder would dump its information to the other ship and fall silent, its job completed.

If this was the *Phoenix* flight recorder, apparently no one had come close enough yet.

They climbed four flights of stairs and exited onto the roof. The sky was not completely dark, but as high as they were the city's sidewalk lights produced almost no pollution, and the star field filled the deep navy sky. Elena's eyes swept over it, the familiarity soothing her nerves. Next to her Trey put his arm around her waist again, and she leaned against him. He was becoming familiar as well.

Ilya walked to the edge of the roof, where a table stood, covered in equipment. Beneath the table she saw a crude bank of batteries, sheathed in a simple Faraday cage. He had power, she realized, even when the lights were out, no matter what kind of rules they had at the observatory. She wondered how many of the natives had some kind of setup like this.

With practiced fingers he switched on the audio visualizer and pulled up a waveform.

"Wait," Elena said. "I want to avoid confirmation bias." She turned to Trey and hummed a complex sequence of tones. "Can you repeat it?"

He frowned and tried, and she corrected him twice. When she was confident he remembered, she nodded at Ilya. "Go ahead."

She listened until it played all the way through, just to be certain; but it was the same abstract sequence she had taught to Trey.

Trey was staring at her, his expression grim, but Ilya was delighted. "You know what it is! Can you tell me?"

She met Trey's eyes. "Strictly speaking," she said faintly, "I am not allowed."

"It is the flight recorder," Trey told Ilya, never dropping her eyes, "for the CCSS *Phoenix,* lost twenty-five years ago." She wasn't surprised he had guessed. "Elena, Central has maintained that the incident was an accident. How can they know this without the flight recorder?"

She had asked Greg the same thing. The explanation he had given her seemed so thin now. "They cannot be certain," she admitted. "They told Greg it was a solid guess, based on the other information they had: radiation levels, cargo, and the engine on the ship. It was a hybrid; catastrophic failure was always a possibility with the hybrids."

"And yet it only happened once."

Why didn't I ever push Greg this hard? "They say this accident moved them away from hybrids once and for all," she told him, "but I know how long it takes them to build a ship. They'd phased out the hybrid designs five years before the accident, minimum. The *Phoenix* was the last one running."

"Perhaps it is just a coincidence," Ilya put in.

Elena caught a glimmer of amusement in Trey's eyes. "In truth, Ilya Putin, I think the only true coincidence lately is that you, my friend, were talking to a man I have been accused of killing."

Ilya looked worried, and Elena was reminded of the concern she had heard in Valeria's voice. "You must be careful, Treiko," he said. "Stoya is a thug."

"It is Luvidovich who beat him," Elena pointed out.

But Ilya was shaking his head. "Neither of you knows the history. Stoya was brought here two years ago for a reason.

The government wants the perception that law and order are followed at all times, that there is no tolerance for crime. It is rumored that Stoya was a Syndicate enforcer, and that the Syndicate tribes recommended him to the body of ministers. Why else would they bring him in from off-world?"

She had been right about Stoya, then. "Is he off Osaka Prime?" she asked.

Ilya nodded. "He was a sheriff in the southern capital, at Fuji Seaport."

Hell. Even Elena, who avoided shore leave whenever possible, had heard of Fuji Seaport. It had the least crime of any city on Osaka Prime, but its population had been steadily dwindling over the years. Many people said that was due to the restrictive laws on public conduct. Others said it was because sometimes people just disappeared. The ranks of the Corps spoke openly about government-sponsored kidnappings and killings, and whenever they dealt with Osaka traders, they were careful to establish the cargo's port of origin up front.

She wondered if Greg knew where Stoya was from.

Trey had noticed her expression, and was frowning at her. She tried to think of how to phrase it. "It means," she told him, "that Stoya will cheerfully kill to close a case, and never look back." She felt a bubble of panic rise up in her stomach. "We need to get out of here," she told him. "If they know Ilya is your friend—"

"They spoke to me this morning," Ilya told her. "I had nothing to say to them, and they did not push. Like most people, they think I am useless as well as old."

"But they didn't know then that you'd spoken to Danny."

"You are assuming," Trey put in, "that they will talk to Ynes, and follow the same path. They had not spoken to her yet, so we have no indication that they're—"

Her comm chimed, and she glanced down. "It's Greg," she told him. "Twenty minutes early." Her mind was racing; she did not want to talk to him yet. She looked up at Trey. "There's only one reason he'd call me early, Trey. We need to go."

But what she saw on his face was not fear for himself. "They will go after my sister," he said. "We cannot risk comming her—they will trace it. Elena—"

"Let's go." She turned to thank Ilya, but he waved her away.

"I am not so easily captured," Ilya said. "Protect your family, Treiko."

Trey tugged her toward the stairs. She wanted to say something reassuring, to apologize to him again—but she knew how he felt. In every battle, whenever they were hit, the first thing they all did when the shooting stopped was check names.

Trey took the stairs quickly, and she hurried to stay by his side. "It is close," he told her. "Even if we do not catch a tram, we can make it to the restaurant in five minutes, perhaps less." Trey shoved open the building's front door.

Instantly they were blinded by a bank of massive white lights. Elena blinked, but it was fruitless. She could make out nothing.

"Step away from her, Treiko Zajec," said a familiar voice.

She tightened her grip on him. "Don't you dare," she breathed at him. He was not moving.

A silhouette appeared against the lights, stocky and thick-necked. "We do not care about the woman," Stoya said, and she thought he sounded bored. "Step away from her and come with us, and she will be free to go."

His fingers loosened. She reached over with her other hand and closed her fingers around his. *"Trey."*

"I want your word, Stoya," he called. "Commander Shaw goes home, and you leave my sister alone."

"We do not need them," Stoya said irritably. When Trey said nothing, he waved a hand. "Yes, yes. You have my word."

She tightened her hand. "You can't."

"It is not only me," he said quietly. And without looking at her, he pulled his hand from hers.

He had descended only one stair when he was rushed by two men who yanked him away. The lights dropped, and she blinked to clear her vision. Four officers, including the two holding him, and Stoya.

Not so many.

She pulled her handgun, and aimed it at Stoya's head. "Let him go," she said loudly.

The two free officers drew on her, but she did not look at them. There were bystanders, she realized, all hanging back, but still too close: fascinated, confident they wouldn't be hurt. God, she hated civilians. "Give the order," she told Stoya, never taking her eyes off of him, "or I will drop you in the street."

She had killed before, but only once someone she could see. Most of her kills were from the air, self-defense shots while flying her people out of a combat area. She had never hesitated, had never doubted her orders. She did not know how many people were dead due to her actions. She still had nightmares now and then.

She thought killing Stoya would be easy.

But he was either confident she would back down, or supremely uncaring about his own safety. When he answered her, he sounded as irritated as he had back at the station, when all she had done was demand Trey's release. "And how will your Admiralty react to such an action?"

"You are assuming," she said, "that I care."

Stoya shook his head and gestured at the officers. "You are outgunned, Commander Shaw," he pointed out.

"You're assuming that I care about that, too."

"They will kill you, I assure you."

"And *I* assure *you*," she told him, "that I will blow your fucking head off before I hit the ground."

She could do it. She was certain. The two cops aiming at her were kids. They had likely never shot at anything outside of a target range. They would hesitate. They might even miss, although at this range that would be unlikely. Still, she'd certainly have time to kill Stoya before she died.

Do it, she thought at them. *I dare you, you assholes.*

But it was Trey who spoke. "*M'laya,*" he said, his voice gentle. And then he added something in that odd dialect he had been speaking with Valeria. It took her a moment to work it out.

Find another way.

She could still smell the ocean on the wind, and the unfamiliar metallic odor of brick warm from the afternoon sun. She could smell the sweat of the men standing before her, frozen, weapons still, waiting. The wind touched her face, and a strand of hair tickled her ear. She had felt that same loose lock of hair on the tram, with Trey's arm around her waist, his body warm and straight. He had still smelled like vanilla, just a little, and she wondered if it ever left him. He must use it often. Her mother had baked a lot when she was a child, but she had never had that lingering sweet smell about her. Her mother always smelled of fresh air and practicality.

She lowered her gun.

The two officers kept their weapons aimed at her. As Stoya pulled her handgun from her grasp, her eyes sought out Trey's. He stood, unresisting, between the two men, and he looked at her with such open affection her heart turned over. God, what had she been doing? *I'm sorry,* she mouthed at him, and incredibly, he smiled.

And then they were pulling at him, and the two armed officers were still watching her warily, and it dawned on her that they were going to take him away and she would be alone. She took a step forward, and one of the men who had pointed a weapon at her moved toward her.

"Leave her," Stoya barked, and the man scowled and turned away.

"Remember," Trey called, as they pulled him toward a waiting vehicle. "It is not only me."

She watched, numb, her brain slow and stupid, as the door slid shut, and the vehicle soundlessly moved away.

He was gone.

It made no sense.

She heard a faint, distant noise, and tried to ignore it. *It is not only me.* He had said that for a reason. She needed to think clearly, and that damn sound kept distracting her. What did he mean? *What were we doing?* And then she remembered: they had been heading for the restaurant. His sister. Ilya was going to comm Trey's sister. They had been going to make sure she was all right.

And in a rush the whole plan came back into focus.

She turned down the sidewalk and pulled up a local map on her comm, her eyes sweeping the street for an approaching tram. Nothing was coming. The streets were lined with people staring at her, wondering what the hell had just happened. There was no shortage of witnesses, but no way for her to get anywhere except on foot. She swore determinedly and broke into a run, weaving in and out of the crowds, half expecting someone to try to stop her. Instead, they all moved out of her way. *Of course,* she thought. *I am the mad Corps soldier who pulled a gun on a cop.*

Bloody hell, she should not have let him leave.

The chime repeated, and she hit the comm as she was running. Officially she owed Greg an apology; she had promised she wouldn't ignore his signal again. But for now, he was the only person she knew who had the power to help her. "We need to do something," she said without preamble. "They've arrested him."

There was a pause, and she thought he would shout at her; but then he swore, and she felt a glimmer of hope. "How long ago?"

"Two minutes, maybe three. I've got to find his sister and—"

"Come home, Chief."

She stopped running. "What?"

"I said come home. That's an order."

Ice hit her veins, flooding through her until she was certain she was shivering. "You don't understand," she said, wishing it was true. "They'll kill him, Greg."

"They won't." He sounded decisive. "I'll contact the Admiralty, and they'll—"

"They'll what?" She was aware she was shouting, that people were beginning to look alarmed. Forcing herself to calm down, she turned away from the storefronts and lowered her voice. "Order Niall MacBride to blow him to bits?"

That caught his attention. "What are you talking about?"

"You can't tell me you didn't know."

"I still don't know. What the hell do you mean?"

"Captain Solomonoff said—"

"You *spoke* to her?" She knew him well enough to know when he was losing his temper. "Do you have any idea what you have stuck your goddamned neck into, Elena?"

"How in the hell would I know when you won't tell me?" The ice was receding, giving way to anger and a hurt deeper than she wanted to examine. "You send me down here with *half* the information I need and leave me to stumble onto everything on my own, and tell me to betray the only person I can trust—"

"You don't even know him!"

"Well I sure as hell don't know you!" she hissed. "Danny was looking into the *Phoenix,* did you know that? Did you know he was at the same damn bar talking to the same woman MacBride had been crying to a month ago?"

"Back up, Chief. MacBride was *there*?"

"Weeping to *strangers* over some awful thing he had to do." It was an inference, but surely Greg already knew the truth. "You knew he was under orders, didn't you?"

He grew quiet. "I suspected, Elena. But not until after you left."

"Well when in the hell were you going to tell me?"

"After you came back here," he snapped, "like I ordered you to."

She wanted to throw something.

"You knew exactly why I was coming down here, and you didn't give me information I *needed*? You leave me down here unarmed, *Captain,* and you're going to get what you get."

"What the hell does that mean?"

"It means you and the Admiralty can either help, or go fuck yourselves," she said decisively, "but I'm not abandoning him."

"I'm giving you an order, Chief. You get back here *now* and—"

"No."

"You're disobeying a direct order?" He sounded incredulous.

"You're damn right I am," she told him. "If you and Central are trying to start a war with PSI, I will not have anything to do with it."

"Chief, nobody is trying to start a war."

"And you know this, do you?"

"Goddammit, Elena, enough is enough!" He sounded desperate. "Let me be a diplomat, for Christ's sake, and I'll get him out, I swear to you. But you have got to get off that planet before they arrest you, too."

If they had not arrested her for threatening the life of their police chief, Elena reflected, it was unlikely they would arrest her for anything else. "You wanted me to get him out of prison," she said, "so I'm getting him out of prison. And you go ahead and fucking write me up on that one, Greg, because whatever the fuck Central is up to with PSI, I want it on the record that I'm on the other side of it!"

"Elena—"

"You go play *diplomat,*" she spat at him. "I'm going to make sure nobody else dies."

And she cut him off.

She kept her finger on the comm behind her ear. She had worn one in some form or another since she was seven years old. She could not remember ever having disabled it. Gently she slid a fingernail underneath it and peeled it from her skin, then dropped it onto the sidewalk. She lifted a foot and pressed her heel against the unit. There was a single crack, and then the tiny device was ground to dust.

She looked up to see a young woman watching her curiously. She was tall and thin, with warm, dark eyes like Trey's; she was ordinary, unhurried, and unaware that Elena had just detached herself from everyone she knew. *And,* Elena realized belatedly, *my map.* Cursing her impulsive gesture, she tried to look composed. "Excuse me," she began, "I find myself a bit lost. I am looking for a restaurant owned by Katya Gregorovich. Do you know where it is?"

Elena watched as the woman decided she was not insane or dangerous. "It's that way," she said, gesturing away from the spaceport. "Half a block, then take a right. It's the first building after the alley. But you won't find a table at this hour."

Elena gave her a polite smile. "Thank you very much," she said. And then she took off down the street at a dead run, leaving the remnants of her career behind her.

PART II

Please tell me, Captain Foster," Admiral Herrod said, "that this early check-in means your man's murder has been resolved."

Greg kept his face carefully neutral, but the remark annoyed him. He wondered, not for the first time, if Herrod annoyed him on purpose. "I'm afraid not, sir," he said. "We have a diplomatic situation, and I could use some guidance."

The afternoon sun shone through the admiral's window. Greg had not been sure if he would be catching Herrod midmorning or halfway through the night; even when he used to comm Caroline on a regular basis, he had always caught her in the hospital, or woken her in the middle of the night. Early in their marriage his mistimed comms had frightened her and made her worry. In the last ten years, she had never been anything other than annoyed.

Herrod's eyebrows shot up. "Aren't *you* usually our diplomatic solution, Captain?"

Only when I don't piss off the local cops, Greg thought, and hoped he wouldn't need to tell the whole story. "Under the circumstances, sir, I thought it was better to contact you first.

Volhynia is accusing a retired PSI captain of the murder, sir. Treiko Zajec, formerly of the Fifth Sector ship *Castelanna*."

"That's old news, Captain. His name has been public for hours."

"Yes, sir. But he's not guilty. One of my people can alibi him."

"You're sure of this."

Greg resisted the urge to rub his eyes. "Yes, sir."

Herrod looked briefly relieved. "Well, that's something. What's the diplomatic issue? Is he asking for help?"

"He—no, sir. In fact he's specifically declined it."

"Then why are we talking?"

"Because they've arrested him for a second time, sir, in spite of his alibi."

Herrod's jaw set. "You know our situation with Volhynia, Captain."

"They are not finding my man's killer, sir, and they're endangering a man I know is innocent." It occurred to him that Zajec was, in fact, the only one of the planet's forty-eight thousand residents Greg knew had nothing to do with Lancaster's death. "I've got a soldier down there, sir, trying to protect him, but she can't do it on her own." *And I need to get down there after her before she completely burns her career to the ground.*

Herrod kept frowning. "We can reach out to them on the investigation," he said, and Greg thought he sounded tired. "But a PSI captain? We can't help him, Captain Foster. It's all over the offices here that they hit *Demeter,* and in another week it'll hit the press. We can't be seen helping him. They've thrown down the gauntlet, and our priority status is deciding how to counter."

Greg had been ready for this argument. "Zajec was PSI for forty-four years, sir. He's got intel, and he's got contacts. If we got him off of Volhynia, he might be able to help us."

"And why would he do that?" When Greg didn't answer, Herrod shook his head. "You really think you know where PSI is coming from, Foster? You think you can read the Corps file on one man and understand five hundred years of history?"

So Herrod had been watching his comms. "All I understand, sir, is that we're provoking an organization who has done nothing but help us based on hearsay from a man who says he got shot at and ran away."

"MacBride's story is backed up with evidence, and people are listening. I am sorry about Captain Zajec, but there are more important things going on right now."

"More important than a man's life?" *More important than Elena?*

Something crossed Herrod's face, and Greg wished he knew him better. "If I say yes, Captain Foster, would you believe me?"

"No, sir. Especially when saving that man's life could defuse this entire situation."

Herrod's expression hardened again. "That's the problem with you remote scouts," he snapped. "There are too few of you, and you start thinking you're making your own laws. We cannot help Captain Zajec, Captain Foster. That it is regrettable is obvious, but that does not change anything. We will address Volhynia about the murder investigation, but what they do with their prisoner is outside of our influence. Do you understand?"

Greg had understood before he had placed the call. "To be clear, sir," he said calmly, "you're telling me we're abandoning a man who protected colonists, freighters, and sometimes Corps ships for forty years because we don't want to offend one little provincial government?"

"Yes, Captain, that's exactly what I'm telling you."

"You do understand that they'll kill him." For all Greg knew, they had already.

"Don't think," Herrod told him, "that you'd make a different choice in my position, Captain. You don't know every fucking thing there is to know."

"So tell me what I'm missing."

"What you're missing," Herrod said, finally losing his temper, "is that I am still your superior officer, Captain, and there is more going on in this galaxy than you and your crew. You stand down from Volhynia and you get the hell away from there, and that's an order. Are we clear?"

"Yes, sir. We're clear."

Herrod disconnected first, and Greg stared into the space where the projection had been. He thought about Danny Lancaster's sister, resigned in her grief. He thought of Elena, who had turned to him for help, only to have him hand the decision off to someone else. He thought of Ivan Rostovich's mother, sacrificing her older child to protect her younger.

He thought of his own mother. His mental picture of her was less memory now than an amalgam of old vids and stray emotions. He had been seven when she had reenlisted. All he remembered about that time was that his sister, Meg, had been furious, and had hurt his mother's feelings. Five years later, when their mother had been killed, he had focused all of his anger toward his sister. Meg had been expressive in her grief, broken and anguished, bleeding all over anyone who tried to get close to her, and he had found it an irritant. In a few years, she had flushed all the rage from her life. In those same years, Greg had finally happened upon his own anger at his mother. Once found, it had never left him.

He got to his feet. "*Galileo,* wipe that last comm from the record." He opened his desk drawer and drew out his duty weapon, a monster of a handgun that could have blown a hole through *Galileo*'s hull, and shrugged on the shoulder holster. "Foster to Commander Broadmoor," he said, pulling his uniform jacket over his weapon. "I want two armed platoons in armor in Bay One in four minutes."

One of his favorite things about Emily Broadmoor was her consistent assumption that he did not ever owe her an explanation for anything. "Acknowledged," she said, and disconnected.

He strode out of his office and marched down the hallway, eyes on the hall before him. Crew members he passed stopped and stood at attention. He returned their salutes crisply, never slowing down. If they were called on later to report on his state of mind, they would say he seemed certain, calm, professional. None of them needed to know he was about to flout a direct order, and potentially piss off an entire colony government.

He turned into the shuttle bay, and walked past the duty officer to call up their primary troop transport. He watched through the window as *Lusitania* glided effortlessly into position, settling near the aft bay door. *Lusi* was their second troop transport, the first having been irreparably damaged two years earlier. Elena had chosen the new ship's name, and when Greg had questioned her judgment, she had explained it was for luck. "Like gargoyles being ugly to ward off evil," she had explained, as if that made the name an obvious choice. *Lusi* had persevered, often under heavy fire, but her purpose this time was not to withstand artillery.

He needed her impressive bulk to send a message.

"Captain? What are you doing?"

Greg turned to see Will Valentis giving him an incredulous look. "I'm heading down to the surface, Commander," he said, turning back to his task.

"You can't do that!"

Greg noticed the bay officer watching anything but his two senior officers. "We're left without options, Mr. Valentis," he said formally. "They have taken a prisoner who is not guilty, and they have refused our request for negotiations."

"He's not exactly an innocent, sir," Will responded. "And for all we know he's been under suspicion for God knows what long before we got here."

"They have arrested him, and they are suspending their investigation into Lancaster's death." The bay officer would remember that, too. "I won't have it, Commander. They want to pursue old grudges, they can do it after we have found justice for my man. And before you start talking to me about politics, I'll be clear: I do not give a fuck about politics. Once I have my killer, they can go back to funding the Syndicates and selling their souls just the way they were before we got here, no harm no foul."

But Will would not let it go. "Don't make this about Lancaster," he snapped. "This is about the chief, and you are *not* thinking straight."

Greg nodded at the bay officer, who opened the door for him. Will followed him in.

"What do you think she's going to do?" Will shouted. His voice echoed through the cavernous bay. "You think she's going to be *grateful* to you? You think she's going to turn around and give you a pity fuck for saving her boyfriend's neck?"

Without thinking, Greg turned around and punched Will squarely in the nose.

Will clasped his hands over his face, silent with shock, blood dripping through his fingers. Belatedly, Greg noticed his two platoons of infantry, lined up at attention, all looking straight ahead, ignoring the ship's two top officers having a very public fight. Emily Broadmoor stood to one side of them. He thought, for an instant, he saw her smile.

"Commander Valentis," he said calmly, "the ship is yours." He would have preferred to turn command over to Commander Broadmoor—or even Jessica—but for now he needed to maintain the fiction that he was acting within the bounds of ordinary Corps protocol. Will wouldn't have access to anything beyond regular Admiralty comms anyway. "We'll be in touch once we get to the surface." He caught Broadmoor's eye and nodded. She turned to the platoons.

"Let's go, soldiers!" she said crisply, and the sixteen men and women turned and jogged through *Lusi*'s passenger door. It wasn't just Emily, Greg noticed as they filed past—a lot of them were smiling.

Will was just gawking at him, his hand still over his insulted nose. Greg raised his eyebrows. "Anything else, Commander Valentis?"

For one instant Greg saw something cold in Will's eyes, something angry and poisonous and endlessly dark. It vanished as the man straightened. "No, sir," he said.

"Very well, then," Greg said. "Dismissed."

Will turned on his heel and marched out of the bay. Greg looked down, and saw a stray drop of blood on the deck. Without a doubt the bay officer would have it taken care of before they were a hundred meters from the ship.

He walked up to Commander Broadmoor, who was looking at him with something like admiration. "You need a pilot, too, sir?" she asked.

He shook his head. "I'll take her down."

"Very well sir. And may I say, sir?"

He raised his eyebrows at her.

"Nice punch, sir."

Emily Broadmoor was fifteen years older than he was, and she had not been blessed with flawless features; but when her eyes twinkled like that, he thought she rivaled the greatest beauties of the galaxy. "Without condoning my own behavior, Commander," he told her, "thank you. And do me a favor. Back him up—but keep an eye on him. He's already mad at me, and that punch isn't going to help." He thought of that flash of dark rage on Will's face, and added, "Keep him busy if you can. I don't need him playing up the details of this exchange to the rest of the crew."

"Of course, sir," she said. "Safe trip, sir." She saluted, and followed Will out.

Greg turned and climbed onto *Lusitania*. Fifteen soldiers were strapped into the passenger seats, and Lieutenant Carter was running a preflight check from the copilot's station. They all fell silent when he entered, watching him expectantly.

"Ladies and gentlemen," he told them, "we are engineering a jailbreak."

CHAPTER 19

....

Volhynia

Katya's restaurant was a good deal more casual than Gregorian's, but it was also significantly busier. There were no empty tables at all, and four harried servers working efficiently across the two-dozen tables in the large, well-lit room. The decor was bright but not garish, all pale wood and burnished lampshades, and the air was warm without being stifling. More than that, the fragrances in the air were delectable; Elena thought she could smell yeast and oregano along with a myriad of spices and vegetables. Ordinarily it would have made her hungry, but thinking of cooking made her think of Trey, and those memories made her want to knock the maître d' over and find Katya herself.

He led her through a bustling, hot kitchen—where she was completely ignored—and then into a dark hallway that ended in a secondary exit. He stopped at a door toward the end of the hall, and knocked.

The door opened, and Elena found herself scrutinized by a tall, broad-shouldered woman with long, straight red hair. "Thank you, Mikhail," the woman said after a moment. "You may leave us."

He gave her a worried look, but did as he was told.

Katya waited until Mikhail was gone. "Is he dead?" she asked, guarded.

Elena shook her head. "Not yet," she said. "But I need your help."

A wave of relief swept over the woman's features, and then her expression shut down again. Elena would not have guessed they were related. Katya's features were more square and gaunt than Trey's, and where he always looked as if he was about to smile, she wore a perpetual scowl. But her eyes were black and deep-set like his, and Elena thought she could recognize gnawing worry.

"I cannot help," she said flatly. "I cannot stand up to the police. You must understand, Commander Shaw. Trey is a grown man. Sarah is a child. I must protect her."

"I don't need the sort of help that would put you in jeopardy," she said. "All I need is to borrow your comm."

"You should change your clothes, too. You stick out worse than a tourist in that uniform." The voice came from behind Katya, higher and lighter, but with the same inflections. Elena looked down as a girl appeared, and here she found the family resemblance. Sarah had her mother's iron-straight hair, but hers was black, like Trey's, and every feature, from her high forehead to her prominent, distinctive nose, was his as well.

Katya said something quick and sharp to the girl that Elena didn't catch. Sarah gave her an eye roll that almost made Elena laugh out loud, and said something back. Katya looked briefly conflicted before nodding, but Elena thought she was more exasperated than upset. Sarah turned and hurried from the room.

Katya looked back at Elena. "Will they kill him, do you think?"

"Not if I get there first," she said, with more assurance than she felt.

Katya closed her eyes. She was younger than Trey, Elena remembered, but in that moment she looked far older. "I did not think he would come back," she said. "Not after all these years. I am not sure I would have asked him if I thought he would truly return. But having him here . . . I would not like to lose him." She opened her eyes. "If you let me initiate the comm, it will appear the call is mine, should anyone have a trace going."

Elena did not think a trace would make a difference, but nodded.

She gave Katya the ident, and hoped she knew the press as well as she thought she did. After a moment, a response came through. "Ms. Gregorovich?" Ancher said, sounding puzzled.

"How much do you want a story, Ancher?" Elena asked.

There was a brief pause as Ancher regrouped. "Chief?" She heard the smile in his voice. "Always nice to hear from you. This have anything to do with them arresting Zajec again?"

"I don't have time for backstory, Ancher. Here's the deal: you help me, you do as I say, and I let you roll vid the whole time, no editing. The only condition is you wait twenty-four hours before you air a damn thing."

She held her breath. In all her work with the press, she had never offered unedited coverage before. Hell, she wasn't sure anyone in the Corps had. There were probably regulations against it. She figured she was past the point where such things mattered.

"You're on," he agreed. "When and where?"

Sarah reappeared, holding a pair of tan trousers in her hand. Elena smiled her thanks, and stripped off her gray and black pants, tugging on the others. They were wide through the waist, and they ran shorter than she would have liked; but they fit well enough that they would not trip her up. She pulled off her uniform jacket and shirt, smoothing her unadorned white undershirt so it lay flat under the waistband of the trousers. "Five minutes," she told him, trying to triangulate in her head, "across the street from the police station."

"No shit." He sounded gleeful. "What should I bring?"

"You have a gun?"

"Hell, no. I drink too much. Can I bring a vid crew?"

"No you can't. And remember: if this leaks out early, Ancher, I'll cut you off, I swear to God, and you'll never get another story out of the Corps, not even the smallest crumb of basic training gossip. Clear?"

"God, Chief, you need to lighten up." But he was laughing. "I'll be there." The connection dropped.

Elena turned back to Katya. "I don't suppose *you* have a gun," she said, with little hope.

Katya looked chagrined. "I do not like them. Today, I wish I did."

"It's all right," Elena told her. "I don't like them, either."

"Wait," Sarah said, and before her mother could object, she dashed out the front door of the flat.

"She looks like him, you know," Elena told Katya.

The woman gave her a sad smile. "I look like our mother," she said, and she did not sound happy about it. "Our father—I have only pictures, and not many. But he looked like Trey, his nose too big for his face, always smiling, like there was nothing but delight in the world. I am happy she looks like him. It reminds me of the family I wish her to have."

A moment later Sarah returned. "It is not a gun," she said, hefting the object with some effort, "but it might help."

Elena took the rolling pin from the girl, weighing it in her hand. It was stone, probably marble, gray and mottled and cool to the touch, and it must have weighed nearly three kilos. She nodded with confidence she did not feel. "This will do nicely," she said. "Thank you."

She headed for the door. "I don't know what they will do when I get him out," she said, ignoring the doubts in her mind, and her complete lack of plan. "Is there somewhere you can go?"

"I have a friend in Riga who will look after us, if it comes to that."

"There is an old man," Elena told her. "A friend of Trey's. Ilya Putin."

"We will look after him, too," Katya promised, although that was not what Elena had meant. "Please, just take Trey somewhere safe."

"I will," she promised, remembering the conviction with which Trey had lied to Ynes.

"When you see him," Sarah said, ignoring her mother's frown, "tell him that I love him."

Elena felt her throat grow tight. "I promise," she told the little girl. "And thank you, both of you." She turned and left the flat, heading out the back door to catch a tram to the police station.

Chapter 20

He had hoped that it would be Stoya. Stoya would be professional about it. He knew what Trey was, knew Trey's true crime. He would hurt Trey only enough to make the interrogation look legitimate, and Trey did not think he would enjoy it. In the end, he would finish it as quickly and as cleanly as he could. There would be no way for him to make it painless, of course; but he would do it with respect, and even a measure of mercy.

Instead it was Luvidovich, and Trey learned quickly how restrained the boy had been that morning.

He chained Trey first, hauling his arms over his head and running the chain through a hook in the ceiling so his toes barely touched the ground. Trey studied that hook, its incongruous shine, the hairline cracks in the tile where it was fixed into the ceiling. This was the purpose of such a hook: torture, or hanging. They had planned for this, the designers of this bright, modern building. They had known their affluent utopia would be killing people in the name of justice.

Luvidovich stared him down as he pulled out a knife, turning it over in his hands. It was just the two of them in the room, no other officers, no recording devices. Luvidovich could compose any confession he liked, arrange the evidence however he wanted.

Trey was powerless. *But Elena is free.*

He thought of her, steady and fierce, her gun pointed squarely at Stoya's head. She had been terrifying. She had been astonishing. There was a moment when it seemed that the sheer force of her will might have taken down Stoya's men, but not even she was immune to the laws of physics. He hoped she had gone to Katya to warn her, or had someone from her ship come to look after them. He wondered if Katya would leave the city for a while. He smiled to himself as he pictured Katya's reaction to the suggestion that she ought to leave her restaurant. His sister was not a soldier, but she had grown into a warrior all the same.

He wondered if she would miss him, and he thought she would not. Most of her life they had been apart. All she knew of him was that he was a killer . . . and a cook. Sarah would forget him as well, eventually; but he thought she had been fond of him, at least a little. He found that some comfort.

He realized belatedly that Luvidovich had been speaking to him. "I am sorry, Janek," he said apologetically. "I was not listening."

Luvidovich smiled—that strange, stiff smile that never reached his eyes. He was like an animal who had learned to smile through mimicry, yet seemed to have no real sense of what the expression was for. "I was giving you the chance to confess," he said, "but I would prefer that you not take it. I have been looking forward to finishing our discussion."

"I see." Trey watched the young man turning the knife, over and over, the serrated edge scraping against his dry palm. "And what is it you wish me to confess this time?"

"It is a shame," Luvidovich said, "that you bear this alone, while your accomplice walks free."

"Ah." He was almost disappointed at the predictability. "Which is an interesting point, isn't it, Janek? Why isn't she here as well?"

Luvidovich frowned. "She has Central Corps protection," he said. "We could not touch her."

Trey had seen enough to be suspicious of any protection Central might have offered her. He thought it far more likely Stoya didn't want her around reminding Luvidovich that he had never believed Trey was guilty in the first place. "And who was it that told you that, I wonder?" he asked.

Luvidovich's lips tightened, and a look of annoyance crossed his face. He turned away, and after a moment he stood, composed again. The knife still spun in his palm. He wandered up to Trey and stopped, as if he were looking into a shop window.

"So she *was* your accomplice," he said.

"You are a fool."

Luvidovich reached back and swung the hand holding the knife against Trey's face. Trey felt the hard hilt connect with his jaw, and a wire-thin burning as the blade caught his lip. A trickle of blood traced down his chin.

A slow beginning, then.

"Has it not occurred to you," Trey said conversationally, "that if she had wanted that man dead, she had many more tools at her disposal on board her starship?"

"She would have implicated herself," Luvidovich said, and Trey thought it a small victory that the man was responding to his questions.

"You have never traveled on a starship, have you, Janek?" he said. "There are a thousand accidents that can happen every day. He could have vanished without a trace, and she would have been implicated no more than you."

"Perhaps she found this method more entertaining."

"You would, wouldn't you, Janek?"

A slap from the other direction, without the knife, but harder and sharper. Trey felt a jolt of pain up his cheekbone and into his eye socket. "If you tell me how you did it," Luvidovich said, retaining his temper, "I may leave you an eye."

Trey shook his head. "You are a miserable liar, you know. I have known enough sadists to know what you will do with me."

Luvidovich moved closer until his face was millimeters from Trey's. Trey could smell coffee on his breath, and something sour; the remains of his dinner, or perhaps the beginnings of another drunken binge. "When I am finished with you," he said, his breath clammy against Trey's skin, "I will find your whore, and I will hang her from these chains, and I will rape her at my leisure. Perhaps even after she is dead. Why don't you keep that image in your mind for a while?"

Trey spat blood in his eye.

Luvidovich caught him in the abdomen with the hilt of the knife, and Trey felt his lungs abruptly empty. He fought the instinct to gasp for air, waiting for his body to recover, and found enough adrenaline to apply one knee sharply to Luvidovich's groin. The shot connected, but not directly enough; the officer was hurt, but not incapacitated. Luvidovich took half a step backward and punched Trey once in the jaw and once in the throat. He turned away long enough to wrench a chair away from the wall, and in a few quick movements—before Trey's body had remembered how to breathe—he had cuffed Trey's ankles to opposite legs of the chair.

Trey found his lungs again, and took great, gaping breaths of air as Luvidovich stared at him, fury in his eyes. Trey forced himself to smile. "You have a problem with anger, Janek Luvidovich."

"I have a problem," Luvidovich snarled, his face blotchy with rage, "with killers who walk away."

"Is that what you will do, when you are finished with me?"

The officer took a few deep breaths, attempting to calm himself. "Obtaining a confession is not murder."

Trey shook his head. "You will not have noticed this," he remarked, as Luvidovich walked behind him and began cutting off his shirt, "but I have found that the more affluent a society, the easier it is for them to dehumanize their criminals." Instead of tearing the cloth, the boy was using the knife to saw through it, and every other cut nicked the skin around Trey's spine. "I find that an odd thing. You would think that those who have been shown kindness would be more likely to be civilized, not less. And yet you will be allowed to kill me, and as long as you tell the public it was in the name of safety, they will cheer you." The tip of the knife nicked the base of his skull, and he winced.

"And why would I not let you live?" Luvidovich told him. "Believe me, this is much more enjoyable than presenting Chief Stoya with your corpse."

"Is that what he has asked you to do?"

Luvidovich said nothing. He slid his thumbs methodically under the waistband of Trey's trousers, and yanked them to the floor, leaving them trapped in a heap around his chained feet.

Trey wondered, for a moment, if he would be left his shorts, but then he felt the steel blade slip against his thigh, and the stabbing and sawing began again.

Apparently not. "Did he tell you he was the one who let Elena go?"

Trey thought there was a brief hesitation in Luvidovich's destruction of his clothes.

"I asked for his assurance that she would not be harmed, and he agreed. Whatever your fantasies about her, Janek, I think you will be thwarted."

The point of the blade pressed against the small of his back. "You are a liar," Luvidovich hissed.

"And you truly are a fool if you think I murdered that man."

He felt the pressure of the knife increase, and the blade slip downward, the point resting against his coccyx. "There are other ways to rape, you know," Luvidovich whispered to him.

He took a step back and walked around to face Trey again, giving him a leisurely, lascivious look up and down. Trey thought Luvidovich's weakness was not his use of psychology—he seemed to have a fairly decent repertoire at his fingertips—but his use of all of his tricks at once, without considering his audience.

He supposed, statistically, that scattershot methodology was most efficient.

Abruptly Luvidovich straightened and walked around the table, making himself comfortable again in the chair. "Now," he said, "let us begin at the beginning. Where did you meet this woman?" He turned the knife against his palm, over and over, and waited for Trey to answer.

Chapter 21

Are you telling me," Ancher greeted her as she jumped off the tram, "that nobody looked at you funny walking through the city with a rolling pin?"

Elena could see the camera mounted next to his ear, and she had no doubt he was recording, but he was carrying nothing else. Whatever else he might do to help, at least his hands would be free. "I suppose I don't look dangerous."

"Your pants are too short."

"Shut up, Ancher." She peered across the street at the entrance to the station. "Do you have a scope on that thing?"

Ancher touched his ear and focused. "There's one guy standing near the entrance. Not moving much. He's slouching; seems kind of bored."

Elena knew better than to take that for granted.

"So what's the plan, Chief?"

That was an excellent question. She had made it this far on instinct and adrenaline, but a stealth infiltration of a police station seemed to require more finesse. "Easy," she lied. "You get me in unnoticed, and I break him out. Bonus points if I get a hand weapon out of it."

He glanced down at her. "Where's your gun?"

"Confiscated." She gestured at him with the rolling pin.

Slowly his face spread into a grin. "You're off-grid, aren't you, Chief?"

There was no harm, she supposed, in telling him. "The first the Corps is going to hear of this is when you air it."

"What about Captain Foster?"

"What about him?"

Ancher shook his head. "You weren't kidding about the story, were you?"

"Can you get me inside or can't you?"

"You look weird," he objected. "And besides, they'll recognize you."

"Can you distract him, then?"

Another grin. "Yeah, I can distract him."

"Then you'll get your story."

They walked up the block and crossed the street, Elena keeping Ancher between her and the early evening crowds on the sidewalk. The station windows were high, too high for her to see in. Too high for anyone to see out as well. When they approached the open foyer she hung back, fading into the building's shadow, just a woman out for an evening stroll. Ancher touched his ear again, and a flood of camera-friendly lighting splashed on the sidewalk before him. He strode up to the police station and turned in.

Elena heard him introduce himself to the desk officer. "I hear you guys have caught your killer," he said. "That's something. Fast work. Not even a day. Were you in on that?"

Elena inched forward, still in the shadows, until she could see the edge of the scene: Ancher talking to the same arrogant kid she had spoken to that morning. This time, though, the officer looked friendly, even eager: he was nodding at Ancher's words, returning his smile, falling for the thought of his face on the news. Elena hoped Ancher would find a way to use every second of that footage.

Ancher kept talking, and just as she was wondering whether he was expecting her to barge in and bash the kid on the head with her improvised weapon, she saw him gesture to one of the grand wooden office doors beside the massive staircase. The officer gave a quick glance around the lobby and nodded, and he led Ancher away from the desk. A moment later he was hidden by the stairway, and all she could see was Ancher's back, and the ambient light from his camera.

Elena edged into the foyer, moving with her back to the wall across the opposite floor. Ducking under the stairs, she crouched in shadow, but she was still horribly exposed; anyone emerging from one of the back offices would see her easily.

Ancher kept chatting up the officer—paying him compliments, eliciting specious details about Trey's arrest—but after a few minutes, the kid seemed to find his conscience. He told the reporter he needed to get back to the desk. "Of course," Ancher said cheerfully, unflustered, and Elena was impressed at his equanimity. "I'll get a few shots of you there." He followed the kid back, continuing his patter, before finally asking if he could look around. The officer hesitated only a moment.

"Stay on this floor," he said. "If you want to go upstairs, let me know and I'll see if I can get someone to escort you. I can't promise, though—they're kind of busy tonight."

Elena's stomach clenched, but she calmed herself. *If they're busy, Trey is still alive. Probably.*

She waited with growing impatience as Ancher sauntered around the atrium, taking shots of the grand staircase, of the windowed ceiling, of the darkened door to the morgue. Eventually he ended up standing a few feet away from her, his camera on a nondescript door. At one point he fingered his earpiece, fiddling with the lighting, and caught her eye.

Elena gestured toward the back of the room, and pointed downward. Ancher nodded smoothly; an observer would have assumed he was still working his camera. He was not bad at this.

Staying in the shadows, she crept toward the rear of the building, back against the wall, keeping Ancher between her and the front desk. Eventually they were far enough from the entrance that she thought she could risk speaking to him.

"The door is on a voice lock," she whispered. "Without my comm, hacking it is going to be a bitch. Any chance you could charm one of these nice officers into opening it for me?"

"And how does that work? 'Hi, you want to be on vid helping an AWOL Corps soldier bust out the highest-profile prisoner you've ever had?'"

"How about 'How would you like to prevent an unconscionable miscarriage of justice?'"

"You're cute when you're idealistic. You're going to have to crack the lock yourself, Chief."

"Fine." Elena sighed. "Just keep a lookout, will you?"

They made it to the steel door, and she got down on her knees to have a look at the mechanism. In what felt like her first stroke of luck, she found the lock was brand-new; the newer Ellis voice locks were lightweight and easy to install, but they were far less secure than the more complex models. The money would have been better spent upgrading their polygraphs. She slid a spanner out of the toolkit strapped to her arm and dialed the tip to its narrowest setting, getting to work removing the sensitivity detector from the lock.

"Is this going to take a long time?"

"Shut up, Ancher."

"It's just that there were footsteps on the stairs, and I didn't hear the front door open."

"Don't lose your composure now, when you've been doing so well." But she felt a bubble of panic, and frowned more closely at the lock. It had a tamper-resistant edge; she was going to have to try a narrower setting, and she was still going to risk tripping the alarm. *Focus,* she told herself, and blinked to clear her vision. Just a few minutes, if she was patient; just shift the shielding and then trip the mechanism—

"Please stop that."

Elena froze. The voice was not Ancher's. She had run out of time after all.

Chapter 22

Trey had become grateful for Luvidovich's scattershot methods. The boy had alternated between punches and cuts. The cuts were unpleasant—Luvidovich went about nicking his skin at its most sensitive points, from his scalp to his testicles to between his toes—but the pain was so generalized, little white-hot flares in so many different places, that his discomfort had become weirdly nonspecific. He hurt, and he desperately wanted it to stop, but each new insult brought with it no new fear. This would go on as long as it went on, and then it would stop, and that would be that.

He had lost track of time, but he knew it had been a long while since he had been afraid. When Luvidovich had pulled out an electric stunner, Trey's heart had crept up into his throat. But Luvidovich left the device on the table, squarely in Trey's field of vision, without turning it on. If he ever decided to use it, Trey felt confident that he would not find it much worsened his experience.

Luvidovich had stopped asking for a confession. Trey found the omission a curious comfort; he had no need to pretend any longer that this was an interrogation. Trey had thought once or twice that he ought to confess anyway, just to disappoint him. But Trey had lived his life telling the truth, and he was not going to end it otherwise.

When he had first arrived on *Castelanna*, Fyodor had asked him why he was running away. Trey, unable to quickly manufacture a lie, had told him the truth.

Are you sorry? Fyodor had asked.

No. Trey had been certain he would be expelled for his feelings. *But I am sorry he did the things that made it necessary to kill him.*

"You are beginning to convince me that you truly believe I did it," he told Luvidovich.

"Of course you did it," Luvidovich said pleasantly. "You would not have me believe in coincidence, would you? What I do not understand is why. She is pretty enough, of course, but there are whores all over this city. You, a celebrity? Surely you could have had your fill of women."

"I thought I was a limp old man."

Luvidovich bared his teeth. "I would think at your age you would understand that women are all the same. There is no difference. Inside they are all alike, no matter how old or young, or ugly. Or screaming, or crying. So why would you kill for this woman?"

Trey blinked. His vision had been blurry for a while. "Was your mother terribly unkind to you, Janek?" he asked. "Because my mother was not a prize, but I cannot even begin to fathom this warp you seem to have. Unless you are just trying to make me angry, which seems rather pointless, as I'm in no position to do anything other than spit at you again."

Luvidovich's eyes had gone dead when Trey mentioned his mother. "I don't have to kill you," he said. "All Stoya told me was to get a confession. I can keep you alive as long as I want."

Pain did not seem to please Luvidovich; but when Trey's eyes widened, when he knew he could not hide his dread of what was before him, a spark of life lit up the officer's cold gaze. He wondered if feigning fear would make Luvidovich back off, or if he would redouble his efforts.

It didn't matter. His mind was back with his stepfather, remembering staring stoically into the distance as the man struck him, over and over, calling him names, begging him to hit back.

"You still disbelieve that Stoya knows I am innocent," he said.

Luvidovich's eyes flashed. "You are not fit to speak his name," he snarled, standing up, the knife back in his hand. Trey wondered what it meant that he was relieved to see the blade instead of the stunner.

"Why is that?" Trey asked, genuinely curious. "He is a stranger. Why do you revere him?"

Luvidovich strode up to Trey, staring him in the eye. "Because he keeps the peace," he said.

Trey laughed out loud, amazed that he was still physically able. "At what cost? He knows I am innocent. I believe you do, too." And that, Trey realized, was part of what was making the boy so angry.

"You are not innocent! You are a murderer!"

That Trey could not deny, but he did not think this was the time to get into his childhood. "I did not kill that soldier, and you know it. If I were guilty, do you really believe Stoya would have let Elena go?"

241

Luvidovich swung at him, and Trey felt the heat of the blade against his cheek. "Stop saying his name!"

"Stoya let her go," he repeated. "I am a scapegoat. This entire investigation is a lie. Your job, Janek, is a lie, and you are a dupe for an off-worlder who has been brought here to fool the people into believing all is well."

"*Shut up!*" Luvidovich swung at him, again and again, at his face, his arms, his chest, slashing at his legs. If the officer had been in control, he would have cut Trey's skin to ribbons, but in his rage he missed more than he hit. Then Trey felt one deep stab into his shoulder, muscle-deep and hotly painful, and the moment it took Luvidovich to pull the blade from his skin made the boy slow down.

"I do not care if you confess," he said. He threw the knife on the table and picked up the stunner. "You do not know pain, old man, but you will." He stabbed the device between Trey's legs, against the raw burns and cuts, and Trey heard himself cry out as the world vanished into a blast of white, searing light . . .

And then the door slammed open, and Luvidovich turned, pulling the stunner away, and the room came back into focus. Elena stood in the doorway, a long club in one hand, staring at Luvidovich with anger and energy and life in her eyes. Behind her stood the reporter, Ancher, with an enormous grin on his face and a light shining out of the vicinity of his right ear.

Clearly Trey was hallucinating.

Luvidovich brandished the stunner, and Elena swung her club at him. The end of it connected with Luvidovich's weapon, and the stunner flew across the room, clattering to the floor. With enviable agility Luvidovich swept the knife up off the table and faced her in a half crouch.

"I am very glad you came," he said, his voice almost seductive.

Trey wanted to demand he stay away from her, but he found to his chagrin he could not speak. He watched as she swung her weapon again—*good Lord, is that one of my rolling pins?*—but this time Luvidovich dodged. He feinted in low, and his blade caught her hip. Yet instead of falling back, she shifted her weight to her other leg and brought the weapon up again, this time landing a solid blow on Luvidovich's left shoulder. The man let out a shout that Trey thought was as much surprise as pain, and made a fist around the knife's hilt again. He swung at her, and she brought her free arm up to block him, but he still knocked her back.

Throughout it all, the reporter stood still, his light flooding the room, a grin on his face.

"Help her, you fool," Trey said, but his voice was too weak.

Luvidovich closed in, lunging with the knife, but Elena dodged at the last moment, moving right and bringing the rolling pin down to catch Luvidovich behind the knee. He stumbled this time, and she rolled to her feet to stand between him and Trey. Trey saw her shoulder muscles tense in anticipation of Luvidovich's next attack.

Valeria had taught Trey how to fight when he was a child. She was a fierce and quick fighter, knowing how to use her small stature and superior balance to its best effect. Watching Elena, he could see she was stronger than Valeria, with a longer reach, and he thought she would have held her own against his teacher. But he had taught fighters of his own as well, and he could see that Luvidovich—taller and angrier—outmatched Elena, even with her improvised weapon. Left to herself, she was going to lose.

"When I say," he said, in that same useless voice, "get out of the way."

She gave no indication that she had heard him. He had barely heard it himself.

Luvidovich was facing her, still brandishing the knife. Trey wondered why he had not picked up the stunner with his other hand, and he supposed the man might have been hurt worse by her blow than he was letting on. But his eyes were bright with bloodlust and adrenaline, and Trey did not think he was minding the pain. He wondered then if his own questioning would have gone differently if he had volunteered to fight the boy, rather than just hang helpless from the ceiling.

He had almost no feeling left in his arms. His shins were bruised; he could no longer feel the legs of the chair against him. His head was light from loss of blood. But he did not need all of his strength; just enough.

Just once, he told himself, tensing his shoulders, tightening the muscles in his calves. *Only once, and then we are finished.*

Life or death.

Luvidovich rushed her. Elena dropped to a crouch, the rolling pin in her hand, and Trey croaked "Now!"

He thought she had not heard him. She waited until Luvidovich was nearly on top of her, and then she dropped to the floor and rolled against the wall. Trey tightened his hands on the chain and heaved upward with his arms and legs, catching Luvidovich under the chin with the chair. Luvidovich's head snapped back, and he staggered, stunned. Elena rolled to her feet brandishing the rolling pin, and swung it across his face, hitting him in the jaw. He spun and dropped, the knife falling from his hand. She kicked the knife clear and climbed around his chair to stand over him, still gripping the rolling pin, but after a moment he gasped once and fell unconscious.

Without pause she turned to Ancher and shoved the rolling pin into his hand. "Give it to me," she said, and Ancher reached into his pocket to hand her something small. Elena turned back to Trey. He was hanging on to the chain over his head, struggling to right the chair so it could take some of his weight. She straightened it for him, then studied the object in her hand. She pressed something, and abruptly his hands and legs were freed, his arms falling numb to his sides. He dropped to his knees next to the chair, weak as an infant, and Elena knelt in front of him. The fierce warrior was gone now, her wide eyes searching his face, worried and desperate.

"Trey?" she asked.

He lifted his uninjured arm and put his hand on one side of her neck. She felt warm, and her hair was soft and sticky with sweat, and he was pleased to discover he still had nerve endings. "You should have left," he said to her. He should be scolding her. He thought he might, later, when he was past thinking she was the most beautiful thing he had seen in his life.

"You shouldn't have gone without me." And she lifted her own arms, put them around his neck, and leaned in to kiss him.

Every part of him hurt. His arms, his neck where she touched him, his lips that were cut and bleeding.

It didn't matter.

He lifted his other arm and tightened his hands in her hair and kissed her back, deep and passionate, amazed to be alive.

At some point—he had no sense of time at all—Ancher spoke. "I hate to interrupt you guys," he said, "but we don't have a whole lot of time."

Elena, her eyes still locked on Trey's, nodded her head. "You need some clothes," she said. Her eyes strayed to Luvidovich's still form, and Trey felt his stomach turn over.

"I would rather go naked," he told her.

Her eyes softened a moment with worry, but then she tucked her concern away, and she became the soldier again. She nodded, and turned to Ancher. "Give him your clothes."

Ancher laughed. "What, so *I'm* supposed to go naked?"

"Are you afraid people will notice, or that they won't? Give him your clothes."

Trey stayed on his knees as Ancher stripped off his shirt and his trousers, grinning as if they were playing a game. When Ancher hesitated and said, "You don't actually want my underwear, do you?" Trey managed a smile.

"Thank you, no," he said. "I will make do without them." He studied Elena's eyes. "Katya and Sarah?"

"They are fine," she told him. "They are worried for you. Katya said they would find Ilya." She touched his hair. "Sarah told me to tell you she loves you."

Of all the things that had happened to him this day, that one came closest to moving him to tears.

Elena climbed to her feet and turned to the unconscious Luvidovich. Rolling him over, she pulled a handgun from the back of his belt, and then straightened. Ancher, who was apparently more modest than Trey would have thought, stepped behind her and began removing Luvidovich's trousers for himself.

Trey was able to grasp the shirt and pants, but he failed utterly at standing on his own. "Will you help me?" he asked. She stepped closer to him and held out her arm. Cautiously he lifted one knee to put his foot down, and tried to push himself to his feet. He had to pull against her, and even standing he had to lean on her. But he made it to vertical, and that small change made him feel that much more himself.

He pulled on Ancher's trousers, aware of the cloth rubbing against every abrasion. He had started to shake, and he recognized the sensation of adrenaline wearing off. With the trembling came waves of emotion, leftover fear and anger, shoved aside as unnecessary when he had been certain he was going to die. Every time he blinked he could see Luvidovich in his mind, hear the man's voice in his ear, feel the burns again and again. Dammit, he was traumatized, and he didn't have time for it. He shrugged the shirt over his shoulders—Ancher was built more broadly than he looked—and buttoned it across his chest.

Elena was shaking her head. "You still look like a train wreck," she said, but she was smiling. "Can you walk?"

Every part of him hurt, the pain pulsing insistently like the vestiges of his revulsion. It didn't matter. *I would endure anything to get out of this place.* "My dear," he told her honestly, "I could run."

She slipped her hand into his—gently, he noted; she was being careful with him—and turned to Ancher. "Let's get out of here."

Trey laced his fingers in hers, and followed her out of the room he had thought was the last thing he would ever see. Behind them, Luvidovich gave a low moan, and was silent.

Chapter 23

H ow much time have we got?"

Ancher consulted his camera. "Three minutes, eighteen seconds," he said. "You beat him up fast, Chief."

"No thanks to you." She had been losing, Elena knew, until Trey had become involved. She had told Ancher to stay out of it, that she wanted it all on vid. In retrospect, she should have specified that he was welcome to interfere if it started to look like she was going to get killed. Not that she was sure he would have.

Trey squeezed her hand. "What is the time limit?"

She turned to him. "Reya Keller let us into the basement and gave us the key to the interrogation room," she said. "We tied her up and left her in the morgue. We've got another three minutes before she starts yelling."

Their success, in the end, had come down to Trey. Facing the officer's service rifle, Elena had said, "They are going to kill him," and the young woman had immediately relaxed. Officer Keller had come up with the plan so quickly Elena wondered if she had already spent time thinking of ways to break people out of the interrogation rooms. The only hiccup had been when Reya told her someone needed to hit her.

"I am junior," she said, "but I am a trained officer, and not a bad fighter. You must make it look as if you overpowered me."

Elena had looked at her, and reminded herself that this woman knew exactly what happened in those interrogation rooms. When she swung her fist, she had been surprised at the force behind it. Reya had raised her eyebrows at her bloody lip and said, "You do not hit like a mechanic." But she had smiled.

With Reya's help they had found some cuffs, and bound her hands and feet. Before they tied a cloth around her mouth, she had told them she could give them five minutes, no more. "Longer than that," she said, "and they will suspect that I helped him. They already know I don't believe he is guilty."

Elena made Ancher climb the stairway first, and check to see who was on the first floor.

"But I'm half-naked! What will they think?"

Elena, who was familiar with what most people thought of the Corps reporters, suspected no one would notice a thing. In truth, Ancher's undershirt did not look entirely out of place as street clothes. A bit light for the weather, perhaps, but it was dark navy and high quality, and matched Luvidovich's blue trousers. He might have been any citizen out for an evening stroll.

She let Trey climb ahead of her, keeping him between her and Ancher until they were well clear of the place. He could not have been long with Luvidovich; it had taken her less than forty minutes after his arrest to break into the station. When she had seen what Luvidovich had done—what he was doing—she had gone hot with rage and guilt. Her suicidal threat to Stoya had been impulsive, but surely she could have talked them into arresting her as well. Trey should not have been alone. Greg might have come after her, and once he was there she might have been able to appeal to whatever conscience he might have left.

But it would have taken Greg an hour to get there. They would have been long dead, and the question of whether or not he would have helped at all would never have come up.

She focused her attention back on Trey. She had never seen anyone with so many small cuts. She watched him climb the stairs, alert for weakness, for him favoring one leg over the other, for a stumble or a slip. Nobody could take that kind of abuse and just walk away, and yet he was doing just that. He had to be running on adrenaline. She needed to get him to a doctor, no matter what he said.

They emerged onto the fine marble floor, and Elena let the door close quietly behind her, marveling at the contrast between the opulent building and the dungeon they had just left. Ancher started to creep toward the front again, but Trey laid a hand on his arm. When Ancher turned to catch his eye, Trey jerked his head toward the back of the building.

Elena peered toward the rear. It was shadowed, and there were too many doors with lights on between them and the rear exit. There was not, however, the armed guard that she had snuck past five minutes earlier. She looked at Trey and nodded, and he moved ahead to lead them.

He did not let go of her hand.

They moved swiftly and quietly down the dim hallway, and the murmured hum of the evening's business buzzed around them undisturbed. Only one obstacle stood between them and the exit: an open office door before them, a handful of voices audible from within. No way they could sneak past. Elena looked at Ancher again.

"They'll just arrest me," he objected.

"They will not," Trey said firmly.

"What if the desk officer notices I changed my clothes?"

"The desk officer is still at the desk," Elena told him, hoping it was true.

"Will you whack them with a rolling pin when they lock me up, Chief?" Ancher asked, but after a moment he took a breath, smoothed his hand over his undershirt, and walked up to the open doorway.

"Excuse me, gentlemen," he said. Elena heard the voices go silent. Ancher cleared his throat. "I'm Ancher, with the Corps news team. I hear you've had a breakthrough in the murder case."

There was a pause. "Who told you that?" The voice sounded suspicious.

"I can't divulge my sources," Ancher said glibly. "I heard the guy put up a hell of a fight."

One of the voices scoffed. "Bullshit. He rolled over like a baby, didn't he, Stan?"

"Will you shut up? He's a fucking reporter. Second floor," the other voice said dismissively. "Officer Keller will give you our official response."

"Sure. Thanks, guys," Ancher said. He backed away from the door, grinning, and headed back toward Elena and Trey. "They're in an evidence room," he said softly. "They can't see the door from there."

She made Ancher go first, and clung to Trey's arm, walking between him and the open door. They stuck to the shadows and crept past, and after several seconds she heard the men chatting again.

The rear door was locked with a traditional voice lock, less sophisticated than the new lock Reya Keller had opened for them, and crudely more effective. Elena handed the rolling pin back to Ancher and pulled out her spanner again, nudging it under the edge of the front panel; the tool started to emit a faint yellow light. "It'll trip," she said, pulling the spanner away. "Best I can do is delay it a little."

Ancher shook his head. "Forty-three seconds, Chief. How much can you delay it?"

The spanner's internal scanner was crude at best. "Five seconds," she said, looking at the readout. "Possibly ten. No more." She looked over at Trey; their short walk had left him gray and clammy. The last thing he needed was pursuit.

But he could read her, and he shook his head. "I will run without complaint, *m'laya*," he told her. "Two interrogations in one day is quite enough."

She found herself wanting to argue with him. *He flew this sector for forty-four years*, she reminded herself. *All that time he was fine without you.* She set the spanner and slipped the edge under the faceplate. "As soon as I trip this, you both run. Nobody stops, nobody looks back. Understood?"

The men nodded. Carefully she nudged the spanner into place, hit the jamming signal, and twisted.

The door slid open. Ancher dashed into the alley at a dead run. Before she could stand, Trey had his hand under her arm, hauling her to her feet and dragging her forward so fast she nearly tripped. He headed up the alley, and she sped up to stay with him. Ancher was a few feet ahead of them.

"We need to get to the spaceport," she said. Behind them, the alarm sounded.

"Left at the sidewalk," Trey called, and they turned. The sidewalks were well lit and filling up with evening tourists. Trey weaved in and out of them with admirable agility, and she began to hope he was not so badly hurt after all.

"We're going the wrong way," Ancher yelled. He dropped behind them, and Elena remembered belatedly that he was still taking vid.

"We are not," was all Trey said. He held on to her hand and kept running. She found she was able to ignore the crowds entirely and just follow his steps.

Trey's circuitous route brought them out in a side street next to the spaceport. There was a loading dock there, and a massive bulkhead that read IMPORT/EXPORT, but there must have been no cargo on deck. The street was abandoned, and ahead of them Elena could see the lights of the open hangar spilling out into the street.

They stopped. Trey was breathing heavily, and he was looking gray again. Yet he stood tall, and in truth he was less winded than Ancher. The reporter was leaning over, inhaling huge gulps of air, unable to suppress a huge smile.

"Next time you come to town, Chief," he said, "remind me to train first."

"Do you have a ship?" Trey asked her.

He would have no idea, she realized. No idea of her conversation with Greg, of the fact that they were entirely on their own. "We will need to appropriate one."

"Wait," Ancher said. "You're leaving?"

Elena met Trey's eyes. He looked resigned, but she could tell he agreed with her. "It isn't safe here," she answered. "Not right now."

"Where is it safe?" Trey asked.

"I don't know," she told him honestly. She did not want to explain in front of the reporter, but she would if she had to.

His eyes widened a little, and then he nodded. "I do," he said. He looked back up the street. "We will need a medium-range ship, at least."

"They usually park those in the back, near the tarmac," she said. If they could find one there, it would certainly improve their odds of escaping.

The three of them walked to the end of the road, and Elena peered around the corner into the hangar. Despite the empty loading dock, the hangar was crowded and active, with civilians as well as spaceport workers milling around the floor. The parking areas were nearly full, with small ships lined up like well-behaved dominos along the walls; the center of the floor was scattered with engines and parts on platforms and tables, being worked on by about a dozen mechanics. She looked toward the back. It seemed their luck was holding: there was a small cruiser right by the entrance that would be fast, and next to it a bulkier ship designed for multi-day trips.

Trey had spied the same pair. "Which one?"

"The larger," she said. "It's newer, and less likely to be customized." *Or malfunction on us,* she thought. It also had the advantage of providing them with space and shelter for a number of days, if it came down to that. If they needed more than a few days . . . well, she would worry about that when it happened.

A mechanic came around the ship's nose, taking notes. She waited a moment, but he showed no signs of wanting to leave, and she cursed. "If I can get him where the rest of the floor can't see him," she asked, "can you ambush him?"

She looked over at Trey, at his unhealthy pallor and his shaky hands, and hated to ask. But he straightened, and smoothed the lines of Ancher's shirt over his chest. "Give me your weapon," he said.

She smiled at him and turned over Luvidovich's gun.

She would have preferred his role, she thought. Distracting the mechanic would require finesse. It would require charm, and she was not charming by nature. By nature she found charm to be a futile and often deceptive exercise. She could perform for a crowd, but crowds had a dynamic all their own, and she found she could easily read the mood of a large group. One person? She closed her eyes and thought of talking to Ancher that afternoon, instinctively knowing how to make him listen to her. This was just another act. She shook herself, and straightened, and walked confidently into the hangar.

Chapter 24

She really did have a remarkable walk, Trey thought, watching Elena saunter easily across the shop floor. Her attire was hardly flattering—a utilitarian military-issue white tank top, and a pair of his sister's ill-fitting tan trousers over square-toed black shoes—but her long stride accentuated the swing of her hips, and her hair tumbled over her shoulders with every step. A moment ago, before she had left him, he had thought she seemed daunted, yet she clearly knew how to play this role. He wondered if she had always been such an odd combination of instinct and self-doubt, if she would ever learn otherwise, if time would help her recognize how extraordinary she was.

He supposed he might be biased.

Elena had reached the mechanic, who turned when she spoke. Trey saw her smile, and when the man took a step toward her, she dropped one hip and tucked a lock of hair nervously behind one ear. She laughed a little at what he said and tilted her head, asking a question; the floor mechanic moved a little closer to her, hands on his hips. If she was still nervous, he could not tell.

"So what are we doing?" Ancher whispered.

"*We* are doing nothing," Trey told him. "Where she and I are going, you cannot accompany us."

"But—"

"Mr. Ancher," Trey said firmly, never taking his eyes from Elena, "you have been a part of saving my life this evening, and for that I am in your debt. But there are favors it is not in my power to grant. You must stay here."

"How much debt are we talking about?"

Trey turned on him. "Do not assume," he growled, "that because I am injured I cannot put you out of commission."

Ancher grinned. "How about an interview? When you get back, of course."

Trey's heart turned over. He was not at all sure that day would ever come. "I will grant you that interview," he promised, "but you must look after my family while I am gone. I would not have them endangered because they have taken me in."

"Safe sister, safe niece, and I get an interview?" Ancher held out his hand. "Deal."

This time Trey shook it. A million little shocks of pain went through his fingers, which somehow he had not felt when holding Elena's hand.

He turned back. The mechanic was opening an access panel on the ship's snub nose so Elena could see the interior. Now, Trey thought, would be a good time, before the man tried to impress her by taking the engine apart. Without looking back at Ancher, he stepped into the hangar, staying close to the wall, trying for stealth. The polymer floor was cool against his bare feet, and he thought if he could remain as nonchalant as the other civilians wandering around, looking for their shuttles or trying to find short-range transport, perhaps no one would notice his attire.

Or the blood on his face.

Or how much he was shaking.

He straightened and walked more quickly. He saw Elena ask the mechanic a question, and she gestured at a part of the ship facing the wall; obligingly, the mechanic stepped over, and the two of them were hidden from the rest of the floor. Trey crept silently around the nose of the ship to stand next to her, pulling out Luvidovich's handgun.

The mechanic stared at it dumbly for a moment, then looked over at Elena, confused.

"I am sorry," she said, and Trey thought she meant it, "but we will need to take this ship."

The mechanic's eyes shifted to Trey, and the man turned white. "You're the ones who broke out of the police station," he said faintly.

"We won't hurt you," Elena assured him, "but we can't have you stopping us, either."

She had the mechanic stand against the wall, tearing two strips of microfiber from the bottom of her undershirt. The first she used to tie the mechanic's hands, and Trey noticed that even as she made the knot secure, she was careful not to cut off the man's circulation. A mechanic herself, she would know his hands were his livelihood. The second she wound around his head, and into his mouth. This one she tied more tightly.

"Can you breathe?" she asked.

The mechanic nodded, but his wide eyes were so full of fear Trey thought he would have said that anyway. He supposed the fellow had not been robbed at gunpoint before; the reaction was not really surprising, but it bothered Trey more than he wanted to admit. In all his years of piracy, he had never taken an innocent hostage.

"Sit on the floor, please," she told him, and the man slid down the wall. Trey kept the gun on him.

She turned away and took a moment to close the access panel. She keyed in a code at the ship's forward door; the door slid open, and the interior lights came on. "I'll get her started," she told Trey. "Keep him still; I don't want to worry about running him over as we leave."

She climbed into the ship. Trey's hostage went whiter.

"She will not hurt you, you know," Trey said. The man was beginning to irritate him. "Stay against the wall and you will be fine. We will be gone in a few minutes."

The ship started up with a low hum. Trey saw its long, wide feet light up—a modern street-level hover system. This was a luxury craft indeed. "Now," Elena said from the inside. Trey turned and stepped in.

She closed the door behind him. The ship was furnished like a sitting room, with two comfortable pilot's chairs by the console, and a table with two long sofas in the main cabin. In the rear was a standard-sized door that must have led to a bathroom. They were stealing from some very wealthy people. He sat down next to Elena, who had the manual controls projected before her.

"Automatic was locked," she told him. "I was hoping the pilot's code was the same as the entry code, but they were more careful. It's going to be a rougher ride."

Silently, Trey pulled on his shoulder harness, and she grinned.

"She is called *Sartre*, by the way," she told him.

"I hope that is not prophetic."

"This place is full of exits," she pointed out. "We just need to make it through one of them."

She eased the little ship off the ground, and it rose, almost noiselessly. Through the front window he could see the mechanic, still frozen in panic, his eyes on the ship. Elena nudged it into reverse, overlaying the rear view across the front window. Trey saw people turning; someone shouted. The other station mechanics began moving toward them.

She cursed and gunned the engine, and they shot straight up, stopping within a meter of the high ceiling. She spun the ship around and headed toward the tarmac, but the opening was much lower to the ground, and they would clip at least three ships if they tried to plow through. He could not see how they could escape without risking injury to the people in the hangar.

Beside him, Elena pulled on her own shoulder harness. "I hope you don't get motion-sick," she said. She was keying in commands to the ship's navigation interface so fast he could not follow them. When she finished, she engaged the program she had just coded, and her hands gripped her seat.

Trey, with no other available evidence, did the same.

The ship shot forward so quickly he thought they would collide with the wall; but before they got there the nose pivoted forward, and the ship was pointing straight down. They dove, making small corrections to avoid the ships that the mechanics were frantically shoving out of the way; and when they reached the opening to the tarmac, their ship righted itself. He heard a crunch as their tail hit a vehicle beneath them, but that was the limit of the damage they caused.

And then they were out in the open.

They sped along the tarmac, and Elena took the controls again, this time shooting them straight up. Trey had a strong stomach; still, he was beginning to become uncomfortable. *Unsurprising,* he thought, *after an evening of torture.* He saw her call up another set of controls, and he felt the vehicle's movements begin to smooth. It was an experienced pilot's trick, using a ship's artificial gravity generator to ease turbulence within a planet's atmosphere. He thought he had grown beyond being surprised by her.

I believe I shall never grow beyond being surprised by her.

The transition to artificial gravity was remarkably smooth; apart from the reorientation and the lessening of g-forces, they might still have been in the atmosphere. The stars appeared before them, and to their right hung Volhynia's lilac-pearl moon. There were no ships in front of them, but Trey knew there would be many right behind.

Sure enough, the ship's emergency comm system engaged automatically. "You will stand down immediately," said an unfamiliar voice, "or you will be fired upon."

"Take her," she said to Trey. "I want to enter our trajectory."

He took the helm from her and she disappeared onto her knees, opening a panel beneath the steering. "Can't you code it in?" he asked.

"If I code it, it broadcasts our flight plan," she told him. "It's a safety thing. They put it in all the vehicles sold to the private market. I want us to get lost."

There were, he knew, a few different ways to get lost at multi-light speeds, but he did not like any of them. "This is something you have done before."

"Once," she said. "And I'm still here. Can you see if this creature has weapons?"

Trey queried the ship's inventory, and came up with one anomaly. He gave a bark of laughter. "We are carrying fireworks."

"A lot?"

"Enough to create a distracting heat signature, at least."

"Excellent. *Sartre*," she said, "tell us if any of those birds behind us are aiming at us."

The ship answered without pause. "Four ships have locked tracking weapons on us," it said. The voice was friendly and male, explaining their fate like an enthusiastic tour guide.

"What kind of weapons?"

"I am not equipped to discern that information."

She cursed, and mumbled something Trey thought was "Bloody tourists."

"Releasing fireworks," he told her, and shot a half-dozen missiles in the general direction of their pursuers. Behind them the star field lit with orange and yellow and green, temporarily obscuring their pursuers. A missile sped past them, but the rest plunged toward the dissipating explosives.

"Will you be much longer?" He readied another half-dozen fireworks, but he was not sure the trick would work a second time.

"Seven seconds," she told him. He could see her fingers working furiously.

"This is your last warning," the comm system blared. "Stop your engines and we will escort you back to Novanadyr."

"Four seconds."

Trey released the fireworks.

"Two seconds. One—"

The ship's lights dimmed, and the stars around them exploded into white light. For a moment, less than a second, he saw the familiar blue and white streaks of the FTL field, and then an instant of stars again.

Dear God, she's doing a hot reverse.

The ship's lights went dimmer this time, and although he knew he was probably imagining things, he thought he heard the metal of the hull creaking in objection to this harsh treatment. And then the stars burst again, and he heard the engine hum, spinning to capacity, and he wondered if the field would fail and they would be pulled into strings.

But the hum decreased, and the interior lights came up, and the front window polarized to shield them from the worst of the bright light. He looked down, and met Elena's eyes, and for the first time since he had been arrested he thought he might live to see another day.

Chapter 25

Y ou found him like this?"

"Yes."

Greg stood in the cell doorway looking down at the body of
Janek Luvidovich. The officer lay flat on his back, in a pool of
his own blood, sightless eyes staring upward, the muscle and
sinew of his neck sliced cleanly through. His arms and legs were
straight, as if he had frozen and fallen, rigid and unresisting—
not a natural pose for death. He had been slaughtered, and then
arranged, whether out of respect or perversity Greg could not
tell. All he knew was that, despite the lack of other cuts, the
similarities to Lancaster's death could not be coincidence.

"How long had the alarm been sounding?"

"Less than three minutes."

Greg glanced up at that, raising his eyebrows at Lieutenant
Norin. Norin was young, and had almost certainly never expected to be left in charge; yet here he was, with Luvidovich
dead, and Chief Stoya conspicuously missing and not responding to comms. Greg had seen a lot of youth and inexperience
over the years, and he was far more forgiving of it than he ought
to be, but in a building this size, three minutes was an eternity.

"What were you all doing for those three minutes?" he asked.

Norin's complexion warmed, and he shifted his gaze away. "We ran after them," he said. "Nobody thought to come down here until they had lost us."

No one had secured the crime scene. Greg rubbed his eyes; he would have Bob give the place a once-over, but he suspected the area was far too contaminated to tell them anything useful. All they had been able to fix was the approximate time of death: 1942, with about thirty seconds of slush on either side. Bob's instruments would be more precise. "Find out exactly when that alarm was tripped," he told Norin. "I want to correlate it with time of death."

Norin looked confused, but to his credit he seemed to be in the habit of obeying orders. He disappeared, leaving the two uniformed officers who had shown Greg downstairs to watch over Luvidovich's corpse.

He had known in the shuttle that something had gone wrong. He had commed Elena, figuring she would want to be with them when they pulled Zajec out of the clutches of the police, but she had not picked up. *Lusi* had clarified that her comm was deactivated: he had been broadcasting into the ether. He had had a moment of panic, and then thought to tune into the local news feed, where he saw the blurry footage from the spaceport security cameras. At that moment, his concern turned into anger. He knew her flying when he saw it. She had taken Zajec, and she had run away.

Away from Volhynia, and the Novanadyr police. Away from the Corps.

Away from him.

Luvidovich's death had not been on the news report. The

alert said only "armed and dangerous" and "do not approach." But once they ran the gauntlet of rabid reporters at the police station door, Greg leaving Carter and his platoons to perform polite but firm crowd control, he had been allowed inside by a worried-looking uniformed officer and introduced to Lieutenant Norin.

He could not blame them for believing Zajec was responsible. They had not read Luvidovich's notes, and they could not know Zajec's alibi was unimpeachable. In this specific situation, he shared their goal of finding Zajec and Elena and bringing the pair of them home, and as far as he was concerned, that was all they needed to know.

Greg allowed himself a moment of sadness for the dead man at his feet before he wondered if the crime was a copycat, or a follow-up.

He turned to one of the uniforms, a gangly young man who looked no more than sixteen. Greg wondered if they really made police officers out of such young people, or if he had finally become old enough to think anyone under thirty looked young. "I'd like to talk with Officer Keller," he said.

The young officer looked grateful to have a reason to bolt from the room.

Greg followed him up the stairs and into what appeared to be a break room. A young woman was sitting there, wrapped in a blanket, staring blankly at a coffee table. Next to her another woman sat, holding her hand. She looked up when Greg came in, and frowned.

"Is this necessary?" she asked.

"Yes," he said, but he kept the threat out of his voice. He sat down across from them and looked directly at Keller, striving to look sympathetic. Keller's ivory skin was mottled from crying, and her eyes were wide and miserable. It took her a moment to focus on Greg. "Officer Keller," he said to her, "can you tell me what happened?"

She blinked once, slowly, but when she spoke, her voice was clear and strong. "He was torturing him," she said.

"You mean Luvidovich was torturing Zajec?"

She nodded. "That was his task. They brought him in, and Chief Stoya said to Luvidovich, 'Get his confession, and make sure it looks like you had to fight for it.'"

Charming. Not just state-sanctioned torture, but coerced confessions as well. "What did he mean by that?" he asked.

Her eyes lost focus again. "Zajec is a stranger, effectively an off-worlder," she said, by way of explanation. "We are allowed, in cases of murder . . . If he confessed, we would stop."

He tried to unravel that. "Meaning if he didn't confess, they were authorized to kill him?"

"Yes."

"And put it on the record that he confessed even if he didn't."

She nodded.

"Hell of a system you've got here," he said, and he couldn't keep the contempt out of his voice.

The attendant glared at him. "She is a victim here, Captain," she said, and Greg reflected that for a population who disliked Central in general and the Corps in particular, there were a lot of them who recognized his rank insignia.

"Tell me what happened after Luvidovich went down to interrogate him," Greg prompted.

"I came down to check out something in evidence," she said, her words stilted. "And I turned a corner, and she was there, holding a gun on me."

"Commander Shaw?"

"Yes. She made me open the basement door, and she took my keys and my restraint controller. Then she hit me. I don't remember much else until I woke up on the floor of the morgue, tied up, and I started kicking and yelling."

All on her own? Even for Elena, that seemed unlikely. "How did she get in the building?"

Officer Keller looked away. "I don't know."

Well, that was clearly bullshit. "What evidence were you checking out?" he asked her, still conversational.

"I don't remember. Something from the first murder, I suppose."

"You didn't yell when you saw her?"

"I was startled. She had a gun. I thought she would shoot me."

"Really?" He thought of the echoes of his footsteps in the huge open atrium. "That would've attracted some attention, wouldn't it? And pretty much destroyed her chance at a rescue."

"I wasn't thinking. I've never had a gun pointed at me before."

"Why were you carrying a key to the interrogation rooms?"

"We all do it."

This time it was her companion who gave it away, unable to hide the startled look on her face. "Officer Keller—" he began, and was interrupted by his comm. "Excuse me," he said, and stood, walking out of earshot of the two women. "Yes, Carter."

"Sir, there's a reporter out here who wants to talk to you. Ancher. He's one of ours."

Greg knew him: cheerful, dogged, utterly amoral, but not prone to frivolity. "What does he want?"

"He says he wants to show you something, sir."

Greg had no patience for this shit. "Have him show it to you," he said, "and if you think I need to see it, comm me again. If it's bullshit, shoot him."

"Sir?"

He closed his eyes. He was definitely going to have to spend more time with Carter just so the man would know when not to take him literally. "Feel free to tell him I gave that order, Lieutenant. As far as actually following it—" He thought for a moment. "Use your own judgment."

"Yes, sir."

Greg turned back to Keller. She was watching him again, her eyes wary. That she was lying was clear, but her distress also seemed genuine, and he did not think she was faking how hard it was for her to focus. Making a decision, he walked back over and sat across from her again. This time he thought of Caroline, of his sister, of all the women whose hands he had held on bad days.

"Would it be easier if we spoke alone?" he asked her gently.

Her eyes widened, and immediately her focus improved. Her expression became nearly desperate. *Jackpot,* he thought, and she nodded.

The attendant was looking at Keller incredulously. Keller looked at her, squeezed her hand, and gave her a dismissive smile. "It's all right, Yana," she said, and pulled her hand away. The woman stood stiffly and walked off. Greg waited until she was out the door.

"What really happened?" he asked.

To his shock, Keller's eyes filled with tears. "I didn't think they would kill him," she said, and began to sob.

Greg had returned Reya Keller to the custody of her friend by the time Carter commed him back.

"You need to see this, sir," he said, and Greg caught the urgency in his voice.

He found them outside, Ancher grinning like a Cheshire cat. He was dressed strangely, in snug trousers barely reaching his ankles and a tank top too thin for a cool evening. "What am I watching?" Greg asked.

"The big jailbreak," Ancher said gleefully.

He had caught all of it, from Keller's discovery of Elena and Trey to the moment Elena used Keller's key to unlock the interrogation room door, armed with nothing but a cooking utensil. Greg watched the fight; it took less than forty seconds, but it was clear she would have lost it had Zajec not managed to clock the kid in the head with the chair. Elena's follow-up blow was equally decisive, but Luvidovich was moving when she stepped away from him. Greg watched her release Zajec and drop to her knees in front of him; he looked away when she kissed him.

"Cute, aren't they?" Ancher said. "This is going to play brilliantly."

Greg decided not to punch him, and sped up the remainder of the vid. He only slowed it down to replay the flight from the spaceport hangar. It was a hideously reckless move, and she was lucky she hadn't killed someone. And yet, it didn't surprise him in the slightest. He couldn't think of another pilot who could have pulled off that exit. He checked the time stamp on the vid: 8:07.

"This is it?" he asked.

Ancher nodded. "I'm sure you noticed the absence of either of them knifing the hell out of that sadistic bastard Luvidovich before they left."

"Don't speak ill of the dead," Greg said automatically. *What the fuck was going on?* "Did they say where they were going?"

"Captain Zajec told me I couldn't go with them, but I don't know if that means anything. I'm not sure he liked me much."

"Who else has seen this?"

"No one. I promised the chief I'd sit on it for twenty-four hours."

"The police?"

"I tried to show it to them, but with all that scrambling to deal with the crime scene, they didn't want to let any of us in."

Greg rubbed his eyes. *Where did you go, Elena?* He activated his comm. "*Galileo,* do you have Commander Shaw's location?"

The lag in the response told him all he needed to know. "Commander Shaw is not in range," the ship told him. He opened another connection, then turned to walk back toward the police station. Jessica picked up instantly.

"Did you find her, sir?"

"She's off-planet," he told her. "Busted that pirate out of jail and stole a ship."

"No shit."

Greg knew he ought to chastise her for the admiration in her voice, but he found he shared it. Wherever Elena was, she was free. "I need the locations of all the PSI ships in the area."

"Sending you the ship locations now, sir," she told him.

"Thank you, Lieutenant. Jessica?"

"Yes, sir?"

He was not sure what he wanted to say to her, what connection he was looking for. He settled on "Keep your eyes open up there."

"You watch your back, sir," she said, and disconnected.

He commed Carter again, and outlined what he needed: one platoon to stay at the police station and make sure Lieutenant Norin saw the video—preferably with Keller's role excised—the other to head to Katya Gregorovich's place and keep an eye on her and her daughter. "They are not in custody," he emphasized. "But I'm not sure if they're considered leverage on Zajec, and with Stoya missing I want them protected."

"And if Zajec contacts them, sir, I'll let you know."

"Good man." Carter was catching on. "I want reports from both platoons every fifteen minutes, no exceptions. If Stoya shows up, if Zajec contacts someone, if anyone hears from the chief, I want to know right away, understood?"

"Yes, sir."

Greg headed off into the shadows of the building to look at the data on the PSI ships. *Castelanna,* which had been his first guess, was hell and gone out by Shenzhu—a week, easily, even in a long-range ship. *Novoselov* was closer, just a day's journey at full speed; a much more plausible choice with a ship like the one they had stolen. And *Aspasia,* hovering on the other side of Volhynia's pulsar, was an even better bet. They'd be within minutes of her by now. *Aspasia* would be the logical place to start.

Penumbra was out by the hot zone.

He stared at that. It didn't mean anything. The radiation belt wasn't a bad place for a PSI ship to sit; the Syndicate raiders tended to avoid it, and the Corps ships, who got constant updated information from the drones that patrolled the hot zone, had no reason to approach. It was coincidence that *Penumbra* was the ship that had hit *Demeter,* that Lancaster had been researching radiation, that *Penumbra* would have stayed put after being fired on by a Central starship. Elena ought to be heading for the closest safe port, and that was *Aspasia,* by a long shot.

He engaged the connection again. "*Galileo,* can you detect any FTL activity in or around the general flight pattern between here and the PSI ship *Penumbra?*"

"Specify variance."

Elena would not take a direct route, Greg knew. He gave *Galileo* a wide area to work with.

"Seven matches," the ship said at last.

"Anomalies?"

"One. No fixed origin. No flight plan. No transponder activity. No active ident."

"Check the specs of the FTL field against an M-series civilian cruiser model."

The answer was immediate. "FTL field within the parameters of a field generated by an M-series civilian cruiser."

He commed Jessica without thinking. "She's headed for *Penumbra.*"

Jessica let off an impressive litany of swears. "What are you going to do, sir?"

"With Zajec, she's probably safe with them," he decided. "We need to find Stoya, and get some traction on these murders. In a couple of hours I'll—"

The chime that interrupted him had become a familiar tone over the last several weeks, but it had been days since he had heard it. He left Jessica on the line, and pulled up the message headers. Same bogus auth code, same artificial ident. He displayed the message.

You don't believe that boy was killed over curiosity, do you?

"Sir?" Jessica prompted.

"Change of plans," he said, walking as he spoke to her. "I'm going after her."

"What happened?"

Elena was headed for *Penumbra,* and the wormhole. She was headed directly into whatever Central had asked Mac-Bride to deal with, whatever Lancaster had been investigating that got him killed. "I need her back before this comes apart," he said. There was no time to explain further. "Find Chief Stoya, Lieutenant. And get me whatever you can on those anonymous messages."

"Sir, Commander Valentis—"

Shit. He had counted on returning to *Galileo* much sooner. "Tell him you're doing research for me," he told her, "but don't say what. Make something up if you have to."

"Yes, sir." She sounded unhappy.

"And Jessica—be careful."

"Of Commander Valentis, sir?" When Greg was silent, he heard her exasperated sigh. "What's going on with him?"

"All you need to know," he told her, "is that his comms are restricted, and I wouldn't have left him in charge if I'd had another choice."

"You had two hundred and twenty-two other choices, sir."

"I can't get into it now, Jess." She didn't need to know that he was flagrantly disobeying orders. If she didn't know, they couldn't punish her. "Just—whatever else you do, don't let him take those auth codes away from you. You have my full authorization to do what you need to keep that access, is that clear?"

"Yes, sir . . ."

"What is it, Lieutenant?"

There was a pause, and Greg thought he knew the look she had on her face. "Nothing, sir," she said at last. "Don't worry about the ship, sir. I'll look after her."

He had to admit it made him feel better to hear Jessica say it.

CHAPTER 26

Take off your clothes."

Elena stood up and headed for the bathroom in the back of the shuttle. The spec sheet on the ship had specified a Level Three medkit—not enough for surgery, but enough to stabilize some pretty serious injuries. At the very least it ought to have a tissue scanner. With luck it might even detect broken bones.

She had been impressed at how well their stolen ship had handled the change in direction. She had expected the FTL field to shudder, or to dissolve within a few minutes; but instead it had stabilized, albeit at a slower speed than she wanted, and the engines were running well within tolerances. They would reach the radiation perimeter in a little more than six hours. In five, Novanadyr would hit the Dead Hour, and they would be able to send a signal to Captain Solomonoff. She did not know how doggedly the police planned to pursue them, but after what she had seen she had no intention of risking recapture.

She wanted to wrap Trey in blankets and make him lie down, and sit anxiously over him until she could get him to a doctor. She had seen enough combat wounds to have a good sense of how badly someone was hurt. None of Trey's wounds looked deep, but the sheer number of cuts had to be straining his system, and she knew he had taken far too many blows to the head. He needed rest, and he needed better medicine than she would find in a Level Three medkit. Maybe she should have taken him back to *Galileo* after all.

Except that Greg had refused to help him.

She could have brought him back anyway, she supposed. She had enough friends there. Bob would have looked after him, no matter what Greg might have ordered. But he would have been a prisoner, and she would have been unable to do anything for him at all. And whatever Central was up to, whatever game they were playing . . . she would be hiding behind her uniform, hiding behind her concern for one man, and pretending none of it mattered.

She had never been any good at letting things go.

She found the medkit, still sealed, tucked behind a door in the corner of the shower. The owners had gone for the upgraded model; it did, indeed, have a deep bone scanner. She walked back into the cabin, finding Trey slowly undoing the buttons of his shirt.

"This was easier when we were running," he said ruefully.

She set the medkit down on the pilot's chair and took over undoing the buttons for him, keeping her face professional. "Adrenaline is remarkable," she said briskly. "It allows you to pull on a stranger's shirt, *and* knock out a policeman with a chair. Thank you for that, by the way," she finished, tugging the tail of the unbuttoned shirt from his borrowed trousers.

He pulled the shirt off of his shoulders and looked at it; his cuts had bled. He bunched it into a ball and tossed it in a corner.

"I believe it was you who saved me," he said to her, and began unfastening his trousers.

She tore her eyes away from his injuries. She did not think there were three square centimeters of his flesh that were free of marks. She circled behind him first, as he stepped out of his pants and nudged them into a corner with the shirt. Pulling out the scanner, she aimed first at his head, panning slowly.

"You have a minor concussion," she told him. "You need sleep."

"I could have diagnosed that myself," he told her, but he smiled as he said it.

His injuries were, individually, not severe. There were not as many cuts as she had thought, and almost all of them were shallow, capillary-level bleeders. He had one deep cut in his shoulder, but the coagulant healing accelerator in the kit would take care of that. She scanned him head to toe, and again from the front, to confirm what she had found. With enough rest he would easily heal, and probably within a few days.

But it was not only new injuries that she had seen. Throughout his body, mostly in his arms and ribs, there were decades-old signs of broken bones. The fingers of his right hand, so long and expressive, had taken the worst of it; whatever mobility he had now was something of a miracle. Most of the breaks had been overgrown, sustained before he was an adult.

"You said he never hurt you that badly," she said quietly.

It took him a moment to figure out what she meant. "He was quite careful, actually," he told her. "He knew how much he could get away with. My hand was an error." He flexed his fingers. "My mother shouted at him after he did it. She told him my teachers would notice. That was the first time I realized she knew what he was doing to me."

She pulled out the deep-cut kit, and began carefully cleaning his shoulder. "But you did nothing until he turned on Katya."

"When it started, I was too young. When I got older . . . it became a point of pride, to do nothing in the face of his rage. I would think, from time to time, that if he lost control and ended up killing me, it would be a sort of victory. But no, I could not watch him turn Katya into the same kind of creature."

She blinked; it would do no good for him to see her weep over him. She used a small syringe to douse the puncture wound with enzymes. "I did not speak to her long," Elena told him, "but she seemed all right. Like you, really. Stubborn."

He laughed a little. "She is, isn't she? It is an odd thing for me; I wrote to her, over and over through the years, but she never wrote back. I did not know her. I am only just beginning to see who she is. I do not remember much of her when she was little, except that she would hide behind me when she was frightened, and that she always did what our mother told her to do."

"It's hard to imagine her being timid." She laid a dermal patch over his wound and smoothed the edges with her fingers. "There is a shower back there if you want," she told him. "There is a place you can sit. I can help, too."

He flexed his shoulder carefully. "I will try on my own, thank you," he said. Then he met her eyes. "*M'laya,* when you threatened Stoya on the street—did you want to die?"

She shook her head. "No. I wanted to kill."

She did not drop his eyes, and after a moment he nodded and headed into the bathroom. While he turned on the water she began opening drawers. The owner was closer to Trey's proportions than Ancher was, but he did not keep much clothing here; still, she found black trousers she suspected were pajamas, and a stack of folded undershirts. She thought they might fit her well enough, too, if she could find a belt.

There were sheets and blankets tucked in the drawers as well, luxurious soft materials that appeared to be custom-made to fit over the sofas. The ship might not be outfitted for long journeys, but for a few days, at least, they would be more than comfortable. If they needed more than that, she thought they could trade some of the ship's interior furnishings at someplace like Hadron or Calexys; it wouldn't get them a lot, but they could buy food and any parts they might need for a week or so. With luck, *Penumbra* would take them in, and all of her planning would be moot, but she always felt better when she had options.

She could hear the water splashing. He was moving around, at least, and she resisted the urge to call out to him. Instead she pulled out the clean clothes, and then began hunting for food. The owner had been far less interested in provisions; there were some utilitarian staples in the cabinets, and some preserved meals, but they were only a few steps above MREs. Still, they were nutritious, and she thought if he was hungry the quality would matter less.

He took a long time in the shower, but when he came out his wounds were cleaner and he had washed his hair. Some of the cuts had begun to ooze, but her bandage had held, and despite his injuries he seemed in far better spirits. When he saw the clothes she had found he smiled. "We are living in luxury," he remarked. He tossed his towel into the bathroom and began to get dressed.

She took a shower after him, removing her undershirt and borrowed trousers only after closing the door to the bathroom. Despite having spent the last half hour with him naked before her, she was shy about stripping in front of him. The ship had an inductive water heater, and she thought she could have stood under the warm spray for hours. As it was she soaped twice and washed her hair, closing her eyes and turning her face into the stream. When she emerged at last she found he had laid out clothes for her as well; they would be far too big, but they were clean, and without the memories of the clothes she had removed. He turned away while she dressed, and she felt a momentary flutter of disappointment.

They opened two of the preserved meals, Trey with some trepidation. "I do not understand people," he said, staring into the container. "All of our technology, and this is the best we can do?"

"They are better than what we get on *Galileo*," she told him. "We try to take on fresh food every six weeks or so, but sometimes we can't. Sometimes—" She stopped, remembering, and put her food aside.

"Tell me why we are not returning to your ship, *m'laya*."

He was looking at her with those gentle eyes, all sympathy, as if he had not just been tortured by an accomplished sadist. "Central is neck-deep in all of this," she told him. "If we go back to *Galileo*, I don't know what they'll do with you." Central Corps, her chosen home and family, everything she had loved for the last ten years of her life. She felt her face grow hot, and she swallowed, refusing to give in to it. "There's something going on about *Demeter*, and about the wormhole. Central is tangled in this, and it could get ugly very, very quickly. If we went back to *Galileo,* you'd be intel. You'd be leverage. They might not beat you, but you'd be no less a prisoner."

"What of your captain?"

My captain is an idiot, she thought, frustration welling up again. "He seems to think he can work all of this through channels," she told him. "I don't know if he's being complicit, or willfully blind, or if he can't bring himself to tell me the truth. He doesn't seem to want to accept the possibility that his chain of command is behind this mess."

"And you are not willing to trust the rules."

"Not just now, no." *Maybe never again.*

Trey watched her with that look that seemed to ask her to say more, but she could not think what to tell him. Nothing she could say would make sense. Eventually he turned back to his own meal. "*Penumbra* will have its own challenges," he told her. "I do not believe Valeria will leave me to the wolves. She has never been one to let her personal feelings interfere in what is right. But she will be wary, more of me than of you."

"Why don't you get along?"

"Hm." That sound again, the one that she took for embarrassment. "Valeria and I used to be married."

Of course . . . That explained all of it: the acrimony, the bitterness, the determined sniping even in the face of a serious situation. He had been on Volhynia only six months, which suggested it was recent. "I see," she said, and wondered why her voice sounded so strange. "That's—" She was suddenly unable to sit still, and she got to her feet, crossing the narrow cabin. There was a supply list displayed against the wall; she began perusing it. "That would explain how well you—of course."

"Elena."

She could feel the heat rising to her face. All she could remember was standing next to him, throwing her arms around him, weeping on his shoulder. "I hope I didn't—I mean, not that there's anything, since we don't really know each other, you and me, and I didn't, I mean I'm not presuming anything, not that there would be any reason for me to presume anything." *Why am I still talking?*

She heard him stand up. "Elena," he said again.

"And I hope she didn't think I was trying to—or maybe she thought we were, or I was being mean, or trying to, I don't know, hurt her somehow. Not that I could, I mean."

He was standing right next to her, but she could not turn around. "You are babbling."

"That happens to me when I don't know what to say. So maybe you could say something instead. Not that you have to, I mean you don't owe me anything, we're not—"

"Elena." He slid one hand over the back of her neck, and when she looked at him he leaned forward and kissed her.

He tasted of their horrible dinner, and of salt, and of blood, and she had one moment to feel a flare of anger at Luvidovich before she found herself kissing him back, winding her arms around his neck, trying so hard to be careful but wanting desperately to consume him. His hands threaded into her hair and his kiss became more insistent; she opened her mouth to his, kissing him with utter abandon.

He held her against him after the kiss broke, shoulder to hip, all heat and skin, and suddenly everything was normal between them.

"So how does it work," she asked, "being married to someone on another ship?"

"PSI ships travel in pairs." He said it as if he thought she should have known. "*Penumbra* and *Castelanna* are sisters. She and I would be apart now and then, when we would separate for a solo mission, but never more than a week or so."

"Why aren't you married anymore?" she asked.

"When my sister asked me to come home, I assumed Valeria would come with me. She assumed I would stay. There seemed no way to resolve it." His smile turned sad. "I cannot do what your captain does, Elena. I could not promise myself to a woman I would never see, and I would not ask her to live out her life alone simply because of what I needed to do. We dissolved the marriage long before I left. It has been more than a year."

"But you are still angry with each other."

"In truth," he admitted, "I do not know. She does make me irritable, but she always did. I knew her twenty years before we became lovers. I would like to think, with all we have been through, that we might forgive each other someday." He studied her face. "But we do not belong to each other, Elena. Not anymore. You have not presumed anything incorrectly."

She wanted to kiss him again, to pull off his clothes and feel his skin against hers—innocently, if that was all he could manage. All that mattered was having him close. "It will be hours yet before we can comm anyone," she said. "You could sleep."

"Sleep." He laughed a little. "I do not remember what sleep is like. But you must promise to wake me when it is time."

She instructed the ship to sound an alarm when the Dead Hour hit, and she pulled sheets and a blanket out of another drawer. Trey let her make up one of the sofas, although she could not stop him from collecting the remains of their meal and tipping it neatly into the ship's recycler. She was shaking out the blanket when he walked up to the bunk; she moved aside so he could sit. He lay down slowly, swinging his legs stiffly onto the cushion before letting out a little groan as he relaxed the muscles in his back. She saw his eyes close, and his face took on a peaceful expression.

She spread the blanket over him and began to pull it up over his shoulders. He reached out a hand and placed it on her arm. "Join me," he said, his eyes still closed. "I assure you I am quite incapable of taking advantage of you at the moment."

"That wouldn't stop me anyway."

He smiled at her remark, and she sat on the edge of the narrow couch, lowering herself down next to him and pulling up the blanket. She wanted to face him, but she did not think there would be room; she turned on her side and pressed her spine against him. He turned a little and laid one arm over her waist. He felt warm, and she could hear him breathing, and feel his heartbeat against her back. He smelled of the same soap she had just used, with a touch of the disinfectant from earlier—and still, a trace of that vanilla.

"You surprised me," he said at length, "when you challenged Stoya. I believe I might have handled the situation differently had I known you were going to threaten him."

"I never threaten," she replied. "And it wouldn't have mattered if you'd asked me. I didn't know I was going to do it until I did." Which sounded, she knew, foolish and impulsive. *And now he's going to think of me as a child again.*

He tugged her closer, and she nestled against him. After a moment she felt his lips against her hair. "I underestimate you," he said.

"Everybody underestimates me," she told him. "It's because I am a mechanic."

She felt the rumble of his laughter against her skin. "I will try to stop, *m'laya,* but I make no promises. You may need to remind me from time to time."

Something in that phrase warmed her heart, and suddenly Novanadyr was a million years away, and the only memories she had were of his kindness. "I will tell you as often as you need," she promised.

He kissed her head again, but he said nothing else, and after several minutes she heard his breathing deepen. His heartbeat slowed, just a little, as he sank into sleep; she lay there, feeling his chest rise and fall against her back, alert for any change, any flaw, any suggestion of serious injury. She did not want to sleep—she wanted to watch over him every moment. Now that he was unconscious, she was free to worry as much as she liked.

But he was warm, and she was tired, and the pulse of the little ship's engine made the place seem almost familiar. Against her will her consciousness sank into itself, and she fell into darkness with him, free of dreams.

CHAPTER 27

Captain Foster had been right: Commander Valentis used to laugh a lot more. But he had always, as long as Jessica had known him, had a hideous temper.

She stared straight ahead, letting him yell at her, responding "Sir, yes, sir" at the appropriate intervals. She had known people who had dated him, but none had done it for long; Commander Grayson, her CO before Commander Broadmoor had taken over, had said, one night over drinks, that he seemed to seek out relationships because he thought he ought to, not because he wanted them. Jessica was always surprised he had the option: he had always made her skin crawl. Ted teased her about that, telling her that Valentis was precisely her type, but she didn't find it funny. She had no idea why Valentis put her off, but even here, in the captain's office with the door wide open, revealing her disgrace to the world, she felt deeply uneasy at his proximity.

"What did the two of you discuss?" he demanded.

"It was personal, sir," she replied.

She supposed by some lights that was not precisely a lie. Surely a direct order to keep something from a superior officer was as personal as you could get.

"Were you discussing the chief? Is that why he went after her?"

"Sir," she began, thinking she might explain at least a little, "I think with that police officer missing he was a little worried about her."

He yelled directly into her face, and she could smell coffee, and something medicinal. "Worried about *her*? She murdered a police officer! She aided and abetted a known felon!"

"Sir, I don't think—"

"I don't care what you think, Lieutenant," he snapped. "I want to know what the captain was thinking before he took off."

That was easier. "I don't know, sir."

"What were you talking to him about?"

She gritted her teeth, and thought bad thoughts about Greg Foster. "I told you, sir. It was personal."

His face had turned an extraordinary color, and she wondered how good his health was. A moment later, though, she did not care. "You know, Lieutenant," he said, "I've watched you spend five years fucking your way through this crew. You probably think you finally hit the jackpot with him. Well you better think again, Lockwood. He's gone completely off-grid this time, and if you've got any brains you'll cut your losses."

Oh, what she would say if he didn't outrank her. "What do you mean, 'off-grid,' sir?"

"I mean," he said, practically spitting in her face, "he disobeyed a direct order from Admiral Herrod."

Oh, hell. "I didn't know that, sir," she said, and she thought he could see the truth on her face.

"So given that," he said, straightening up and walking back behind the captain's desk, "do you have anything to tell me?"

She rolled over in her mind the possibility of telling Commander Valentis what she knew. It might give her a shot at preserving her career, should the captain have truly run off against orders.

"I've told you, sir," she said, resigned, "our discussion was personal."

Commander Valentis changed colors again, and she gritted her teeth, staring straight ahead. She wished for Elena's aplomb. That woman, when she got angry, became the sharpest, flintiest, coldest creature Jessica had ever seen. She hoped she would get a chance to tell her friend that; for reasons Jessica did not quite understand, Elena always seemed to envy her.

"*Galileo*," Valentis said, "revoke all access codes for Lieutenant Jessica Lockwood." The ship responded with a low tone of acknowledgment, and he moved to stand in front of Jessica again. "Lieutenant, you are confined to quarters until further notice. If you choose to speak to me, I may still be able to prevent disciplinary action. Do you understand?"

"Yes, sir."

He dismissed her, and she fled. It was only when she was in the hallway, half running toward the sanctuary of her room, that she realized she had been holding her breath.

When she got to her quarters she put a voice lock on the door and sat down in the overstuffed armchair she kept by the window. "*Galileo*, engage Lifeline."

The ship processed for a single heartbeat, engaging the backdoor access Jessica had hastily programmed in after she had spoken with Foster. Another flagrant violation of regulations, aided and abetted by Foster ordering her to make sure she was always able to get the information she needed. *Bastard isn't going to revoke my access just for being loyal to my captain.*

Who may have just screwed his own career, but she didn't have time to worry about that. "Did Captain Foster talk to Admiral Herrod before he took those platoons down to Volhynia?"

"There is no record of that conversation."

"Did he wipe it?"

"There is no record of that conversation."

So either Valentis was lying, or the captain had deleted the discussion in hopes of covering his tracks. Which brought up another question.

"Did Commander Valentis talk to Admiral Herrod?"

"No."

Galileo was always so short and sweet when she had the answers. "Did he talk to anyone back at Central Gov?"

"Yes."

"Who'd he talk to?"

"Central Gov Command Center."

Useless information. His call could have been routed to anyone from there. At least it explained how he might know about Herrod's orders. "*Galileo*, did the captain file a flight plan out of Novanadyr?"

"No."

That should have meant that she was the only one who knew where he was going, but even a tone-deaf asshole like Valentis would guess. Everybody on the ship would know the captain had gone after Elena, and most of them would be relieved. It was long past time the two of them stopped sniping at each other.

Jessica closed her eyes and sat back. Her mother had been prone to temper tantrums, although never petty ones: she fought for her family, and always loudly and publicly. Jessica thought her own tendency to work toward a peaceful solution was probably a reaction to that: she had been embarrassed more times than she could count by her mother appearing at her school, outraged, to challenge her teachers.

Greg Foster reminded her of her mother, and right now he was fixated on finding Lanie and . . . Jessica did not know. She thought the captain probably didn't, either. She had great sympathy for his emotional predicament, but she didn't think he was in the right frame of mind to offer Lanie any kind of coherent explanation. Lanie was going to stomp all over him—again—and he had no one to blame but himself.

Jessica found it strangely romantic.

She sent him a silent wish for luck, then turned her mind to the task at hand. "*Galileo,* what have you got on this Stoya character?"

"Born 3175.44.12, approximated, in Fuji Seaport, Osaka Prime. Parents unknown. Education unknown. Trained in law enforcement 3201–3202. Served as governor of Fuji Seaport until hired by the Volhynian cabinet twenty-three months ago."

Lovely, she thought. "Why did Volhynia hire a thug?"

"Stated reason: public perception of serious crime."

"How close is that perception to reality?"

"The Volhynian crime rate has been decreasing for the last sixty years. Violent crime in Novanadyr was statistically negligible until the murder of Daniel Lancaster."

"So it's possible the cabinet had something besides crime prevention in mind when hiring this guy," she mused.

"That hypothesis is consistent with the data."

"Can't you just tell me I'm right?"

"Insufficient data to determine validity of—"

"Never mind." With no effort at all, she thought of three good reasons the government might want to hire a goon; she knew there were more possibilities. "What's his official status at the moment? Is he a missing person?"

"Yes."

"What have the police done to find him?"

"They have ordered searches of all outgoing spacecraft. They have issued a public appeal for information."

"They're assuming foul play."

"That hypothesis is consistent with the data."

"So how many ships have left Volhynia since Lanie stole the civilian cruiser?"

"Seven," Galileo told her. "Four freighters. Two registered pleasure vehicles. The Lusitania."

"All searched?"

"Yes."

Jessica frowned. "What about before that? What about ships leaving Novanadyr between . . ." She checked the report. "1942 and 2007?"

"No official flights out of the spaceport."

"What about unofficial?"

There was a pause as Galileo swept Volhynia's radar data. "Three hundred fifty-two intracity transports. One ship sub-stratosphere to Riga."

Jessica sat up. "Anything fly out of Riga after that?"

"Four ships. One under no flight plan."

"What was it?"

"A single-person carrier, Fender class."

She swung her legs to the floor and stood, pacing. "So he bolts in a little one-person Fender? Did it come back?"

"No."

"Ergo, he met someone. Can you trace the Fender?"

This time the pause was longer. "Fender trail disappears at 192.234.3345."

"Explain 'disappears.'"

Another pause. "Insufficient information to explain lack of data."

Her eyebrows went up. "You mean you don't know what you don't know?"

"Yes."

Jessica could swear the ship sounded annoyed. "*Galileo*, can you make anything of the telemetry data on that Fender's journey?" she asked.

"Replies to that question constitute probabilities, not facts."

"Fine, fine; I'll take probabilities."

"The Fender's flight pattern is normal until it disappears from the field. Possible causes: field destabilization and destruction. Probability: 58.9 percent."

"Why so low?"

"Field destruction produces a radiation signature. Radiation in this area is too high to verify any deviations."

"What else?"

"Self-destruct. Probability: 35.7 percent. Secondary source. Probability: 78.2 percent."

"Explain."

"The presence of another structure with an anomalous transportation signature could have obscured the Fender's telemetry."

"What kind of structure? Speculate."

"Malfunctioning terraforming equipment. Previously undetected quasar. Stable cloaking field. EMP from—"

"Hang on," she interrupted. "'Stable cloaking field'? What about unicorns, while you're at it?"

"The distortion of the Fender's telemetry data is consistent with the field that would be generated by a stable cloak."

"You're really going with that."

"Data is consistent."

Uneasiness hit her then, and she began to wish she had insisted on accompanying the captain down to Volhynia. He was out there, with whatever this oddity was. Elena was out there, too. If Stoya was alive . . .

Who would hire an Osaka thug to run a police station on a small, wealthy, safe colony? Of all the positions he could have had, with his record—why this one? Why Volhynia? Was it function?

Or was it proximity?

Twenty-five years ago, the *Phoenix* had been destroyed while investigating an unremarkable wormhole. Yesterday, Danny had been murdered after asking questions about that same phenomenon—and today, Volhynia's shady police chief bolts into the residual radiation field by the wormhole, only to vanish in the shadow of something that shouldn't exist.

Jessica was with Foster: she didn't believe in coincidence, either.

CHAPTER 28

Interstitial

The longer Greg spent reading over Luvidovich's history, the less he was able to feel sorry that the man was dead.

He had left Carter behind to keep the situation stable on Novanadyr and had taken *Lusi* on his own, setting her course to *Penumbra*'s last known location. He doubted he would be able to catch up to Elena and her pirate, even though they were in a civilian ship, but he thought he could close on them enough to be no more than a few minutes behind. He wondered how Captain Solomonoff would take the intrusion. He supposed he would find out quickly if she really was the sort of woman who would preemptively attack MacBride.

But in the meantime, he read.

He had sympathy for Luvidovich's origins. His home life had been horrifically abusive. It would have been heartening to think that Luvidovich had become a police officer to avenge his own miserable existence, but that, it turned out, had been engineered by his father, a prominent politician. What had surprised everyone was that Luvidovich had been good at the job: despite his questionable character, he had a sharp mind. When Stoya was hired, Luvidovich was given a number of cold cases that he was able to tie up quickly, leading to his promotion. That appreciation, it seemed, had earned Stoya Luvidovich's loyalty.

Until Zajec's arrest for Lancaster's murder.

Luvidovich's police reports had a rhythm to them: initial reports made up of methodical lists of evidence and questions, thorough updates on interviews and investigation, notations of hypotheses and dismissed ideas, and finally details of arrests and confessions. But his report on Danny's murder went a different way. After his initial write-up—in which he had observed, Greg noted with interest, that the body had likely been moved—the focus had turned almost exclusively to Zajec, with the stated purpose of bringing a "known murderer" to justice. Instead of dealing with the case at hand—with Danny, his movements, his background—all of Luvidovich's notes were about ways to legitimately bring Zajec back into custody. He had even tried to think of how to get Elena out of the way, including hiring someone to assault her. Greg's heart had gone black at that. He was glad she had stuck close to the pirate.

But Luvidovich's duty logs and comms, provided by the Novanadyr PD, told a different story than his official reports. While he had not investigated Danny's final movements, he had done thorough homework on the knife. The blade was not unique, but it was unusual. Such knives were not typically chef's tools, but belonged to the butcher family, enabling the easy hand-processing of carcasses. Luvidovich had taken the time to verify that Katya Gregorovich did not butcher her own meat, and then he had sent out a general query on other murders using knives. There were not many—in the days of stun weapons and laser cannons, they were almost never used for violent crime anymore. But Luvidovich had turned up seventeen knife murders over the last twelve years, and a total of eight performed with some variant of a butcher knife. All eight had occurred on Osaka Prime, which didn't surprise Greg at all, knowing the nature of the place; but he wondered what it would have meant to Luvidovich.

Greg rubbed his eyes, then left them closed, allowing his mind to drift. He would fetch Elena, and then they could return to Volhynia to finish the investigation. He thought about what he wanted to say to her. He'd have to yell at her for going AWOL first; she would expect that, and she wouldn't need to know about his own indiscretion. Then he would promise her they would help Zajec, and he'd keep that promise. And he would find out who had killed Danny and why, and then possibly promote Jessica Lockwood, for nothing more than making him laugh when the universe was falling down around him.

His mother had been like that, he remembered: when he was moody or upset, she would swoop in on him with gentle teasing and optimism, and restore his perspective. He wondered why Jess was in tech; she'd have made a wonderful counselor, or even a doctor. He pictured Jessica in a pale blue jacket, a civilian doctor's uniform, like Caroline. He had always wondered about Caroline going into medicine. She had always lacked empathy, and had never apologized for it. That was one thing they had in common: neither of them apologized. He found it most difficult when he was in the wrong. That was going to make it hard for him to fix things with Elena . . .

He was jerked awake by a proximity alarm. Annoyed with himself, he sat up and studied the readout. Something was approaching, its flight plan dangerously close. *Lusi*'s usual clear visuals were amorphous and incomplete, and he frowned. "Can we get out of the way?" he asked.

Lusitania paused, and Greg's heart sank. It was never good news when a ship paused. "Insufficient data," the ship told him.

"What do you mean, insufficient? What kind of a ship is it? What's its ident? What kind of a field is it generating? Make a fucking guess."

Another pause. "Possible dreadnought level shipping freighter," it said at last.

"Going that fast?"

"Field signature is a seventy-two percent match."

"Why the uncertainty?"

"Field signature is distorted. Telemetry is not on record. No ident."

"What do you mean, 'no ident'?"

"The ship is not broadcasting any identifying information."

What the fuck is this thing? "Where's it headed?"

Lusi rattled off familiar coordinates. It was headed for *Penumbra*.

"Do we have time to adjust the field?"

"No. Recommend dropping out."

Greg swore. "Try to keep a fix on it. Drop to sublight."

The field vanished, and Greg found himself hanging alone among the stars, no planets visible in any direction. "Regenerate and start up again, same destination," he said. It took just over three seconds for *Lusi* to restore the FTL field.

"Where's that ship?" he asked.

Lusi's response was instant. "Unidentified ship is still on course for *Penumbra*. She is now three minutes ahead of us, with her lead increasing."

He thought for a moment. "Hail her," he said at last, "but keep your ident to yourself unless it's requested."

There was a long pause. "No response," *Lusi* said at last.

Protocol stated he should keep hailing the ship, and report its presence to the nearest traffic control facility. In this case, that would be Volhynia. So much for protocol.

"*Lusi,* keep following that ship," he said. "If she drops out, we do, too."

"Acknowledged," *Lusi* said. Greg kept staring into the light of the FTL field, wondering what he was chasing.

Chapter 29

It was the weightlessness that woke Trey: the sudden, disorienting loss of body mass. But when he opened his eyes his senses were overwhelmed by the flashing orange and red lights in the cabin, and the wailing klaxon. Elena was already up, her hands finding protrusions in the wall to hold on to, hauling herself toward the pilot's console. Outside the window he saw not the steady blue of the field, but stars, spinning in a wobbly circle.

This was not a timed alarm. They had been thrown out of the FTL field, and they were spinning out of control.

He could not hear Elena's shouting over the alarm. He found the edge of one of the cabinets and pulled himself off the sofa, keeping his momentum slow and steady as he worked his way forward. On *Castelanna,* they trained frequently without gravity. Even so, he was amazed at what his body remembered.

Elena had pushed herself toward a panel under the console and had pried off the access circuit; he suspected she was trying to shut off the noise. Methodically he pulled up the ship's diagnostics. Basic systems were intact, but the field generator was completely blown, and even their sublight engine was damaged.

A quick look at the logs revealed they had been shoved out of the field by another ship, and he frowned. They were lucky to be alive, but who would have done such a thing? Not even Novanadyr PD would be that brutal, if they had been able to find them in the first place.

The alarm went silent, and mercifully the gravity reengaged. He told her quickly what he had found. "Local scans show nothing," he said. "They must have moved on."

She swore fluently. "That couldn't have been a coincidence," she said. "Nobody collides in-stream anymore. Someone shoved us out on purpose." She climbed into the copilot's seat and strapped on the harness, pulling up a mirror of his console. "What are the odds they'll politely leave us for dead?"

Trey had been reading in location data. "They may feel a follow-up is unnecessary." He met her eyes. "*M'laya,* we are in the radiation belt."

Her eyes widened, and then she went back to the console. "Ship, what's our interior radiation?"

"Ambient 2.8," the ship said pleasantly.

Trey frowned. "What about external?" he asked.

"Ambient 3.7."

"Something is wrong," he said, half to himself. He spun through the star charts. "*Sartre,* run a navigation diagnostic." He shook his head. "How can it be clean here?"

"We need Ilya," Elena said. "Isn't there some theory about EMPs and radiation?"

"On occasion, EMPs have been observed to neutralize radiation," he remembered.

"*Sartre,*" she said, "what's the official recorded radiation level at this location?"

There was a brief pause. "Ambient 13, critical 22.2."

She looked at him, and her dark eyes were grim. "I think someone has been falsifying the official numbers," she said. "How far are we from the wormhole?"

"Two hundred thousand kilometers," he told her. "We must be leeward of it. I'm not reading any—"

Far too close to them there was a flash, a light pattern Trey knew: a field closing down after an emerging ship. He set the ship's scanner on it, but the device kept spinning, confused.

"Where the hell is it?" Elena asked, looking at the same data.

"Location information is distorted," the ship said.

"How about a visual, then? Give me three sixty."

The ship projected a mocked-up three-dimensional view of themselves and the space it could detect around them—including, in the periphery, the swooping, conical gravity well of the wormhole. Elena plunged her fingers into the image, twisting it around like a puzzle, zooming in at anything that looked unusual.

"There!" He caught sight of it just for a moment, a large dark shape, rippling and distorted as if it were underwater. After a few seconds it disappeared again.

Elena went back to the ship's console. "Comms are down," she said tersely. "*Sartre,* how much maneuverability have we got?"

"Engines are at eighty percent power," the ship said. "Manual navigation only."

She unbuckled herself. "Have you got her?" she asked Trey.

"As much of her as there is to get." He pulled up the ship's thruster control. It made for crude steering, but it was better than nothing.

Elena got up and headed aft. "I might be able to pull apart the field generator," she suggested, opening up an access panel in the floor. "Maybe get us something we can vent at it."

Trey glanced at the holographic readout. The massive ship rippled into existence again; it was closer to them, matching its path to their rotation. He did not think there was much that would be effective against it, but he shared her need to try.

"We are being targeted," *Sartre* said cheerfully.

"Hang on to something," Trey called to Elena.

He waited until the cloaked ship let off a shot. It was a directed plasma stream, designed to open them up like a butchered animal. He watched it move closer and closer . . . and then he slammed the ship's thrusters on full. They leapt forward, angling out of the shot's trajectory, and he caught a glow of red in the holographic display.

"Heat damage to the ship's stern," *Sartre* said. "Rear observation disabled."

"How are you doing?" Trey asked.

"We've got almost no charge left," she replied, "but if you can buy me another twenty seconds, I can get us two good shots. Maybe we can take out her guns."

The ripple was coming around again. Trey tensed, wondering if she should have tried to fix their navigation first, and then he noticed something odd. The rotation of the stars out the window was changing. "*Sartre,* overlay a gravity map on the display."

He saw it then, the familiar cone shape, the characteristic parabola of a gravity well. It was a strong one, too, which did not surprise him, given its origin. "The wormhole is pulling us," he told her.

"Can we use it to accelerate away?" she asked him.

"I will try, but we will need to be careful."

"Why?"

She had heard it in his voice. "It is very strong," he told her.

"So are the guns on that monster out there."

"I am not certain which is the greater threat, Elena."

She made one last adjustment, then turned to look at the display. She swore again, and went back to the copilot's seat. "I don't think we have a choice," she said grimly.

The ripple was coming around again. Whatever was maneuvering it, pilot or computer, it had figured them out: it was matching the curvature of their path, angling to fire an intercept shot. Elena watched its trajectory, and glanced at Trey.

"They're not out of Novanadyr, are they?"

He shook his head.

"You fly," she told him. "I'll fire."

Chapter 30

U nidentified ship is dropping out of the field," *Lusi* said.

Greg frowned. They were still an hour away from *Penumbra*. "Where?"

Lusi rattled off coordinates, and his eyebrows went up. It had to be unmanned, then, and there was no way he could follow it there. "How long would your shields last against the radiation?"

There was a long pause, and immediately Greg became alert. "Specify parameters," *Lusi* said at last.

"The unidentified ship dropped out in the middle of the radiation belt," Greg said. "How long could your shielding protect me if we dropped out in the same place?"

Another pause. "Conflicting information," the ship said at last.

"Explain."

"Reported radiation levels are ambient 13. Detected radiation levels are ambient 2.7, fluctuating to 5.4 in the vicinity of B1829."

Greg knew which he was inclined to believe. "What's the source of the reported radiation levels?"

"Central Government push update received 2.7 hours ago."

He made a decision. "*Lusi,* drop out of the field on top of that ship."

"Recorded radiation levels are not compatible with survival."

"Acknowledged," he said. "Apologize to my crew if I accidentally kill myself."

The ship said nothing. They were still two minutes behind.

Chapter 31

She would have to wait for it to fire, Elena realized, taking the best aim she could. With the ship nothing more than a ripple circling them, any kind of guess would be a waste of the small amount of power they had. She set another filter on their holographic display; if it was a heat-seeker, she should be able to get an early look at its source. The question was whether or not the shot that gave her the aim would kill them.

Combat pissed her off. When she was fired on, she got cold and rigid, focused on stopping whatever was trying to kill her. Fear and distress came later, usually when everybody else was in the pub and she could hide in the gym or in her room and have a quiet meltdown. She had known many people who were better fighters than she was who froze during battle, or became so terrified they made bad decisions. She did not believe her re-action had anything to do with character. She thought of it as something physical, like her brown eyes.

Trey, it seemed, was similarly cool-headed, and she was grateful for it. As a general rule she did not care for other pilots; but his hand was steady, and he had demonstrated more than once that he strategized well. She kept her eyes on her readout, waiting for the flash, counting on him doing whatever was possible to evade their attacker.

The weapon fired without warning, and she aimed and shot. This time Trey throttled back and to starboard, letting inertia slow them down, but it would not be enough. The shot was getting closer, would tear them in half . . . and then the makeshift torpedo she had fired met the enemy's ammunition, and with a great flash both weapons exploded. Trey exclaimed something she did not understand, then said, "That was a prodigious shot, my dear."

She grinned. "Got lucky. Maybe in more ways than one. They're not firing heat-seekers. Can we utilize the gravity of the wormhole to pull his weapons off course?"

"I am not sure we'll have enough thrust to keep it from pulling *us* off course."

"It's a risk," she acknowledged. "But given our current trajectory, we might be able to skip off the edge."

"We would have to time it precisely."

She grinned. "I'm beginning to think I should have worked on the nav before the weapons."

"If you had, *m'laya,* we would already be dead." He glanced at the readout. "He is coming around again."

"Okay." She armed the weapon again. "Let me see if I can connect with him this time. Wait until the last possible second before you accelerate."

The cloaked ship fired from the other side this time, and she loosed her weapon at the same target. She watched hers approach the other ship, its missile approaching them . . . and just as Trey thrust them forward, her shot connected. There was a flash on the surface of the other ship, and large chunks of gray metal spun off in different directions. The ripples grew more frequent, and the ship came suddenly into sharp focus: she had hit its cloak.

And now she got a good look at it.

It was the size of a heavy freighter, of the sort that hauled terraformers and building materials, but its design was unmistakably military. She recognized the way the nose was narrowed, and the joinery used between the stern and the body of the ship. Like *Galileo,* it bore a resemblance to a great bird, and was likely sufficiently aerodynamic to fly in and out of atmosphere with some grace. Or it would have been, had she not just shot the hell out of its starboard wing.

There were no identifying marks on it at all.

"That is not one of ours," Trey told her.

"It's a Central design," she replied. "I'd bet my career on it. But I've never seen anything like it before. And a *cloak,* Trey. We don't have anything even close to that." *Or I thought we didn't.* Ellis Systems had been stringing the Corps along for years with their attempts at cloaking tech, and they'd had little to show for it beyond model after model of overheating reflector. She stared at the image of the ship, wondering how much of what she had been told by Central had any relationship to reality at all.

The gray bird pulled away, and she noted it also had some trouble tugging itself out of the wormhole's orbit. Their own trajectory was curving more dramatically, and she wondered how close they could get before the thing would simply swallow them.

Or if they would have the chance.

"That was our last shot, was it not?" Trey asked.

"Afraid so."

The ship was coming around again, this time giving them a wider berth, keeping itself as far away from the wormhole as possible.

"Can we skirt the gravity well?"

He was studying his instruments. "I do not know," he said at last. "The gravity field is fluctuating. If we do not get close enough, he will catch us, even with the damage he has taken. If we get too close . . ."

Her brain spent a few moments scrambling desperately for an alternative, but she came up with nothing. "All right then," she said. "I've always wanted to know what the inside of one of those things looks like."

He smiled at her, and it struck her then how much she had missed being side by side with someone who trusted her, someone she could trust in return. They would not survive this. There was no chance. But if they did . . . it was down to this man, whom a day ago she had not even known. She reached out a hand to him, and he took it . . .

And then another ship appeared between them and the gray bird.

Chapter 32

This is Captain Greg Foster of the CCSS *Galileo*. Your vehicle is unauthorized in this area. Stand down and identify yourself."

The other ship—almost certainly a Shadow Ops prototype—responded by firing.

So much for protocol.

Greg dodged the ship's first shot and fired at its remaining intact wing, wondering how Elena had done that kind of damage to the other side. His own shot caught the missile housing, but at best he had damaged their ability to aim. It occurred to him the ship might have been more vulnerable when cloaked.

It wasn't vulnerable now.

Greg tried to raise the other ship. "Chief? Elena, can you hear me?" There was no answer. He looked at the civilian ship's flight pattern. No auto nav, he guessed; someone was steering, crudely, with what was left of the ship's thrusters. The stern of the thing was a blackened wreck, but if she was being steered, someone in there was still alive. All he could do was give her a chance at getting away.

He opened up *Lusitania*'s substantial weapons banks on the S-O ship's intact wing, keeping himself between its guns and Elena. The other ship fired again, and he jerked the helm to one side. But either he was not as lucky this time, or the shot was packing substantially more tonnage than the earlier salvo. *Lusi*'s port side was caught, and a containment alarm sounded. A glance at the atmospheric sensor revealed a slow leak. It was easily reparable . . . if he found himself with five safe minutes to fix it.

"Keep on that S-O ship, and stay between it and the civilian ship," he told *Lusi*. He stood and moved to the rear storage locker, his eyes never leaving the tactical readout. *Lusi* kept up a steady barrage of fire, most of which bounced off the other ship's hull, as Greg blindly pulled a suit out of the locker and hauled it on over his uniform. He pulled the clear hood over his head and sealed it around his neck; an instant later he was inhaling the stale air of the suit's storage system. "Hit it on the damaged side," Greg told the ship, and *Lusi* came about.

The S-O ship was not interested in him anymore, it seemed, wasting no firepower going after him, instead dodging in an attempt to move around him. *Lusi* swooped ahead, still firing, and the ship let loose another cannon shot. This one caught *Lusi* broadside; there was a lurch, and the artificial gravity went off, and Greg realized he wasn't going to have to worry about containment after all.

"Stay between the ships!" he shouted, as he hand-over-hand pulled himself back to the pilot's seat and strapped in. *Lusi* was still firing, but the larger ship had figured out their strategy, and was keeping her intact bulkheads facing Greg. He would get in no more lucky shots.

He engaged the broad-spectrum comms. "Mayday, mayday, mayday," he said. "This is the transport *Lusitania,* off of CCSS *Galileo.* We are under attack by an unidentified ship. There is a civilian transport here that has been severely damaged. Casualties unknown. Enemy ship is still firing; we won't hold out. All ships in this area, please respond." He looped it, and opened comms to the civilian ship.

"If you can hear me, Elena, Zajec—get the hell out of here and tell someone what's going on. Safe money that's an S-O black ops ship, but firing on you is still an act of war, no matter how undercover they are." He thought for a moment. "Report it to Admiral Herrod. Keep yelling until they let you talk to him. He's an asshole, but he'll listen. Just get away."

He took control of the weapons from the ship. Firing was a futile gesture at this point, but he'd be damned if he'd go down meekly.

Chapter 33

T hat's *Lusi*," Elena said, dumbfounded.

"Who is Lusi?" Trey asked. He was adjusting the direction of their thrusters; the gravity well was proving more unpredictable than he had feared. If he did not know better, he would have suspected an intelligence in how the strength of the field grew every time they were on the verge of pulling away.

"Not who." Elena had unbuckled herself, and was making her way aft again. "*Lusitania*. She's *Galileo*'s main troop carrier."

"Why is she out here?"

"From the look of it," Elena said, "she's trying to save us."

Elena was right. The troop carrier was tenaciously keeping itself between the winged ship and their transport, despite taking at least two solid hits. Trey applied himself to the thrusters. Their savior had a better ship, but it would not last forever. "What are you doing?" he called to her.

"Trying to get one last shot out of this thing," she said. "Maybe distract that bird long enough for *Lusi* to get a decent shot."

"Is she strong enough?"

"No," Elena said tersely, "but he'll go for the bird's damaged side if he can get to it. That might be enough."

He. "You know who is flying."

"It's Greg."

Trey did not ask how she knew. "Elena, if you use the power from the thrusters, will you be able to get another shot?"

She paused. "We'll get pulled in if we do that."

"It is futile anyway," he told her. "We are too close. The only thing we could do to escape is blow ourselves up, which would be counterproductive." He turned to look back at her, and was surprised at the anguish in her face. "If we can save your captain, let us try."

He saw her swallow, and then she nodded. "If you disengage them from there," she told him, "I can pick them up from here."

He turned and swept his hand through the ship's navigational display; it disappeared, and immediately he saw the star field swoop and bank as they stopped resisting the wormhole's gravity. He moved out of his chair and crouched on the floor next to Elena. "Let me do the transfer," he suggested. "You are a better shot than I am."

She met his eyes, then nodded. "All you need to do," she said, showing him the readout, "is sever the safety on my mark. The alarms on this thing will bleat, so be prepared." She moved back to the front of the cabin, and he saw her pull up what was left of the ship's navigational display.

"Whenever you are ready," he told her.

"Just a few seconds . . ." She was watching their rotation, her hand over the firing mechanism. "Now."

He switched the line, and sure enough an orange light began flashing. He disabled it with one hand. "Go," he shouted.

Elena let off the shot, and he watched the explosive head toward the gray bird. Their front window spun so that the ship was invisible; all they had was the holographic readout, where their swan song was nothing but a tiny blip of light. He kept his eyes on the blip, noting peripherally that the light through the window was brightening; slowly the polarizer kicked in, and their rotation steadied.

They were heading nose-first into the wormhole.

"Come on," Elena whispered.

There was a flash on the readout, and the gray bird staggered.

"Direct hit!" she shouted, laughing.

Trey left their cobbled power system behind, and stood next to her. On the readout, he saw *Lusitania* firing at the bird, shooting at the ship's damaged side. The troop shuttle was still trying to shield them.

"He is a stubborn man."

"It will save his life." She glanced up at the window, and her expression grew serious. "Trey," she said, and held out her hand to him again.

Instead, he embraced her, pulling her against him, his eyes still on the window. He felt her arms go around his waist, felt her heart beating rapidly against his chest. It was, he had to admit, beautiful, all dancing color and snakes of white light, like the FTL field and yet wilder, more organic, more alive. He felt his stomach turn over, but he kept his eyes on it; if they survived this, if he made it home, he wanted to be able to tell Sarah what he had seen, what mysteries there were left in the universe, even for a man of his age.

He kissed the top of Elena's head. "I was never any good at physics," he remarked, and he felt her gasp with laughter.

"I'm pretty sure that doesn't matter now, my dear," she said.

He held the words close to his heart as the bright light swallowed them.

Chapter 34

The thing about rage, Greg's father had told him, *is that you have to do something with it. You have to use it. If you sit on it, if you swallow it, it will hollow you out, make you weak. But if you take it, focus it, let it focus you, it becomes useful. If you control the rage, it makes you strong.*

Greg watched the civilian shuttle disappear into the mouth of the wormhole, and let the rage wash over him.

"*Lusi,*" he said, "let's blow that motherfucker out of the sky."

They were still no match for it, of course, but he had a chance now, thanks to Elena. He had no doubt now that she was alive—that she had been alive. Who else would think to throw bits of an FTL field generator at an attacker? It was a crude weapon, and might have easily detonated before she blasted it out of her ship, but she had made it work. She had saved his life.

There was something else there, under the rage.

Lusitania focused all of her weapons systems on the S-O ship. With nothing left to protect, they were free to circle around to the ship's damaged side and chip away at it. They swooped close, focusing on the starboard engine, and with some concentrated fire it dropped off the ship and exploded. Their enemy was not incapacitated, but they sure as hell had slowed her down.

Where would the field generator be on a ship like that? He thought about all the ships he'd ever studied, thought about the prototype plans he had seen, all the top-secret stuff he was told was only theoretical. The field generators were usually protected, nestled adjacent to some sharp angle; but they needed to have external access, and a bird that size would need a big one.

Did you hear me? Did you at least know I came after you? That I didn't abandon you?

The starboard engine had gone with too much ease; he guessed the generator was nestled under the port wing. Ducking *Lusitania* under the other ship, he pivoted in flight and laid down targeted fire as they sped past. "Come on, you bastard," he muttered at it.

The other ship dipped its wing and reversed, dropping behind *Lusi*. Greg pivoted, but a shot caught his aft engine and he lost attitude control.

An alarm sounded. "System targeting unavailable," *Lusi* said.

He pulled up the manual controls and started firing, but most of his shots went wide. Taking his cue from Elena, he used his thrusters to even out his flight, but the other ship, damaged as it was, had quickly matched his trajectory, getting ready to fire . . .

. . . and then a massive blast hit the ruined starboard wing of the S-O ship. As Greg watched, a third ship rose above them, her hull burnished black, her lines half-familiar. She strafed the S-O ship as she passed over them, and Greg saw the ship's port weapons take another hit.

He came about again, aiming for the port wing. The S-O ship spun away from him, all the while firing on the newcomer, who was making some impressive evasive turns. Greg tumbled under them both, his shots ineffective.

"*Lusi,* comm the new ship," he said.

There was a pause. "Outgoing only," *Lusi* said.

That would have to do. He opened the connection. "The field generator is under the joint of the port side wing. I can't target anymore."

He turned again, firing futilely, attempting to draw the S-O ship's attention. Above him the newcomer sped and rolled, then stopped and inverted in place. She was firing before she moved forward, dashing at an angle toward his attacker, concentrating on the ship's port side.

With one final bright shot, the rear of the wing exploded with a telltale blue-white fire.

"Got you, you son of a bitch," Greg yelled.

His exultation was short-lived. There were alarms going off all around him. The internal oxygen was nearly gone, and he had almost no shielding left. He did not think he would last more than a minute or so; he could do more damage in that time, but unless the pilot was absurdly stupid he would be unlikely to get in a kill shot. But without a field the ship wasn't going anywhere. The newcomer might uncover what was going on, might figure out who the hell in Shadow Ops was willing to go this far, and for what.

But he would never know.

There was a lurch, and they started to yaw. "Did we lose nav?" he shouted over the alarms.

"No," *Lusi* told him. "We are in the gravity well of the wormhole."

The newcomer sped vertically out of his line of sight, then down again; she was looking for a way to get to him. He engaged the comm one last time. "Don't come after me," he told the other ship, "or you'll be trapped as well."

All the rage drained out of him. He took his hands off the controls, watching the spinning remains of the S-O ship out his front window. He had done what he could. He had done what was possible. It was not all he wished, but in that moment, he thought it would do. He thought he could be remembered like this, and it would be all right.

"*Lusi,* shut down the engines," he said.

And he fell.

PART III

CHAPTER 35

Galileo

Jessica had been six when her baby sister, too malnour-
ished to fight off a cold, had died, her breathing rattling
into silence in the night. She learned early she could never
count on her friends to live through Tengri's hideously long
rainy summers, and by her teens she had lost more aunts and
uncles than she could remember to the ravages of insufficient
resources. She had thought herself inured to death. Elena favored the idea that her polyamory was a result of choosing
not to bond with people, but to Jessica, it was precisely the
opposite. She loved too deeply to risk being alone, and this
was the Corps. People died.

Losing Danny had made her sad, and she had been irritated
with the strange possessiveness of the *Demeter* crew. Losing
Captain Foster made her angry.

Valentis had assembled the crew in the pub; still confined to
quarters, Jessica had to listen to his announcement over intraship comms. He had spoken with grief and sincerity, his voice
breaking in all the right places. Jessica wondered when she had
started hating his voice. But just when she thought she had heard
the worst of it, he had more to say:

"A few minutes ago, we received orders from Central Command, directing us to pursue the PSI starship *Penumbra,* responsible for the death of Captain Foster. Central has also ordered *Demeter, Constellation,* and *Abigail* to join us. We will spearhead the attack; they will rendezvous with us at *Penumbra*'s last known coordinates in eighteen hours, should reinforcements be required.

"I am sure the import of this is not lost on any of you. Central Command has declared *Penumbra*'s attack on *Demeter,* and her subsequent murder of Captain Foster, to be acts of war. Our mission is to take *Penumbra* and imprison her crew, or destroy her. We should arrive in six hours and seven minutes. All crews are on standby; all engineering staff are on shift until further notice. We will avenge our comrade. That is all."

He had taken a dramatic pause before his last words, and Jessica could not hear it as anything but artifice.

She sat in her overstuffed chair, watching the streaks of the field flit past her window. She should have gone with him. She should have told him not to go at all. She should have insisted Elena would be safe with her pirate, that he should come home and deal with it from here.

He would not have listened. And now Will Valentis was in charge, doing everything short of publicly salivating at the prospect of having his own ship.

She was in the process of detailing the promiscuity of every one of Valentis's ancestors when her door chimed. "Who the fuck is it?" she snapped.

"It's me, Jess. Open the door," Ted said, just as *Galileo* helpfully displayed *Lieutenant Shimada.*

"I can't open it. I'm confined to quarters."

But Ted had known her a long time. "Fuck that, Lockwood. Let me in."

"Do you have that little *Demeter* girl with you?"

"What do you take me for?"

She opened the door. Ted stepped inside, and she regretted making him wait. His face was drawn and anguished; she thought he had been crying. Immediately she softened her body language. "Aw, Ted. Maybe you *should* go find your girlfriend."

"After what she was saying about the captain?" He began pacing back and forth in front of her.

"Valentis is captain now."

"Fuck that, too," he said. "No way Central is going to let him keep this ship." He stopped and stared down at her, furious. "I think he's lying. Don't you think he's lying, Jess? He's always wanted this ship."

"Come on, Ted." Strangely, his paranoia was deflating her. "You can't lie about a guy being dead. It comes out if you do that."

"Well, then, it's bullshit about PSI," he declared. "That shit doesn't make any sense anyway. It didn't make any sense when Enkha said it, and it doesn't make any more sense from Valentis. He just wants to fucking *shoot* at somebody."

"*I* want to fucking shoot at somebody," she told him.

He glared at her, speechless, then dropped into the chair across from her, his rage vanishing. "Elena is going to dissolve," he said.

Jessica closed her eyes. "We're all going to dissolve, Teddy. What's this ship without that man? I mean, sure, he was an arrogant, single-minded son of a bitch sometimes, but he was ours, you know? And usually he did the right thing."

"Seemed that way to me," he agreed; then she heard him shift in his chair. "Jess . . . were you guys sleeping together?"

Jessica opened her eyes. "Valentis is telling everyone that, isn't he?"

"Well, sleep specifically was not mentioned, but yeah."

She considered detailing all of the reasons why it would be impossible, but settled on, "It's bullshit."

"I thought so," he said, but looked relieved.

She was curious. "Why?"

"Because he doesn't do that," Ted said simply, relating a universal truth.

She thought of that lost, hollow look in Greg Foster's eyes, and felt her throat tighten. "He should have said something to her," she said, half to herself. "Don't you think?"

"He was better off keeping his mouth shut. He was going after her, though, wasn't he?"

Jessica nodded. And then she sat up straight. "Not just him, either." She jumped to her feet. "*Galileo,* show Ted the telemetry data on that Fender."

Ted blinked as the schematic appeared before his eyes. "You want to explain how you did that when you're in lockdown?"

"No, I don't. Ted, can you make anything of that?"

He looked again, this time with a more critical eye. "What am I looking at?"

"You tell me."

He shot her a look. "Looks a lot like a Fender class cruiser getting swallowed by a whale."

"That," she told him, "is our missing Volhynian chief of police."

"You have lost me."

She told him of Stoya's background, and of Treiko Zajec's history. Much to her frustration, though, he kept shaking his head. "This is all fascinating, Jess, but it doesn't mean anything. It's a bunch of gossip and old crimes. What does this have to do with the captain? Or even Danny, for that matter? You're looking for connections that aren't there."

Jessica clenched her fists in frustration. "The connections are somewhere, Ted. I know it. Otherwise none of it makes sense. The captain gave me some grave speech about how we don't know PSI, they've avoided us, they have their own agenda, that sort of bullshit; but I think he was just trying to be cautious. Seriously, Ted, it's been more than eighty years since we shot at each other, and even then, depending on who tells the story, it was either a diplomatic incident or a couple of stupid kids not wanting to admit they were wrong." A thought occurred to her. "*Galileo,* show me Captain Foster's mail."

A list of names sprang up before her eyes: hundreds of messages, all from the last twelve hours. She didn't bother scanning them. "Weed out the dross," she said.

Ted moved to stand next to her. "You are hacking the captain's mail," he observed.

"Since he's dead," she corrected, "I'm hacking official Corps documentation."

"You are going to get court-martialed."

"That's a distinct possibility," she agreed. "But in this case, I have permission. The captain told me to check out those anonymous messages." The filter had left fewer than eighty messages, most of them back and forth with the Admiralty. The most recent one had been sent shortly before he announced Danny's death.

Request permission to access all of Commander Valentis's records on his investigation for Shadow Ops, due to the proximity of the deceased officer to the suspect Demeter crew and the potential involvement of PSI with the killing. We all know the local officials do not have all the facts. Commander Valentis's investigation has had a direct and deadly impact on my ship and my crew. Prompt and just resolution is required if we are to continue to operate at peak efficiency.

Their reply had been prompt, terse, and negative.

"What fucking investigation?" Ted asked.

Taking Ted's expletive as a request, *Galileo* brought up the six reports Valentis had sent since they had last left Earth. Jessica had been over them more than once, and had long since stopped feeling outrage. Ted was properly shocked by it all.

"He's been reporting on us," he said.

"He has," she confirmed.

"You knew this."

She nodded. "The captain pulled me into it five months ago, when it started, although at first it was just decoding the redacted parts and validating where they went. Later he had me dogging Valentis's footsteps. There's nothing to these reports, Ted. They're busywork. Distractions for the captain. Maybe even for Valentis. They're a cover for something else."

"How can you be sure?"

"He gave the captain these reports," she pointed out, "but there's nothing else. No log entries, no meetings, nothing. What does that tell you?"

"Shadow Ops is nothing but a bunch of bureaucrats playing spy games." Ted scoffed. "When was the last time anything significant came out of there? Hell, Ellis *left* the Corps so he could get out from under them and start his own company."

Jessica thought of the founder of the terraforming company, and how quickly he had managed to push his prototypes into the mainstream market. "Or maybe he didn't," she suggested. "Maybe Shadow Ops likes looking impotent. Get themselves a couple of corporate guys as beards, anything real they do looks like independent economic bullshit. And who in this mess we're in is the biggest enemy of independent economic bullshit?"

Ted frowned. "I don't like your imagination, Jess."

"Me neither. Will you hate my guts if I read his personal logs?"

"Not if you let me listen in."

Foster had not been a frequent diarist. His most recent entry was a week old, and it was short. Jessica played the audio.

"Personal log, 3215.23 . . . 24 . . . what the fuck is the date? *Galileo,* time stamp this thing for me when I'm done. Had another message today. 'Why didn't anyone look for the flight recorder?' Just like the others, it sounds like bullshit, except when I look closer it makes me wonder. And it means that whoever is sending these knows the *Phoenix* took her flight recorder down with her. Someone playing with my head again. I'd suspect Will, but he knows me well enough to recognize that I can go insane without additional help."

There was a pause; the sound of ice against glass, the sound of Foster swallowing. "It's bullshit, and I should stop listening. I wouldn't be listening at all if we weren't going to be there. I never should have approved Will's request to divert for *Demeter,* but maybe he'll forget what a prick I've been lately. I'll visit the site. I should have before. Whatever else she was, she was my mother. She was Corps. I owe her. Elena will fly me. She may be angry with me . . . but she knows I have to go, and I can't go alone. Maybe, on the way, we can ease up on each other a little." More ice clinking. "Fuck. I don't know why I do these things. They don't fucking help."

The recording ended. Jessica wished she had pulled up a transcript instead.

"Wait," Ted said, oblivious to her reaction. "They don't have the *Phoenix*'s flight recorder?"

"No," Jessica said. "Foster told me earlier." She didn't want to talk about the *Phoenix*. All she could see in her mind was her captain, elbows on his desk, no company but his diary and far too much scotch. That was how the man had chosen to live. She could not agree with Ted. Foster should have grown a spine and told Elena his feelings years ago. This was bullshit, and now he was dead, and it was pissing her off.

But Ted was clearly bothered by something else. "Nobody ever said that," he told her. He stood, and started pacing, agitated. "When she went down—I was ten. I remember where I was when I heard. My dad was making toast for breakfast, and I was doing some preteen bullshit thing about how my old man had no imagination, and my mom came in and played the announcement off the stream. Four hundred and fifty-six people. They told us it was engine failure. They *said* that, Jess, I remember."

"I remember, too, Ted." She had still been on Tengri. Corps starships and their exploits had been the stuff of science fiction to her, but she had sensed the deep sadness among the adults.

He would not let it go. "Why doesn't this bother you more?"

"It does bother me. I just—I'm pissed off, Ted, and maybe I don't have the capacity to be pissed off about everything right now."

"What other messages did he get?"

She had been planning to look at them. She had been thinking about crypto hacks to try, how to break the code in small pieces, to acquire bits of data if she could not translate the large ones, but she'd had no time to try anything. "Pull up the anonymous messages," she said.

All of Foster's messages disappeared but four. The first had been sent twelve days earlier, just before they had docked at Aleph Nine, and it read like a cheap fortune teller's prediction:

Incomplete information is worse than no information at all.

He had opened it once, and had marked it for deletion without actually throwing it away. The second message, which he had quoted in his log entry, had arrived just a week ago. The third message was stamped yesterday:

What is the half-life of the radiation produced by the destruction of a hybrid nuclear starlight engine?

Ted read it, and frowned.

"Is this suggesting the radiation is due to more than the *Phoenix*?" he asked.

"Wait," she said, and opened the last one.

You don't believe that boy was killed over curiosity, do you?

Ted started pacing again. Jessica pulled up the message's ident. She could tell by skimming it had been counterfeited; it was clean for validation, but the auth code was gibberish. Well-formatted gibberish, though, designed to pass seamlessly through all of Central's top-level checks. "Someone has friends in high places," she mumbled, and started to pull the ident into tokens.

"What are you doing?" Ted asked her.

"I'm doing a traceback," she replied. "Like the captain told me to."

"I think you're missing the big picture here, Jess," he began, but she interrupted him.

"I am missing fucking nothing, Shimada," she said. "What have we got?"

"We've got Lancaster nosing around something with Valentis; we've got Valentis and MacBride cozying up to Shadow Ops; we've got PSI . . . doing something; we've got—"

"What do we have that's concrete? That we can prove?" She stopped her work long enough to glare at him. "We have a bunch of fucking hearsay, that's what we have. And four messages with the same bogus, anonymous ident, all addressed to our mysteriously dead captain, and all about the *Phoenix*. I deal with data, Ted," she said shortly, returning her eyes to the screen. "This is all the data I have, and I'm going to dissect it until it tells me something I can use."

She felt Ted staring at her, but she would not meet his eyes. He was softhearted, and she thought if she looked any longer at the pain on his face she would fall apart.

"Okay," he said at last. "I can pick up the investigation on Danny. I've got to be on duty, but I can snoop from engineering.

Maybe we can figure out why all of this seems to point toward the *Phoenix*."

She stilled her hands. "He knew it," she said quietly, her chest tight. "Foster. He knew it was all connected, but he didn't trust himself. Do you know people sent him bullshit conspiracy messages about the *Phoenix* every year? Since he was a kid? All this time, we sort of rolled our eyes when he got out of sorts around the anniversary, and there are people out there who deliberately fucked with his head. This kid who lost his mother." She shook her head. "He might have trusted himself if they hadn't. I'd like to find every one of those motherfuckers and rip their lungs out through their ribs."

Ted flashed her a smile, a shadow of his old self. "I'm glad you love me, Jess," he said.

"Get the fuck out, Teddy."

She had lost herself in her work before he was out of the room.

CHAPTER 36

Elsewhere

Elena did not know how long they were inside the worm-hole. Whether it was adrenaline or some artifact of the object itself, she had no sense of time passing. She felt Trey's arms around her, and his sturdy form against her body as she held on to him. She could feel a pounding—her heart or his, she did not know—but her ears were full of a strange, soundless thunder that swallowed all the noises around her, and when she tried to speak she felt as if her lungs were out of air.

They seemed to be plunging through a tunnel, although it was nothing like any tunnel she had ever seen. It was too wide and too narrow for them; it twisted and turned and folded in on itself with mathematical impossibility. They were moving in and out of it, and shaping it at the same time; it thrashed and grabbed at them like a living thing. Occasionally parts of it split off, like great capillaries. Once she thought she saw stars at the end of a branch, and she wondered if there were different destinations. If they could learn to navigate something like this, it might take them anywhere. The longer she stared at it, the more she was certain that somehow it made sense, that if she stopped thinking and let her mind open, she would understand, would be able to explain it, would know what it was . . .

And then abruptly they were back in normal space, and she could hear Trey's heartbeat and *Sartre*'s alarms and the whining of their damaged mechanical systems. She could see the wormhole, a glowing dot growing smaller as they spun away from it; and as they pitched and yawed, the bright green-gray of a planet was flanked by the glow of a yellow sun.

They let go of each other, Trey sitting back in the pilot's seat to pull up the instruments again. He used their thrusters to still the ship, leaving them hovering over the huge rock below. They were over the planet's dark side, the sun's corona visible over the horizon. The planet itself was featureless from this height; ice, she supposed, or cloud cover. At first blush it appeared to be the sort of planet Central explorers would dismiss as too inhospitable for terraforming.

"Do you know it?" Trey asked her.

She shook her head. She knew the Fourth Sector cold, and parts of the others, but she had heard of no planets spinning under the watchful eye of a wormhole. "Let's see if we can figure out where we are."

Trey assessed the engines and the nav while Elena took a closer look at the ship's computer and sensory systems. The vocal interface was off-line, but much to her surprise the core appeared to be intact. Beyond their field generator and their flight controls, the damage they had taken seemed relatively light. They had no fine sensors, and the power system would support nothing more than the anemic emergency lights; but they still had atmosphere, and heat, and sufficient insulation from the vacuum outside. "Whoever built this thing saved our lives," she said, and she heard Trey laugh.

"I cannot imagine they thought of making it wormhole-proof," he said. "Can you get sensors?"

"I think so. Crude ones, at least."

"Navigation may be reparable," he told her. "And our stellar collectors are intact. We may not have a field, but we will be able to move. Perhaps head back through."

She said nothing to that. Part of her never wanted to get near that thing again. Part of her longed for it. Mostly she wanted to stay very still, and breathe, and figure out where the hell they were.

The ship's voice feedback was down, but the text display was working, and she sat back, relieved, feeling like she wasn't blind anymore.

"*Sartre,* where are we?"

Nothing. She frowned.

"*Sartre,* can you hear me?"

Instantly, the ship displayed *Yes*.

"Can you tell me where we are?"

Silence again. She checked the comms activity; it was calling out to the stream, trying to connect to a data source, and finding nothing.

Suddenly she felt blind again.

"*Sartre,* consult your internal star charts and see if anything around here looks at all familiar."

She watched as the ship spun through its stored maps. *No matches,* it said at last.

Nothing? "Anything recognizable at all?"

No.

"How far are you scanning? How far out can you match?"

Fourteen million light years.

"You're telling me that in fourteen million light years, there are no astronomical objects that you recognize, even partially."

That is correct.

She felt Trey watching her, and she looked over at him, expecting to see dread, or anger. Instead, he was smiling, that familiar kindness in his eyes. "We seem to be a long way from home," he remarked. "But we are alive, *m'laya*. That is not a bad place to begin."

A light began to flash on Elena's sensor display. "What is it?" she asked.

An object has appeared. Current trajectory will take it within five kilometers of our location.

"Can you get a visual?"

Not from this orientation.

Trey spun them 180 degrees, and they saw it: approaching from the wormhole, with alarming speed, was the gray bird.

Or rather, she realized after a moment of panic, the remains of the gray bird. Its wings were gone, and the light emanating from its stern was fire rather than a working engine. The exterior was scarred and burned, and huge chunks of metal sheeting had been sheared off. It was possible the pilot was alive somewhere in that mess, but if he was, he was not in control of the ship's movements. It tumbled over and over, skimming past them close enough to make Elena flinch; and then it plummeted toward the planet. She saw a glow as it hit the atmosphere, saw the glow flare, and then it vanished.

"What happened to it?" she asked.

The ship paused before answering. *Insufficient data,* it said at last.

"Explain."

The planet is producing radiation. I cannot read into the radiation field.

She glanced over at Trey. "How much radiation?"

Radiation at the stratosphere is 5.9 ambient, 6.2 critical.

"What's the radiation out here?"

Radiation at this location is 4.4 ambient, 5.4 critical.

She swore; her brain had gone slow. She should have asked that first. "How long can your shielding last?"

Seven hours, eight minutes, twenty-three seconds before internal radiation becomes damaging.

"We need to get away from that planet," she said, and Trey nodded. "*Sartre,*" she asked, "how far away can we get in seven hours, eight minutes, and twenty-three seconds?"

Insufficient momentum to evade radioactive damage. Power supply required.

"We should see what we can read from the wormhole," he said, turning them away from the planet. "Without our attacker on the other side, it may be just as simple as going back through."

The light flashed again, and Elena cursed. She knew, this time, what it was.

"It got him, too," she said.

They watched as *Lusitania* came drifting toward them.

Elena kept her eyes on *Lusitania* as Trey guided them closer to the troop ship. *Lusi* was adrift, neither under power nor on fire, and the cabin appeared intact; but she was moving more slowly than the gray bird, tumbling out of control. Elena had to resist the urge to shove Trey out of the way and gun their own damaged engines. They needed to stop *Lusi*'s free fall before she hit the planet's atmosphere and was swallowed as well.

She remembered the moment Jake died, swept from the universe as if he had never existed. She had learned to live with the hollow wound he had left, but she never deceived herself that she was not still bleeding. Greg had to be all right. There was not enough of her left to keep going if he was not all right.

"Can we dock with her?" Trey asked her.

His steady voice drew her out of her panic. "Yes. I think so. There's an access panel in her hull. As long as our door didn't get completely clobbered, we should be able to get a hard seal between the ships."

He nodded, and kept his eyes on the window, steering as much by sight as by instruments. She got to her feet and went to the ship's door, methodically checking the locking mechanism. Everything tested green, each joint moving smoothly and easily, and she sent another silent thank you to the owner's willingness to buy quality. The faster transport they had left in Novanadyr would have been pulled apart by the wormhole, if it had managed to survive the dogfight in the first place.

With a few judicious nudges Trey matched *Lusitania*'s rotation, and they began spiraling closer to her. Elena engaged the interior magnetic locks that would compensate for any small inaccuracies in their position; after a moment the locks blinked, indicating a handshake with *Lusi*'s docking system. Leaving the ships to handle the final contact, she turned to the closet in the back of the cabin and pulled out two emergency suits. Draping one over the seat next to Trey, she climbed into the other, pulling it hurriedly over her clothes.

"Do we have any readings over there?" she asked.

"One moment," he said. With a quiet *snick,* the two ships locked together, and he pulled up *Sartre*'s crude sensors. "No gravity," he told her. "Oxygen density is sufficient for life support, but low. There is a slow leak."

She pulled the clear hood over her head and ran her fingers over the seal at her neck. Her fingers were shaking; she tried twice before Trey stood and put his hands over hers. "Let me," he said gently.

She took a deep breath and dropped her hands. Quickly and expertly he zipped the seal closed, then reached for the other suit. When he pulled his hood on she returned the favor, her hands steadier. *Safety first,* her trainers at Central Military Academy had always said. *You can't rescue anyone else if you are suffocating.*

Greg had air. She had time.

Trey handed her the medkit from the bathroom, and pulled a small leak repair kit from the cabinet next to the wardrobe. Elena opened the inner door, exposing *Lusitania*'s belly, and with a few practiced twists, had the access panel open.

There was a rush as air flooded from their ship to *Lusitania.* Elena took a hesitant step through the doorway, gripping the handholds beside *Lusi*'s door as she stepped out of their artificial gravity field. *Lusi*'s access panel was in her floor, and it took Elena a moment to orient herself to seeing the ship sideways. She looked toward the pilot's seat.

He was strapped into the seat, wearing a suit, facing away from her toward the ship's front window. She pushed toward him, her heart pounding. He should have heard them come in. He should have said something.

She came around and saw his face. His eyes were wide open, their mottled depths reflecting the gray planet, and for a black, bottomless instant she thought he was dead. Then he blinked, slowly, and she recognized disorientation. "What's the oxygen in here?" she asked Trey.

"Ninety-six percent and rising," he told her. He pushed across to the front corner of the cabin and stabilized himself, opening up the repair kit.

She pinched the seal at Greg's neck and yanked the hood off his head. "Greg?" she said.

He blinked again, and shook his head. "What—" he breathed.

"Greg." She activated the scanner and started with his head. No concussion, no measurable brain damage.

"How is he?" Trey asked.

"Conscious," she said tersely. She set the scanner aside carefully. "Greg, can you hear me?"

This time he seemed to focus. He met her eyes, frowning, confused; and then she saw him recognize her. His eyes lightened, and he smiled, and for one moment she was thrown back six months, looking into the face of the man she knew. "Elena," he said, full of wonder. "Did you see it?"

She knew what he meant. He had fallen through that great, flashing living thing as well. "I did," she replied gently. "Are you all right, Greg?"

His eyes shifted to the window, and then over to Trey, before they returned to her face. "A little startled to be alive," he said. "Where are we?"

"Just outside the wormhole," Trey told him. "Our ships are docked. We are unable to establish our location."

"Unable—" He turned back to Trey, frowning. "I remember taking *Lusi* after you. I remember . . ." His eyes widened. "There was another ship."

"It came through before you did," Elena told him. "It crashed on that planet."

He shook his head. "Not that one." His eyes focused on Trey's. "It was *Penumbra*."

Trey's expression froze. "Did they take damage?" he asked.

"I don't know," Greg said quietly. "They were hit, but I didn't have incoming comms. It didn't seem to affect their maneuverability, or their weapons. *Penumbra*'s the one who shot down that bird," he told them. "Saved my life."

It was on the tip of her tongue to ask if that was enough to convince him MacBride was full of shit, but there were more important issues to deal with.

"That planet is radioactive, Greg," she explained. "We need to get away from here."

He looked back at her, still puzzled. He was not yet quite himself, she realized; he still looked pleased to see her. She felt a flicker of worry, and of annoyance; but he was alive, and mostly himself, and soon enough everything would be the way it was.

And then maybe she could get some answers.

"We have gravity over there," she told him. "Come on."

He fumbled with the harness, and in the end she had to pull it off for him, gripping his arm as she untangled the straps from his limbs. He braced his hand against the floor and slowly walked himself hand-over-hand toward the hatch. By the time he got there he had remembered his training; he swung himself through legs first, his feet steadily on the ground by the time he transferred the rest of his body weight into the gravity field. She floated behind him as he stood, his hand still gripping the edge of the little ship's doorway, and she resisted the urge to hold out an arm to steady him.

Trey drifted next to her. "If you would like to look after him," he said, his voice low, "I will finish sealing the oxygen leak, and see how her systems are running."

She raised her eyebrows at him. "You can triage a Corps troop ship?"

He raised his eyebrows back, looking amused. "I am familiar enough with this model, *m'laya*. I would not attempt to transfer any of the power systems without your assistance, of course, but I can evaluate how badly she is damaged." He laid a hand on her arm and lowered his voice. "Elena, my dear, he is alive. Whatever he says to you, remember that you are happy about that."

Her face warmed; he could read her so well. She put her hand over his and squeezed his fingers. "I won't kill him until you come back," she promised; and as she had hoped, he shot her a grin before turning away to leave her alone with her captain.

She followed Greg in, pulling off her hood as her feet touched the ground and stripping off the safety suit. Layers bothered her; she always felt too hot and too confined. She felt Greg's eyes on her as she carefully folded the suit, replacing it in the closet where she had found it.

"You're out of uniform, chief," he said.

Well, he had come back to himself quickly enough. "Yes, sir," she said simply. She turned around to face him, arms folded, waiting. He was scowling at her.

"You care to explain yourself?"

"Could you be more specific?"

He snapped. "Fuck *that*, Elena. You broke a criminal out of prison, stole a ship, and ran for PSI? And what the fuck happened to your comm unit? I report you AWOL and your career is *done*, do you get that?"

She did. But what she didn't get was why he thought that mattered now. "Why wouldn't you help him?"

"What the fuck do you think I'm doing here?"

"I don't know!" Months and months of shouting at her, and she was tired of it. "I don't know anything, Greg. I don't know why you didn't tell me why we took *Demeter*'s cargo, or what really happened with *Penumbra,* or why Danny was digging into the *Phoenix.* I don't know why you sent me down there to move Trey from their prison to our prison when you *know* he didn't have anything to do with any of this. I don't know why you have been lying to me and shutting me out for six months!"

"I haven't lied about anything."

"Bullshit, Greg. Don't play me for a fool, and don't talk to me like I'm some fucking *subordinate,* because we are hell and gone the middle of nowhere, and I am done playing the good soldier."

His expression darkened, and for a moment she thought he was going to shout again; but then he turned away from her, his gloved hands coming up to rub his face. He looked down at himself; he was still in his safety suit. Irritably he pulled down the zipper and tugged it off, tossing it on the couch where she and Trey had been sleeping. He sat down on the other sofa and looked up at her, his eyes bleary. She wondered if he had had as little sleep as she had.

"Did either one of you have anything to do with that cop getting killed?"

She frowned. Who was he talking about? "What cop? Who's dead?"

"They found Luvidovich lying on the floor of the cell you left him in," he said.

He was watching her face closely, but she had no lies to betray. "I didn't think I'd hit him that hard," she said faintly. Killing a police officer, even in self-defense, was going to complicate the situation.

"It wasn't the hit that killed him," Greg told her. "His throat was cut. Just like Danny's."

She stared at him for one long moment, adding that piece of information to her stack of mismatched puzzle pieces, then turned and headed back to *Lusi* to fetch Trey.

CHAPTER 37

Galileo

Jessica was a superlative cryptographer, and this god-damned message header was bullshit.

The captain had told her it was Admiralty, but Jessica thought he was wrong. It was official, certainly; she knew enough of Corps crypto techniques to recognize the telltales. But it didn't use any of the official conventions, and without some kind of Rosetta stone, she was shooting in the dark. It was almost as if the sender had come up with a completely different language. She knew a handful of cryptographers with that kind of skill, but she was only on speaking terms with a few of them. With the ship on battle alert, she'd never get clearance to comm anyone anyway.

Not that it would help. She lay down on the bed and looked at the ceiling, letting the glyphs and equations fade from her mind. She wasn't going to find the sender; she wasn't even going to find the origin. Without Foster's access, she wouldn't even have been able to read them. This guy was really good.

And he hadn't become really good overnight.

"*Galileo*," she said, "have you seen this kind of crypto code before?"

"Specify parameters," it said.

"You should know what I'm thinking, not what I'm saying," Jessica grumbled, but it was a fair question. "Okay, how about this. This is a weird ident, yeah?"

"The referenced ident is comprised of cryptographic techniques not in wide use," the ship agreed.

"So have you seen anything similarly unusual?" Before the ship could ask for clarification, she added, "Not identical—although, yeah, that, too—but the same kind of not widely used technique?"

"Specify time frame."

"God, *Galileo,* you're only seven. Search your whole history. Knock yourself out."

At least the ship understood slang. "Seventy-nine matches found," it said.

Holy cats. "Seriously?"

"Seventy-nine matches found," the ship repeated helpfully.

"How many recipients?"

"Four."

"Specify, you stubborn thing."

"Gregory Foster. Robert Hastings. Anton Jacobs. William Valentis."

All senior officers—and two deceased. In spite of herself, she shivered.

Her thoughts were interrupted by a chime at the door. She sat up and swept her work aside just as Galileo displayed *Captain Valentis.*

"Well, this can't be good," she said to herself. She stood and came to attention, facing the door. "Let him in."

Valentis stepped into the room, and the door closed behind

him. "At ease," he said. His eyes ran over the walls, the table, her chairs, and finally rested on her. "I've come to see how you're doing, Lieutenant."

Well, *that* was flat-out bullshit. "As well as can be expected, sir." If it had been anyone else, she would have asked the same question in return; but she already knew this was not that kind of a visit.

He clasped his hands behind his back and walked up to her window. "Yes," he said. "We're all pretty shaken by this. Probably not the best time for us to be going into battle, but I suppose it can't be helped."

Damned if he didn't sound regretful. "Is it inevitable, do you think, sir?" she asked. Maybe he could give her some hope. "Going to war?"

"War is a frightening prospect. Nobody wants it. But it's our job out here to protect people, to keep the peace. It's possible *Penumbra*'s a rogue, and we're not challenging all of PSI. But they've taken out two of our people already, and—"

"Two?"

His eyebrows twitched, and she regretted the interruption. "They murdered our captain, Jessica. Between that and what was done to *Demeter*, it seems clear that pirate on Volhynia murdered Lancaster."

"What about the chief, sir?"

He arranged his face into something plausibly sympathetic. "She may not have known," he allowed, "but that's going to be for a military court to decide. We can't help her unless she turns herself in."

"Does she even know she's in trouble?"

At that he looked irritated, and she realized, once again, how little patience he had. "Unless you think she's a fool, Lieutenant Lockwood, Commander Shaw is quite aware of the consequences of her actions. Do you think she's a fool?"

Jessica straightened and looked ahead. "No, sir."

For the moment that seemed to mollify him. He began pacing in front of her, slowly, like a university lecturer. She had seen Captain Foster do it hundreds of times; Valentis looked like a spidery mimic. "I admire your loyalty to your friend, I truly do," he said. "But I'm asking you to remember your loyalty to *Galileo,* and to the Corps. I know you don't care for me. You're hardly the only one." He managed a self-deprecating smile. "But I'm in command now. It wasn't my choice, but that's where we are. And I need to know you'll work with me moving forward."

He sounded flinty, tense, like a rubber band ready to snap. Which was understandable, given what he had been through. She suspected she was a little close to the edge herself. But that wasn't what bothered her.

What bothered her was that he was lying.

She was not sure if it was what he was telling her, or simply his pretense of sympathy, but something in what he was saying was completely and utterly wrong in a way that made her hair stand on end. "I understand, sir," she said, as professionally as she could. "I'm sorry I've disappointed you, sir."

He fixed her with those eyes of his, so dark they were nearly black. Lanie had dark eyes, too, but hers were always filled with light. Even when she was unhappy—even in the depths of her grief over Anton Jacobs—Lanie's eyes held warmth and love. Valentis's eyes were empty. "I believe you, Jessica," he replied.

"And I'm willing to start over with you. I need everyone on this mission. I need to know you are on our side."

She swallowed. "Of course I'm on our side, sir," she said.

"I'm glad to hear that. I'm lifting your restrictions for the duration of this mission. We can revisit the incident when all of this is done." He reached out and touched her arm. "If we can get along for the next few weeks, I may not have to report this at all."

It was everything she could do not to rip her arm out from under his hand. She took a moment to steady her breathing before she replied. "I appreciate what you're doing for me, sir. Thank you, sir."

She stood stock-still and measured the time in heartbeats. After far too many, he took his hand off of her, and the oxygen returned to the room. He glanced around as he turned to go. "You've done nice things with your quarters, Lieutenant," he remarked. "Very attractive. Very feminine. I bet not a lot of people know that about you." He shot her a cold smile. "We'll talk again after we stand down."

He left the room.

More than anything in that moment Jessica wanted a shower. Instead, she stepped out of her quarters and looked up and down the hall to make sure Valentis was gone. With everyone at battle readiness the halls were nearly empty. She left her room behind and headed for the infirmary, sending a message to Ted while she walked. When he answered, she said, "Can you get away?"

"I don't know." Ted sounded irritable. "Valentis put Limonov in charge. *Limonov.* Never mind the crazy stuff; that man hasn't touched a starlight drive in fifteen years, minimum, and *he's* telling *me* what to do?"

"Not relevant at the moment, Ted."

"*Not relevant?* If Lanie were here, she'd be kicking his ass right out the door."

If Lanie were here, Jessica thought, *she'd be organizing a mutiny against William Valentis.*

"Listen," Ted was saying. "I dug up a couple of things on—"

"Not over a comm, Ted." Her caution was probably misplaced, but she didn't want him saying anything in front of the *Demeter* crowd in engineering, either. "I need you to meet me in the infirmary. I just had a seriously creepy chat with Valentis. It wouldn't surprise me if he's monitoring everything I do."

"He can't do that. He doesn't have that kind of crypto skill."

"He doesn't have to," she pointed out. "He just needs to know someone who does. He's not stupid, Ted. He's very not stupid. Also," she added, the thought finally surfacing, "I'm not so sure he's really following orders."

Ted paused. "I'll tell Limonov I've got, I don't know, motion sickness or something," he said at last. "He'll want me to get it checked before we reach *Penumbra*. I'll meet you there." He ended the connection, and Jessica broke into a run.

CHAPTER 38

Elsewhere

He should not have been surprised at Luvidovich's death.

Trey sat on the couch opposite Foster as Elena's captain told them what they had left behind on Volhynia. Elena paced between them, peppering Foster with questions and filling him in on their escape and eventual ambush. Trey tuned most of it out. He felt no need for clarification; it was easy enough, once Foster related Stoya's history, to piece together what had happened. Luvidovich had amassed enough circumstantial evidence to credibly accuse Stoya of Lancaster's murder. Killing Luvidovich made sense in that context; Stoya was both covering his tracks and reinforcing public perception of Trey's guilt. What Trey could not figure out was why Stoya would have killed Lancaster to begin with.

He felt robbed.

Despite Elena's ministrations, his shoulder ached where Luvidovich had stabbed him, and the smaller cuts across the rest of his body sent faint signals of pain every time he shifted. He had bruises on his face from being beaten that morning. *That morning.* He remembered Luvidovich putting his hands on Elena at the bar, how much he had enjoyed knocking the boy to the ground, how he had known, somehow, that he would see him dead someday. He had been still, fists clenched, silent, as Luvidovich had beaten and tortured him, and now he would never have the chance for revenge.

He wondered if Stoya had saved his soul.

He tuned in again when Foster told them he had instructed *Penumbra* to contact Central. Elena just scoffed at him. "You really think that will help?"

"Central isn't the enemy, Chief," Foster said.

"Well they sure as hell aren't friends," she snapped. "Enough's enough, Greg. We answered your questions. What the hell has been going on?"

So Foster told them, going back six months, explaining his second-in-command's investigation, and his original belief that it was related to *Demeter*. When he told them about the anonymous messages he had received, Elena turned her back to him, her arms crossed. Trey could see the look on her face: lost, hurt, and angry.

"So you knew it was about the *Phoenix* all along," she said.

Foster stared at her back. "I didn't know shit, Elena," he told her. "All I knew is someone was trying to jerk my chain, and they weren't doing a bad job of it. I didn't have a thing apart from a stack of messages from an anonymous crank."

From there any pretense of peace between them collapsed. Foster insisted on repeatedly taking her to task for cutting him off to rescue Trey, and she could not hear the deep worry behind his words. Instead she accused him of abandoning them, of following the rules out of cowardice.

"*Cowardice?*" he shouted. "I brought down two fucking platoons! With *actual weapons,* not kitchen implements."

"You were too late," she shouted in return. "While you were making sure you weren't going to get in trouble for breaking the rules, Luvidovich was *torturing* him! He'd have been dead before you showed up!"

And that was the other fascinating part of all this: Elena had been quite clear on her feelings for Foster, but she seemed spectacularly oblivious to his for her. Trey didn't know what kind of a poker face the man had in other situations, but every word and gesture he made betrayed how close to the bone she cut him. On some level, Trey reasoned, she had to know; every shot she took was true, designed for maximum impact. And Foster kept engaging her, kept coming back, kept fueling her anger.

Trey had been the same with Valeria. And Elena, like Valeria, knew exactly how to hurt someone who loved her.

They began arguing over Will Valentis, for whom Elena clearly had little affection.

"What makes you think he won't report *you* AWOL, Greg?" she was saying. "On the off chance we all reappear, he'll want to keep *Galileo* for himself."

Foster shook his head. "That won't happen," he said decisively. "Central won't give him *Galileo*. He's not captain material, and he knows it."

Now that, Trey thought, was curious. "How does he know?" Trey asked.

Foster looked across at him, surprised. "It comes up in Eval."

"Every year?"

"He's ambitious. Most people are. But he knows he's not viewed that way, and not only by me."

Trey frowned. He had chosen Rosaria as his first officer ten years before he retired because he knew she would make a strong leader someday. "Why would you keep him as a second if he could not take over for you?"

"Will's a good foil," Foster told him. "He does good work." He turned to Elena. "You remember how he was after Jake died?"

A shadow crossed Elena's face, and Trey thought Foster had evoked the painful memory deliberately. "He kept the crew organized," she said, for Trey's benefit. "He kept them all together. Kept them busy. He did a good job."

"So he is a steady man under pressure, your Commander Valentis."

"Yes," Foster told him.

"He handled the loss of your previous engineering chief."

"He kept people on shift, but made sure everyone had downtime. Didn't ding anyone for being late or not getting everything finished, but made sure everyone was accounted for. Made sure we were looking after each other."

"I imagine Lieutenant Lancaster's death was different," Trey remarked. Elena was watching him closely.

"Of course it was," Greg said. "They were friends."

Trey raised an eyebrow at Elena, and she nodded. "More so after we broke up," she told him.

"But Commander Valentis was not friendly with your Commander Jacobs?"

Foster nearly laughed. "No. They were oil and water."

"Still, one would think that sudden death would be handled much the same way."

"I thought so, too," Foster admitted. "But Will was really shaken up. Had no idea what to do with himself. I hadn't known they were so close, but I've never seen Will like that before. He—"

He broke off, staring at Trey, but it was Elena who said it. "You think he's a part of it." Her voice was mostly air.

"I think," Trey said, "that he knows more of what happened to that poor boy than he has told. Why is it you do not consider him command material?"

"Because he's an antisocial asshole," Elena interjected.

Foster looked annoyed. "You have never liked him," he retorted, and Trey recognized an old argument.

"It's the truth," she insisted. She turned to Trey. "He has the regs memorized, which isn't in itself a bad thing; I've got most of them memorized myself."

"Especially the ones you've broken," Foster put in.

She ignored him. "But with Will, they're the first thing he goes to. Like he can't understand what's going on unless he puts it in the context of some rigid definition." She turned back to Foster. "You said Will's a good foil. You're an intuitive decision maker. You know what's right, you just don't always know why. Will pushes at you, and makes you figure out the why of it all."

"How is that bad?"

"Has he ever changed your mind, Greg? Even once?"

"I—" Foster broke off, and Trey thought she was getting through. "I don't change my mind much."

"You change it with me all the time."

Trey refrained from remarking on that.

"That still doesn't make him guilty," Foster insisted.

Elena's jaw set. "Greg, think about it. Has he ever once made an argument to you that made sense? Beyond the letter of the law? You see the big picture, how it all works together; he just sees scaffolding."

Foster fell silent, and Trey carefully avoided looking at him. "Captain," he said, "how many people knew you were coming after Elena?"

"Jessica knew," Foster replied, subdued. "Lieutenant Lockwood. And I told Will. He was—" He broke off, looking chagrined. "He thought I was being unreasonable."

"Did he know you were violating orders?" Elena asked.

"Yes." His eyebrows knit together. "Even though my call to Admiral Herrod was encrypted." He met Trey's eyes again, and this time all Trey saw was a soldier, old and tired. "You're suggesting he set me up."

"He's always wanted *Galileo*," Elena said, and Trey knew she believed it.

"But he's not a killer, Elena."

Trey had found, throughout his life, that there were very few people who would not kill under the right circumstances. "He is ambitious," he said matter-of-factly. "He has been thwarted in those ambitions, repeatedly, by one man; and he has recently been granted an opportunity to excel by a governmental organization with great political power."

"Fifth Sector crime is hardly a political bombshell," Foster protested. "They're using him because he's desperate."

"You have said yourself you do not believe local crime is the subject of his work. And the line between desperation and murder can be quite thin. On this point you may trust me."

Trey could see it in Foster's eyes: the beginning of disillusionment, the grief of loss. "I can't believe it of him," he said flatly.

"That's because you're usually a good judge of character," Elena told him, and Trey thought she meant it as a kindness.

"Will wasn't dangerous before, but they weren't dangling a carrot in front of him before."

Foster shut his eyes for a moment, his expression grim. "*Demeter*," he said at last. "He asked me to take on *Demeter*'s mission."

"Why'd you say yes?"

"I'd been a jerk about his investigation." When Elena raised her eyebrows at him, he looked away. "I knew he was under orders, but I was pissed off. I thought I ought to make it up to him, and he said it would help."

Foster's jaw had set, but Trey didn't think he was angry anymore. There were more questions, but Trey knew better than to pursue it. "Captain Foster," he said, "are you feeling well enough to help with repairs?"

Elena flashed him a look, but accepted his change of subject. "I want to see if there are enough field generator parts left between the two ships to construct one," she explained. "And if we can wire our scanners into *Lusi*'s, we might be able to find ourselves a power source that can get us out of here faster."

The two of them began to discuss strategy, and Trey let himself tune out again. He must have been told, at some point in his career, how old Greg Foster was. He knew a little of the man by reputation, despite the fact that he flew in a different sector; but on Volhynia, listening to his well-worn arguments with Elena, Trey had constructed a mental picture of a much older man. A man his own age. This man was young, and handsome, and angry and full of fire. He was at the start of his career, the start of his life, with nothing but heroism behind him and hope at his feet. He had none of Trey's aches and pains, none of Trey's mistakes.

Trey watched Elena. She was gripping her elbows tightly, body language still and closed as she listened to Foster and gave him instructions. Trey had thought her perceptive. He had felt she could see him, that if she had forgiven him, perhaps what he had done was forgivable. He closed his eyes for a moment, then rose to his feet. "I will reset the scanner interface here," he told them, and walked around them to the pilot's console. He did not look back. If Elena was watching him, he did not want to know.

Chapter 39

Greg had to convince Elena that cannibalizing *Lusitania* was the right thing to do.

"She's bad off," he told her bluntly. "The hull repair will hold here, but on a trip back through that wormhole? I don't want to bet anybody's life on it. Your ship is in much better structural shape."

She had conceded his point, but he could see as they rummaged through *Lusi*'s carcass how unhappy she was. For a woman who made a point of having very few personal possessions, she had a hard time letting go of inanimate objects. *Lusi* was only two years old. He supposed she would have memories of Jake associated with it.

He wondered, not for the first time, how different their lives would be if they had not lost the old man. Elena would not have that constant air of sadness about her, of irreplaceable loss. And Jake would not have tolerated their fighting; he would have locked them in a room together until they shouted through it, and Greg would not be standing in the middle of nowhere trying to think of something to say to a woman he had known for seven years.

It's not memories of Jake, he realized abruptly. Standing in the middle of nowhere, Elena was hanging on to the only thing she knew she could still count on: her machines. She had done the same thing after Jake's accident, methodically repairing the engine damage, hiding from everyone she knew until she had figured out how to cope. He could not believe he had not put it together before.

After all these years, I am still learning who she is.

Lusi's resources notwithstanding, they were going to need another power source. Despite current wormhole theory, which held that they should have been trapped inside the thing, bouncing from end to end, this particular wormhole had a functional exit. Zajec's readings had shown an asymmetrical gravity pattern, which meant they would need some significant engine power to propel themselves back the other way. Even that was only a theory. Despite the fact that both their ships and the gray bird had come through without incident, he had no confidence that the reverse trip would be as uneventful. On top of that, Elena had reported seeing other exits as they came through. Even if they survived, there was no guarantee they would make it home, much less be anywhere near any kind of energy source.

Halfway through transferring *Lusi*'s utilitarian food supplies into the other ship, he noticed Elena was carefully dismantling what was left of the stellar collector. He stopped and watched her set aside half-melted slivers of circuitry and fused carbide sheets. "You can't take all of it," he told her.

She kept her eyes on her task. "If we have to, we can break the photocells down and grow new ones."

"That's a two-week task." She said nothing, and he crouched

down beside her. "Elena, we don't have two weeks of supplies. You're wasting time."

"I'm thinking of contingencies. That's my job."

She still would not look at him, and he fought off annoyance. "Maybe you should have thought about that before you took off."

That earned him a glare. "Maybe *you* should have thought about that before you followed me."

She looked tired. Her lips were bloodless, and the skin under her eyes was puffy, but there was energy in that glare. Anger always gave her fuel, no matter how spent she was, and she always knew where her opponent was vulnerable.

And he never could just let it go.

"What were you planning to do?" he retorted. "Defect to PSI?"

"They're not the enemy, Greg. We needed the help of someone we could trust."

We. He would not have thought allegiance was so fluid for her. "So you shoot halfway across the sector instead of coming home?"

She opened her mouth to say something, then closed her eyes. When she opened them again, she was looking at her hands. "Why doesn't matter," she said flatly. "What matters is getting out of here."

"Yeah, which is why you don't need all that crap."

"Fine. *Fine.*" She threw the spanner down and got to her feet, stalking to the other side of the cabin. "So what's *your* brilliant idea?"

He stood. "Same plan we started with. Pull what you can use right now in the other ship, and leave the rest."

"And if we don't find a power source?"

"We can't plan for everything, Chief. Let it go, and let's—"

"Don't you *dare* start pulling rank on me. There are three of us here, Greg, and you don't get to make unilateral decisions this time."

"Of *course*." Irritability was getting the better of him. "Your pirate. The guy you've known for a day, that you ditch your career over."

"Do you know why I trust him, Greg?" Her glare never wavered. "Because he is honest with me."

"And you know this how? Some secret psychic ability you discovered by sleeping with the guy?"

That pushed her over. "Right, of course." She threw up her hands. "It always comes down to a personal attack with you. Well I'm tired of it, Greg. Here in the land of nowhere, with no contingency plans, I am officially *sick* of you attacking me!"

"Well then maybe you could try sticking to the subject for once in your life!"

"Fuck you, Greg, I've had it. Either you tell me what your problem is, or you leave me the hell alone."

"You are my problem!" It burst out of him, hot and angry and futile. "You've been my problem since the day I met you!"

She stared at him, silent, and he swore, looking away.

"I didn't mean that," he said.

"Then what did you mean?"

Her voice was calm and quiet, and all of the anger drained out of him. Suddenly he wanted more than anything to lay it all at her feet.

"Last time we were on Earth," he told her, "I found another man in the house with my wife. She said she thought it was understood, with me being away so much. I told her I'd never cheated on her, and she said, 'How is that my problem?'"

He heard a noise, but when he looked up her expression had not changed. "So that's your excuse?" she asked him stiffly. "Your marriage falls apart, and you decide to be an asshole?"

"It didn't fall apart," he told her. "She doesn't want a divorce. She wants me to try it her way, and because I'm a fucking idiot I said I'd do it."

She crossed her arms again. "Still not seeing the connection."

He should be used to feeling foolish in front of her. "When I got back to *Galileo,* and all of my old routines kicked in . . . everything looked different. Suddenly half my crew wasn't just half my crew. They were—potentially, anyway—*options.* I settled on Caro when I was twenty-four years old. That's a lot of years since other women were options."

"So is that what this is all about?" Her voice was tight. "That after seven years, it finally crossed your mind that I was a woman?"

"*No.*" It was all coming out in the wrong order. "All of the others—that was new. You, I never forgot. Never. Not from the first time we met."

He watched her absorb that, uncertainty crossing her face, a blush creeping over her skin. "So how does this explain your systemic nastiness?"

"I needed you to stay away from me, Elena."

"*Why?*"

"*Because I didn't want them!*" There was no getting around it anymore. "One hundred and seventeen women on my ship, Elena, some of them so beautiful they make you look like a *genetic mistake.*" She flinched at that, but he could not stop now. "And I didn't want any of them. I only wanted you, and there you were curled up with that mental defective boyfriend of yours, the latest in a long line of mental defectives, and yes, goddammit, the only way I could cope with that and fucking *function* was to get you to back the hell off!"

She had frozen at his words, her hands back to gripping her elbows. That uncertainty was still there, and he wondered what he had said that was unclear.

"You couldn't just tell me this?"

He rubbed his eyes, tired of trying to figure her out. "I believe I just did."

She gave a gasp that was almost laughter. "So the meanness, the exclusion, the public animosity, the insults—all of that was down to *lust*?"

That was not the word he would have chosen. "Elena—"

"No, I want to make sure I have this right." She let go of her elbows and took a step toward him. "After seven years of working together, of evacs and supply drops and bullshit politics and friendship, for God's sake—all of a sudden, I become this *thing* you can't have."

Good God, she hadn't listened at all. "No. What I feel—"

"Don't tell me what you *feel*." Her voice had turned to ice, and she wasn't looking uncertain anymore. "Don't try to tell me that you care, because that's so much worse. You *abandoned* me, Greg. This is what it means to you, to care for someone? God, you're making me have sympathy for your wife."

He closed his eyes. This was the crux of it, and he had to figure out how to undo it. He could no longer remember what Jessica had told him to say, although he was certain it had been good advice. "Elena, I'm—"

"Don't you dare tell me you're sorry! Everything I ever said to you, everything I thought you were to me, it's all been a lie. Do you think you're the only person who's had a bad time of it, who's felt betrayed and alone? Like there's nothing—" She broke off, turning to the wall, and he realized she was swallowing a sob.

He knew what to say this time. "I was drunk that night, Lanie. I didn't mean any of it."

"That's always such a good excuse for you, isn't it?" she spat, furious. "Too drunk to know any better. Too fucking drunk to *mean it*. To mean that you'd only been friends with me because I was *pathetic* and nobody else liked me. That I'd done nothing but nag you for seven years, that if you had to have a *surrogate wife* I'd be the last woman you'd choose. That I only got this job because you had to do a favor for your dead friend!"

Jessica had left out that last one. "I didn't mean any of it, Elena." He stood his ground, refusing to flinch from her anger. "And whether or not you can hear it right now, I am sorry for saying it."

"I'm sorry, too." The tears had stopped, but her breathing was still shallow. "I'm sorry I trusted you. I'm sorry I presumed we were ever friends. I'm sorry I never saw you for what you really are."

A throat cleared, and Greg turned to see Zajec looking in from the other ship's cabin. He had painted his face with polite disinterest, although Greg had no doubt he had heard every word. Unlike Elena, though, Zajec would not have found Greg's confession a surprise. Greg thought he had known all along.

"I apologize for interrupting," Zajec said, "but I have found something I believe is of interest."

Elena was looking at him, brusquely brushing the tears from her cheeks. "What is it?"

His face changed, just a little, and it took Greg a moment to recognize sympathy. "*Lusitania* was recording as she fell through the wormhole," he told them. "Along with the telemetry data—she has acquired the contents of the *Phoenix*'s flight recorder."

CHAPTER 40

Galileo

Jessica found Bob Hastings sitting at his lab table, the ceiling lights dim, staring out into the infirmary at nothing. He was almost certainly stinking drunk, but he wore it well. He wore everything well. If Jessica considered older men, he would have been first on her list. Not that he didn't look his age, with his white hair and the wrinkles furrowing his dark skin; but he had good-humored blue eyes and some damn fine cheekbones. He was in good shape, too; he ran with the captain sometimes, and although he usually quit before he hit ten kilometers, the distance never wiped him out.

He had known Greg Foster for all of the captain's thirty-seven years, and Jessica was unsure how much he was able to deal with just yet. She wondered if she might be better off encouraging him out of the room so she could talk to Ted alone.

"Hey, Doc," she said kindly, "how are you holding up?"

He shot her an acid look. "How the hell do you think?" He spoke clearly enough, but his eyes were not quite focused as he looked her over. "Why aren't you drunk?"

"I've had no time." She waved her palm at the wall, and the ceiling glowed a little brighter.

He lifted a glass off the table. "I thought you were confined to quarters."

She walked over and sat next to him. "What else did Commander Valentis tell you?"

He snorted. "You know I did that, too? Called him 'Commander' instead of 'Captain.' He fakes compassion pretty well in front of the crew, but one-on-one, he's kind of an asshole." When she did not respond to that, he took another drink. "He told me you were confined until you decided to tell him what you and Greg had been up to."

"'Up to'?"

"He has been suggesting that the two of you were . . . involved."

Involved. Trust Doc Hastings to use the euphemism even when he was soused. "He sure did jump to that conclusion fast," Jessica grumbled.

"You consider the possibility he's spreading rumors to discredit you?"

She stared at him for a moment. "The fact that you even ask that," she said, "raises a number of disturbing possibilities. You don't like Commander Valentis, do you?"

"I don't know him very well, which I find more disturbing, given how long I've worked with him. That he'd try to spread a rumor that you and the captain were lovers seems ham-fisted, even for him. But Valentis does, from time to time, screw things up rather spectacularly." He drank again. "Nobody believes it, of course."

"Yeah, because Foster doesn't do that," she said, remembering what Ted had said.

He gave her a curious look. "Actually, I was thinking because *you* don't," he told her. "Don't discount your own reputation here,

Jessica. Valentis can say what he wants, but people know you. They're not going to believe it, no matter how often he says it."

And damned if that didn't make her feel better. "Those *Demeter* assholes will believe it," she said.

"Funny thing about them," he said. He drained the glass and put it down. "All that gossip they were spreading before, about the chief and the captain, and her being responsible for Danny's death? They're not saying it anymore. All of that got switched off, like someone cut the power."

The infirmary door opened, and Ted strode over to the lab table and stood with his hands on his hips. "I've got five minutes." He glanced over at Bob. "Hey, Doc. How are you doing?"

"Everybody asks that," Bob said with some asperity, "like it's some huge damn mystery. Always nice to see you, Lieutenant Shimada. Care for a drink?" He reached behind his back and produced an unlabeled flask, tipping clear liquid into his glass. Jessica caught a brief, sharp whiff of raw alcohol.

Ted shook his head. "I can't. I have to be sober when we attack some people. Speaking of which . . ." He frowned at Bob's glass, and Jessica remembered what a puritan he could be when he was on duty. "Shouldn't you be, too?"

Bob stared at him calmly. "Unless *Penumbra* has acquired a few missiles in the last month," he said, lifting his glass, "this is going to be a really short battle." He downed the contents of the glass.

Jessica gave Ted a look, and he relented. "Can we talk here?" he asked her.

Hastings raised his eyebrows. "Is this where I should be leaving?"

"Maybe," Jessica told him.

He took a deep draft of the unidentified liquor. "Doctor-patient privilege," he stated. "If anyone asks, I'll tell them you two were in here for fertility advice."

Jessica grinned; Ted looked horrified. "Will they believe that?" he stammered.

"We would have beautiful babies," she declared. "Spill it, Shimada."

He cleared his throat. "So along with Limonov, Valentis has put five of the *Demeter* people in the machine room with me, and they're feeling pretty gregarious, here on the eve of nuking the PSI ship that dinged their windshield. I steered them toward Danny, and right away they start taking shots at Limonov. With the guy right there."

Limonov, it seemed, was beginning to earn Ted's sympathy. "Did you find out what he said to Danny?"

"That's what they were giving him crap about. He gave Danny the same weird line he gave you," Ted said, "about the wormhole singing. Only Danny doesn't ask him about the wormhole. Danny asks him about Volhynia, and how long the observatory has been there, and what happens to it during the EMP when they shut down the power grid. And Limonov starts feeding him all of his scary stories about what really happened to the *Phoenix*."

"Anything plausible?" Jessica asked.

Ted shook his head. "He's got some interesting ideas about aliens," he admitted, "which would be cool if there was any evidence to back them up. But here's the thing: When the *Phoenix* blew, where do you think the first readings came in from?"

It was Bob Hastings who answered. "Novanadyr Observatory," he said.

Jessica blinked. "So the first news of the *Phoenix* came off of Volhynia?" She felt a tingle up her spine again.

Bob raised his eyebrows at her. "They're the closest manned access point," he told her. "Central's got some relays now—around the hot zone—but at the time there wasn't much interest about the wormhole. They'd shot some probes into it and found nothing, so it pretty quickly became this boring, immutable object. Novanadyr wasn't studying it in particular; they just took the data when the blast happened."

"That pub that Danny went to," Jessica said. "Didn't Elena say it was a big scientific hangout?"

Ted looked chagrined. "I figured he was just telling her that to try to lure her to join him."

"So Danny was trying to corroborate Limonov's stories," she concluded. "But—why would he care, Ted? Limonov is a nice cluster of crazy, but nothing he's got is unusual or new."

"Except," Ted pointed out, "six months ago, Volhynia's happy little pulsar has a spike, and suddenly Central gets cagey about PSI ships hanging out around the wormhole."

She shook her head. "Draw me a line."

"EMPs, Jess," he told her, and she thought he was pleased with himself. "If the right sort of EMP catches the right sort of radiation field, it can neutralize it."

"You think Danny found out the radiation field is gone?" She frowned. "*Galileo*, what's the radiation reading around B1829?"

"Current radiation levels at 345.89.225 are ambient 13, critical 22.2."

"That's not a live reading," Bob said into his glass.

"Can you put that down for one damn second, Bob?" she snapped. When he looked at her, she tried again. "*Galileo,* what is Novanadyr Observatory reading from the wormhole?"

There was a pause. "Insufficient information."

"What the fuck does *that* mean?"

"It means," Ted told her, "that she has asked, and nobody will tell her."

She had a thought. "*Galileo,* has anyone else asked you for direct data from Novanadyr?"

"Yes. Lieutenant Commander Daniel Lancaster asked for that data sixteen days ago."

"Did you have data then?"

"No."

She frowned. "This doesn't make sense," she reasoned. "If the flight recorder has been broadcasting, the whole damn sector would have heard it. What could Danny have put together that got him killed?"

"Maybe it wasn't what he put together," Ted guessed. "Maybe it's what he wanted to do about it."

Hastings took a moment to drain his glass. "I can't speak to why, but given how odd the actual murder was, I took the time to investigate a little myself. In the Fifth Sector, there have been only three knife murders in the last twelve years. One was Danny, and two were opportunistic."

"Who gets opportunistic with a knife?" Jessica asked.

"In the other five sectors," Hastings went on, ignoring her, "there have been a total of seventeen over the last twelve years. Nine disparate and scattered. And eight that took place in the span of five years in one city. Same MO as Danny."

Jessica's spine tingled. "What city?"

"Fuji Seaport, on Osaka Prime."

She swore so loudly both men stared at her. "Stoya, that police chief who disappeared? He was hired off of Osaka after being governor of Fuji for five years. *Shit*."

Ted looked at Hastings. "Can you tie the murders together?"

"The knives are all different, of course," the doctor said, "but I've had a look at Osaka's records, and I can make a good case all the killings were done by the same hand. As the only evidence, though, it's not enough, especially without motive."

"So we'd need to interrogate him." She started to compose questions in her head. "Get someone scary in front of him. Hekekeia, maybe."

"You're forgetting Stoya's missing," Bob said.

"So we find him," she insisted. "We get our hands on him, and the captain can—" *Oh*. "Shit," she said quietly.

"Well said." Bob refilled his glass. "We can unravel all of it, and it doesn't change a damn thing."

"So why don't we tell Valentis?" Ted suggested. When Jessica just looked at him, he said, "You're really telling me we can't trust him with this? This isn't impressions or intuition. This is actual fact."

"Another actual fact," she said, "is that he's a lying bastard."

"What did he say, Jess?"

She thought back. "It wasn't so much what he said as how he said it." She gave an involuntary shudder. "All I can tell you is that he's gung ho on this fight, and he's already setting Lanie up to take the fall for aiding and abetting."

"But she can alibi that pirate."

"He loses the pirate-as-murderer, he loses the reasoning behind this attack."

"This attack," Bob pointed out, "was ordered by Central Command, not William Valentis."

Jessica looked at him. "You're sure?"

"I've seen the order myself," he said. "And before you think about running to them, Danny wasn't a part of their rationale. It was all *Demeter* and Greg."

Damn, damn, damn. It had all made sense before she talked to Bob and Ted. Now all she had was a stack of unrelated questions. Like why Valentis would have been so keen to implicate Zajec if Danny's murder didn't play into the ordered attack. "Bob, can I ask you something way off the record?"

"I seem to be getting asked that a lot today."

"You ever get any encoded messages from headquarters?"

"You mean the Admiralty?"

"Them," she said, "or maybe Shadow Ops."

He was silent for a moment. "Now why would you want to know that?"

"Well that sure sounds like a yes."

He sighed. "Jessica, there are some things—"

Ted spoke up. "They're a part of this, Bob."

"What makes you say that?"

"Did you know Valentis has been reporting back to S-O about potentially illegal actions undertaken by this crew?"

Bob's eyebrows shot up. "That does explain a few things," he said.

"Like the captain's blood pressure?"

"And Commander Valentis's. Man does not take good care of himself."

"You have had some messages, haven't you?" she pressed.

He nodded. "Seven, all in the last year, all requests for medical records."

"Whose?"

"The senior staff. The captain, Will, Emily Broadmoor. The chief, after Jacobs was killed."

"They say why?"

He shook his head. "The regular records they get, of course," he said, "but they wanted my personal notes and observations. It's not unheard of, especially when an officer is killed, but I did wonder why the requests were spread out like that."

"When was the last request?"

"About eight months ago. At the tail end of the Pyraeus mission."

While they were still in the Fourth Sector, nearly eight weeks before they had gone back to Earth. Long before the pulsar would have exposed the flight recorder. She wondered if S-O had been trying to figure out whom to recruit. "What did you say about Commander Valentis?"

"If you're going to ask me to violate my oath, Lieutenant, you could at least flirt with me first." At her look, his jaw set. "I was a doctor before I was Corps, Jessica."

"Do you think you said anything about him that would have made him sound like an easy mark?"

"I will tell you only that I am quite certain that what I said about the captain would have kept him out of any scheme they might have had to subvert the Admiralty."

"And I know for sure Lanie wouldn't have gone for it," she said thoughtfully. She thought about Emily, who was on the surface as by-the-book as Valentis, but she was dead loyal to the captain. Jessica had never understood why, specifically, but it had always made her trust the woman.

"I am having ideas," Ted said slowly, "that are making me very unhappy. That weird ident, Jess—can you trace it outgoing?"

Good God, she should have thought of that herself. "*Galileo*," she said, "you have anything outgoing on that weird ident signature?"

"Specify time frame."

That would depend, she thought, on how much premeditation had gone into all this. "Start with a week," she said.

"Seven outgoing messages."

"From who?"

"William Valentis."

"When was the last one?"

"1925 hours."

"Do you still have it?"

"Message was not saved."

She looked at Bob. "You know what else happened around 1925? The captain blew off the Admiralty and went after Lanie."

"So what are you thinking? That *Valentis* is in on all this?" He shook his head. "That's a stretch, Jessica, even for me. This is our own command chain we're talking about."

Jessica remembered something the captain had said. "If the Admiralty really believed that *Penumbra* had gone rogue," she said, "they'd have had warships headed this way a month ago. You really think a PSI ship hit one of ours, and then turned around four weeks later and shot down our captain in an unarmed troop ship?"

"The simplest answer is usually the truth, Jess."

"And how is that the simplest answer?"

He stood. "You're suggesting that rather than having been murdered by an organization we don't know and don't trust, he was murdered by his own people." He did not seem angry, just sad and tired. "Jessica, dear, I'll help you investigate Stoya when all of this is done, but in the end, it comes to the same thing. The captain's gone, and we have to figure out how to live with it." He grabbed the bottle off the table. "You'll excuse me," he said, and headed back into his office, returning the lights to twilight dimness as he left.

Ted waited until the door closed. "Man's not without a point, Jess."

"Are you suggesting we let this go?"

"Hell no." He paused, and looked at her. "You said, earlier, over the comm, about Valentis. You *do* think he's involved, don't you?"

"I think the fact that it's not a crazy question means it's worth investigating."

Ted glanced at his comm. "I have to get back. Limonov is inattentive, but not inattentive enough." He put a hand on her arm, gently, and she had a moment to notice how kind his touch was. "You gonna be okay?" he asked her.

"Yeah," she said to him, and gave him a smile. "I'll hold up, Ted. You head back. I'll shout if I need anything."

He squeezed her arm and then left.

Jessica looked across the infirmary. The time was displayed above one wall: four hours until the attack. She shook her head. If this were a cryptographic puzzle, what would she be doing? Validation. Figuring out which pieces didn't fit, and finding out why. No guesses, no intuition; just keep looking until the code unlocks.

"*Galileo*," she asked, "that order from the Admiralty, to attack *Penumbra*. Was there a formal vote?"

"Yes."

"What was the breakdown?"

"Five to four. Dissenters were Khalar, Herrod, Mitchell, and Yarrow."

She frowned. She was almost certain Foster had spoken to Herrod before he left. What if he had said something to make the man start thinking?

She had met Herrod once, more than four years ago. He had scowled at her jokes and told Captain Foster he should keep her on a short leash. She clearly remembered the captain's reply: "I would, but she'd hack my bank account and steal my money." She had been horrified until she had seen the gleam in his eye.

She straightened, deciding. There was no way to do any of this halfway. She supposed preventing war was worth destroying her career.

She walked out of the infirmary to lay out her theory in front of her boss.

CHAPTER 41

Elsewhere

The flight recorder had been wiped.

Elena pulled up the waveform and began separating the channels, but she could see from the pattern what had been done to it. As she scanned through it, tagging spots where some of the data remained intact, Greg turned away. She heard him pace to the back of the cabin. He had come to the same conclusion she had.

Next to her, Trey frowned—he had recognized the pattern as well. "Wouldn't it have been shielded from an EMP?"

"It was," she told him.

"Then how did this happen?"

"Somebody hit it on purpose." Greg said it decisively, making it fact and not speculation, and she could not disagree. Nothing else made sense.

Trey turned to look at Greg, but Elena kept her eyes on the audio. No matter what Greg was dealing with, it was more than she could take right now. She needed steady hands for this work, and she was still shaking from their argument.

"One of her crew," Trey concluded.

"Specifically," Greg confirmed, "the captain of record at the time." His voice sounded brittle.

"See the pattern at the edges of the damage?" She pointed it out to Trey. "Someone would have needed physical access to the memory core, and the ship would restrict anyone but the captain of record from getting close to it. Once they open it up, though—something small could do it. A handheld coil, even."

"Why would Kelso do this?" Trey asked.

It was Greg who answered. "Because he didn't want anybody knowing what happened."

It was incomprehensible. What could have happened that Kelso would have wanted to hide? "There's still data here," she told them. "Bits and pieces, and a whole block from after the damage was done." She sat back and frowned. "That doesn't make sense. Anybody looking at this would know it had been hand-wiped. He was setting himself up."

"He did not expect to die," Trey pointed out. "Perhaps he could have returned to it later and done a more convincing job."

"Andy Kelso was a decorated officer," Greg said. "It's a court-martial offense, tampering with a flight recorder. To even take the chance is career suicide."

"He must have felt strongly about destroying the information."

"Or he never thought he'd have to face charges."

Damn, had Greg always been so irritatingly pessimistic? "Be quiet," Elena told them. "I think I can play some of this." She swept the waveform back to its most intact section and activated the audio.

The sound of a crowd filled *Sartre*'s cabin. She could make out overlapping voices, and the mechanical sounds of a ship's idling engine—healthy, she thought. There were footsteps, many running, and the monotone of the ship's internal comms. There was an alarm sounding, but it was not a critical alert. The voices themselves were not panicked: brisk and business-like, certainly, but not frightened.

Elena tried a refining filter, and some of the white noise fell away. Voices became clearer, and the ship's comms came into focus: "—*seconds to detonation. Please evacuate the area.*" The *Phoenix,* she discovered, had been a baritone.

The voices continued, and she heard snatches of overlapping conversation . . . *forget about that? I'll buy you a new one . . . sixteen canisters, give or take . . . what's taking them so . . . think I'm planning on dying here while you assholes run off?*

That last statement, made by a woman with a strong, musi-cal voice, was followed by ripples of laughter, but Elena was brought up short by Greg's reaction. He stilled, as if he had stopped breathing, staring straight at the wall, and she knew whose voice they had just heard. Her anger at him evaporated.

The voices continued, unalarmed, as the ship counted down. *Ten . . . nine . . . eight . . . seven . . . six . . . five . . . four . . . three . . . two . . . one.*

And then silence.

Elena kept her eyes on the waveform. "The earlier data is more fragmented, but it might tell us something."

"Like what?" Greg asked. His voice was flat. "They blew the ship on purpose."

"It sounded like an evacuation," Trey said.

"That was a self-destruct countdown." Greg was angry again, but she did not think he was angry with Trey. "If they were going for the lifeboats, they didn't leave themselves enough time."

Her eyes strayed over the waveform, taking in the shape of the sound. She frowned. "Wait," she said to them. She magnified the end of the signal.

"Perhaps the ship was timing the detonation of something else," Trey was saying. Greg was having none of it.

"No. It would have been phrased differently."

She asked *Sartre* to analyze the signal, and discovered it agreed with her. She felt a shiver down her spine. "Wait," she tried again.

"The crew would have known that, too, though," Trey pointed out. "You heard them. Those people did not think they were going to die."

"Who the hell knows? Maybe they'd all gone crazy. Maybe that monstrous thing out there fucked with their minds. Maybe it was Kelso, insane and homicidal. Maybe he killed all of them; that'd explain why he nuked the flight recorder."

Oh, for God's sake. "GENTLEMEN."

They both stopped and turned to her, Greg looking annoyed; he hated to stop mid-tirade.

"I'm sorry to interrupt your wild speculation," she said, "but I don't believe the self-destruct is what destroyed the ship."

That left them both speechless.

"Look here," she said. She pulled one strand out of the signal, stretching it until it spanned a meter in front of them. "This is the ship's audio. Here"—she pointed out the telltale spikes in the wave—"is where it was speaking. Look at the interval: three seconds, two seconds, one second, and there's the terminus."

Trey frowned. "It's too close."

She nodded. "I'll verify against the magnetic shadow, but the recorder is designed to stop as soon as the ship has lost a critical percentage of its requisite structure—essentially, as soon as it's irretrievably pulled to bits."

"Maybe the timer was off," Greg suggested, but he sounded unconvinced.

"Possible," she agreed. "There's a little bit of engineering data here, so I can look at it to see if there were system flaws that might cause a discrepancy. But I don't think we'll find them, Greg. I think something else took the ship apart."

He shook his head. "We're guessing."

"Perhaps," Trey said. "But it does make some sense. If we rule out—for the moment—mass insanity, or the criminality of your Captain Kelso, what we have are people who were speaking much as if they were evacuating, and who clearly had no expectation of dying."

"We also have a lousy wipe job done on a flight recorder, clearly implicating a man who, at the very least, should have been too smart to do it like that." Elena looked at Greg. He and Andy Kelso had had the same training. "If it was you wanting to wipe the recorder, how would you do it?"

"You mean besides not trying to blow up my own ship?" Despite his bitter tone, she saw him considering the question. "If I wanted to erase the record of my journey, I'd probably drop the box inside the plasma cooler for an hour or so. It'd flatten the whole signal. I'd tell Central it must have been the wormhole. It's plausible; that thing spikes all kinds of radioactive nonsense."

"What would make you hit it with a handheld EMP first?"

"If I had no time. If I was going to pull a dangerous stunt. Do a quick wipe just in case, and take the time to make it look like an accident later."

"So what," she concluded, "would have been your dangerous stunt?"

He closed his eyes, thinking. "That was the self-destruct sequence, no doubt," he reasoned aloud. "That's a pretty unsubtle tool. But the *Phoenix* was a J series, running a D10."

Elena glanced at Trey. "The D10 was the last of the nuclear starlight hybrids," she told him. "The J series included a fail-safe: the ship could be separated from the engine compartment. What remained would run a limited FTL field—it would have been a long trip home—but the self-destruct would have been designed to nuke the engine compartment separately."

"So why not separate sooner?" Trey asked.

"They shouldn't have had to separate at all," Greg explained. "Close off the engine compartment, the self-destruct does a controlled implosion, you maybe get a little bump. Maybe even a boost, if you're stuck."

"The thing is, Greg, they were on the other side when this happened. Given what we experienced, I can't believe they didn't get sucked through."

"Perhaps they did," Trey suggested.

All three of them were silent at that. If the *Phoenix* had made it back . . . so could they.

But hopefully not in pieces.

Chapter 42

Foster retreated to *Lusitania* to sync the troop ship's scanners with *Sartre*'s less sophisticated systems. Trey watched the incoming signal, manipulating the inputs in hopes of attenuating their interpreter enough for the two to handshake. Behind him Elena was still focused on the audio, scraping nearly invisible sections of the waveform, searching for something more substantive in the recording. He could believe she was a superlative mechanic; she had a persistence that was apparently impossible to shake. After all of the shouting she had just done, she had returned to this room and begun deciphering the damaged recording as if Foster's words had meant nothing.

They should have meant nothing. No, not nothing—good news. Her falling-out with Foster had been a simple miscommunication. Foster was not involved in any Central conspiracy; he was not going to pursue *Penumbra*; he bore no ill will toward PSI. He was simply a broken man who had no idea how to properly tell a woman he loved her. A woman Trey had known only a day.

"I didn't know what he was going to say," she said quietly.

He did not look up from his task. "I know that, Elena."

"Then what is bothering you?"

Nothing is bothering me, he thought. *Nothing has changed. He is still your captain, and I am still a murderer and a fugitive.* "What does it change for you?"

"Why would it change anything?"

Irritation caught up with him. "I do not believe you feel nothing."

"Don't tell me this has anything to do with how I feel." It seemed she was annoyed as well. "Neither one of you gives a damn how I feel. You're stuck in your own egos, the pair of you."

She was not wrong, and it changed nothing. His ego had always chosen the most inopportune moments to assert itself. He looked over at her. She had left the waveform and was glaring at him, her lovely face outraged, ache and exhaustion in her eyes. "Is it such an impossible question for you to answer?"

"You want to know how I feel?" She took a step toward him, dark eyes flashing. "*Pissed off.* Exhausted. Fucking terrified, and close to panic, and like I'm being backed into a corner and forced to answer questions *I don't even understand.*" She balled her fingers into fists. "*Of course* it makes a difference. Everything I thought I had, this relationship that I have leaned on for *years,* turns out to be something utterly alien, and I haven't the slightest idea what I'm supposed to do about it. And you stand there like some jealous teenager asking me to *choose.*"

"Do not put words in my mouth."

"Is that not what you're asking?"

"I am not asking you to choose. I am asking what he is to you."

She took a step closer to him. "That's fine. That's *lovely.* Because I do not know what he is to me, not anymore. I don't even know *who* he is. But I can tell you this: if he came in here right now *on his knees,* Trey, I would tell him I am sorry, but I am not free. My heart is not free."

That could not be right. He wondered if he was misunderstanding her.

"And if that isn't enough for you," she finished, her face close to his, "then you can go straight to hell with him."

She turned away, and he looked at her rigid spine. He thought she was shaking, and he remembered belatedly that he was not the only one who had been traumatized recently. But he was not quite ready to let it go. "Why?" he asked her.

"Why what?"

"Why me?"

After a moment he saw her posture begin to soften, her hands opening up. She turned around. He could still see anger in her face, and frustration, but he caught a glimpse of sympathy there as well. She took a step toward him again.

"Because you are kind," she said firmly. "Because you are strong, and you are honest and brave and you stand up and do what must be done. Because you trust me to do the same. Because you've stood next to me through all of this, looking at me like I really am strong enough to do it. Also," she finished, "because you make the best lemon hazelnut custard I have ever tasted."

His heart warmed, and all of his insecurity washed away as if it had never been. "I am a foolish old man," he told her.

She laid a hand on his arm. "You are not," she insisted. "You are a man who has been through hell and who would like to go home. So let's do that," she said. "Let's go home."

He put one hand on her waist and she leaned into him, and he tucked that same stray lock behind her ear. It would not have been so hard, he reflected, being stuck here with her, had they been alone. With her looking at him like this, he thought he might even have made room for Foster, as long as the man knew when to leave them be. It was a wistful sort of madness, and he smiled, and leaned in to steal a kiss before they could be interrupted again.

He caught the flash through his closed eyelids, and opened his eyes to look down at the scanner signal. There were still data dropouts, but *Lusitania* had given them much better vision. Reluctantly he pulled away from her, and worked on focusing the scanner beam. The system was sluggish, but after several seconds it narrowed in on the planet's magnetic poles, and began methodically pulling fuzzy data from the surface.

Next to him, Elena was smiling. "Not blind anymore," she said, and met his eyes.

Foster ducked back into the cabin. Trey half expected him to scowl when he saw Elena's arm around Trey's waist, but if he noticed at all he did not react. *Honorable,* Trey thought again. He wondered how many times Foster had had to watch her with another man. Foster moved to Trey's other side, looking down at the scanner output. "Better than I would have expected," he said. Trey wondered if all the man had needed was one good shouting match.

The scanner was agonizingly slow. It had been running almost ten minutes before *Sartre* alerted them to a match: a massive power source near the planet's equator. Details proved elusive, even with Elena's attempts to clarify the information.

The ship did not have the intelligence to identify the nature of the power source, or even if it would be convertible for use with their engines. All it could tell them was that the source was large and radioactive.

"Is that the source of the planet's radiation?" Elena asked.

The pause before the ship responded told Trey what he needed to know. *Insufficient information to determine radiation source,* it told them silently.

"It has been a long time," he told Elena, "since I have performed reconnaissance."

"It's been a long time since I've flown onto a cold planet with nothing but fuzzy sensors."

Foster shot them both a look, but when he spoke, his tone was neutral. "Let's see if we can pull *Lusi*'s shielding over as well," he suggested, and moved toward the back of the cabin to kneel in front of the same access panel Elena had used to dismantle their field generator. Elena shot Trey a quick smile, and slid out from under his arm to return to her waveform. He watched her, the blue glow of the display cooling her skin, and allowed himself to consider the possibility that he might make it home after all.

Chapter 43

E lena should not have been surprised to find Trey to be a competent mechanic. There were similarities, she knew, between mechanics and cooking; both required subtlety and precision, and both benefited from the occasional application of intuition. Besides, he had been in command of his own ship for decades; every decent captain knew, at the very least, how to make basic repairs. Greg was a fine mechanic himself. Jake used to say mournfully that he would have been excellent if he hadn't strayed into command.

Greg was patching together the remnants of the two ships' shielding systems, absorbed in his own thoughts, and Elena kept her eyes on the work in front of her. He had not spoken often of his mother, but Elena knew the woman was behind his choice of career, that she had steered him toward the Corps since he was a baby. And then she had been taken from him by the Corps, and he had not changed any of his plans. What his mother had given him, more than a direction, was a well of emptiness, of insatiable loneliness, that he expended a huge amount of energy hiding from everyone around him. Elena had glimpsed it, once or twice, and the familiarity of that feeling had been a part of what had brought her close to him. It had been hard not to want to do something, to keep him company, to comfort him.

Since the day I met you, he had said. What the hell was she supposed to do with that?

"Some last words," Greg said.

It took her a moment to figure out what he meant. They were almost certainly not his mother's last words, but she understood. "She made them laugh," she pointed out. "Because of her they were not afraid."

"They should have been," he said bluntly. "I didn't remember what she sounded like. I lost that memory a long time ago. But when I heard her voice—I knew it instantly. I can't believe I forgot."

"You were twelve years old."

"She was my mother. Shouldn't I remember my mother? All the stupid shit floating around in my head that I wouldn't miss."

Elena could not share with him her opinion of his mother. She thought PSI had it right: it was madness, leaving children behind. She wondered then if that was why Greg had never had children. She had always supposed he had not wanted them, but perhaps he simply refused to re-create history with children of his own. "You remember what counts," she said, knowing it was useless.

"Yeah, like how much I have her temper."

"And her intellect," Elena added, "and her courage."

He watched her fingers. "I've never stopped being angry with her," he said. "Doesn't make a lot of sense, does it, being angry with someone who's dead?"

"Sense has very little to do with it. I'm still mad at Jake."

He was silent for a moment. She found a larger chunk of data, and set the ship about interpolating what it could. "I would have given you the job anyway," he said awkwardly.

Well, she thought, *it's probably the safest place to start.* "You don't have to say that, Greg."

"Yes, I do." He was looking at her, and she stopped what she was doing to warily meet his eyes. "Elena, after he died, and I told you I needed you to take his job, you looked . . . you shrank. Like I had just tied a boulder around your ankle. With everything else you were dealing with . . . I wanted to give you confidence. I wanted you to know that he had always believed in you. I thought it would help. But it wouldn't have mattered what Jake said; I gave you that job because I knew you could do it."

"Ted has three years on me," she said.

"And he's very good," Greg agreed. "Next to anyone else it would have been him, no contest. But he doesn't have your instincts, Elena. And people don't follow him the way they follow you."

"They are good people, Greg. They'd follow him without question."

"They are, and they would. You don't have to tell me I have the best crew in the galaxy. But you? They follow you not just because it's their duty. They follow you because they want to please you. They love you."

Elena wondered, not for the first time, how much he missed. "We all love each other on that ship," she told him. "That's why it works." He should know that already. Unsettled, she turned back to the waveform. "Have a look at this bit—I think it might be audible."

Trey got up from his seat to stand next to her. Instinctively she reached out and touched the small of his back with her fingertips; he slid an arm around her waist, almost absently, and she shifted closer to him. As long as she had him, she had balance.

On her other side, Greg was ignoring Trey's gesture, and she felt a flicker of relief.

The signal had the tinny sound of something badly reconstituted, but enough of it was intelligible. " . . . sonal log, 3190.2 . . . robably shouldn't have done it." The voice was a man's, baritone like the ship, with the same sharp-edged accent most Earth dwellers had. "It was a terrible risk, on top of everything else here. But I . . . talk to someone. I'm the jolly guy in all of this, the one who's certain, who calls all the shots. I tried . . . voting, and of course they all agreed. Even Katie. I would've . . . all we could do with it, but she said she knows people too well. So I know it was the right choice. No regrets, no . . . it's going to take us months to get back without the mains, and I had to tell someone. He won't . . . one else, and when I get home I'm letting him get drunk on every centime I've socked away. And then maybe I'll hang it up, stay on Earth, let someone else face the horrors of the universe. I am tired. All this . . . more than I ever wanted to know. Wish it was a surprise, that we could do this to ourselves. Maybe I'm just getting old."

The signal degraded into noise, and Elena shut it off. Trey looked over at her, and she met his eyes.

"Not suicide, then," he said. He looked relieved.

"Or homicide."

Greg was frowning intently. "Can you tell where they were when that was recorded?"

She lined up the audio with the recorder's magnetic shadow. "Incoming telemetry suggests they were receiving the stream, at least."

"So they were on the other side," Greg concluded. "And he sent someone a message. Why would he do that? Careful enough to wipe the flight recorder, and he spills the whole thing over comms?"

"It means there was someone back home that he trusted," she said.

"It means," Trey put in, "there is someone back on Earth who knows the truth of what happened, and has known all along."

There was nothing else useful on the recording. Elena was able to validate the system chronometer; the early destruction of the ship was not a recording anomaly. The *Phoenix* had been trying to detonate something, and before they could do it their ship had been destroyed.

"What the hell were they blowing up?" she wondered aloud.

The three of them were silent. Elena glanced at Greg; he was studying the waveform, but she did not think that was what was on his mind. "You're investigating this wormhole," he mused, "and you get pulled through. What's the first thing you do?"

"Same thing we're doing," she replied. "Check out the radiation source on that planet, see if we can use it for fuel."

"You think whatever he found is down there," Trey said.

"Or whatever destroyed them."

"That's the risk, yes. But what's our other choice?" Greg asked. "We need a power source."

She felt Trey straighten next to her. "What sort of weapons did you have on *Lusitania*?"

Greg nodded, understanding. "The infantry took the plasma rifles, but we've got handguns."

If any of the crew of the gray bird had survived, a trio of handguns would be a meager defense; but they were a good deal better than nothing. They would never be better prepared. "All right then," she said, looking from Greg to Trey. "Let's go in."

Chapter 44

··

The last time Trey had made planetfall was six months ago, when he had returned to Volhynia. The transport had dropped through the clouds at the pole, speeding south over the mountains at Riga. It had been late spring, just warming into summer, a few yellow-flowered trees still dappling the emerald green, and his memory brought him back more than forty years. He had stared out the window, watching the ground speed underneath him, and the past that rose to greet him was not the pain of his last years there. Instead he remembered being small, walking with his father in the spring rains, laughing and splashing through the mud, and felt lighter than he had in years. No matter what awaited him, he was home, and everything inside of him knew it.

The planet they skimmed over now was dead.

Below the cloud cover the air was surprisingly clear, revealing a flat, featureless landscape. He thought at first that they were flying over rock, but here and there when the wind kicked up he saw gray dust rise and swirl before settling back into its nondescript place. They passed over hills, and in one place a great chasm, as if some cosmic ax had split the surface; but there were no plants, no water, no animals visible at all.

Elena was flying, her deft fingers ready to compensate for turbulence; there was none.

The atmosphere was nominally breathable, but the radiation levels rendered it deadly. Once they descended below the stratosphere, *Lusi* had been able to give them measurements from the surface: ambient 6.1, climbing to 6.7 as they approached the power source. Upon hearing this Foster had silently passed out radiation suits, and Trey had pulled his on along with the others. Even with help from *Lusi*'s shielding, *Sartre*'s limited protection would not last them long down here.

Elena flew through the dim predawn, coming around to the planet's morning. The pale yellow sunlight energized Trey, clearing his head for the first time since his imprisonment, and he focused more on the landscape. Here the land grew more disparate, flat plains flanked by mountains, snaking channels that had at one point almost certainly been rivers. Trey queried their sensors repeatedly, but *Sartre* always told him the same thing: there was nothing organic there at all.

"Has it always been like this?" Trey asked softly.

Sartre tried to calculate the age of the damage, but gave up. *Insufficient data to determine radioactive half-life,* it said. *Minimum duration: ten thousand solar years.*

"A natural phenomenon, do you think?" Elena was whispering as well, her eyes never leaving the desolate landscape.

"When there used to be water?"

"Maybe an orbital shift," Foster speculated. "Or a geological event. The power source might be a meteor."

Trey knew he was right. The galaxy, for all its vast, empty spaces, was cluttered with all sorts of dangerous debris. Planets like Volhynia—or even Earth, for that matter—were blessed to have escaped serious damage. Impact was not necessary, either; he thought of Volhynia's normally placid little pulsar, and the chaos it had caused with a relatively brief deviation from its normal pattern. Not that he had been surprised to hear of rioting in Riga— his father had always told him Riga had too much money for its own good, and that the people did not know how to do without. Three days of doing without had been too much for them.

They came over a mountain into the full dawn sun . . . and discovered a city.

Stretching as far as he could see in three directions, it was as lifeless as the rest of the planet; but the buildings sprawled across the earth and stretched into the sky like fingers sprouting out of the ground. Elena slowed down and brought them in low. The buildings were laid out in grids, wide cobbled streets between them, their stone and brick facades catching the dust-filtered sunlight. Many of them were nondescript, blocky and utilitarian. He could see dozens, though, scattered wherever they looked, that were works of art: spires and colored glass windows, spiraled minarets, asymmetrical crystal blocks designed to look flat when viewed from an angle. There was one arched building that reminded him of Novanadyr's spaceport, but much bigger. They flew under the arch, and he peered at the underside as they passed, wondering what feat of engineering was holding it up.

She slowed, and they flew closer to the buildings, looking in through wide windows. Trey saw what appeared to be a furnished apartment, items that might have been a table and chairs arranged to catch the morning light. The chairs had been pushed out and left askew, and the table was covered with unfamiliar knickknacks, but there was nothing moving. No bones, either; no life, and no death. The whole place felt artificial, wrong somehow; almost but not quite familiar. The word drifted through his mind: *alien*. A word used by jokers, by conspiracy nuts. Nobody believed in them anymore, yet what else could have built this beautiful place?

More important: What else could have destroyed it?

Ten thousand solar years. He wondered where—or when, for that matter—the wormhole had dropped them.

"Do you suppose they abandoned it?" Elena asked, her eyes on the same window Trey was watching. "Perhaps they had enough warning that whatever-it-was was coming, and they packed up and left."

"I don't think so," Foster said, and Trey knew enough of him to feel foreboding.

He and Elena turned to follow Foster's gaze. He was looking down the road, in between block after block of magnificent buildings. In the distance, Trey saw something odd: a flat spot, as if the city had melted into a blank sheet of paper. He frowned and looked more closely; he thought he saw objects in the middle of the road, as if parts of a building had fallen off. With a chill up his spine, he realized that was exactly what had happened.

Elena had gone gray, and he stood close to her as she followed the road toward the debris.

At first they saw only minimal damage: chips in a facade, a door that had come loose, a broken window. But the destruction increased with each passing meter, and soon every building they passed looked torn, as if the top stories had been ripped off by great talons. Soon they were passing piles of amorphous rubble, pieces of foundation visible here and there; and then they reached patches of glass, where stone and brick and metal had been melted and fused into something solid and shapeless.

They came across the lake almost abruptly: an expanse of silvery gray, stretching out toward distant mountains, smooth and featureless. Elena flew out over it, and in seconds the city was left behind. His eyes searched the surface for some trace of the civilization they had just left, some mark or shape or chunk of ruined building to indicate that something had been here, that the enduring beauty they had just left could not be so easily obliterated.

There was nothing.

He caught a glimpse of smoke in the distance. Elena followed his gaze and steered them toward it. He imagined she, too, had guessed what it was, and when they saw the remains of the gray bird, broken and scattered, she did not look surprised. She slowed down and hovered over it, her eyes darting over the bent and torn scraps of metal.

"You won't see any serial numbers," Greg told her, but he was examining the wreckage just as closely.

"It's not that," she said. "The cabin's still whole."

Trey had not identified it among the ship's unfamiliar architecture, but when she pointed it out he saw a small, intact section, with an open door that appeared to be undamaged. Having the weapons from a Central troop ship seemed suddenly less like a luxury.

They sped away, and after a few minutes Elena found the blast crater, lower and deeper than the rest of the glass lake, the bottom seared to blackness. A radiation alarm sounded and she sped up past it, climbing back into the atmosphere. After a few minutes they were back above the stratosphere under their own gravity. Trey felt exhaustion hit him again as they left the sunlight behind, but he had never felt so grateful to see the stars.

Elena leaned back in the pilot's seat, all of the energy drained out of her. Trey laid his hand on her shoulder, and she put her hand over his. She did not look at him, but her eyes dropped closed. He could imagine what she was thinking of, for he was thinking the same: every colony found too late, every war fought over wealth or territory or anything else meaningless. He had loved the part of PSI that meant helping people, but too often he had been left to witness what happened when a colony fell prey to its worst impulses. It felt like waste; it felt like personal failure; it felt like futility. Sometimes it drove him to despair.

Eventually it had driven him home.

Foster spoke first. "Was that the power source? The epicenter?"

Trey looked over at him. Foster had taken the shock of what he had seen and tucked it somewhere invisible. He stood now, tall and steady, ready to tackle what was ahead. He met Trey's eyes, and for a moment Trey understood him perfectly: this man, this captain, was doing what he had been trained to do. He was quietly and confidently pursuing his mission, and any doubts and worries would be his own. Gently Trey squeezed Elena's shoulder.

"No," she said, opening her eyes and sitting forward again. "It was southeast of there. We flew over it."

"So not a by-product of the blast?"

She shrugged. "I suppose it might have been something that was destroyed."

"You think we'll need to mine it?"

She ran her hands over her face, and Trey saw her color coming back. "If that's fused glass, we could probably blast through it with a couple of handguns. Only one way to be sure, though." She looked up at Trey. "Do you suppose we'll find what Andy Kelso found?"

He squeezed her shoulder again. "I think, *m'laya,* we already did."

Chapter 45

They left *Lusitania* in orbit, sacrificing the extra radiation shielding to lighten their fuel burn, and Elena guided the civilian ship back through the atmosphere and over the lake of glass. The route over the city would have been just as fast; she might even have saved a minute or two. But she did not think she could bear to see it again, all of those beautiful, desolate buildings. So much created, so much accomplished, and for nothing. It was too close to her own life, to what she feared more than anything else. Whoever had lived here had died long ago, and all they had made was meaningless.

The meaning of her life, for the moment, was in finding Trey a way home.

She set them down by the power source, steadying the ship against the uneven terrain, and they stood in a circle to check the seals on each other's radiation suits. Trey, she observed, performed the ritual in the same sequence she and Greg did. She wondered if it was human nature, or if there was something in the construction of the things that led to the same process. She wondered how many rituals PSI had that she would find familiar.

Five minutes of unshielded radiation at these levels would be deadly; even with the suits, they would have to be back on board the ship in less than half an hour. Which meant that even with radiation suits, any survivors from the gray bird were likely beyond help at this point—although after seeing the cloak, she couldn't rule out the possibility that the other ship was equipped with more robust safety equipment than either *Sartre* or *Lusitania*. When she got home, she was going to have to comm some of her friends back at Central and find out exactly what kind of research was going on behind the scenes.

Greg jumped out of the ship first, taking a few unsteady steps. Gravity was slightly higher outside, and the glassy surface was far more uneven than it had appeared from the sky. She stepped out after him, Trey following. *Sartre*'s door slid shut behind them, leaving them with absolute silence.

She used her comm to call up a crude display, and gestured forward. "The radiation spikes about two meters ahead," she said. Her voice sounded loud and flat, and she wished she had not spoken.

Greg moved forward, his stride becoming more confident; and then he stopped abruptly, teetering as if he was going to fall. She rushed forward, instinctively reaching for his arm; he spread out his hands at her, gesturing for her to stop.

"I almost missed it," he said, looking down.

There was an abrupt drop in the landscape, ten meters at least. The glassy, reflective surface of the lake had camouflaged the change in terrain so that it was nearly invisible. From the sky, she had not seen it at all.

They walked along the edge and found themselves moving down an incline, and then the land flattened and they were able to move underneath. Before them was the entrance to an enormous open hangar, built in a curve blending into the landscape. The glass before it was polished and even, providing a tarmac large enough for a small cargo runner or a two-person fighter. The arch itself had been manufactured out of large chunks of opaque glass, precision-cut and fitted together like jigsaw pieces. She was almost certain it was machined—there was a grace to the curve, an aesthetic pleasantness, like a wave rising out of the dead ground.

"Deliberate camouflage," Greg said.

"Who would be looking?" Trey asked.

Elena felt grateful for her handgun.

The interior of the hangar echoed with a soft, mechanical hum. The floor, like the tarmac outside, was level, but instead of the glassy silver-gray it was dark and unpolished. From the feel of it under her feet, she thought it was a standard poured polymer, used for everything from home foundations to cargo ship hangars, but unadorned by the usual colorants. The space stretched at least a hundred meters straight back, angled downward into the ground; not large enough for a passenger ship, but enough of a taxiway to accommodate something with a fair amount of horsepower. The ceiling was illuminated all over, as if it was painted with light, and it took her a moment to realize why the material was glowing.

"How hot is it in here?" she asked.

"6.3," Trey said. "And we are not at the radiation source yet."

"What is that made of?" Greg asked, studying the ceiling.

"Cesium, I'd guess," she replied. "Look closer—it's liquid."

The silvery substance rippled here and there with the vibrations of the walls. "Cesium is not especially dangerous," Trey remarked, "but neither does it last long before decaying."

It seemed oddly wasteful, sealing such a liquid into the ceiling when it would need to be replaced. Except— "They are expecting to replace it with something else," she realized. Whatever this place was, it was neither abandoned nor static. Suddenly the bright, rippling ceiling seemed oppressive. She moved farther inside.

A hallway opened to their left, and she peered into the darkness. She heard a hum, low and monotonous, echoing as if from a distance. All three of them switched on their suit lights, and the dark space lit up with a cool glow. Ten meters away from them stood a table on which sat three small cubes. As they watched, a robotic crane lifted one of the cubes and placed it on a belt behind the table, which swiftly carted it out of sight. Moments later another cube appeared on the belt, and the crane placed it in the vacant spot. Apart from the hum, everything appeared inert.

Elena circled to one side of the table, playing her light over it, a frown of concentration on her face. This was a test bed of some kind, but she couldn't imagine what the crane might be reading from the small, static objects. She leaned in closer to look at one of the cubes. It was gray and nondescript, its edges seamless. As she watched, the crane hovered over it for a moment, then lifted it and dropped it back on the belt to disappear. Rejected, for reasons she could not see.

"The radiation in here is unstable," Trey told them. "It is spiking over seven, and it is irregular. We cannot stay here."

Radiation. "It's testing them for containment," she guessed.

"They are not doing well," Trey observed.

"Wait." Greg was on the other side of the table, leaning over a cube waiting its turn, and he had grown completely still.

"Greg?"

"Come here," Foster said, and his voice sounded like dust.

Elena rounded the table to stand behind him, and heard Trey move in behind her to look over her shoulder.

Etched in the side of the cube, almost invisible, dark gray on black, was a slowly spinning cube, shifting with the viewing angle. In the center was an ancient pictograph, a phonetic spelling of a family name in a character set no longer used. She would not have been able to read it had it not been familiar to anyone who paid any attention to the news.

"What is Ellis Systems doing here?" Greg asked.

That, she thought, was the wrong question. What they were doing seemed obvious. Ellis manufactured most of the high-yield terraformers in use these days, and they kept the details of their power sources very quiet. Elena had tried to dissect one once, curious about what was under its heavy shielding, and had found a heavily radioactive combination of strontium and iodine. With no confidence she could duplicate their containment, she had left off before she had completely dismantled it, and never opened one again.

Ellis was looking for a new power source. The question was why they were doing it here, and who else knew about it. "How are they getting results back?" she asked.

"There must be a way through," Trey said. "At least for data."

Greg had thought of the same problems she had. "But why here? Even if they can go back—it's got to be expensive, both in energy and in wear-and-tear on this equipment. They could dig allanite on Shenzhu for less than it would cost them to maintain this place."

Trey looked between the two of them. "Unlikely to be an ordinary lab, then," he said.

Greg's expression grew more preoccupied, and she wondered what he was thinking. He met her eyes for an instant, then looked away. "Come on."

They headed back up the hallway and into the hangar, following the radiation signal. There was another hallway at the rear of the structure, its shadowed entrance marked by a single row of floor-level lights, and Elena had a brief memory of the brick sidewalks in Novanadyr. They left their comm lights on, flooding the passage before them. Even so, the darkness swallowed everything just a few meters before them. Greg, a few steps ahead of her, pulled out his handgun, and instinctively Elena moved closer to Trey.

"Personally," Elena whispered to him, "I'm missing that rolling pin."

"We had best keep our ears open," he agreed.

"If there's anyone here," Greg said, "they already know we've arrived."

She did not find that observation comforting.

Elena heard a low industrial hum coming from the space ahead of them, both louder and more complex than the hum of the test bed. They turned a corner, and the floor ended abruptly, the space opening downward into a vast cavern lit intermittently by operating machinery. A variety of drones hovered in the air, against the walls, on ledges built out of the sides. The bulk of the space was a massive hole, the sides made up of streaks of blown glass blending into dirt striped with silver-gray mineral deposits. The stripes were luminescent, adding a faint blue shimmer to the lower part of the cavern. She could see the bottom, glowing solid far below, drones shadowing the surface.

"Ambient 6.5, spiking to 7," Trey told them. "This is the source. *Sartre,* how long can we last in this?"

Fourteen minutes before symptomatic exposure, the ship projected before his eyes. *Seventeen minutes before fatal exposure.*

"How far away do we have to be at seventeen minutes?"
Ambient 6 or less.

He looked up at Elena and Greg. "We must be off the planet."

Greg turned away. "Let's see if there's a way down."

There was a steep ramp set against the wall, smooth and sturdy, but without a handrail. Greg went first, and she beamed her light at his feet. For wheels, she thought, looking at the ramp, not daring to glance at the drop. She lifted her left hand and let her fingers brush against the wall as she walked, giving herself the illusion of safety. She heard Trey's step close behind her.

"Elena," he asked, "can you detect the age of any of this equipment?"

She had already tried. "I can't get a read on the material," she told him. "Too much radiation. But based on the construction . . . some of it's new, newer than anything I've seen. But a lot of it—the drones in the air, for example—a lot of it is old. Decades."

"Twenty-five years?" he asked.

"Plausibly, yes."

"Older?"

She paused. "I cannot say," she admitted at last. "I haven't seen anything obviously older." She knew what he meant: none of this is coincidence. "You think this material is what Kelso discovered."

In front of them, Greg stopped, and swore quietly. "It's dellinium."

She stood still, and felt Trey's hand come to rest against her back. "How do you know?" he asked.

"The properties fit," Greg said. He resumed walking, this time at a faster clip. "The glow, the interference."

"It could be a dozen others," Elena objected. "Promethium, cobalt, polonium—"

"You remember that question my pen pal asked me?" Greg interrupted. "The half-life of a nuclear starlight explosion? *Galileo* gave me a list of materials that would produce the kind of radiation they used to have out there. The first two on the list? Dellinium isotopes and Ellis terraformers. And you remember the rumors, after the explosion?"

She had been too young. Everything she had read was secondhand. "There were rumors of dellinium?"

"It was Volhynia that reported detecting dellinium," Greg told her. "They were the closest recording station at the time. But less than twelve hours later, they retracted the information. Said it was distorted by the heavy radiation."

There was no longer any question in her mind about who was behind all of this. Ellis could not have hidden evidence of dellinium on their own.

"How can Ellis have been using dellinium all this time?" she asked. "Someone would have known." *Someone would have blown themselves up.*

"They have not," Trey said. "I would guess this is a refinery. Dellinium, properly refined and shielded, could power a terra-former for a hundred years."

Elena thought about that. A hundred years. There were ter-raformers in the field that failed after five years, sooner if the climate they were fighting was severe enough. A dellinium-powered terraformer would hold off methane and sulfur, pro-viding atmosphere and humidity for virtually any crop. It could make rain on a desert planet. It could turn dust into orchards within three months. People would not have to starve ever again. She would never again have to land on a planet where people had grown so used to death they did not even name their children anymore.

It sounded like a miracle. But that was not the most obvious use for dellinium.

"That city above us," Elena said. "No wonder it was so vast. They would not have had to conserve anything."

"I don't think they did," Greg said. "I think they had every-thing they needed, and then someone got angry with someone else, and that was that."

The ramp flattened out, and they came to a massive shelf dug into the earthen wall. They shone their lights along the floor and found stacks of boxes, each about a cubic meter, made of the same featureless plastic as the small cubes above. Trey stepped forward and scanned them. "These are not spiking as badly as the small ones," he said after a moment, "but the yield is lower."

A reasonable start, she thought; but if they could power no more than similar amounts of allanite, there was not much of a win. And with the risks of transporting something as inherently unstable as dellinium—even a dilute isotope—they would need solid containment if they were going to put it to commercial use.

"How close do you suppose they are to getting the containment working?" Greg asked her.

"No way to tell," she replied. "It could be years. They could have it already. That system up there is on autopilot."

"If they had it already," Trey pointed out, "they would be using it."

"Don't discount the political issue," Greg said. "Dellinium power is going to freak people out, and with good reason. They'll have a marketing problem, in addition to an engineering problem. Even a contained isotope is going to be dangerous. And who the hell trusts a corporation to follow all the safety protocols? Even one like Ellis?"

"They need a reason," Elena said. Reality opened before her, a great dark pit swallowing the last of her illusions about Central. "Like a physical threat."

Trey nodded. "Introduce the material first as a weapon, something required to keep the people safe." He sounded tired, and she remembered then that he had grown up viewing Central with suspicion. He had spent his life waiting for this possibility, and it had been hidden here all along. "Once there is public acceptance, Ellis will be able to use as much of this stuff as they wish."

Greg scoffed. "Dellinium as a weapon is insanity. That's a fast, one-sided battle, and anybody left over is going to be blown back to the dark ages. Nobody is that crazy."

It would not have to be insanity, Elena thought. All it would require was good intentions.

"The pirate is correct."

The voice came out of the dark behind them, and all three turned and shone their lights up the sloped path.

Stoya stepped out of the shadows. He was in a radiation suit, but through the clear material of the hood, Elena could see the pallor of his skin. He was gray, and his eyes were sunken; she thought some of his hair had fallen out. Despite his color, his skin was shiny, as if he were coated in egg, and he blinked too often. That he was on his feet at all was a testament to how healthy he had once been. Now he was nearing death, probably within hours.

Elena thought she should have found that horrifying.

All three of them pulled their guns, but he did not react. "There is no need for you to be alarmed," Stoya told them, and he was healthy enough to sound irritated. "I am hardly a threat to you."

"You're the pilot of that bird," Greg said. "You shot at me."

Stoya nodded. "That was my mission. I was to kill all of you."

That small revelation was the only piece of information she had heard lately that fit at all. "You fucked that up," Elena said, "didn't you?"

Stoya would not look at her. "They did not tell me the wormhole had such a gravity well," he said. "When you were pulled in, Zajec, I assumed it was because your ship was small. Or your pilot was inexperienced. I did not expect to be trapped."

"Or shot at," Greg snapped.

Stoya nodded, unrepentant. "Just so. The cloak . . . it is useful, but it drains too much from the ship's defenses. They should redesign it."

"Who asked you to kill us?" Elena asked.

Stoya finally fixed his eyes on her. "You are the engineer. How are you planning to get back?"

"You don't actually believe we're taking you with us?" This question came from Greg. Elena wished he meant it, but she knew him.

"I believe you want to know what happened to your officer," Stoya said impassively, "and I believe I am your only source. If you take me with you, I will tell you what you want to know."

He had to know what was happening to him. Trey took a step toward him. "What do you expect to accomplish by leaving this place?"

Stoya looked at Trey, his gray eyes holding something like respect. "People who can build a cloaked ship . . . they may yet have something that could help me."

Elena knew far less about medicine than she did about dellinium, but radioactive materials figured prominently in her work, and as far as she knew science was further from a treatment for advanced radiation poisoning than a functioning hardware cloak. She thought Stoya knew it, too; but if he insisted on deluding himself, she was not beyond using his belief. She exchanged a brief glance with Trey, who moved closer to Stoya, his handgun pointed steadily at the man's gut. "Put your hands against the wall," Trey said. Stoya obliged, and Trey patted him down thoroughly. She had no doubt he would know where to look for hidden weapons. "He is unarmed," he said at last, stepping back.

Reluctantly, Elena holstered her gun. "Stay out of the way," she told him. "We will not wait for you."

Greg was more direct. He walked up to Stoya, and stared down at him until the man looked back. "If you try anything," he said evenly, "if you so much as slow us down, I'm throwing you off the ledge. Understand?"

Stoya managed a grim smile. "I would expect no less," he said.

She turned back to the cubes of isotope and caught Trey's eye. Something was bothering him; she frowned slightly, and he just shook his head. "It is nothing," he told her, in the same language he had used to speak to Valeria.

She wanted to hold out a hand to him, to comfort him; but she was acutely aware of Stoya, still leaning against the wall where Trey had searched him, watching all three of them with his sharp, humorless eyes. For now, she would have to trust what he told her, and trust he would let her know if he needed her.

For now, she had a box to open.

CHAPTER 46

Galileo

Explain to me," Emily Broadmoor said to Jessica, "why I shouldn't report you for this."

"Because I am following orders, ma'am. Just like you."

For a crew on alert, an awful lot of them were passing the time before the attack in the pub. Ted and the engineering crews were running diagnostics on the ship's nav and weapons systems, and the infantry was busy with combat drills in the gym, but most of her fellow techs were here, clustered in the corners drinking coffee and speaking in quiet voices. Bob Hastings's nurses and medical associates were here as well, looking patient and stoic, hoping they would not be needed.

Jessica was hoping none of them would be needed, but Emily wasn't going to make it easy. Her boss was sitting at the table across from her, arms folded, her expression downright unsympathetic. "He's following orders, too, Lockwood. This order is from the Admiralty. He's not following some glory-seeking whim."

Well, at least she'd properly assessed Valentis's personality. "The Admiralty didn't have all the facts," Jessica pointed out. "And the one guy the captain talked to voted against this attack."

Emily's eyes narrowed. "And exactly how did you get that little piece of information, Lieutenant?"

Oops. "He just—" It was no good; she was a dreadful liar. "Look, ma'am, Captain Foster gave me some leeway, and I've been using it. And isn't figuring out whether or not we should be attacking a ship full of potentially innocent people more important than how I got the intel?"

"Why haven't you gone to Captain Valentis with this?"

That was where she and Emily always got stuck, Jessica realized. To Emily, there was a process, and she trusted it. It wasn't that Jessica mistrusted the process; it was that individuals were far more important. "Permission to speak candidly, ma'am," she said.

Emily sighed. "Lockwood, if this discussion was on the record, you'd be in the brig already."

"He wants this too much." It wasn't everything she suspected, but it summarized the worst of it. "Without a direct order from Central to stand down, he's going to take that PSI ship, whether or not he believes me. Or them, for that matter."

Just then a new crowd wandered in: about a dozen of the soldiers from *Demeter*. They were in high spirits, talking and laughing, and Jessica wondered if they were bothering to stay sober. Sure enough, they went straight to the bar, and one of them began rummaging through the bottles. They ignored the stares of the *Galileo* crew, making jokes and toasting each other as if they were celebrating.

"Bastards."

Jessica looked back at Emily, surprised. The older woman was staring at the *Demeter* soldiers, and Jessica didn't think she'd ever seen such strong emotion in her face. Emily's glare was beyond resentment; Jessica thought it was outright hatred. The security chief stared for several seconds, then turned back, her expression professional again.

"Okay," Emily said, "this is how we'll handle it. I'll send a message to Admiral Herrod, outlining what you've told me here."

Jessica felt a wave of relief. "Thank you, ma'am. I—"

"And then," Emily went on, "I'm taking the whole thing to Captain Valentis."

At that, Jessica's stomach dropped. "Ma'am, you—"

"I won't mention your name, Lockwood. I'll tell him Foster and I discussed it all before he left. He's an officer. He has an obligation to uphold his oath. He might not like what I tell him, but he'll listen."

Jessica felt certain that Emily was wrong, but without facts to back up her feelings, there was nothing she could say. "As you like, Commander," she said.

But Emily did not move to leave. "You know Captain Foster punched Valentis before he left."

Jessica nodded. "I heard. I also heard he deserved it."

Much to Jessica's amazement, Emily's eyes twinkled. "I think he broke Valentis's nose."

"Wish I'd seen it," Jessica said with a smile.

Emily sighed. "I liked working for him," she said, half to herself. "And I suspect I know what he would have done with this order. But it's not my place to say, Lieutenant. Nor is it yours." Her gaze grew hard again. "You keep your nose clean."

"Yes, ma'am. And truly, ma'am—thank you for listening."

Jessica made her way to the atrium, taking in the simulated mid-morning light, and waited on a manicured path by the herb garden. Ted arrived a few minutes later, peering around furtively. He was, in many ways, a horrible spy, and she found it rather charming.

"How'd you get away?" she asked.

"Limonov's been ignoring me for the last fifteen minutes. His guys keep fucking up the battle drills, and he's getting pissed off at them. I can give you maybe ten minutes before he comes looking for me."

"Come on, then." She hurried out of the garden and down the hall, and he followed her.

"What's going on?" he asked.

"Emily's going to call Herrod," she told him. She wanted to run, but there were too many people in the hallway. She could not afford that kind of attention.

"That's good, yes?"

"And then she's going to tell Valentis she did it."

"Ah." He thought. "Where are we going?"

"Foster's quarters. Valentis will relieve her of duty. Might even put a guard on her. We can't wait and see."

"What's in Foster's quarters?"

"If I'm right," she told him, "he has an off-grid in there somewhere."

"Which you need for what reason?"

"I want to talk to Captain Solomonoff."

Ted stopped dead and grabbed her arm. "Jessica. You can't."

"Ted—"

"That's more than mutiny. That's treason, Jess."

She shook her arm free. "I'm not going to *tell* her anything," she said, annoyed. "But I need to hear it from her side. If she killed our captain, I want to know why, and we're getting nothing but bullshit from our own brass." She started walking again. "With an off-grid, she won't know anything about us if we don't tell her."

Ted fell into step with her again, but she could tell his enthusiasm was dampened. "If we survive this," he mumbled, "I'm never letting anyone I know take shore leave again."

The hallway before Foster's quarters was empty, and they ducked in and closed the door behind them. Jessica took a moment to let her eyes sweep the room: a bunk with a table next to it, a standard-sized dresser, a couch and two chairs, and a low bookcase. He had given the space almost no personalization. There was a stack of real, bound books on the bookcase, but no artwork, no color, no decoration on the walls or around the window.

Over the dresser was projected a single still photograph of a strikingly beautiful, ice-pale blond woman in a white medical coat. Jessica found herself surprised Foster would keep a picture of his wife so close after what he'd confessed to her.

"We're looking for something flat and reflective," she told Ted, heading for the bookcase. "Like a sheet of glass or polymer. Something that you could embed some circuitry in."

Ted started with the nightstand, pulling open the single drawer. "It's empty," he said, sounding puzzled. "Has someone cleared this place out already?"

"I don't think so," Jessica said. She picked up a book, examined the binding, felt the edges of the stiff cover. "I think he just lived like this." She found nothing in the first book; setting it aside, she picked up the second.

Ted had knocked his fingers against the sides of the night-stand and switched to the dresser, pulling open the top drawer. She heard him rummaging around, and then he grew still. "Oh," he said, and something in his voice made her stop and turn. He was staring into the drawer, unmoving.

She carried the book with her to join him. "What is it?"

Ted just nodded toward the drawer. It contained a dozen pairs of underwear, stacked in threes, each folded so uniformly a robot might have placed them there. Nestled behind them, in one corner, was a plain gold ring. In the opposite corner was a burgundy satin hair ribbon, as precisely folded as the under-wear, tucked against the back of the drawer. It took her a mo-ment to realize what was bothering Ted: wrapped around the ribbon, barely visible, was a long, dark hair.

"His wife's a blonde," Ted said quietly.

Jessica remembered the ribbon. She had loaned it to Elena for a party, years ago, some formal reception for a bunch of admi-rals. Elena had pulled it out in annoyance less than an hour into the party, and had mislaid it. Jessica had reassured her that it wasn't important, but her friend had been irritated with herself when she hadn't been able to find it again.

Apparently the captain had found it first.

Jessica looked between the ring and the ribbon. Two sepa-rate lives, never the twain shall meet. She shook herself. "Later, Ted."

She found a partial transceiver in the third book, and Ted found the other piece tucked into the bed frame. They sat on the couch and placed the pieces on the table; Jessica let Ted do the delicate work of joining the halves. After a few moments the polymer sheet strobed once with a violet glow, and then the controls were projected before her eyes, pale orange and sharp, as clean as any modern comm setup.

"You can leave if you want," she said.

He shook his head. "If *Penumbra*'s innocent," he said, "we're following an illegal order. I'm not taking off after all this. Do it."

Jessica keyed in a message for *Penumbra,* adding only *Galileo*'s general ident for authentication. She expected to have to wait for a response while Solomonoff validated the auth, but the connection was accepted almost immediately.

"*Galileo,* this is *Penumbra.*" The voice was a woman's. She spoke Standard with a flat accent, as if she had been raised on Earth. "I have been trying to reach you."

That brought Jessica up short. "I—who is this?"

"This is Captain Valeria Solomonoff. To whom am I speaking?"

"This is Lieutenant Jessica Lockwood," she said. "Why have you been trying to contact us?"

There was a pause, and when the woman spoke again, she sounded almost gentle. "I am sorry to have to inform you," she said, "but your captain has been lost."

Jessica looked at Ted; she suspected her expression was as puzzled as his. "Yes, we know, Captain. We were told he was shot down. That you shot him down."

"No," Solomonoff said. "It was not us. It was the other ship."

She did not sound worried. Jessica was beginning to feel deeply uneasy. "What other ship?"

"It had no ident."

Ted spoke up. "Captain Solomonoff, I'm Lieutenant Tetsuo Shimada. Is the ship still out there? Can you give us its position?"

"I am afraid not," she told him. "Between ours and your captain's efforts, it was shot down as well. It went through with him."

"Through where?"

Captain Solomonoff sounded genuinely grieved. "We tried to follow," she told them. "To pull him out. But he was too close. There was nothing we could do. Your captain, I am afraid, was pulled into the wormhole."

don't suppose it is a voice lock."

Elena looked up at Trey and smiled. "No such luck," she told him. "And even if it was, I'd be afraid to bash the daylights out of it."

"Surely it's not a contact explosive."

She shook her head. "For detonation, it would need a trigger. But I don't know how stable it is. Stuff like polonium has been known to just break apart on impulse. I don't want to give it an excuse."

Her eyebrows knit together as she studied the interface. There had to be a release somewhere, some kind of handle into the thing's locking mechanism, but damned if she could find it. She slid her fingers gently over the edges of the box, feeling for anything uneven, and cursed the gloves of her radiation suit. "It's not a physical trigger," she said. "Any chance we can get a thermal scan through all this noise?"

Trey already had his scanner open, but beyond the radiation levels the picture it had of the box was fuzzy and distorted. She pulled his display closer and spun the image of the box. If it was a thermal trigger she would never find it. "Can you calibrate it enough to detect changes in surface material?" she asked him.

He frowned. "A fingerprint?"

"Of a sort. If these were assembled by machinery made of something different," she explained, "they might have left trace elements on the surface. Maybe those will lead us to the lock mechanism."

He made some adjustments, but the image did not change. "Can you get a finer granularity on the radiation readings?" she asked, playing a hunch.

In an instant the image of the box changed from amorphous orange to discrete blotches of color ranging from bright yellow to dull red. In the bottom corner of the facing panel was a small red patch the size of her thumb. She crouched down and examined the box itself; she could still see nothing, but she pulled out her spanner and aimed it at the corner. Carefully she began pushing through the surface material.

"You cannot open it," Stoya said, from his position against the wall.

"Shut up," Greg said to him.

Greg had never holstered his gun, and had never taken his eyes from the Volhynian policeman. Elena could guess what he was feeling. She was angry with Stoya herself, and would have taken great pleasure in shoving him to his death; but she simply wanted revenge. For Greg it was more than that. Losing a crew member was more than a personal loss; it was an affront to his professionalism. With Jake he had been angry, but there had been no one to be angry with, and he'd had no outlet but alcohol. It worried her, how easy it would be for him to shove Stoya into the cavern.

Stoya, though, did not know him so well. "You people of the Corps," he said, with some contempt, "you are so fond of posturing. That boy of yours. Do you know, he thought he would be famous? That he had discovered some great secret that no one else had recognized? What arrogance. It was astonishing to me that no one had killed him already."

Elena blinked and focused on the task in front of her. "Greg will kill him, Trey," she said quietly.

"Do you wish me to stop him?"

She looked up. He was studying her face, his expression closed, and she realized then that if she asked him, he would let Stoya die. She remembered how she had felt training her gun on Stoya, how vividly she could imagine pulling the trigger, him dropping to the ground. She wondered if she could kill him here and now, when he was defenseless, and dying.

Yes, she thought she could.

"There's a slim possibility Stoya actually knows something," she told him. And radiation sickness, as it progressed, would be deeply unpleasant. Her sense of vengeance, it seemed, leaned more toward the cold.

He nodded and stepped away, and she returned to her task.

"Do not goad the boy, Stoya," Trey said irritably, and she thought his mood was as much of a performance as Greg's was not.

"Don't insult me, old man," Greg growled. "This son of a bitch killed my officer. He killed his own officer. I don't need another reason to get rid of him."

"Your reason," Trey told him, "is that your engineer is trying to concentrate. So if you are going to kill him, kill him and have done with it. We do not have the time for distractions."

"He will not kill me," Stoya said. "He is bloodless, this one. No wonder that woman chose you, Zajec. Men of the Corps have no balls at all."

Elena heard Trey swear. "Very well, Captain Foster," he said dismissively, "throw him over."

Oh, for God's sake. "All of you, shut the fuck up," she snapped. "Greg, kill him or don't, but stop rising to his bullshit. And Trey, good God, you know better."

There was a brief silence, and then she heard Trey's footsteps moving closer. She heard Stoya say, "Perhaps the Corps is not without balls after all," but this time Greg did not answer. She looked up at Trey when he rejoined her.

"Was that sufficient?" he asked.

"Perfect," she told him. "I didn't know who to root for." Carefully she wedged her spanner into the small slice she had made and took a breath, leaning back. "Okay," she said, "let's give this a try."

She leaned forward and touched the mechanism, and Ellis's logo appeared, large and bright, on the face of the box. After about half a second it spun, shattered theatrically, and disappeared. A moment later, the entire side of the box obligingly vanished. It was a flashy piece of technology, that lock, but ultimately it was just an interface for a physical key. What the box contained was something else entirely.

The crate was filled, top to bottom, with cubes like the ones they had seen by the entrance, each one stamped with four concentric circles. Trey adjusted his scanner again, and Elena studied the results. The shells were made of an inert material the scanner could not decipher, but the cubes were far less radioactive than pure dellinium. Even this close they only gave off 4.2.

Someone in a regular uniform could handle them for several minutes without receiving a lethal dose. Someone in a radiation suit could carry one for hours.

"What is it?" Greg asked.

She described the cubes to him. "If this really is a stable isotope, I'd only need three of them, maybe four, to get us out of here."

"Can you verify what they are?" Greg asked.

"Not without opening one up." She looked up and met Trey's eyes.

"Let me do it," he said, but she shook her head.

"I'm the one with the spanner."

She pulled out one of the cubes and held it in the palm of her hand. It was almost buoyant, as if it contained something lighter than air. She moved several meters down the walkway, clear of Trey and the others, and held her hand out over the ledge. Her fingers found the seam on the cube, and she pulled her spanner out again, resting its morphing edge against the join.

"Someone record this," she said, and twisted it open.

The contents were glowing, as bright as her suit light, and the material lost its shape when the cube wall fell off. It shimmered for an instant, veins of light and dark shifting in its amorphous depths; and then she dropped it into the pit, afraid to breathe until the light it emitted was swallowed by the hole.

Greg looked up. "Dellinium-345, sixty-eight percent certainty," he said.

"Why so low?"

"The radiation blew most of the readings," he said, "which is exactly why the sensor concluded it was dellinium."

She turned back to the crate. "I want to take six, just in case," she said, plucking cubes from the box. She handed three to Trey. It made her hair stand on end, thinking of the power they held.

"What are you going to do with it?" Stoya asked. "You said yourself that without the proper equipment, even the stable isotope is explosive."

"And what do you know about the proper equipment?" She tucked three cubes into her pockets, then stared at the crate. It was still packed full; there had to be a thousand cubes in there. A thousand terraformers, a thousand years. No more restrictions for FTL fields; no more twelve-hour recharges. It was all here, more power than any one planet would need. More than all of their colonies scattered throughout the galaxy could ever use. No one need ever starve again. Disasters like Canberra would never have happened at all.

She had been deployed less than six months. She had seen three Aleph stations and a resort planet. Canberra was her first residential colony, the first place that had wanted to be nothing more than someone's home. But that home had become toxic, and the Corps had not made it in time. PSI had tried, but they, too, had brought too little too late. When Elena had arrived, she had learned what happened to humans who lost hope. And she had learned how far she would go in the name of fulfilling her mission.

She was not a killer, but she had killed. She had had a good reason. There was always a good reason. More firepower, more advantage. The bigger the stick, the easier it was to keep the peace. She looked over at Stoya, who was still occupied with glowering at Greg. Bad men were never the real threat.

She swore quietly. "We can't leave it," she said.

Greg looked over at her, but said nothing. She met Trey's eyes, willing him to understand. *I am sorry,* she told him silently. *All I wanted was to get you home.*

She watched as he realized what she was saying, as he wrestled with the idea, just for a moment, looking for alternatives. And then, his bright eyes sad, he nodded. "How do we detonate it?" he asked her.

That, of all things, finally unnerved Stoya. "Detonate? Are you mad? This entire planet will go up. There will be radiation for thousands of light years. You could destabilize the wormhole."

"Thanks for the astrophysics lesson." Greg sounded calm and secure, and she almost smiled. This was the man she had worked with for the last seven years. "Where do we set it off?"

"In the pit," she said. She turned and started walking briskly up the ramp, the way they had come. *Sartre* obligingly flashed *Nine minutes* in the air before her eyes; she would have to set it up quickly if they were to have a chance at escape. "We can use the isotope to detonate the raw material. I can cannibalize something in that lab up there for a trigger, maybe even a timer."

"This is suicide!" Stoya was stalking after them, but his earlier composure had deserted him. "Do you think they have spent decades putting this refinery together so you can blow it up? Do you think they will *thank* you for this?"

"Who is 'they'?" Greg did not slow down to wait for the answer.

"You know who they are!"

"Shadow Ops."

Elena looked over at him. "Not Central?"

He would not meet her eyes. "I don't know," he admitted. "Possibly. But not everyone. I know that much."

"Stupid, naive woman," Stoya growled. "Do you think any private corporation would have a setup like this without approval from the government? If you destroy this refinery, you will destroy your career."

Elena wondered, for a moment, at the sort of person who would think she was concerned with her career in the face of all this. "For all I know," she said, "it's Ellis running this place and lying to our government about what's involved. Ellis used to work underground, so who's to say he hasn't got some rogue friends still involved?"

"That might fly," Greg agreed, and she grinned.

"Let's get out of here alive," she suggested, "and then we can worry about how much to leave out."

Trey was shaking his head. "I do wonder how easily you Corps soldiers lie to one another."

Stoya was not finished, however. "You speak of my crimes, my deeds that you would call evil. What is it you call this? You know what this material could do. You know the lives it could save. Hundreds of thousands. Millions. And you would destroy it because you mistrust your government?"

For a moment she thought of ignoring the question, but she wanted to say it aloud, for Trey and Greg to hear it. They would all be responsible, after all. "Actually," she said, "I don't mistrust my government. Not in any major way, anyway. I trust they'd take this dellinium isotope and use it to build some truly amazing, life-saving things. They might even manage six months before they decided to use it as a 'deterrent' for some

Second Sector turf war. Maybe a whole year would pass before some psychopath like yourself got ahold of enough to make a threat." She glanced at Greg; he met her eyes, his long stride never slowing, and she turned back to Stoya. "You may believe I'm killing people," she finished. "From where I stand? I'm saving them."

Stoya was gaping. "I will not be a part of this!"

"Fine," Elena said, as they emerged from the hallway into the main hangar. "Then stay out of the way."

In the end she had to dismantle the robotic arm to build a timer. Detonation was not an issue; one comm circuit triggered to overheat would set off the isotope once it was out of its protective casing. She had finished the explosive in a few minutes, and could have burned Ellis's project to vapor in an instant, but she took an extra moment for the timer. She found, even in the face of preventing the kind of war that had taken the civilization of this planet, that she had never felt more strongly about staying alive.

She hurried back into the hangar, where the light was better. Greg and Trey had opened an access panel in one wall and were pulling out lengths of wire. She had no idea how much they would need to lower the isotope to the bottom of the mine, but six hundred meters would put it close enough to the unrefined ore to set off the chain reaction.

Stoya was sitting on the floor close to the two men. Odd circles had formed under his eyes. He looked utterly dispirited, and she thought if she were a better person she might have felt sorry for him.

The timer and detonator were easy enough to cobble together. She tested the mechanism once, shooting a little jolt of electricity into the trigger's main controls. "Not my prettiest work," she admitted, looking at the jumbled row of connectors, "but solid." Jake had always told her beauty was optional; it was how well something worked that mattered. She always heard subtext when he said that. "How much wire have you got?"

"About a thousand meters," Greg replied, "if we tie it all together. Will that get us to the bottom?"

"It will get us close enough so that it won't break if it drops," she said, picking up her messy blocks of work. "No time like the present," she said.

"I will not go," Stoya said. His voice was thin.

Greg opened his mouth, but Trey spoke first. "I will watch him," he said. "Be quick."

An act of faith, she thought, or perhaps an acknowledgment that Greg really would kill Stoya if he could. On impulse she pressed her masked face against Trey's to kiss him on the cheek. "If we are not back in five minutes, get off the planet as fast as you can."

She jogged down the hall, Greg in step with her. She handed him the timer, and as they ran, she fixed the trigger mechanism to one end of the wire.

"How long do you figure?" he asked.

"That's a good question," she replied. "I want to give us time to get away, but as soon as we show up on the other end of that wormhole—"

"—the whole fucking sector will be clamoring to dive through. So either someone gets back here in time to stop the detonation, or a lot of people die." He shook his head. "What do you figure our chances are?"

"We'll make it," she said with certainty. They came to the ledge, and she turned; Greg was looking incredulous. "You gonna bust me if I'm wrong?" she asked.

Much to her astonishment he laughed. "You've got a point, Chief. Okay, we get out of this intact. The whole mission is a cakewalk."

"And when we've fucked up all of Shadow Ops' plans, no-body fires us." She pulled out the microscopic spanner and wedged it carefully into the casing of one of the isotope cubes. "You really think it's only them?"

"I can't believe so many officers could lie to me for so long," he said. "It's possible, of course. But I don't think I'm that easy to fool."

"Someone already knows, though." She set the receiver on the trigger, then gave the cube a tug to test the strength of the wire. Stepping to the end of the ledge, she dropped it over, and began to let the coils of wire out. "Someone has known all along. If S-O wanted to do something, why didn't they do it twenty-five years ago?" She handed him the timer. "Let me know if it loses contact with the trigger."

"What do you think Kelso said?" he asked. "'Hey, everyone, there's a massive supply of high-yield dellinium on this planet'?"

"I'm guessing it was more along the lines of 'Lunatics have killed themselves. Let's not do the same thing.'"

"He should have blown the wormhole on this side," Greg said. "Four hundred meters."

"Setting up a detonator without a stable isotope would be dangerous," she reasoned. "The thing to do would be—oh, hell,

Greg, that's what he did!" It was exactly what she would have done, faced with nothing but raw dellinium and a destroyed civilization. "He brought some back, and tried to blow the wormhole from the other side. But next to the nuclear engine, the stuff destabilized." She shook her head. "All of the lies and the cover-ups, all these years—and it really was an accident."

He was silent a moment. "You remember what you said to me after Eindhoven?"

Good God, Eindhoven had been five years ago. Another evac, far less catastrophic than Canberra, but enough to give her flashbacks. They had evacuated thirteen people, and left more than three thousand behind to a local government that was turning toward dictatorship rather than allowing its people to emigrate. It had been the first time she had seen up close how much he took failure to heart. "Something about powerlessness, if I remember right."

"You said the miracle of the human race was not our existence, but the fact that we had never managed to exterminate ourselves."

"That sounds like the sort of pretentious Pollyanna bullshit I would have spouted," she said. She would have wanted to make him feel better, and blind optimism would have been all she had to offer.

"You were right, though—eight hundred meters. But we will someday. It's just we all think it won't happen in front of us." He began counting down, and when they ran out of cable he was at 1,024. She tied off the wire, taking the timer from his hands; he was watching her, his expression troubled. "This city, Elena—is that our future, do you think? Or our past?"

She looked at him. It was the first time she had really looked at him since their argument. There was none of what he had said in his expression, none of the angry, brittle stranger she had lived with for the last six months. All she saw was Greg, the man she knew, who had never, as long as she had known him, lived without dread. She had always tried to give him hope, a sense that what they were doing mattered. For the first time it crossed her mind that hope was not something he was ever going to get from her, or from anyone else.

"Not our future," she said.

"How do you know?"

"Because we won't let it happen," she told him.

"So simple."

"Yes."

He looked confused, and she kept looking at him, willing him to see it, to understand. Maybe she was being optimistic. Maybe she was lying to him, or to herself. But that was the only hope they had of winning.

At last he nodded. "Okay. About time we got out of here, don't you think? We've got four minutes before we're all fried beyond help. Put two hours on the timer; we've got to be through the wormhole before it blows."

The wormhole was the wild card. By *Sartre*'s chronometer, the trip through had taken seventeen minutes, but the accuracy of that measurement was anybody's guess. And they had never ascertained whether or not there was a time skew—large or small—between the two sides. A time skew could render this entire endeavor pointless. "Seems close," she said, rapidly keying in the numbers.

"The second we come out of there," he pointed out, "every-body knows the radiation warning is bogus, and the wormhole is a two-way trip. If someone's waiting for us—some S-O ship curious to see if we blew ourselves up—the first thing they're going to do is head back here to see what we did. We can't give them time to shut it down."

"I'm not sure we can get *Sartre*'s FTL field working," she confessed.

To her surprise, he grinned at her. "Maybe we can't, Elena," he told her. "But if you can't get us out of this, there's no way out at all."

It took her a moment to recognize it was a vote of confidence.

have misjudged you," Stoya said.

Trey looked down at him. His voice had grown reedy, and he sagged against the wall as if he were unconscious. In fact, Trey suspected he might be unconscious soon, and he felt resentful of the peace that would bring. On the other hand, he would not have to listen to the man's attempts at psychological manipulation. He wrapped his fingers reflexively around the grip of his hand weapon and looked away again.

Stoya did not give up. "I took you for someone strong. And yet you allow your woman to walk away with another man. Perhaps you have simply grown old."

"I think you and Luvidovich draw from the same bag of tricks," Trey said.

Stoya made a noncommittal noise. "It was a shame, having to kill him," he said. "But he was flawed. He could not see that the path to justice is not always clean."

"You know very little of justice."

"Perhaps you are right," Stoya admitted. "I never ran after doing what needed to be done. But you did, didn't you?" Trey was silent, and Stoya continued. "There was no proof of your story, you know. Your sister was not badly injured. Your mother had not been struck at all. She did not defend you, did you know that? She was perfectly happy to see you hang, so long as she was left alone."

Trey knew all of it. He had known it before he struck his stepfather, and before he left home. He had always understood his mother's nature, even when his father was still alive, even when he still hoped someday she might love him.

"What I do not understand," Stoya went on, "is why you joined PSI. You had so many options. You are a born killer, Zajec. You demonstrated this with your stepfather. All of those Syndicate traders you killed—that was wasteful, you know. You could have done so much with your talent, and instead you invest your life with a pack of idealists. I always expected to hear something of you: that you conquered a world, or perhaps took over the Fifth Sector PSI fleet. Instead, you will die a meaningless old man, remembered for nothing at all."

"And what is your legacy? Murder and psychosis?" He looked back down; Stoya was staring at him, his expression ugly. "You will be remembered as a madman, Stoya—if you are remembered at all—for that is what you are." He turned away again. "I am happy enough to leave some peace behind me." He thought if he held on to the thought long enough, it might become true.

Elena emerged from the hallway then, Foster at her heels. "Two hours," she said tersely.

"One hour, fifty-nine minutes, and twelve seconds," Foster corrected. "Including the three and a half minutes we have to get off this rock. Let's get moving."

Trey saw Elena's eyes go from him to Stoya, and she frowned.

He reached out a hand to her, and tucked his anger away again; she clasped his gloved fingers and said nothing. Behind her, Foster pulled his hand weapon, steadying it on Stoya.

"Staying or going?" he asked.

Silently Stoya climbed to his feet, pushing against the wall to keep his balance. He wavered, but ultimately stood unaided, and Trey felt an instant's disappointment. He turned away, and with Elena's hand in his he headed for the exit.

As they headed up the hill back to *Sartre,* Trey could not help but notice the bounce in her step. She had not been so buoyant when she had headed back to set the explosive, and a whisper of self-doubt returned. But when she caught his eye she smiled, entirely unself-conscious.

"There is always a moment," she told him, "when the plan is in motion, and cannot be reversed. No matter how mad it is, there's something liberating about having made a choice."

He could not help but smile back. "You are an optimist."

"She is optimistic because she is a fool," Stoya put in. He was becoming difficult to understand. "If we survive, they will kill you for this."

Elena's eyes had gone hard at the sound of Stoya's voice. "They might," she agreed. "And it will still be done."

Trey felt a surge of affection, and pride to which he had no right. She was a warrior, this woman, and Stoya had no idea who he was talking to.

They came over the hill and within sight of the ship, and Elena started the engines remotely. "I'll do the external preflight," she said. "Greg, you do the internal, and set up the decon." She turned to Trey. "I'm going to check the feet; can you do a quick visual on the undercarriage?"

She set about examining the surface thrusters on the ship's landing gear while Foster opened the door and climbed in. Trey squatted, aiming his comm light at the underside of the ship. Under the circumstances, a preflight seemed a luxury; he was acutely aware of the explosives they had rigged. On the other hand, she was the mechanic. He had learned repeatedly over the years never to argue with his mechanics.

Something caught his eye, and he frowned. He leaned closer, examining the hairline crack running diagonally below the ship's engine mount. "Elena," he called, "you should look at this."

There was no answer.

"Elena?"

He stood, and turned.

Stoya had one arm around her neck, the other pointing her hand weapon at her head. She had her hands over his arm, and Trey could see how tightly she was squeezing, but she otherwise stood still. Trey's hand went to the grip of his own weapon, and Stoya shook his head. "Do not move, Zajec, or she will die before I will." His bloodless face stretched into a grin. "I would like that."

Trey had frozen. "If you do that," he reasoned, "none of us will help you." He was too far away to extract her safely, nearly two meters. How could he get closer? How could he get her away?

"I will take her into the hangar," Stoya said, backing away. "She will turn off the timer, and then I will let her go."

"You are a liar," Elena said.

"*Shut up*," Stoya snapped. "All of this is your fault. All of it. If you had stayed out of it, Zajec might have had a light sentence, mercy because of his history. But you complicated everything by making it look like revenge, like that boy had been a rival. He was not worth it, you know."

"He was worth a thousand of you," Elena said, and Trey wondered if she was deliberately trying to make Stoya angry.

"He was a coward. And a fool. No one cared about the flight recorder. No one cared about that old ship and all the foolish theories. If he had left it at that, they would have let him live. But he thought he could be a patriot. As if it were not his own government behind all of it."

"Central doesn't stage interplanetary incidents," Elena insisted.

Stoya scoffed. "I see you are a fool as well. Shall I kill her for you, Zajec? She will be less trouble dead."

"You will let her go," Trey said. He kept his voice icy. The ship's engines vented out the back; could he use that somehow? "And I will agree not to murder you. Anything else, Stoya, and your death will be at my hands."

Stoya laughed again. "I have always liked you, Zajec," he said. "You are ruthless. If you did not have such a bothersome sense of honor, we might have been friends." His expression hardened. "Back up and get on the ship."

"Don't do it," Elena told him. "He's going to kill me anyway."

Trey saw Stoya's arm tighten around her neck. "He will do it," he told her, "because like all the men around you, he is weak. Women like you, you take what makes men strong, and you call it love. There is no such thing as love. There is only helplessness."

Trey caught it, an instant before it happened: Elena's eyes flickered to the other side of the ship, and he knew it was time to move. He drew his heavy, Central-sanctioned weapon, watched

Stoya's eyes widen, watched his hand clench against the gun, watched Elena shove his arm away from her, enough to shake his aim. Stoya's shot flashed wildly, and Greg Foster, from the other side of the ship, crashed into Stoya from the side. The captain hooked Elena around the waist and rolled the two of them to the ground, keeping himself between her and Stoya. By the time Stoya had steadied himself, Trey had his weapon trained on the man's head. Stoya still had Elena's gun, but his hand hung at his side.

Trey held his weapon steady. "Drop that gun, Stoya."

Stoya straightened, his weariness apparent again, but this time Trey did not believe it. Stoya grinned at him, less enthusiastically than before. "I told you," he said. "Once a killer, always a killer."

Out of the corner of his eye, Trey caught movement: Elena rolling over, rising to her knees. She was all right. "I shall not ask you again to drop that weapon," he said.

"It doesn't matter to you, does it, that I have answers for your friends that they will never otherwise find," Stoya went on. "Or that I killed Luvidovich for you, after he stripped you naked and cut you. He could have done anything he wanted, and you could not have stopped him. No, all you care about is revenge, like a good murderer."

Stupid, childish attempts at manipulation. He wanted Trey to drop his guard, to prove that he wasn't a killer, that Stoya was wrong. Stoya's opinion was not relevant. Trey was what he had always been, and Stoya was a fool to challenge him. The man had no sense of proportion.

Elena was still on her knees, scrabbling frantically at the ground around Foster as if she was searching for something.

Something was wrong. Was Foster moving? He couldn't tell, and he didn't have time to be diverted by something else. "You didn't kill him for me," he said to Stoya. "You killed him because he was figuring out who you were."

Stoya bared his teeth. "Come now, Ivan," he said. At the sound of his childhood name, Trey straightened. Of course he was Ivan again. He had never stopped being Ivan. "You expect me to believe you feel sorry for the boy? As you stand there, ready to kill me for crimes I have not yet committed? That will certainly show your friends what you really are."

She already knows what I really am, Trey thought. And under the circumstances, he thought she might forgive him for killing again.

At the sound of the weapon firing Trey jumped, startled. The explosive shot tore into Stoya's side, through the radiation suit, leaving a bloody gap where his kidney and most of his rib cage had been. He dropped onto the silver-gray surface of the lake, that smug smile still on his face, even as his eyes went vacant.

Trey turned. Elena was still on her knees, the handgun she had fired—Foster's, Trey realized—discarded beside her. Foster was limp and still, and Trey could see her running her gloved fingers over his rib cage. Dropping his own gun, he stepped over to them; the tunic of Foster's suit was torn, the edges charred, and beneath it his uniform had burned and fused to his skin. Elena was trembling as if she were cold.

"I think he's breathing," Elena said, her voice ragged. "The shot got him under his arm."

"We must get him onboard," he told her.

She looked up at him, and her eyes were wide and frantic. Everything else had disappeared for her, he realized: the dellinium, the detonation. The vengeance she had just exacted for her faithless ex-lover. The fact that she had kept him from once again being a murderer.

"*M'laya*," he said, more gently, "the radiation. We must hurry."

She scrambled to her feet as Trey slid his arms under Foster's armpits and lifted. The Corps captain was heavier than he looked; densely built, despite his thinness. Elena grabbed Foster's heels, and together they carried him into the little ship.

Trey helped her settle Foster onto one of the couches, then headed forward to the console, leaving Elena to retrieve the medkit. He slid the door shut, ignoring the remains of their preflight check, and raised them off the ground, shooting them upward. His mind went to the crack he had seen in their undercarriage, but dismissed it as moot at this point—if they stayed in the thick of the planet's radiation much longer, Foster would have no chance at all.

He keyed in a quick route back to *Lusitania,* then joined Elena at Foster's side. She had tugged off his hood and was pressing an analgesic to his neck, her other hand gripping the med scanner. As Trey crouched beside her, she said, "Without an autopilot, the ship won't compensate for obstacles."

"*Lusitania* is the only engine signature out there," he reminded her. "I don't think we need to worry about running into any satellites. How is he?"

"He's in shock," she said shortly, "and he's bleeding internally." Foster's breathing was fast and shallow, his hands clumsily clutching the air. Not entirely unconscious, then, Trey realized. "Sealing the outside of the wound will only do so much, and I'm not sure how much of this painkiller he can take."

Gently, Trey took the scanner from her hand. Foster's blood pressure was dangerously low, but his brain scan clearly showed he was conscious. Trey laid the scanner down and pulled the liquid bandage from the medkit. He laid the vial down on the ground, and began pulling the charred, ragged edges of Foster's uniform away from the wound. It looked raw and oddly swollen, but the bleeding was slow. Most of what oozed from the area was sera. Elena was right; sealing the wound would guard against infection, but Foster would not last long enough to be killed by a germ.

Elena emptied the analgesic, and Foster's breathing steadied. His hands stilled, and he mumbled something. It took Trey a moment to recognize Elena's name.

"Be quiet," she said shortly. "We're getting out of here."

She sounded angry. Trey thought Foster should have opened his eyes; he might have seen the frantic worry on her face.

"Stoya," Foster said.

"Don't talk," she chided, just as Trey said, "Dead."

Finally Foster's eyes opened, but instead of looking at Elena, he looked directly at Trey. For one moment, Trey could see into the other man's heart to the grim satisfaction there. *Elena may have forgotten about revenge,* Trey thought, *but you have not, have you, Captain Foster?*

"Do not be so quick to declare victory," Trey told him quietly. "We are still on the wrong side of the wormhole."

The cabin darkened, and the artificial lights came up. They had cleared the planet's atmosphere. Trey looked at Elena; she knelt, tense, her elbows on the edge of the couch, the spent analgesic pad in one hand. *Helpless,* he thought. He knew how she felt.

"*Sartre,* how far are we from *Lusi?*"

Three minutes, the ship told him.

"I'll lay the charges," she said faintly.

"There is another problem, *m'laya,*" he said. "Our undercarriage is cracked." He described to her what he had seen.

That seemed to get through to her. "That's our engine mount," she said, and her voice sounded more focused. "I may be able to patch it, but a crack like that . . . it won't be a perfect fix. It should hold us through the wormhole. But getting away on the other side could be more interesting." She had not moved.

Trey reached out and took the analgesic pad from between her fingers. "I will look after him," he said firmly.

She turned and met his eyes. She had not looked frightened before, he realized, not even when Stoya was holding a weapon to her head. Trey wanted to wrap his arms around her and promise her that Foster would survive, that they would make it home safely, that everything would be as it was. He didn't, though. She would know it for a lie before he said a single word.

"Do you wish for me to attempt the repair?" he asked.

Something flickered across her face, and he thought it was gratitude. She smiled at him, and ever so slightly her body relaxed. "This is my job," she told him. "I'll take care of it." With one more glance at Foster, she pushed herself to her feet, and headed to the back of the cabin.

CHAPTER 49

Galileo

Jessica stood in the gym, staring up at the infantry brigade leader, and wished for Alex Carter. If Alex were here, Jessica was certain they would have been done talking already. Off-duty Alex had a reputation for being shy, or even stupid, but the truth was he was always listening. Jessica and Ted could have outlined their argument concisely, and only once. Alex would have considered—silently—and decided whether or not to believe them.

But Alex was still on Volhynia, and Lee Henare, despite his distinctive eyebrows and piercing stare, was a good deal less bright. He was a nice enough fellow, but his failures were almost always of imagination, and now was no different. Standing over her in the gym, his uniform already damp with sweat from his battle drills, he was frowning down at her like a disapproving schoolmaster.

"Why isn't Commander Broadmoor telling me all this?" he asked.

"She's meeting with the captain," Ted told him. It was the truth, or close enough, assuming Emily had carried out her original plan.

Ted had pointed out to Jessica repeatedly that no ship that had gone into the wormhole had ever come back out again, but she could not give up hope. If the *Phoenix*'s flight recorder had survived, then the *Lusitania* could have as well. She did not think about whether or not the captain would ever come back; she just hung on to the possibility that he was still alive.

And maybe Lanie was with him.

Captain Solomonoff had played Captain Foster's mayday for her, but had said they had not seen a civilian ship. "Would he have fabricated that, perhaps to elicit a faster response?"

"No," Jessica said. "He wouldn't lie to put another ship in danger like that."

Defending the captain's honesty made her feel uncomfortable about withholding the names of the likely passengers on that missing ship. She did not know where Zajec stood with his former tribe, and since—for now, at least—they could do nothing about his fate, she kept her suspicions to herself.

All that was clear to Jessica was that *Penumbra* had not attacked the captain, and that called into serious doubt Will Valentis's story of Foster's death—not to mention the honesty of every single member of *Demeter*'s crew. "We can't attack them if they were trying to help," she had argued to Henare. "Central didn't know any of this when they gave us the order."

But Henare wasn't biting. Half of his people were warming up with calisthenics, the others assembling assault weapons and riot gear in preparation for boarding the other ship. "Once Commander Broadmoor has spoken with Captain Valentis," he said, "we'll get the stand-down order from him. But I'm not setting my people up to go in cold."

And she lost her temper. "*Your people*? Lee Henare, you are twenty-six years old, and before now you've been in command exactly once, and that was only because Alex sprained his foot dancing with Becky on her birthday."

"Carter," he said through clenched teeth, "is still on that damned colony. So maybe, Lockwood, you could cut me a god-damned break."

Ted pushed himself between them. "That's enough." He stood with his back to Jessica, blocking her view. "How about this, Lee. You guys keep up your preparations, but you think about it. Maybe discuss it with some of the others—you've got some people who've seen this sort of combat, and they may be able to think of some things we haven't. We're going to need ideas if Foster really went through that wormhole."

And that, it seemed, was the key. Henare's face lit up with something like hope. "Do you think we can get him back?"

Jessica shoved her way back around Ted. "As long as this clusterfuck doesn't explode," she told him, "then we have a chance. What do you say?"

He thought, and she fought the urge to shake him. "I'll think about it," he said.

Before she could speak, Ted stepped on her foot. "That's all we can ask, Lee."

"*Ten-hut!*"

This outburst was so rare on *Galileo* that all two-dozen infantrymen in the gym failed utterly to come to attention, instead stopping their exercises to exchange confused glances. Jessica looked over at the source of the order, and her heart sank. Standing in the gym doorway, wearing a full uniform complete with commander's stripes, was an officer from *Demeter*. Yuri Nikov, she recalled: tall even among those taller than average, and as wide as two men. The last time she had seen him, he had only been a lieutenant.

His eyes were blazing with rage at being ignored. "I said attention, people!" he shouted, his voice echoing through the space.

Henare and his platoons caught on quickly, and arranged themselves in two neat rows. Jessica and Ted stood at an angle to them, at attention. She wished fervently she had left before giving Lee a piece of her mind.

"On Captain Valentis's orders," Nikov said, "you men are now under my command." He paced in front of them, perhaps waiting for an objection; but it was Ted who spoke.

"Permission to ask a question, sir," he said smartly.

Nikov strode over to Ted. He looked annoyed, but Jessica could see in his face he appreciated Ted's deference. "Granted, soldier."

"Is Commander Broadmoor injured, sir?"

Whether or not Nikov was taken in by Ted's disingenuous phrasing, he answered the question easily enough. "Commander Broadmoor has been temporarily relieved of her duties," he said. He turned back to the infantry. "Now, I want guerrilla drills, thirty-second intervals, until you carcasses hit all your points one hundred percent. We are twenty minutes away from this battle; I will not lose because one of you children decided to slack off. Now go!"

Hastily the platoons split into teams, and Lee began timing them in the drills. Jessica kept still, trying not to shake. Emily had been relieved of duty, which meant she had talked to Valentis, and he had moved her out of the way. "We were right," she whispered to Ted.

"Did you think we weren't?" he asked.

"No. But I was hoping. How do we get out of here?"

"Be polite, be military, and for pity's sake, keep saying 'sir.'" Ted caught Nikov's eye. "Excuse me, Commander, sir."

Nikov marched back over to them. "Yes, Lieutenant."

"Permission to return to my engineering duties, sir," he said.

"Granted." Nikov turned to Jessica, his eyes narrowing. "Where are you supposed to be, Lieutenant?"

Jessica had no idea. "Comms, sir," she said promptly.

He nodded. "Very well, Lieutenant, you'd best be on your way, too. Dismissed."

Out in the hallway, Jessica turned to Ted. "Can you stall them in engineering?" she asked. "Keep the weapons from spinning up? Slow them down a little?"

"I can try. What are you going to do?"

She looked up at him, into his earnest face, and ached to tell him. "Never mind what I'm going to do," she said. "Just slow them down, understand?"

"Jess—"

On impulse, she rose up on her toes and kissed his cheek. "Shut up and fight, Shimada," she told him, and turned and fled before she could see him react.

It took her longer than she'd hoped to reassemble the off-grid in Captain Foster's quarters, and for a moment she wished she had not let Ted go. But in the end she managed to piece it together and send the ping, and she sat on Greg Foster's bed, staring at the photograph of his wife on the dresser. Time was moving at a glacial pace; after less than thirty seconds she grew tired of the otherworldly smile on the woman's face, and deactivated the photograph. She wondered if his wife had been told he was dead, and how she felt about it. She wondered if Captain Solomonoff would answer in time.

After more minutes than she dared count, the response came. "*Galileo*, this is *Penumbra*."

Jessica exhaled. "This is Lieutenant Lockwood again, Captain Solomonoff," she acknowledged. "I have to tell you something I didn't before. I need to warn you."

The woman's tone changed instantly, becoming sharp and wary. "Warn us of what?"

"Captain Valentis has been ordered to secure your surrender and take your ship," Jessica said. "We'll be there in about sixteen minutes."

There was a long pause, and only the steady pulse of the off-grid told Jessica the connection was still intact. "I see," Captain Solomonoff said at last, and Jessica thought she had pieced it all together.

"The Admiralty doesn't have all the facts," Jessica told her, "and Captain Valentis won't comm back to the Admiralty for clarification. He's preparing to attack you. You need to get your ship out of there."

Another silence. "I am afraid that is not possible."

Good God, are all captains stubborn idiots? "Respectfully, Captain, we outgun you substantially. You may be bigger than we are, but we'll be able to shut you down with very little effort."

"I am aware of your firepower, Lieutenant." But it was not bravado Jessica heard in her voice: it was sadness.

"Captain, you've got civilians there, haven't you? Just leave. Pick a direction. You don't even have to get lost; we'll clear this up with Central in a day or two, and then—"

"You misunderstand, Lieutenant. We cannot leave. Our FTL field generator has been damaged. We are a week away from travel, at a minimum."

Jessica's throat closed. "Was it the S-O ship that hit you? Did you get this damage trying to save our captain?"

"Had we not been recovering from the earlier attack, it would not have been insurmountable." Another pause. "I will not be boarded voluntarily, Lieutenant," she said quietly. "Your Captain Valentis will need to take us by force."

Frantically, Jessica said, "But it wouldn't be permanent. You'd just need to surrender, and then we could fix all this, and then—"

"And how will you fix it, Lieutenant? It is not our way, to be prisoners. Nor will I admit to crimes I did not commit."

She sounded so sane, so steady, so confident. Jessica could not believe she had given credence to MacBride's story. No one who heard Captain Solomonoff could think her insane.

A glimmer of hope ignited within her.

"Captain," Jessica said, "would you be willing to tell us that? Send a message to the effect that you didn't hurt anyone?"

"Respectfully, Lieutenant," the woman said dryly, "I have been trying to do that for four weeks."

"But you didn't have me before."

"You can get me through to Captain Valentis?"

Fuck Valentis, Jessica thought. "I can do better. Do you think you can come up with something off-the-cuff? We don't have a lot of time."

"I have been making speeches for many decades," the captain said. "Tell me when I may begin."

This should have been a difficult choice, Jessica thought. Snooping around the captain's mail was one thing. Even spreading rumors among the infantry was at worst in poor taste. This was flat-out insubordination and mutiny, and if she turned out to be wrong, it would mean her career, and anything resembling a normal life.

I can't just sit back and do nothing. "*Galileo,* can you route this call to intraship comms?"

The ship took a moment to set up the connection. "Yes."

"Captain Solomonoff, are you ready?"

"Yes, Lieutenant."

Captain Solomonoff's strong, steady voice filled the air around Jessica. Her message would be heard over every transmitter on the entire ship.

"Starship *Galileo,* this is Captain Valeria Solomonoff of the PSI starship *Penumbra.* We are aware of your mission, your destination, and your intent. We are prepared to defend ourselves." Her voice was cold and arrogant, and Jessica suspected she would play a formidable game of poker. "I wish to be clear, however, that the reasons your command has given for this attack are erroneous. We did not murder your Captain Foster—he was shot down by an unidentified vessel. We did not attack the starship *Demeter;* we defended ourselves against Captain Mac-Bride, who told me directly his mission was to remove us forcibly from the hot zone. This ship has never, under my command or any other, carried out an unprovoked attack against anyone, nor will we commence doing so, despite your current actions."

She was silent a moment. "We will not run. Neither will we allow ourselves to be boarded. We claim the sovereign right of all people to choose our own existence, to take our own path. Our goals have never been contrary to yours. If this becomes war, *Galileo,* the choice will have been yours."

She disconnected. Jessica stared at the transparent off-grid, wondering what she ought to do next.

Captain Valentis promptly let her know.

"Attention all hands." His voice came over the comms, louder and larger than life. "Lieutenant Jessica Lockwood has committed an act of treason. She is to be located and brought to me immediately."

Shit. How had he traced her? "*Galileo,*" she said, hastily dismantling the off-grid, "report my recent locations as the gym, engineering, and the infirmary. Do not, under any circumstances, let anyone know I was in the captain's quarters." She shoved the pieces of the off-grid back into their hiding places, and restarted the photograph of Captain Foster's wife. "Keep monitoring comms. I want to know about anything that comes in from the Admiralty, official or unofficial." For a few frantic seconds she blanked on a hiding place, then remembered the lower maintenance hallways. They would be empty now, with everyone preparing for battle, and if she kept moving, she could stay ahead of Valentis . . . at least until they were face-to-face with *Penumbra* and she found out how much Ted could do.

She stared for a moment at Foster's wife's face. At some point Valentis would come in here, and dig through all of Foster's possessions. On impulse she opened the top dresser drawer and closed her hand around Elena's hair ribbon, tucking it into her pocket and zipping it in safely. When he returned, she would put it back. If by chance he didn't . . . it was nobody's business if he'd saved an old hair ribbon, was it?

"You'd better come back," she said to the empty room . . . and then she turned and fled.

CHAPTER 50

T his will work, Elena thought, laying isotope cubes over *Lusi's* weapons batteries. *We will get home, and find* Galileo, *and Bob will take care of Greg.*

Which was a foolish hope, she reflected. Even if her repair of the engine mount held through the wormhole, she had seen enough damaged engines to suspect it might not withstand the stresses of entering an FTL field. It was possible, of course, that the wormhole would absorb the destruction of the planet, as it had absorbed so much else; but even with all of the anomalies it had displayed, that seemed unlikely. The most likely scenario was that the return trip through the wormhole would tear the engine mount apart again, and they would be stuck drifting in normal space until the blast from the planet overcame them.

And that was if the explosion she was currently setting didn't destroy them first. She was acutely aware that her idea was very close to the stunt that had destroyed the *Phoenix,* and that her assertion that the contained isotope would be more stable than whatever chunk of raw dellinium Captain Kelso had used was nothing but guesswork. The casing helped, but even the nanometer gap she had to pry open to insert the detonator made the substance spike alarmingly. The thing seemed to have noth-ing like a predictable matrix; power spun and roiled within it like an angry animal. No wonder Ellis was still working on the containment. She knew why people wanted it; it was powerful and fascinating, and seemed like a miracle. Annihilation often looked that way, if you were the sort of person who always as-sumed you would survive.

She focused on her task, laying a cube over one of the fuel re-serves and sliding her spanner—at its thinnest setting—through one seam. Objectively their deaths did not matter, but subjec-tively she discovered she cared very much if they survived. She had never felt so strongly that she had more left to do with her life.

She wondered what Danny would have done if he were with them. She had never thought of him as particularly bold or brave, even early on, when all of his flaws had been endearing. He never took an assignment with anything less than enthusi-asm and good cheer, but he never volunteered for anything, ei-ther. He was a good soldier, and would always have been a good soldier; but he would never have been extraordinary.

Except that they would not be here if he had not followed the clues. Insight or dumb luck—it didn't matter now. He had died because someone needed this to stay a secret, and because he had died, they had a chance to change it all.

Danny Lancaster, savior of humanity.

He would have enjoyed that.

She steadied the last cube in place, then pushed herself to her feet and climbed back over to *Sartre*. "How is he?" she asked, as she sealed *Lusi*'s door for the last time and secured their inner hatch.

She turned to Trey, who had stood when she walked in, then followed his eyes down to Greg's face. Greg was awake, his eyes on her, and she felt a ripple of relief. She took a step closer and knelt next to him. His skin looked gray and bloodless, and he was still covered in a sheen of sweat, but his gaze was steady on her face as she leaned over him.

"Greg?" she asked.

"He fades in and out," Trey told her. "His pressure has stabilized, and the internal bleeding has slowed. The radiation damage is a more immediate concern; that fine medkit does not seem to be equipped for radiation exposure. When we get to the other side, we will need to find him a doctor quickly."

"*Galileo*," Greg said.

"When he speaks," Trey said, and she caught a hint of dryness in his tone, "that is almost always what he says. I do believe he said something about your Commander Valentis as well. Something about hitting him harder."

"Did you hit him?" Elena asked Greg.

"Bastard," Greg mumbled.

She made herself smile at him. "I'm sorry I missed that."

Greg took a shuddering breath, and said, "Off my ship."

"When we get back," she assured him. She stood and turned to Trey. "I've got the trigger set on remote, rather than a timer. It's all guesswork anyway, and given everything that's gone wrong I'd rather have the flexibility of blowing it ourselves. What's our countdown?"

"Three minutes, eighteen seconds," Trey told her.

She reached out to squeeze his fingers, for him or for herself, she wasn't sure. "Let's hope nobody's coming the other way," she said, and turned to the cockpit.

She was only half joking.

Because they did not know if Stoya had sent a message back. They did not know if the lab systems pinged periodically with status. If anything solid was coming through when they were trying to return, the best-case scenario would be that they would be stuck inside the wormhole for the rest of their lives.

She brought the ship about, and they tugged their explosive payload toward the wormhole. Trey strapped himself into the copilot's seat to monitor their position. Elena watched through the window, counting stars, until a spot of darkness came into view: the rear of the object. She flew a spiral around it, giving it a wide berth, then slowed as the corona began to show. The window polarized as they centered on the entrance.

"One kilometer . . . now," Trey said.

The magnetic clamps gave a deep thrum as they released the *Lusitania.*

"It's pushing back on us," she reported, "but we're holding steady."

"Five hundred meters," Trey said.

There was nothing to do now but watch. Elena reached out a hand, and Trey took it.

"Ten meters. Detonation."

The flare caught them first, pouring around their ship like sunrise. Before them the wormhole spun and thrashed, beautiful and menacing. "Gun it," she said, and the ship's engine lit up to full throttle just as the percussion wave struck them. She held her breath . . .

They remained whole. A lurch of inertia hit her as the artificial gravity struggled to keep up, and then they were inside.

She felt their engine vibrating with effort, but there was no turbulence, even when the ship drew power away from the internal lights and the three of them were illuminated with nothing but the color of the anomaly. She had that same strange sensation of deafness; still, in the midst of it all, she thought she heard Trey say *It's beautiful.* She could feel his hand through the fabric of her glove and she squeezed tightly, hoping.

And then, without fanfare, they burst out the other side, stars and space surrounding them as if they had not just done something remarkable. Freeing her hand, she pulled up a star chart. "Where and when are we?" she asked the ship.

"Fifth Sector, adjacent to B1829, radiation zone. Time and date 3258.00.19. Earth-relative 0028."

She closed her eyes, relieved. The time skew, if it existed, had been a small one. They were back, and they were where they needed to be. Now all they needed—

"We have a proximity alarm," Trey said, his voice tense. "Right outside the radiation zone."

"Have they seen us?" she asked.

"They aren't moving toward us," he told her.

"How many?"

Trey rotated the visual to take in the other side of the ship, and all of Elena's relief deserted her.

Closest to them was a hybrid ship of some kind, larger than most ships the Corps ran. Elena saw the lines of old Type 18s and Atlantis-class explorers in her, along with some engine banks that were clearly D series, as new as the ones they deployed to the border ships in Sector Four. Some of her was custom, lovely organic sweeping lines, expanding cabin space as well as strengthening her structure. She was dark, mostly silver-black, with a few dull scars that looked recent. Her nose was pointed away from them. Elena had never seen a PSI ship up close before, but she knew who this had to be.

But the beautiful, foreign ship was not what caught her eye. It was the ship beyond the PSI vessel that twisted her gut with dread. Nose to nose with *Penumbra,* her external weapons glowing with charge, was *Galileo.*

Will had apparently been busy.

She hit *Sartre*'s comm, and was greeted with nothing but blankness. Frowning, she hit it again, but next to her Trey was analyzing the signal. "They have blocked it," he said tersely.

"Blocked how?"

"They are not accepting incoming comms traffic," he told her. "Complete blackout."

There was no way *Penumbra* could have done something like that. Elena stared at the ship, her heart going cold. *Galileo* had deliberately shut off comms contact. Such things weren't entirely unheard of, especially during delicate operations; but in this case she suspected Will had a different motivation. He couldn't have known they were coming out of the wormhole. If the Admiralty hadn't ordered the blackout, he was hiding from something else. Possibly someone asking him what he was doing provoking war with PSI.

And yet, if they couldn't get the two ships to move, war wouldn't matter.

Next to Elena, Trey was sending a message to the PSI ship. " . . . have an explosion coming through the wormhole in approximately seven minutes. Magnitude dangerously high. You need to clear the area, Valeria. Get her out of there."

Captain Solomonoff replied promptly, her voice incredulous. *"Treiko?"*

"Yes, Valeria, and there is no time to explain. You need to get the field going and get away, quickly."

There was a pause. "We can't," she said softly.

Elena looked over at Trey. He was scowling, looking furious, and if she had not known him as well as she did she would have missed the fear in his eyes. "What do you mean, you can't?"

"Stoya's ship," Elena guessed. "Greg said you were hit."

"Captain Foster—is he with you?" she asked.

"He is injured," Trey told her, and did not elaborate.

"It was not his fault," she told them. Her voice was stately and gentle, and Elena wondered how anyone could have believed she was mad. "Our field generator was already damaged; the cloaked ship simply finished what *Demeter* had started. But your *Galileo*—she still has a field generator. You can get her away."

"She's not listening," Elena said.

"What about the stream?"

Of course. Unstrapping herself, she opened the ship's console. Tucked in beside the rear scanners was a sleek, boxy commercial-grade streamer. They could priority wideband to everyone if it was operational. "Hang on," she said, searching for the activation lock; with one quick twist of her spanner, the streamer lit up green.

There was something she needed to do before contacting Jessica.

"This is a General Evacuation Alert," she said, watching the green light winking steadily. The signal radiated out from their ship, catching the stream wherever it could, reaching the widest possible audience. "The wormhole will undergo an energy discharge of lethal strength in six minutes, possibly less. Minimum safe distance is estimated to be ten million kilometers. Remove yourselves from this space immediately." She looped the message, and scrambled back into her chair.

"Do you think," Trey asked Elena, "that Valentis might be listening without answering?"

"Possibly, but he's not going to answer *us*."

"Then I will try," Valeria said. She left them in on the transmission. "Captain Valentis, this is Captain Solomonoff. You are in grave danger. We must talk."

"Come on, you arrogant bastard," Elena said under her breath. If she knew Will at all, he would not be able to resist the urge to posture, even if his intent was to blow *Penumbra* out of the sky.

He did not disappoint her. "The only one in grave danger is you, Captain," Valentis said smugly. *Smugly.* How had Greg ever been able to stand the man? Elena would need to have a long talk with him about his perceptions of people.

She broke in on the transmission. "Commander Valentis, sir, I think there's been a misunderstanding."

There was a brief pause. Elena expected many things—anger, disappointment, uncertainty—and she got none of them.

"How surprising to hear your voice, Chief." Will said smoothly. "I'm sorry to find my suspicions about you were correct."

She wondered what kind of an audience he had for this message. "Back at you, sir," she said tersely. "But we can discuss that later. That wormhole back there is going to be spewing a radiation field that will make the *Phoenix* look like a summer heat wave in less than six minutes, and you need to get *Galileo* out of there."

Valentis laughed. "You must take me for a fool, Chief. We've caught you here, plotting with your PSI friends, and you want me to run off?"

Me, Elena realized. *Not* us. *Not* Galileo. *Me*. "Sir," she tried again, "we'll come with you if you want, but there's going to be an explosion, and—"

He interrupted. "If you'd followed orders, Chief, this PSI ship wouldn't have murdered our captain, and none of this—"

"Oh, *please*," she snapped. "He's not dead. Sorry about that, by the way. But the bastard you sent after him turned out to be a monumental fuckup. Are you going to get *Galileo* out of there or not?"

At that, Will paused, and Elena wanted to reach through the space between the two ships and strangle him. "If he's alive," Will said, "let me talk to him."

Shit. Elena turned back to Greg. His eyes were half-shut, and his breathing was rapid; he was in no condition to respond. "He's indisposed at the moment. Look, can't you just get out of there, and we'll deal with all of this later?"

"I don't think so," Will replied, his confidence returned. "Your collusion in Captain Foster's death is noted, Chief. When this is wrapped up, we can—"

"Cut him off," Elena said, and Valeria did.

"Valeria," Trey asked, "how badly damaged is your ship?"

"We are not in bad shape, apart from the field generator," she said. "But even our EMP shielding won't—"

Apart from the field generator. "Excuse me, Captain," Elena put in urgently, "you said your generator. What about your stabilizers? If you could get into the field, could you sustain it?"

Valeria said something muffled in dialect, and Elena heard another voice replying. "I am told there is no reason why we could not," she said, once again in Standard. "You have an idea, Commander Shaw."

Elena looked over at Trey. "*Galileo* can generate a field strong enough to pull *Penumbra* in with her," she told him. *If we can get Will out of the way.* "We've got to get through to Jessica."

"We have an incoming comm," Trey told her. "It's . . . on a very odd ident. Encrypted."

Immediately Elena accepted the signal. "Jess? Is that you?"

"Fucking Christ, Lanie, do you have any idea what's going on over here?"

Elena almost laughed with joy. "Absolutely not," she said, "beyond Will not listening. What have you got?"

"He's not just not listening, he's out of his fucking mind. We've been ordered to take *Penumbra*. Commander Broadmoor sent a message to Admiral Herrod with more recent intel, and now she's in the brig. I've got people in engineering trying to hold our fire until Herrod gets back to us, but the *Demeter* crew is in charge. We won't be able to stall for long."

"I need to get through to Ted," Elena told her, and gave her a quick explanation of *Penumbra*'s situation.

"He's holding off Limonov," Jessica said. "I can't comm him; they'd find me."

"Find you?" Elena frowned. "Why are you hiding?"

"Too long a story." Elena heard footsteps; Jessica was moving. "I'm going to try to get to engineering and talk to Ted myself. How much time do we have?"

"Four minutes and fifty-three seconds," Trey said.

"Perfect!" Jessica said. "Tons of time. I'll just sneak past every fucking guard on the ship in four minutes and fifty-three seconds."

"Four minutes and forty-five seconds," Trey said.

"I fucking hate countdowns," Jessica muttered, and kept running.

CHAPTER 51

Galileo

Jessica ran through the maintenance corridors toward engineering. All she knew of what was going on was that they hadn't fired. She hoped Valentis hadn't given the order yet, and that Ted hadn't had to start stalling. If Limonov had discovered *Galileo*'s people were stonewalling, she would likely find the machine room full of *Demeter*'s security people. For a fleeting moment she thought of comming Ted directly—if Valentis was still monitoring her, surely he had other things to worry about just now—but there was still a possibility stealth would help her. Time limits notwithstanding, she needed to evaluate the situation before she tipped her hand.

They're alive, she thought, and in spite of her frantic pace, she felt a wave of euphoria.

She came to the access stairway under engineering and crept quietly up to the doorway, pressing herself against the shadowed walls. She saw *Galileo*'s people first, calmly at their stations. Not arrested, then; that was good news. She heard Ted's voice before she saw him, and she listened before risking a glance around the corner.

Limonov stood over Ted, glowering. Despite his slighter build, his professional scowl made him seem bigger than thick-necked Ted, whose skin had gone blotchy as he lied to Limonov's face.

"We rushed out of Aleph, sir," he was explaining. "Normally we do a full maintenance sweep, but when we picked up *Demeter*'s cargo we cut that short. Commander Shaw had to cut some corners."

Oh, Teddy, she'll get you for that, Jessica thought.

"You expect me to believe your redundant systems are off-line as well?" Limonov snapped. Jessica didn't think the man was deceived.

"They're coming on-line," Ted assured him. "They're just taking a little time to warm up. A few more minutes—"

Limonov straightened and turned away, dismissing Ted. "Lieutenant Toyo," he said to one of the *Demeter* engineers, "bring up the targeting system and await orders to fire on *Penumbra*."

Oh, hell. She was out of time. She ran out of her hiding place, and said, "Wait!"

Limonov's head turned, and his hollow eyes widened when he saw her. "Lieutenant Lockwood. You're aware your captain is looking for you, aren't you?"

"He's not my captain," she told him. "And he's not yours, either. Listen to me, Commander Limonov. Everything you told me, everything you said about the wormhole—you were right. It's the truth. Tune into the stream."

Out of the corner of her eye she saw Toyo touch his comm and say something. Calling security, no doubt. At least the bastard wasn't firing. Before her, Limonov was frowning, his face still a mask of military irritation; but she thought she saw his eyes shift, and one of his fists was clenched. "We don't have time for the stream, Lieutenant. In case you missed something, we're in the middle of a war."

"Not yet we're not," she said decisively, "and it won't matter if we start this if we don't get out of here. You were right about the *Phoenix*, Commander. Please, tune it in. Just for a moment."

He stared at her, and this time she was sure of it: a flash in his expression, hope, fear, desperation. For interminable seconds he stared at her, and then he said, "*Galileo*, give me the stream."

Internal comms came on, and the priority message echoed through the machine room. When Elena's voice said *ten thousand kilometers,* everyone but Limonov began to shift nervously. *Yes, you fucking idiots,* she thought, furious, *we do need to get the fuck out of here.* Limonov stared at her, unmoving, and she saw his fist unclench.

"That's your chief," he said.

"Yes."

"She's a traitor."

"I'll talk to him," Elena said in her ear, "if it would help."

"Just a minute," Jessica said to her. She took a step toward Limonov. "She's not, sir," she said, lowering her voice. "She's done all of this because she wanted to find out why Danny was killed. You were right about me, that I didn't like him. But she loved him. For a long time, she loved him, and if you talked to him you know he loved her, too."

Limonov looked at her, and she could see him weighing her words. "Can she hear me?" he said at last.

Jessica nodded.

"Commander Shaw. You came out of the wormhole."

Elena spoke loud enough for the entire room to hear. "We did."

"Did you hear it? The singing?"

Jessica had no idea if Elena knew what he was talking about, but she rolled with it. "Yes, Commander. We heard it."

"It did not destroy you."

Jessica heard a note of desperation creep into her friend's voice. "It will destroy all of us, Commander, if we do not start moving. This war you've been tasked to start—it's a lie, Commander Limonov. It's an excuse used to hide what's happening here. But there will be no war, Commander—no war, no peace, no *nothing*—for any of us if you don't stand down."

Behind her, Jessica heard the machine room door open, and the familiar rhythm of booted footsteps. *Shit*. She turned to see six infantry—*six, just for me?*—all aiming their weapons at her and, by extension, Limonov. The *Demeter* officer frowned at them. "You wouldn't actually fire in the engine room, would you?" he asked.

It wasn't Henare in charge. It was Bristol, older and steadier, far less likely to be swayed either by Jessica's temper or by Ted's charm. "Lieutenant Lockwood," he said formally, ignoring Limonov, "you're under arrest. Please come with us."

"Wait," Limonov said. He reached out, and from the master panel he shut down the weapons banks.

The room filled with the sound of shouting and objections. Jessica, despite the pulse rifles aimed at her, closed her eyes in relief. *No war today,* she thought, but that was only half the problem.

Elena had seen the weapons go dark. "Ted, are you there? We need to—"

"Uh," Ted said, his eyes on the infantry, "we've still got a small problem here, Elena. There seem to be some people here to arrest us."

Which seemed to snap her friend's last nerve. "Who is it?" Elena said crisply.

"Bristol," Jessica said, "and his usual crew."

"Bristol, do you hear me?"

Bristol was still aiming his weapon, but Jessica could see in his eyes the conflict. Elena was supposed to be a traitor, but she was a superior officer. At last he said, "Yes, ma'am."

"What are you doing in my machine room?"

"Captain Valentis's orders, ma'am. We're arresting Lieutenant Lockwood."

"Rubbish," Elena said crisply. "Valentis isn't captain. Foster is here with me."

And damned if the nose of his gun didn't waver. "Begging your pardon, ma'am, but why isn't he telling us this?"

Jessica heard some scrambling on the other end, and then she heard a familiar voice—faint, ragged, frighteningly weak—say "Bristol. Stand down. That's an order."

He really was alive. She wanted to shout.

Bristol seemed less enthusiastic. "You could have made that up, Chief. My orders are clear. I'm to—"

And there went Elena's temper. "Now listen here, you thick-headed, slow-witted bastard. You want to follow orders? Fine. I'm a traitor. Blow us out of the sky. But when you're done, you grab *Penumbra* and you get the fuck out of there as fast as you can, do you hear me? Because if you keep interfering and get my ship destroyed, I swear to any and all gods you may believe in, I will find you in your sorry afterlife and I will make every instant of your existence hell and torment for fucking eternity. Have I made myself clear, soldier?"

It was almost amusing, watching it play out on Bristol's face. Valentis. Foster. The threat of hell and torment. It took him less than two seconds to drop the nose of his rifle. "Captain's orders," he said to his team. "Stand down."

Jessica checked the time: two minutes and three seconds left.

CHAPTER 52

On some level, Greg was aware of agonizing pain, but he felt as if he were next to his body, experiencing the pain as echoes, as waves radiating from the inside out. He felt strangely alert, aware of what was happening; but there were jumps in words and actions, and he knew he was missing things. Blacking out, probably, although he had no sense of time passing. Elena had come to him—moments ago? hours?—and said, "Bristol's in engineering trying to arrest Jessica." Greg had ordered Bristol off, and the effort of speech had knocked him out again.

He could hear Elena talking to Ted, planning to fold *Galileo*'s FTL field around *Penumbra* so they could all get away together. "That's theoretical, you know," he tried to say, but he didn't think any sound came out. Well, never mind. She knew it was theoretical. If ever there was a time for a field test, this was it.

" . . . close are we to *Penumbra*?" Elena was asking.

"We will reach her," Zajec said, "but we will not have time to slow down."

That, Greg knew, wouldn't stop Elena. He thought of her takeoff from Volhynia, how easily she had shaken the trackers.

She'd land them at speed, and slam on the brakes, and with a little help from the physics gods they wouldn't become paste against the hangar's back wall. Such landings were the stuff of bullshit Academy stunt flying, usually ending with someone's shuttle in very small pieces, occasionally taking the pilot with it; but when someone pulled it off, they had bragging rights for months.

He supposed she had done it dozens of times. What he would have given to know her back then.

Another blink. He heard Elena say "Twenty seconds."

Greg heard a proximity alert; they were close to *Penumbra*. Another odd time flash, and his mind replayed the alert from the *Phoenix* recording: *Please evacuate the area.* He let the countdown continue in his head, uncertain of how accurate it was, quite sure it did not matter.

Ten seconds. The light in the cabin began to glow red: heat from their external shielding, as they hit the overlap of *Penumbra*'s.

Nine. He felt a lurch of disorientation as the gravity field averaged and recalibrated, shifting him toward one side of the ship.

Eight. The red light gave way to yellow artificial ship light; *Penumbra* had swallowed them.

Seven. He suddenly felt the pull of acceleration, and he wondered how close they were to the wall.

Six. Elena threw the engines into reverse, and he heard a groan and a snap as they almost instantly failed. He heard her curse, and his weak fingers clutched the edge of the couch, waiting for impact—

Five. —and his stomach lurched as the ship slowed as if confined by a slingshot.

Four. Abruptly their motion stopped, and he was thrown to the floor, and the pain that had been hitting him in distant waves became acute and immediate.

Three. He craned his neck to look out the window, and saw the familiar glow of the field, so much weaker than he was used to. The stars began to disappear in the growing light.

Two. No polarizer, he remembered, and turned his face away, closing his eyes.

One. He heard the ship's stabilizers revving up, and wondered what his father would do if he died.

There was a flash that filled the cabin, bringing daylight behind his closed eyes, and everything inside him dropped into blackness.

CHAPTER 53

Penumbra

Elena gripped her seat as the ship's cabin bounced off the rear wall and toppled onto its side, skittering across the hangar floor. As soon as she felt their motion slowing she released herself from her shoulder harness, dropping to her feet. "Trey?" she asked, looking over at him.

He was already grappling with his harness. "I am unhurt," he said. "Check Foster."

She turned to where Greg lay on the floor and cursed, wishing they had taken more care strapping him in. She moved toward him, and light began to flare in the cabin. Instinctively she squeezed her eyes shut, wondering if the light was the FTL field or the wormhole exploding. "Greg?" she asked, as she heard the ship's stabilizers revving up. The engines began to sound distressed as they worked to match velocity, and she thought, *We'll fall right out of the field, or get tossed out, or it'll get ahead of us and pull us to pieces. . .*

And then the flare faded, and the sound of the engine grew quieter, and after a few groans of annoyance it settled into a stable rhythm. She opened her eyes and looked out of what was left of their window to see that the landing bay door had closed against the light. A klaxon sounded in the distance, but the mechanical hum of the ship told her they were out of immediate danger. She turned back to Greg, dropping to her knees next to him.

"Greg? We've made it. It's all right now."

He did not answer, and she frowned. His breathing had gone shallow again. "Greg?" Her fingers went to his neck, and for one terrifying moment she felt nothing. When she found his pulse it was thready and uneven. She looked up at Trey, her heart back in her throat. "He's unconscious."

Without hesitation, Trey used the pilot's chair to climb up to the ship's side hatch, which, somewhat miraculously, was still operational. He raised himself out of the ship, and she heard him shout in his own language, "We need a medic, now! That's an order!"

Elena's eyes searched the cabin. Everything had been tossed: blankets, couch cushions, most of the tools she had been using to cobble together their engine mount. Where was the med scanner?

Trey appeared next to her. "They will be here in a moment, Elena." He took Greg's pulse, as she had, and she looked up at him to see his lips had set. "The blood loss, I think," he said quietly.

"But—" He had been talking. Not five minutes before, he had been conscious and talking and part of their plan.

She heard scrabbling against their hull, and two people dropped in, one carrying a medkit. They immediately went to Greg's side, one opening the kit, the other giving Greg a quick visual examination.

"This isn't from the crash," the medic said, turning her eyes to Elena.

Elena shook her head. "Pulse rifle."

"How long ago?"

"A little less than two hours," Trey told the medic. "He's also had severe radiation exposure."

With far less care than either Elena or Trey had shown, the medic grasped the burned edges of Greg's uniform and tore.

Reflexively Elena lunged for her. "You can't—"

Gently, Trey caught her arm. "*M'laya*, they are helping him. Let them do their work."

With an act of will she let herself lean against him, and he closed his arms around her while she watched the medics work on her old friend. Greg would not do this to her. After everything that had happened, he couldn't. Not now, not when they had made it through, not when she had learned all of his behavior was nothing but a reaction to his bad marriage. They would have time, she was sure of it, to talk that through, for him to realize that everything he thought he had been feeling was nothing to do with her, not really, and they could become themselves again, just as they had always been, unchanged. Because she had never really believed he could hate her.

Please don't leave me, she begged him silently. *Please*.

Minutes passed, and then the woman working on Greg sat back, looking satisfied. She glanced at her partner, who closed up the medkit and climbed back out of the shuttle. "He's going for a transport stretcher," she explained, at Elena's anxious look.

"He'll be all right?" Elena asked.

"He's stable enough for us to move," the woman said, and Elena hated the gentleness in her voice. "Doctor Lukaya is experienced with these sorts of injuries. He will look after your friend."

The other medic returned, and Elena watched, useless, as they shifted Greg onto the stretcher with practiced care and passed him through the ship's hatch. The woman paused before she followed him out, her compassionate eyes meeting Elena's.

"You should come to the infirmary as well." Her gaze briefly took in Trey. "Both of you. Being able to stand doesn't mean you're not hurt."

Stop wasting time with us, Elena thought. She felt Trey's arms tighten around her, briefly. "Thank you," he replied. "We will."

The medic left.

Elena's energy deserted her, and she leaned against Trey, feeling sluggish and unable to move. "He should have let Stoya kill me," she said.

She felt Trey's lips press against the top of her head. "Is that the man you know?" he asked her.

"No," she said, barely a whisper. "If he dies . . . I have no one."

His arms tightened again, and she closed her eyes, dropping her head against his chest. "That, *m'laya,*" he said into her hair, "is not the truth."

Chapter 54

He noticed the nausea first, and only then his gnawing empty stomach, clawing for food he was pretty sure would not stay down. He lay as still as he could, waiting to fall back into unconsciousness, to retreat from the uniformly unpleasant physical sensations; but his mind, it seemed, was ready for him to wake up, regardless of how muddleheaded and uncomfortable he was. The nausea became more and more insistent, and without opening his eyes he lurched to one elbow and threw up over the edge of the bed.

"Welcome back, Captain Foster," said a cheerful voice.

Greg spat, then opened his eyes. Standing next to him, in a jet-black uniform with long brown hair braided neatly down his back, was a man somewhat younger than Zajec. He was shorter and thinner with a far more facile smile, but something in his posture made Greg recognize him for what he was. "Doctor . . . ?" he guessed.

"Lukaya," the man told him. His Standard was almost completely unaccented, and Greg wondered if he had come to PSI as an adult, or was simply good with languages. "You're ahead of schedule. That's excellent. We weren't expecting you to wake up until tomorrow."

The worst of the nausea had retreated with the vomiting, and Greg became aware of a burning ache in his right side. He lay back, and risked a glance down at himself. He was on a narrow, utilitarian hospital bed, dressed in loose black pajamas, his bare feet protruding from the bottom of a thin, warm blanket. He tugged the hem of his shirt up, and saw a red and raw patch of skin obscured by the light tan pseudo-skin of a liquid bandage. "How long have I been out?"

"Two days," Lukaya told him. "You've missed nearly everything."

"My friends," Greg said. "What happened?"

"Your friends walked away from the crash," the doctor said. "And they didn't need nearly the radiation treatment you did." Greg thought the man sounded disapproving. "But you can ask them yourself, if you want. Commander Shaw drops by every hour or so; she's due soon. And in the meantime, you have a visitor."

Greg looked over to the entrance to the small room in which he lay. Standing there was the only woman he had ever seen who was shorter than Jessica Lockwood. She was not young, but he could not hazard a guess as to her age: sixty or eighty, he could not tell. Her skin was unwrinkled but loose across her high cheekbones and strong jaw, and her braided hair, although mostly white, was streaked with red. Her most striking feature, though, was her eyes: bright green, sharply intelligent, with a gleam in them as if she were, somewhere in her mind, always laughing. She carried herself with a regal self-confidence, and he knew who she had to be.

"Captain Solomonoff," he said.

His reward was a genuine smile, bright and dazzling, taking twenty years from her face. "Captain Foster," she said, and stepped forward to stand next to his bed. "I am pleased to find you alert."

"I'm pleased to be alert," he said. He thought, in five or ten more minutes, that might even be the truth. "I'm not quite sure how to ask this," he said, "but—I take it we're not at war."

Captain Solomonoff grew more serious. "No, Captain. And when you are feeling better, I would like to discuss with you the best way to remain in that situation. I am not entirely clear how much of what happened was down to misunderstanding, but I do not believe it was everything."

"Captain Solomonoff, I assure you, the Admiralty's official stance is—"

"I understand your Admiralty," she said. "But I do not believe they are the problem, are they?"

Only in their impotence, Greg thought. "What did you have in mind?" he asked her.

She shrugged, suggesting what she was about to say was of no significance, did not matter to her at all. He suspected it was a calculated affectation. "I am thinking it might be worth our while to be more explicit about our own official stance, and to ensure that we and your Admiralty are seeing things from the same perspective."

It took him a moment to catch up. "You mean a treaty."

That shrug again. "It is an imperfect word, *treaty,* but under the circumstances I think it is not inappropriate. But there is time for that, Captain. Right now, I believe you have other visitors."

He had not seen them come in. Behind Captain Solomonoff, hanging back, hands on her elbows, stood Elena, sturdy and whole and unhurt, and suddenly all of his pain and nausea meant nothing at all. Her eyes met his, and she smiled, just a little, and he thought, perhaps, that they might someday be all right again.

Next to her stood Jessica, who was far less inclined to be reticent. She marched past Captain Solomonoff to loom over him, glowering. "Do you have any idea the position you left me in, sir?"

He smiled at her. "It's nice to see you, too, Jess."

"Fuck you, sir. The only justice here is that you've survived to help me un-screw this up."

There was that, of course: the lies from Captain MacBride, Danny's murder, the guilt of Volhynia's much-admired—at least by the officials who appointed him—chief of police. All of that would have to be sorted out, along with Ellis and what they had done to the factory. And there was the *Phoenix,* on top of it all, the final fate of a ship that had shaped a future it had never seen.

Elena, as she so often did, seemed to be following his thoughts. "No way of telling if the flight recorder got swallowed or destroyed," she told him, taking a step closer, still holding her elbows, "but no one has asked about it yet. I imagine nobody wants to tell me they knew about it. I think they're waiting to see what happens when the radiation clears up."

"Is that likely to happen?" he asked her.

She shrugged. "The pulsar helped last time; it might help again. If it doesn't, though—it'll be a long time. Maybe our life-times. We can't even tell what sort of state the wormhole is in. It's intact, but the radiation has cluttered all the readings. Novanadyr Observatory is fairly drooling over the idea of trying to weed through all the chaos."

Novanadyr Observatory, Greg thought, who'd had it right all along. "How's *Galileo*?" he asked.

At that, she looked away from him. "Ted says the engines came through brilliantly, even hauling two ships into the field." She paused. "I haven't been back yet."

He turned that over in his head. As much as he believed she had been worried for him, he suspected that was not what was keeping her on *Penumbra*. "What about Valentis?" he asked.

Jessica, who had been scowling at Elena, looked back at him to answer. "Commander Broadmoor has confined him to quarters, sir. Two guards, one inside, one out. They say he was yelling a lot."

"You didn't watch?"

"I'd have had to hit him, sir."

Greg laughed aloud, and then stopped, gasping at the stabbing pain in his ribs. Elena looked back at him, worried, and he waved a hand to reassure her. "I guess I can't do that for a while," he said lightly, dizzy from the pain.

"You can do it all you like," Lukaya told him. "It'll just hurt."

Greg thought of Bob Hastings, and decided that doctors, facile smiles notwithstanding, were all alike.

Chapter 55

It took them two full weeks to hammer everything out.

Foster had convinced Central Command that now was an optimal time to officially hash out a treaty with PSI. For the first week he operated out of *Penumbra*'s infirmary, until an annoyed Lukaya declared him fit for travel. After that Foster spent his days shuttling back and forth between *Galileo* and *Penumbra,* in closed-door meetings with Valeria or speaking tersely with one of the admirals back on Earth. Trey had occasion to ask Valeria what sort of treaty they were trying to craft.

"It is difficult to say," she told him. "We are in agreement about nearly everything apart from how the Syndicates should be handled, and I believe most of our differences there are semantic. But they ask for details, so we work out details."

Trey did not think that was all they discussed. Valeria took at least one meal a day with Captain Foster, and Trey had caught the two of them chatting and laughing more than once. Clearly there was affinity there. Certainly Foster seemed much less the sullen, short-sighted hothead he had when Trey had first met him, and far more the charming and easygoing man of his reputation. Trey found that discovery left him with a number of conflicting feelings; he could understand better why Foster and Elena had been friends, but this sophisticated, relaxed officer was a much more credible rival.

But he knew Foster was not the rival to whom he would lose.

Unlike Foster, Elena had stayed on board *Penumbra*. She received daily reports from Ted Shimada, but otherwise spent her days in *Penumbra*'s engine room, helping with repairs. When she had volunteered, Trey had thought Stefan—Valeria's chief mechanic—was going to have a stroke; but he had silently set her to busywork, and after a few days had allowed her to help fix the field generator. His attitude toward her never changed, but he stood over her less and less often, and after the first week she was working entirely unsupervised.

Trey, who had nothing to do at all, eventually adjourned to *Penumbra*'s main kitchen, and did what he always did when he was at loose ends: he cooked. He made loaf after loaf of bread, the rhythm of the kneading easing the tension in his head. He cooked taffy and hard candy, and make finger-sized éclairs for the small children. Within three days he had a line outside the kitchen each morning when he arrived, and he almost wished he hadn't started. It was too much like home, and too many of the children reminded him of Sarah. He found it impossible not to become mired in homesickness.

Predictably, it was Volhynia that proved the most recalcitrant. Despite evidence of Stoya's guilt and Ancher's video, they seemed interested in charging Trey for assaulting a police officer and resisting arrest. Both charges could land him in the same interrogation room, and although he hoped their tactics would ease somewhat without Stoya or Luvidovich, they could still legally detain him as long as they wished.

In the end, to Trey's chagrin, it was Central Corps that came to his rescue. Someone named Admiral Herrod sent a blunt memo to Volhynia's government: Treiko Zajec, captain, retired, was to be pardoned, both for crimes they wanted to charge him with and for crimes he had committed in the past. If the government refused . . . well, then, Volhynia was welcome to see what would happen to their trading channels without the patronage and protection of Central Gov, who would cheerfully grant them their long-standing wish to secede and stand alone.

Volhynia's governor had responded by issuing Trey a personal invitation to come home. Trey had listened with Elena, and found he was almost incapable of watching the smug, nervous little man finish his message.

"Are you behind this?" he asked.

She shook her head. "Greg says Admiral Herrod did this on his own. Probably because he feels like a jerk for leaving you hanging out to dry."

He suspected there was more to it than that. Even having spent forty years away from home, he was aware of the fraught relationship between Volhynia and Central. There was almost certainly a political motivation behind Herrod's generosity, but he could not imagine ever being in a position to do the man a favor. In the end, he decided to simply be grateful.

He and Elena managed to find time for more than sleeping. He had worried, at first, that Valeria would be bothered, but she had shrugged when he had mentioned it.

"Do you think I have been sleeping alone, Treiko, pining for you nightly? I am finding, the longer you are here, that I actually wish you happiness. Take what you can, dear boy."

He could tell, from the sadness in her eyes, that she saw the future clearly. Captain Foster, on the other hand, did not. The more days that passed, the more concerned he looked, his eyes always following Elena when she crossed a room. Trey wondered if he ought to say something, but he did not think she would thank him if he did. Better to let Foster work it out alone, and take the time with her that he had.

They slept as little as possible, and apart from their daily duties they were rarely apart. They ate together, showered together, even exercised together, she pounding laps around *Penumbra*'s short track while he lifted weights. At night they made love until they collapsed with exhaustion, and every day he felt more himself. She was warm and passionate and delightful and giving, and she lit him up from the inside, like fire spreading from his heart throughout his limbs.

The closeness was unsustainable, of course, but they sustained it just the same.

Castelanna had appeared a few days after their flight from the wormhole. Trey had spent a pleasant afternoon reminiscing with Rosaria, but he had not visited his longtime home. He could have shown it off to Elena, he supposed, but returning there, even for a visit, would have felt too much like stepping backward. His time on *Castelanna* had always been tinged, however faintly, with penance, and he was finished with penance.

Elena did not invite him to *Galileo*, either, although her reasons, he knew, were very different. He believed she could see as clearly as he could and, like Trey, was taking what she could. He was not going to lose a moment of it by trying to make her face the future before she had to.

One afternoon Trey was sitting in his kitchen, reading a book while his bread was rising. Greg Foster poked his head in, and Trey shut down the display, waving the man inside.

"Can I get you something to eat?"

Foster shook his head. "I'll take a drink, though, if you have something nonalcoholic."

Elena had not noticed, but Foster had not had a drink since they had returned through the wormhole. Trey wondered why the man would not tell her, but he realized Foster told her almost nothing of himself, assuming she would infer. Trey was beginning to understand Greg Foster, and he wished he didn't—it made him feel sympathy.

Foster sipped at the lemonade Trey handed him, then looked at Trey with those sober gray eyes. "She's a natural leader, Elena," he said, as if they were continuing an old discussion. "Better than Jake was, really. Jake was a fair man, and a good officer, but he was kind of a social misfit. He didn't always communicate all that well. Elena, she gets the point across." He laughed a little. "You should see these kids we get once or twice a year, fresh out of the Academy, or a year or so out in the field. She smiles that big, naive smile of hers, and welcomes them, and you can see it in their faces: they think she's a pushover. It takes some of them as much as a week to figure it out, and then they're scared of her. And either they get over that, or she transfers them out. She comes across as this sweet, shy woman, but on duty, my God, she's hard as nails. When she joined *Galileo*, I thought she'd be too soft for the job."

"Even knowing the missions she had been through?"

"Even so. I got fooled as much as anybody else." He paused. "I suppose I'm still fooled. But the thing is—Shimada's good, and that's the truth. She thinks he should have had her job because he's three years senior. I never would have given it to him, even if Jake's wishes had been different. She knows that ship like nobody else. She knows *us*. She remembers birthdays, and how people take their coffee, and who lost someone, and who likes to dance on their days off. She knows if somebody's homesick, or if they need company or just to be left alone. She doesn't see it, not really, but she knits us together. We need her."

"*We* need her?" Trey asked him. "Or you need her?"

Foster's jaw set. "You've known her two weeks," he said.

"Captain Foster, I do not believe you have known her a day."

Foster stared at him for a long moment, then silently turned and left the kitchen. Trey pulled his book up again, but could only stare past it out the kitchen window into the dark.

CHAPTER 56

Y ou okay with this, Lockwood?" asked Emily Broadmoor.
"Yes, ma'am."

"Because I can ask the captain to have someone else do it."

Jessica looked at Commander Broadmoor. The distinct lack
of good humor in her expression suggested to Jessica that she'd
happily take the task of talking to Will Valentis on herself. Part
of Jessica would have happily turned it over to her. "I volunteered, ma'am," she explained.

He doesn't think of me as a threat, she had said to Captain
Foster. *He thinks he can spew that twisted patriotic shit and
win me over. He'll talk more to me than to you.*

Commander Broadmoor studied Jessica's face, then nodded.
"But I'm not giving you more than three minutes. I don't trust
that bastard."

"That should be plenty of time, ma'am." She waited for the
commander to turn away, and opened the door.

Will Valentis looked up from his seat on his couch. Most
Central starships had a brig of some sort, but Captain Foster
had repurposed *Galileo*'s less than a year after they deployed,
mostly for rec rooms and kitchens. They had not needed it until

now; most of their guest quarters were currently dedicated to confining the *Demeter* crew. Jessica appreciated Commander Broadmoor's caution with Commander Valentis, but she did not think he would become violent, at least not with her. Among other things, he had nowhere to go.

Valentis looked back down at his reading. "Did you come here to gloat, Lieutenant Lockwood?"

"No, sir," she said.

His lip curled in a halfhearted sneer. "I guess nobody's told you you don't have to call me 'sir' anymore."

"Force of habit, sir."

She waited, and he finally shoved aside his reading. "Fine, Lieutenant. What are you doing here?"

"Captain Foster asked me to tell you what's been happening, sir."

His response to that was predictable. He frowned sourly, and glared at her. "Still running errands for him, I see," he said. "He still doesn't understand what he's done to himself."

Jessica was fairly certain who was misunderstanding. "He wanted me to tell you," she said, as if he hadn't spoken, "that nobody's spoken for you. Nobody from the Admiralty, or from Shadow Ops. The party line seems to be that you and MacBride were trying to start a war over the dellinium mine."

Valentis seemed irritated, but not yet worried. "He's missing the point," he explained to her. "They'll court-martial him for that. It was a perfectly legal refinery."

Question one, Foster had said. *Did Will know about the mine?*

"Maybe, sir," Jessica continued. "Although the Admiralty has already granted clemency to Captain Zajec."

That shook Valentis's composure. He stood, and began to pace the room. With some effort, Jessica stood still. If he tried to touch her again, she was going to punch him, and she didn't think that would help her get information from him. "That doesn't make sense," he said. "He's the perfect—"

"Fall guy?" Jessica finished for him. He stopped, wary again, and she cursed her own impulsiveness. With some effort, she softened her expression, trying to look sympathetic. "You know they can't prove anything. I mean, when it comes to you, sir. The path to Stoya's pretty clear, and Captain MacBride is going down. But it seems to me—" She stopped. "I'm sorry, sir. It's not my place."

But he had stopped pacing and was watching her, and instead of hostility she saw a sort of hungry hope. "No, Lieutenant," he said. "You're free to speculate with me. Go on."

She took a breath, and ran down what she knew. "I don't think Danny was your fault, sir," she said. "If I have this right—he was asking you about the *Phoenix* and the wormhole, and you told Shadow Ops that he was getting too close. They were the ones who turned their assassin on him. That's why you were so upset when he died, isn't it? You didn't realize they were going to kill him."

He was nodding, almost eagerly. "They didn't need to do it," he told her. "Lancaster was an idiot. He thought he'd unravel the mystery of the flight recorder, and suddenly he'd be a hero. He thought he'd get her back." His face darkened. "He was pathetic. Just like Foster was pathetic, heading after her."

Jessica made a mental note to ask Elena what the hell had made Will hate her so much. "Is that why you sent them after him, sir?"

"He was unfit," Valentis insisted. "He ran after her. Playing the fool for her. *Again*."

Question two: Was it his idea to have me killed?

"He ignored his duty, made impulsive decisions that endangered everybody—"

"Like engaging a PSI ship single-handedly to start a war, sir?"

At that, his expression closed. "I was following orders, Lieutenant. It's something you should try sometime."

He was glaring at her, and she dropped his gaze, looking down at her feet. "That's probably a good defense at a court-martial, sir."

"You're damn right it is."

"Too bad you're not going to get one."

He took a step toward her, and she saw his hand reach out. She looked up, meeting his eyes. He must have seen something there, because he stopped before he touched her. "What do you mean?"

Having him standing so close was revolting, but she wanted to see every detail of his reaction. "That's what Captain Foster sent me to explain to you, sir. As part of the treaty with PSI, we had to make a few concessions. One of them is you."

Valentis went gray.

"Let me see if I remember the exact wording of the Admiralty's order: 'Given that Commander Valentis moved forward into battle unilaterally, concealing relevant information from his command chain, we accede to Captain Solomonoff's request to transfer the prisoner to *Penumbra* for disposition.'"

He began to sweat. "He can't. They can't. Lockwood. You know what they can do, you know her reputation—she'll put me out an air lock!"

"I'm told that's not a consideration, sir."

Valentis tried bluster. "I will not be treated this way!"

At this point, she thought, there was no reason to playact anymore. "I think you will, sir," she said, her eyes boring into his. "Because I think you'll find if you stay on this ship, you're not likely to get any different treatment from us."

"My own people wouldn't do that to me."

She drew herself up as tall as she could, and took a step closer to him, gratified when he shrunk away. "We're not your people, sir," she hissed at him. "You would disappear without a trace, and no one would miss you."

She stared into Valentis's dark eyes, not blinking, and eventually he looked away. She settled back on her heels and turned, heading for the door. "In truth, sir, I wish you luck on *Penumbra*. They seem a decent bunch; you might even be able to redeem yourself. But don't eat the bread. Their baker is likely to poison you."

The door slid shut behind her, and she walked away.

CHAPTER 57

Penumbra

could request a transfer," Elena suggested.

"To where?"

She thought of *Constellation*, of *Abigail*, of *Demeter*. All the Fifth Sector ships had the same reputation.

"A freighter, then. I've got friends in commerce. They're always telling me they'd take me on."

"And this would make you happy, *m'laya*? Moving cargo for the rest of your life?"

"I—" Contingencies. That was her job. "I would be flying. I would be out here. That would be enough." *If I had you, too.*

"You would be miserable, Elena, and you would grow to hate me."

"If you don't want me, just say so."

"Do not be a fool." He leaned closer to her, and put his forehead against hers. "I need you like my arm, like my hand, like the heart in my chest. But I will not destroy you, *m'laya*. Not for anything."

There had to be a way. "You were good, when you were out here," she whispered.

"I was."

"But you were never happy, were you?" She had seen it in him, even as he caught up with old friends, as he made peace with Valeria, who had all those years with him that Elena would not.

He did not reply for a long time. "No, I was not."

"So there is no answer? Is that what you're saying?"

He wrapped his arms around her and pulled her into his lap. She curled up against him, tucked in his arms like a small animal. "The answer, *m'laya,* is that I love you, and I always will. And that this time we have must be made to be enough."

There was no time, she thought, that would ever be enough.

"Tell me about *Galileo.*"

They lay as they had every night for the last two weeks, undressed under a single light blanket, Elena next to the window so she could open her eyes to the stars. She nuzzled his chest, inhaling the familiar scent of him, and listened to the quiet thrum of *Penumbra*'s systems in the background.

"She makes this sound," she told him, "coming in and out of the field. This low little *coo,* like a dove. It's a strange noise, and I've never found out what causes it; no other ship out there seems to do it, but she does it every time. And her drive—the starlight drive is always on, even when we're not in the field, and it has this rhythm. Like a rhumba, only more complicated. You could dance to it, but your feet would get tangled up. It's this sound that's in the background all the time, like my heartbeat; even when I'm not listening for it, I hear it. When I go visit my mother, or on holiday, I can't sleep properly because it's not there. Jessica thinks I'm antisocial because I spend all my time off at home, but it's not true. I just feel better when I'm there. Safer."

She settled her head against his chest. "At night . . . I watch the stars if they're out, but of course sometimes we're at speed, and all I can see is that streaky blue through the polarizer. But I can hear her. Even through the pillow I can hear her. And when the day has been long, when I feel lost and alone, I put my head under the pillow, and all I can hear is her heartbeat, gentle and constant, and I know somehow everything will be all right." She could not finish. "I'm sorry, Trey. I don't know why I'm crying."

He kissed the top of her head and pulled her closer. "It is all right, *m'laya*. I do."

Galileo

Greg had been sitting in the pub for nearly an hour before he realized what felt different about the place.

In the week since they had been under way, the general air of festivity aboard ship had quieted to its usual easy routine. His crew was still exhausted, still talking wistfully of their return to Earth; but the tension and irritability of their time with the *Demeter* crew had passed. While they were not as fresh as they would be after they had had a chance to see their families, there was a tranquility about the ship's hallways, a sense of harmony.

There was mourning, too. Danny was still missed. Greg was glad to hear the story of his heroism repeated, and all the less charitable stories of his gullibility and lack of intelligence were quickly becoming lost to memory. Any unflattering speculation about why Elena had broken things off with him had disappeared. All of his actions could be explained as an attempt to decipher the puzzle of the *Phoenix,* and in that narrative, his only mistake had been to trust Will. With many of the crew feeling betrayed for the same reason, it did not taint his memory. Daniel Lancaster, perennially average, would be remembered as an investigator and a crusader for good. Greg had already sent a long vid to his sister, explaining what her brother had done, and for the first time in a long time he felt he was leaving someone with a memory that might actually help.

But it was not the ship's newfound tranquility that struck him that evening. What struck him was that he was no longer spying on them. He was not sitting in a corner hiding behind a bottle, real or faked. He was sitting with them, a part of them, no longer separate.

Taifa Reid, captain of *Arizona,* his first deployment, had told him you had to stay separate, that to integrate yourself too much would make your job impossible. Greg found, so far, that he enjoyed the phenomenon too much to want to resist.

They did not require much of him. He could sit at a crowded table and just listen, laughing at other people's stories, or he could sit on his own, and say hello now and then to those who stopped by. He found he could even tell stories, sharing doubts and fears and laughter, as if he outranked no one. Tonight he sat with Elena, largely in silence, and sipped tea with her. She had introduced him to a green tea that was less smoky and bitter than the ones she favored, and he found it had the advantage of both calming his nerves and giving him clarity.

He had been careful with her since she had come home. He had not asked about Zajec, or how they had made their farewells. He could see on her face sometimes a crestfallen look, as if she had lost something somewhere; but he let her be. They were starting over, like strangers, despite knowing everything about each other. All he could do was stand still, hands open, and let her decide how close she was willing to get.

They spoke, a little, about going back to Earth, although neither of them brought up Central's investigation, the outcome of which was out of their hands. He told her about talking to his father, and to his stepmother. His father had wept, and Greg had felt both guilty and strangely grateful. Eventually his stepmother had to take over the call, and Greg had taken the opportunity to apologize to her for years of poor behavior.

"I don't expect forgiveness," he had said, meaning it. "But I can promise I will do my best to be different from now on."

He had made that promise to a lot of people.

Elena was going to do what she always did: head for her mother's house and let herself get inundated by relatives. She said it always cured her of any need to see them, like a vaccination. He thought he might like to meet her family someday, if only to see why she was always so grateful to come home to *Galileo*. He wondered if seeing them would ease the loss of Zajec, or make it worse.

"So what are you going to do?" she asked, and he knew what she meant.

"Get a divorce," he told her. "Be on my own for a while, see what that's like." He would never be comfortable with the kind of marriage Caroline wanted, and he was tired of lying.

"I'm sorry, Greg," Elena said.

"It's overdue."

"I know. That's why I'm sorry."

He watched her sip her tea, her eyes wandering over the crowd. He supposed there was no harm in asking. "What about you?" he asked. "How are you doing?"

She kept her fingers around the mug, clutching it as if she were freezing. "Most days," she began, "I feel like I've been torn in half, like I don't know why everybody isn't staring at me, because I'm walking around bleeding all over everything, and I have to keep moving so I don't drown in it. But sometimes . . . once in a while, anyway . . . you know how they say when you fall in love you lose your heart?" She met his eyes, and he caught a glimpse of the woman he knew, strong and passionate. "I feel like I'd been missing mine, and he found it, and returned it to me. Like I'm whole for the first time in years. Maybe ever. And in those moments, I feel light and free and invincible." She blushed and looked away, smiling into her teacup. "I know, it sounds mad."

"No it doesn't." She looked up when he said it, and he saw the surprise in her eyes; and for a moment he let himself look at her, taking her in, feeling grateful that whatever else had happened, whatever her reasons, she had stayed.

"*Where is he?*"

The pub fell silent, and the crowd's eyes went to the door. Jessica Lockwood stood there, neat and military and absolutely furious. He thought he could see her eyes flash from across the room. She had not seen him yet, but was scanning the crowd, starting at the bar. He suspected she wanted the chance to throw a drink in his face.

Elena had not moved. "I thought you were going to wait," she said.

"Figured the sooner the better," he told her, "while I've still got some friends back at Central."

Jessica's eyes lit on his. "*You,*" she snarled. She stormed toward him, the crowd dodging out of her way.

"Don't go anywhere, and that's an order."

"Are you kidding?" Elena said. "I wouldn't miss this."

Jessica loomed over Greg, ignoring Elena entirely. He stayed seated; he might as well give her the advantage of height. "What the *hell* have you done?" she shouted.

"Could you be more specific, Commander?" Out of the corner of his eye, he saw Elena hide a smile behind her teacup.

Jessica was poking a finger in his face. "That! That right there! What the *fuck* are you doing, promoting me?" She was stomping her feet in fury, and he thought she was not far from taking a swing at him.

"It's standard practice," he told her, "when someone has consistently done exemplary work over a long period of time. Besides, I needed a second."

"After everything I did for you, after *saving your ass* while you were gallivanting on the other side of the universe? You *know* how I feel about bureaucracy! You *know* I never wanted a promotion!" She rounded on Elena. "And don't just sit there grinning at me. I know you had a hand in this."

"I didn't," Elena laughed. "I told him you'd tear his head off, but he didn't care."

"You could have stopped him!"

"Let me ask you a question, Commander Lockwood," he said. "If Elena and I get court-martialed and tossed in a military prison—which is, you'll admit, not an impossible scenario—who would you choose to run the ship?"

She froze, still glaring, and he could see her thinking. "*Shit*," she said, her voice dropping to a normal volume.

"That's what you get for being good at your job," Elena told her.

Jessica scowled. "Don't I outrank you now?"

"Yes you do, ma'am."

"Good." She dropped into a chair on the other side of Greg. "Go get me a drink, Commander. A big one. With fruit."

Elena stood. "Yes, ma'am." She leaned down to leave her tea on the table. "You have created a monster," she whispered to Greg, but she had a twinkle in her eye.

Greg watched her walk away, aware of Jessica's eyes on him. "You guys seem almost normal," she observed, relaxed. "How's it going?"

"Was all that yelling just for her benefit?"

"No," she said, "but it's more fun when it's both of you. You gonna tell me anything?"

He thought. "I don't know," he admitted. "I'm kind of afraid to curse it."

"Best to say nothing then," she agreed. He took his eyes off Elena to look over at her, and she raised her eyebrows. "What? I am superstitious. So are you."

"No I'm not."

"Well you should be. It's safer." She settled back in the chair. "I suppose I should thank you."

"You earned it."

She winced. "Can't I just continue believing you're doing me a huge favor because I told you what to say to Lanie?"

"I forgot all your advice."

"So it was all just you?"

He opened his mouth to say yes, and in his mind's eye he saw an alien cityscape, bleached and sterile and beautiful. "No," he told her. "Not just me." He leaned back in his chair, watching Elena laugh at the bar with an ensign. Karenssen, he remembered: twenty-four, a math prodigy. Shaky pilot, but a damn good shot. "Do you know her?" Greg asked, gesturing at the young woman.

"Sure. Kris Karenssen. Nice kid."

"Tell me about her," Greg said, and settled in to listen. He had 224 people to get to know.

Volhynia

"Are you sure he's on this ship?"

"Yes."

"But what if he changed ships? What if he changed his mind?"

"Hush, child. I spoke with him not an hour ago. He is on this ship, as you will see for yourself shortly."

Sarah bounced on her toes, craning her neck to look over the heads of the crowd awaiting the *Yangtzee,* the transport shuttle from Shenzhu. She did not have to crane much, Ilya noticed; at twelve she was already tall, almost as tall as Ilya himself. Within a year she would be looking down on him from those dark, serious eyes. She had the strong features of Treiko's father, and would never be a delicate beauty; but there was an animation about her, a shrewd, good-humored intelligence in her eyes, that Ilya was fairly certain would garner her as many admirers as she might want. Treiko had seen it, too, he knew. Ilya had seen the dismay in his friend's eyes whenever he spoke of the girl, and how quickly she was growing.

Children grew, Ilya knew. He had watched so many of them

get older, become men and women. He still remembered Treiko as a boy: shrewd, like Sarah, but instead of good humor his face had always held wariness. Seeing him had made Ilya sad, and angry. When he had returned as a man, Ilya had been gratified to see laughter in his eyes, but it had shocked him to see that boy so old. Surely that much time had not passed. Surely Ilya himself was not really such an old man.

They heard the surge of the big shuttle's engine from within the spaceport, and Sarah's hand convulsed on his arm. "They're here," she said. "Do you suppose he will be alone?"

Ilya had not asked. He suspected, if Treiko had brought her back with him, that he would have said so.

The crowd's focus turned to the spaceport entrance, and after a moment the passengers began streaming out, first in ones and twos, and then in a substantial crowd. Conversation swelled; families hugged loved ones; friends laughed in greeting; returning vacationers stumbled wearily to local transports with their packed belongings. Ilya loved watching people, but he detested crowds, and he wondered if they might have a sufficient view of the passengers from off to one side.

Sarah's fingers tightened. "There," she said. Ilya glanced down at her, expecting her to be jumping and waving, but she just nodded in the direction of the spaceport entrance. Ilya looked up, and met his friend's eyes.

Treiko looked better than he had the last time Ilya had seen him. He still had some cuts on his face, and there was a mostly healed bruise on his chin; but he had shaved, and his hair was combed, and his burnished skin glowed healthily in the sun. To Ilya's surprise he was dressed all in black: his old PSI uniform. Ilya had never seen him wear it during the day.

There was no one with him.

Ilya raised his hand, and Treiko's face twitched with something resembling a smile—he clearly had not expected to be met at the spaceport. And then his eyes shifted from Ilya's and lit on Sarah. His expression froze, and for several moments he didn't move.

"I don't think he's happy to be home," Sarah whispered.

"I think he is happy to see you," Ilya told her truthfully.

Treiko threaded his way through the crowds. A few people started when they saw him, and backed away; a few, undoubtedly recognizing him from the frenzied news reports of the last several weeks, gaped and smiled. Most people ignored him, and Ilya wondered if he found that a relief.

He stopped in front of them, looking down at Sarah.

"Shouldn't you be in school?" he asked.

The child looked up at him, and suddenly she did not look half-grown. She looked like a little girl, frightened and hopeful. "We are on holiday this week."

"And your mother does not have you working?"

"Well," Sarah hedged, "I told her I was doing a school project with my friends today."

"Hm." Treiko was trying very hard not to smile. He looked up at Ilya. "Thank you for coming, my friend. How are you?"

Ilya shrugged. "I am old, and my joints ache," he complained. "There is a storm coming, but not enough of one to wash away the insects."

Treiko was studying him intently. "You were not hurt?" he asked.

Ilya shook his head. "I let them think I was senile. They asked me questions, but they did not persist. That nice Central security officer came to see me, but they were gone by then. I liked him very much."

He had made Alex Carter some of his horrible coffee, and in return the young man had told him what he knew of Captain Treiko Zajec of PSI. Ilya had been impressed, and strangely saddened. Such a large part of his friend's life, shut away behind him. Although seeing him in his uniform . . . Ilya had to wonder.

"You are standing out, you know, Treiko Zajec."

Trey glanced around, noting some of the attention. "I suppose I am," he said ruefully. "No matter. Hiding from what I was—what I am—did me little good, and I have recently decided that lying is exhausting. I have better things on which to spend my waning energy." He looked back at Sarah. "Is your mother very angry with me?"

Sarah's eyes widened. "She used words I never heard her use before," she told him. "But I think she was worried. I went downstairs one night, and she was in the kitchen, reading your letters."

"Hm," Treiko said again, and Ilya saw a suspicious gleam in his eyes. "I am sorry if I caused her pain."

The child straightened. "I think it was good for her to miss you," she declared. "Perhaps she will be nicer to you now."

At that Treiko laughed out loud, a true belly laugh, and Ilya felt his worry for his friend falling away. "You cannot change the nature of a thing, Sarah dear," he told her. "Your mother will be herself, and I will love her for it. You must, too, you know. She will need that from you, on the days she cannot love herself."

"We still don't have a new dessert chef," Sarah told him slyly.

"One thing at a time, dear girl," Treiko said gently. "Let her grow used to me being home, and to all of these people knowing who we are to one another. If she wishes for me to cook for her after that, I will cheerfully do so."

Impulsively Sarah reached out and took his duffel. She frowned. "Is it empty?"

"I left with nothing," he pointed out. "These are small creature comforts acquired on the way home. And possibly a gift for you, from Yi Shao City, but you will have to wait until I unpack to see it."

Her eyes glowed, and she became little again, and she turned and skipped ahead of them, heading down the block toward Treiko's flat.

The two men fell into step, eyes on the child running up the sidewalk. "What happened, Treiko Zajec?" Ilya asked.

Trey was quiet for a long time, his footsteps muffled against the concrete, his eyes far away. "I have seen the future, Ilya Putin," he said at last. "Or possibly the past. I do not know which. I do not know that it matters."

"And what does the future hold?"

"I am not sure," Treiko admitted. "I think I ought to fear it. But I must say, Ilya, that having seen it . . . when I set aside the fear, I am left, strangely enough, with hope."

Ilya did not begin to understand. He would have his own measure of the future, and it would not be as big as Treiko's, or Sarah's. Any fear he used to feel at what lay ahead had long since been replaced by curiosity and anticipation. He thought on the last day of his life he would still wake up full of energy, awaiting the beauty of the day. "So it did you good, this seeing of the future," he said.

"I do not know. But I would not give it back."

Sarah had stopped, having run into a friend, and instinctively

Ilya and Treiko stopped as well, giving her room to socialize. Her friend was a few centimeters shorter; he looked younger than she did, but there was something in his smile that suggested to Ilya he was not. Ilya glanced at his friend, expecting to find a glower of disapproval. Instead Treiko was watching the children, a slight smile on his face, something lost and hollow in his eyes.

"She stayed behind," Ilya observed.

"She is a child of the stars," Treiko told him. "She could no more thrive here than a plant without light. She might have stayed, if I had asked; but she would not have been herself, not for long."

"You let her go."

"I did."

"I am sorry she allowed that."

Another smile, brief and sad. "As am I."

Sarah flashed the boy a bright smile, and started skipping down the sidewalk again. The two men resumed walking. After a while, Ilya cleared his throat.

"You are not alone, you know, Treiko Zajec," he said.

Treiko kept his eyes on the little girl. "None of us are alone, Ilya Putin."

And much to Ilya's surprise, Treiko Zajec began to sing, his voice melodic and strong, an old folk song Ilya remembered from his own childhood. After a moment Ilya joined him, and together the two men followed Sarah back home.

Acknowledgments

Writing is indisputably a solitary activity, and yet somehow I have managed to acquire a long list of incredibly talented and generous people I would like to acknowledge. Without them, this book would never have come to pass. With apologies to those I will inevitably miss, I would like to extend my thanks to:

Hannah Bowman, my agent, who saw what this book could become and worked with me to get it there with the fiercest good cheer of any person I have ever known;

David Pomerico and Natasha Bardon, my editors at Harper-Voyager US and HarperVoyager UK, for their invaluable insight and their kind patience with the new kid;

Richard Tunley, writer, musician, and endlessly patient friend, who was the first to read my work and say "Hmm, this is not bad";

Nancy Matuszak, writer and coconspirator, giver of honest feedback, midnight encouragement, tea, and chocolate;

Donna, Tara, Reuben, Denise, Gery, Bob, and Tru, my beta readers, all of whom gave me invaluable insight;

and everyone at Absolute Write, especially the denizens of the M/T/S board, who have stuck with me through failure and success, good days and bad, and continue to motivate me every day.

My family merits their own section for putting up with me. My thanks to:

my mother and father, who have somehow always been proud of me, no matter what in my life I've screwed up;

my brother, who picks up my parenting slack by taking my kid on all the rides I'm too scared to go on;

my always amazing husband, who has managed to survive living with me through all of this while remaining unfailingly patient and encouraging;

and lastly, my smart girl, who will someday pick up this book and say "Oh, THAT'S what she was doing!" There are things in life worth fighting for, my dear. Never doubt it.